I0678067

WITHIN THE THE WALLS

Within the Walls

1010 Auckland, New Zealand

First published in New Zealand 2024.

This edition published 2024.

Copyright © 2024 Emma Jackson

Emma Jackson has asserted her right under the New Zealand Copyright Act 1994 to be identified as Author of this work.

All rights reserved. No part of this publication may be reproduced or transmitted in any forms or by any means, electronic or mechanical, including photocopying, recording, or any information storage or retrieval system, without prior permission in writing from the publisher.

This is a work of fiction. Unless otherwise indicated, all the names, characters, businesses, places, events, and incidents in this book are either the product of the author's imagination or used in a fictitious manner. Any resemblance to actual persons, living or dead, or actual events is purely coincidental.

ISBN: PB: 978-0-473-71632-5; eBook: 978-0-473-71633-2

First Edition

10 9 8 7 6 5 4 3 2 1

www.ingramcontent.com/pod-product-compliance
Lightning Source LLC
Chambersburg PA
CBHW030552260626
47157CB00006B/2278

For 5-year-old me, who wrote stories about her stuffed animals. We did it.

The Wilds

Northern Forest

The Palace

Army Headquarters

Park

Concave Sector

Entertainment District

The Academy

Apes and Killers

King's Army

Tex

The Square

The Trades

To The Gates

THE KINGDOM
As roughly sketched by Ajax

4

Farmer's Village

Aston

Concave Farms

Convex Farms

Musical Instruments Factory

The Village

CONVEX SECTOR

Elle

Mass Graves

Elle's Garden

The Stoned Dog

Southern Forest

Chapter 1

Sometimes, I wonder if the shadows have found a home in me. And yet, the scream rattles my bones. It reverberates through the alleyway and rakes its fingers down my spine. I quicken my pace and weave between the sun-starved, tight-knit buildings, passing bony beggars, and emerge into the town square. The rumbling crowd falls silent as the three Tranqs fasten bronze handcuffs to a girl's wrists and shove her into step. She mutters prayers to the Gods as they direct her through the rendered-still crowd. The girl looks no older than me, eighteen, with knotted brown hair pulled behind her head. She tightens her jaw, and a tear dribbles down her cheek. Her dirt-stained, threadbare apron, grey tunic, and scrubbed-raw fingers indicate she likely works with my sister in the laundromat. Hundreds of eyes, including my own, follow her as the men shove her forward. She does not resist. As she stumbles past, her gaze locks with my own. Bile stings my throat as the watery, wide glint in her eyes sinks, like blades, into my gut.

The Tranquillity, nicknamed the Tranqs, haul the girl into a barricaded wagon, cramming her into the wooden seat. Their helmets are as black as the night, and the eye slits reveal nothing of the souls behind. Dainty knives stick from their belts, glinting in the waning light like the teeth of a beast. Spears are pinned across their backs. With each step, the clang of their onyx metal armour rings through the square and bores into my ears. Horses snort and stamp their feet before jerking the trailer forward, drawing gasps and flinches from the throng. But the girl's eyes remain pinned on us, on *me*, the Convex people.

As soon as the horse and wagon disappear around the corner towards the kingdom gates, the crowd disperses at an astonishing rate. Mothers in grimy grey tunics grip the hands of their uncomprehending children, desperately tugging them away. Elderly men and women, thin and frazzled, shuffle back to their homes in knowing silence.

I duck my head, slipping into the hordes of gaunt figures staggering towards the western exit. My teeth clatter together. A freezing draft lashes into the square like a whip. Dread curls in my stomach, and I brace myself as it grazes my cheeks. I gag at the pungent stench of decay. An array of buildings borders the square, built from brown brick and mortar. There's an apothecary on the ground floor of one building, leaking an aroma of sickly sage and other herbal medicines. The owner, a scrawny woman with yellowish skin, slips from the masses and slams the door shut, flipping her open sign to *closed* and drawing the blinds tight. A tavern, usually crawling with drunkards, flicks its warm candle lights off.

A woman with greasy hair squeaks next to me when the distant city gates ease open on their mechanical hinges. Groaning and screeching. Stone gates against the stone ground. I hold my breath, listening for the girl's final scream. My heart thunders against my chest. The sharp pitch of her scream burrows into my bones.

I loosen my breath.

A rough voice catches my attention.

"I hear she stole food from a Concave gentleman," the man says, shaking his head. His scruffy beard and hollow cheekbones are indicative of his Convex status. His hands are calloused and stained with black oil. He's likely a blacksmith.

"She was his wife's handmaid," another man mutters. He chews his cracked, dark lip. His jawline is too sharp, and his ribs poke out from beneath his thin, tan tunic. "Stealing from a Concave man whose wife is pregnant... well, she's at the mercy of the insanity beyond the walls now."

"Not if the monsters find her first," the first man says grimly. They shoulder their way around a corner, towards the markets, and their voices dissipate.

I hug my thin body against another biting blow of wind, shuddering. Grey and white clouds billow across the city walls, coating the skies over the farms in the east of the Convex Sector. The snow will fall tonight.

At last, I slip into the street across from the one leading to the markets and navigate my way home. Every person I pass, scrawny and notched from the famine, doesn't bother to glance my way. We all keep to ourselves in the winter months when the famine is at its worst. Starvation means people must be selfish. Although, few skip the

9

opportunity to lose themselves to alcohol. I shake my head at a group of young men spilling from another bar, pitchers of ales in their dirty hands. Their braying laughter and crude jokes remind me we are all trying our best to survive. I cross the cobbled stone road, passing an old man shovelling animal feed into his mouth, and step into my apartment building.

The stench of rotting wood hits me at once. Green mould grows up the walls like a grotesque painting, and clumps of dust adorn the corners. The wooden spiral stairwell groans like a dying animal as I climb it, cringing as the sound grates my eardrums. Dust particles burst into the air, disrupted by my movement. A lazy finger of sinking sunlight reaches into the window, catching on my red curls and appearing to set them alight.

My elder sister's eyes widen when I step into our tiny, cramped apartment. She scurries over with a book clutched to her chest. My stomach clenches. Her bones are becoming more prominent by the day, and shadows are finding a home in the curves of her cheeks. Her skin has long since drained of colour and liveliness. But her pale blue eyes, the same eyes that once belonged to our mother, glimmer like the cosmos above.

"I heard the screams from the square," Lyra says. Her voice is soft and quells the clubbing beat of my heart. She pushes her ever-tidy, thick red braid over her shoulder. "The Tranqs banished someone, didn't they?"

I nod, dropping my gaze to my tattered boots, peeling my sword from my back, and placing the worn leather scabbard on the kitchen bench.

"We must be more careful, Elle," she says. "Lie low until the summer."

"If we survive that long," I say, unable to withhold the sharpness in my tone.

The sparkle in her eyes dims, and she presses her lips together. I trudge to the window and peer down at the street, watching the flocks of people thinning out as the sun dips below the horizon. I am certain there will be bodies littering the streets in the morning, especially as my breath mists before my face and the spiderweb-like frost creeps up the glass of the window. My stomach grumbles, and I shiver, slamming the window shut and cursing when it doesn't seal properly.

I shift my gaze to my faint reflection in the glass pane. My sharp, slightly upturned nose, high cheekbones, and grey eyes make me look cold and calculating. Which, I suppose, I am.

Lyra drags a match across the small box in her trembling hands as an icy draft drips in from the window. She limps around the room, igniting the six candles perched on holders and shelves. The shadows around us dart away. She tosses the creeping flame into the hearth and feeds the fire with chunks of wood I chopped earlier this morning.

"Look, I'm going to head into the forest again before nightfall," I say, spinning around and leaning against the mildew-infested wall. "We have no food. Even Aston didn't have anything to offer me in the markets today. There are a couple of potatoes in the garden that we can roast."

She chews her lip and furrows her strawberry-blonde brows. "You would be so stupid to do such a thing after what happened to the girl?"

"I will be quick." I snatch the rucksack from our wobbly bookshelf. "Would you rather starve to death?"

11

She shakes her head as I slip my two knives into the straps of my belt. One of the knives once belonged to my father and has our family emblem hand-carved into the wooden hilt. A twisted serpent between two flaming torches. I reach for the sword, which has the same emblem, but decide to leave it. I used it enough at training today. "You know the Tranqs flock the Convex Sector at this time of year," Lyra says, picking her nails. "I don't want you to draw attention to yourself."

Heat creeps into my cheeks. "We promised Mother and Father we would look after each other."

"You won't be of use if you're arrested or banished, Elle," she snaps.

I bristle, spinning on my heel and marching towards the door before pausing, nocking my chin over my shoulder. "You know, you act so concerned, Lyra. But we both know you are itching for me to return with food we can actually eat."

Frosty air seeps into my pores, and my fingers quickly stiffen. My breath plumes like ghosts from my mouth as I slip through the streets towards the southern forest. An earthy scent swirls around me as I exit the streets into the meadows of farmland in the east, following the yellow path south. Men and women carrying heavy woven baskets pluck the fruit from an array of trees in the orchards—apples, oranges, and pears. Another group of men, covered in a layer of dirt and grease, grunt and groan as they push the ploughs through the vegetable fields. The clumps of earth burst out from the plough. As they sow the seeds, a wave of fire burns into my gut.

My nose wrinkles as I traipse the path, past the stench of rotting potato fields, which are clearly separated from the healthy farms—Gods forbid the blight grows onto Concave produce, eventually reaching the first trees of the forest. At this time of the day, with the sun racing towards the horizon, shadows throw themselves in haphazard shapes among the trees, like sinister monsters with unknown horrors. But I am more than familiar with the maze of the forest. It was once my father's favourite place. His peace.

Now, the forest belongs to me.

Bright green moss coats the floors, absorbing the thud of my tread. The wind blows through the trees, shaking the dripping bare branches, loosening the remaining leaves clinging to the bark for dear life. Branches groan as their limbs bend towards the earth. During the summer, the branches teem with birds and chirping insects. But they have all scurried into their nests and burrows, waiting out the winter.

I draw in a breath and shake the tension from my shoulders. This is my place of peace, too. Frost crunches beneath my boots, and my heart thumps to a steady rhythm. The Tranquillity do not roam this forest. No one does. The stories of a monster terrify the Convex people from ever entering. A monster, never seen by a person who lived to describe it. But my father used to tell Lyra and me that the monster was the night itself. Swathed in shadows, like a storm of misery and death.

"They echo the screams of their victims long after their deaths," my father used to say. His leathered face would wiggle into animated facial expressions as he launched his hands at Lyra and me, feigning claws. We would squeal until his laugh chased the fear away.

I leap across one of the many icy, bubbling streams criss-crossing the forest, slipping into a tight-knit set of trees and then emerging into a small clearing. On the border of the clearing, in a tiny patch, a couple of potatoes sprout out from the soil, brimming with hope. I crouch and yank the potatoes to the surface. Dirt and roots cascade from the

13

vegetables, and I brush the excess off. With a tentative glance at my surroundings, I shove the potatoes into my rucksack.

I stand, ready to hasten back the way I came. My heart lurches into my throat when I see them staring directly at me from within the shadows. A pair of wide, brilliant green eyes. The colour of the forest itself. Demanding my attention and swelling with startling malice. Human.

I stumble backwards, regaining my balance against a trunk. But when I glance up again, the eyes are gone.

A spike of adrenaline caresses my insides, and I startle. With a grip on my knife, I fall into a run, soaring over the stream and bounding through the forest maze as the blood roars past my ears. The farmers are finishing for the day when I explode from the trees onto the path doused in the last puffs of light and make my way back into the town. I reign in my erratic breathing and shove out my knitted brows.

Who was that? Why were they in the forest?

No one goes into the forest.

The eyes, green and feral, burn through my skull, no matter how much I try to distract myself with the evening bustle of the village. Reality demands attention. I am a dead girl. And so is my sister. If the eyes do, in fact, belong to a Tranq.

"Gods, what happened?" Lyra asks as I crash into the apartment, shooting up from her perch on the wooden chair by the window. Her blistered fingers curl around her book.

"Nothing," I snap, tossing the rucksack of potatoes onto the bench.

The girl's scream and the screech of the gate closing behind her rattle in my head. Beyond the walls is the promise of nothing but monsters and madness.

And it all waits for me.

Chapter 2

My fingers ache from the frostbite, stiff and pink, when I emerge onto the street the next morning. I grimace at the bags under my eyes in the window across the street. Stained in red, stinging, and hollow. The green eyes in the forest haunted my dreams, and I woke up in sweats. I round the corner, slipping into one of the major streets. Even though the sun is only peaking over the walls in the east, the street already teems with the Convex people. But gazes remain cast on the ground. A woman pops out of a textile warehouse and squeaks when she bumps into me. Her nose scrunches, and her body trembles. While she wears a drab, torn frock and stained corset, she carries an armful of brightly coloured fabrics. Bold pink, baby blue, and sunny yellow.

"I'm sorry," I stammer, darting out of her way. She blinks before placing her heap of clothing into the back of a wagon, where a chestnut mare snorts and stamps her feet. The woman climbs aboard the cart, flicks the horse reigns and heads north towards the Concave Sector, where wealthy patrons will browse and purchase her garments.

As I skirt past her shop, I almost trip up over a person huddled on the footpath. The man is hunched into a ball, embracing his knees. His eyes are wide open, staring lifelessly in front of him, his eyelashes coated in a layer of white frost. My insides churn. No one has bothered to move his body to the morgue yet.

I increase my pace, trudging through the icy, dry maze of streets, moving deeper into the textiles district, passing Lyra's laundromat, the scent of fabric dye tinting the breeze, infused with the hay and manure of the large horse stables. Stablemen scramble back and forth with handfuls of hay and pails of horse feed. Others sweep the stalls and brush the horse manes. Soon, I cross the square, careful to keep my gaze forward. I fight the urge to glance at the Tranqs stationed in the vicinity to look for those green eyes. Maybe a rogue Tranq was roaming the southern forest last night, enforcing some new law the king has contrived? Freshly sharpened claws slither around my throat, tightening. If it *was* a Tranq, then they saw me break the law—Gods forbid a Convex person try to find a way around the blight.

The girl's scream from yesterday reverberates in my ears, followed by the shudder of the city gates.

I pull the hood of my coat over my head. The shadows of the Trades markets welcome me as I slip into the alleyway. I allow the disarray of senses to swallow me whole. Hooves clatter as horses pull carts of goods, the metal wheels rattling along the cobbled ground. People shout greetings at one another. They huddle in small groups and flit between the stalls. My nose wrinkles at the sharp scent of burnt metal and charcoal from the blacksmith stand. The burly man hammers a sword into shape, grunting with the effort. A tall lady selling her pottery waves at me. She presents a gummy smile as she tries to coax me into buying one of her vases.

I pass the lady from the apothecary, stirring a steaming herbal mixture in a pot. She has a sign on her stand offering bloodletting, with a tank of black leeches floating inside.

"Two leeches for the price of one! Purify yourself today!"

With a shake of my head, I ignore the protest of my stomach. The aroma of stew almost pulls me to my knees. As I round a corner, I have my sights set on a stall selling oils, and someone hollers my name across the aisle of vendors.

"Elle!"

I spin around, regarding a boy loitering behind a stall selling old fruit and vegetables. However, his baskets are looking rather empty due to the lack of crops. I grin and zigzag through the traffic. He yanks me into a hug as soon as I squeeze behind the stall.

"You would not stop by the markets without purchasing some of my delicious produce, would you?" he says with a chuckle, releasing me from his embrace.

"Of course not, Aston." I roll my eyes and laugh. "Although, I think your carrots have shrivelled up against the cold. They're growing a nice green mould to keep warm. But at least you have something to even sell today."

Aston's hazel eyes glimmer, and he presses his lips together, bronze cheeks flushing. "The orchards are struggling, even for the Concave food." He blows out a breath and pushes his ashy blond hair out of his dirt-stained face. "Grandmama says we can only sell the bad stuff, the food the Concaves wouldn't want. Or we risk our necks."

His eyes flash, and I know he is thinking of his mother. He always has that look on his face just before he brings her up.

"Aston!" a high-pitched voice chirps before I can reply. A girl around our age shoulders her way through the throng.

"Hello, Sadie," Aston says, his voice smooth as honey as he flashes her his trademark grin.

"When do you finish work today?" she asks. Sadie blinks her heavily kohl-lined eyelashes at him so fast I fear they will fly away.

Aston sighs and pouts. "I'm scheduled until late. I must sell as much as possible. You know how it is."

Sadie's otherwise wide smile falters. "Another time, then?"

"Of course, see you soon."

Sadie throws me a dirty look before sauntering off back into the crowd. I stare after her slim figure, tanned from too many days on the farms. With a shake of my head, I turn back to Aston. "I will never understand why every girl practically drools over you."

"Not just girls," he reminds me, waggling his finger playfully. As if that were a cue, a darker-skinned boy approaches us. He smirks at Aston as he purchases a couple of floury apples.

"I'll see you after work?" the boy says, eyes pinned to Aston as if I were invisible.

Aston chews his lip, and heat creeps into his cheeks. "I know where you live," he says, reaching over the stall and kissing the boy's hand.

When the boy slips back into the crowd, Aston grins at me, and I roll my eyes. I catch Sadie glaring at us from a few vendors along.

"Not only is he unabashedly picky about who he sleeps with, but he acts like his best friend is invisible sometimes," I say, jabbing him in the ribs and snatching an apple. "Can we meet at our spot later?"

"Did you not hear me confirm my plans for after work?" He wiggles his brows, and I feign throwing up. "I have places to be, Elle. And that is a much-needed night in that boy's bed."

I stiffen, trying not to gag at his bluntness. "I can wait up for you. It's important." My voice is laced with urgency, and he senses it, nodding.

And yet, his demeanour is calm and collected. "I'll be there when the moon crests the sky."

As I turn to leave, the air deflates from my lungs. A group of Tranqs, dozens of them, march into the markets, splitting the crowd in half like meat falling from the bone. Convex people shriek and tremble, cowering against the building walls. The Tranqs disperse, assigning themselves to the slim gaps between each vendor's stall. One Tranq per gap. They grip the long, shining metal beams of their staffs, with spearheads melded to the end. Poised and powerful.

Of course. Tonight is the Winter Solstice. Music and dancing cascade from the streets of the Concave Sector. But the Tranqs swell the Convex streets like an oozing wound. The night of the Winter Solstice marks the beginning of increased surveillance during the cold months. One Tranq, whose boots ring in my ears as he forges the path through the alleyway, sweeps his hawk-like gaze on all of us as if someone might be stupid enough to stash some stolen food into their coat.

Aston squeezes my hand. I move forward. The first to take a step after the crowd dispersed. A rumble and scuffing fill my ears as the throngs of people merge back into the centre, and hundreds of eyes burn into my spine while I stalk to the exit. My insides stiffen and then quake. Sweat trickles down the sides of my face, but I do not stop moving, the din of the markets driving me forward, as if I'm a hare trying to escape the fangs of a fox.

***

The wind is a thousand ghosts wailing at the stars when I haul myself over the ledge and onto the building roof. My fingers grapple for the gutter, and I push myself off the windowsill below. The navy sky stretches over my head.

"Took you long enough," Aston says, an easy grin stretching across his olive-toned face as I brush the grit from my palms.

He's perched on the furthest edge of the building, gaze pinned on the Concave Sector far beyond the river. The bright lights of the wealthy sector glint in his eyes. His legs dangle off the side, kicking clouds of dust from the brick wall below.

"I'm surprised you are here at all," I say, sighing as I sit next to him.

"My date bailed on me, you see." He gulps, a muscle pulsing in his neck. "I think the Tranqs arrested him. Stole from the baker."

My heart twists, and I lean my head on his shoulder. "It will not always be like this. It can't be."

"How do you know?"

"Don't all human civilisations follow the same pattern in the end?" I stare at the lights of the palace, tracing my eyes along the half-dozen towers reaching into the skies. "They always crumble. Rome fell, even the United States of… well, you know. Every single society to ever

21

exist has crumbled to the Achilles' heel that was their greed and hunger for power."

"They destroyed the world," Aston murmured, the steadiness of his voice still somehow keeping me tethered to sanity. "We shouldn't even be alive."

"Humans are tenacious creatures, hell-bent on surviving. We are still alive because of that obnoxious all-too-human trait."

"Maybe we should sneak out," he says, beckoning past the rounded city gates west, as if we were talking about going for a leisurely stroll through the village. "Perhaps there are other cities who treat their people better."

"We wouldn't make it far. There's just endless wilderness, Aston. No food, no water for miles. Only the insanity and the monsters."

"There is clearly someone out there, Elle." The shadows of the night settle into the grooves of his face and pool in those hazel eyes that I love so much. "And who are the monsters, really? You know we aren't just training to defend ourselves against ghosts. I know we do not know who it is out there. But it must be a threat if King Talin has increased our training. My mother knew there was more to the world than within the walls."

I can almost smell the sharp tang of her anti-fungal concoction, the one that was still in the pot on the stove the week I met Aston, days after his parents were exiled.

"We are nothing but a pawn in his little game," I snap, fidgeting with the string bracelet on his wrist. The bracelet that his father gave his mother on their wedding day. "He's only trying to protect his reign and his heir. Chances are, whoever is out there wants our resources.

They probably want the control King Talin has. We are the pieces that will protect him. Useful, but replaceable when disposed of."

Aston laughs a full belly laugh that sends a wave of warmth over my skin. I shake my head and raise my brows. "Your thoughts are practically spilling from that smirk, Aston."

"At least beyond the walls, there might be soil that isn't controlled by a power-thirsty king. Think about it, Elle. We could make it."

"And leave your grandmother behind? My sister?" I shake my head, tutting. Shackles embed themselves in my gut even as a shaky laugh flies from my mouth.

He scrambles to his feet and pulls his sword from the sheath at his waist. Its long, bronze blade glints in the pale light of the crescent moon. "You brought yours, didn't you?"

A thrilling wave rolls through me as I stand and pull my sword from the sheath. The clash of blades reverberates in my chest cavity like a drum as Aston blocks my swing. We grin at each other. I bounce on the balls of my feet, parrying with Aston. The Goddess of Wind pummels us with her affections and sweeps our laughter into the sky. Freedom roars in my ears, so near it splinters into my heart, blowing the dying coals of my hope into a flame before leaping back over the walls, scattering into the precipice of whatever matter is beyond. A sickening reminder of the shackles that keep me—that keep all of us trapped. The fiery glimmer in his hazel eyes fuels the energy tearing through my veins, anyway. He parries his sword high, and I stumble. Pain shoots up my wrist as I topple, and his laughter takes my darkness in its hands, pricking it with flecks of gold like the stars that feast on oblivion. The tip of his blade meets my throat, and he smirks in triumph before tucking the sword back into his sheath.

23

"Let it be known," I say, pushing myself up, the sour scowl far from feigned. "I was going easy on you."

He snorts like an old bull. "Oh Gods, no, you weren't. It's okay to admit when you lose, Elle."

"Fine. I will shout you a beer for your efforts."

We chuckle as we scale the fire escape, speckled in rust, down the side of my apartment building, dropping into the narrow alleyway below. I elbow him in the ribs playfully as the path feeds us into the main street. A cacophony of drunken laughter and shouts swoop around us like gulls as we enter the pub, embraced by the sooty warmth, my eyes stinging at once, the tang of body odour aloft like fog. We weave through the labyrinth of swinging arms, folk music, and creaking tables, sliding into the wooden seats at the bar and grinning at Sam, the owner. A tall, scrawny man who hardly sees the light of day. We greedily gulp our pitchers of ale. I welcome the familiar heat of the alcohol. Wooziness steeps into my mind like tea in boiled water as my muscles gradually turn to stone. The room spins and sways as a rosiness dapples Aston's cheeks, and I stare fondly at my friend. The stubble hugging his cheeks and the third beer in his hand is a far cry from the boy I met as a child mere days after we both lost our parents to exile from the kingdom. He used to sell freshly squeezed juice from the market with his grandmother, and I spent the last of my parents' coins to purchase a cup. His hollow, reddened cheeks mirrored my own like a lake cradling rain clouds.

The beer carries us into dawn, where the hunger will knock on our door like an old, withered friend.

Chapter 3

The blade narrowly misses my eyeball. It snags on my skin just below my temple. I dab at the droplet of blood oozing from the cut with my fingertip. Aston's jaw falls open like land tumbling from the side of a mountain. He stumbles over his tongue, grappling for an apology. I launch myself at him, but his swift reflexes block my attack, and my teeth clatter. He hops backwards and tosses me a sly grin.

"You've gotten smug since becoming a soldier, Elle," Aston says, tutting and shaking his head.

I tuck my blade back into its scabbard. "Says the one who tells anyone and everyone in the markets that you can parry with Tranqs."

He puts a gnarled hand on his heart. "I am a humble young man, oh so dedicated to protecting His Majesty from the monsters in the wilderness."

"Alright, Convex soldiers," the leader and trainer Tranq barks. His hungry leer roams over us as he prowls forward, stepping between us all. I fight the urge to squirm as he passes me, his gaze slithering over my corset. His heavy body armour clanks as he grips his powerful staff, and I'm quite sure I can hear him salivating. "Good work today. We will return in the morning to continue protecting the throne."

Early evening sunlight blares through the grimy warehouse windows, and the dust particles catch bright orange as they hang aloft like fireflies.

The Tranq bows his head, and we follow suit. "Iteus, God of Tranquillity and Peace, may you always protect our kingdom from the wilderness and monsters beyond the walls. May you brandish us with the courage to fight if they arrive, blades drawn."

Wind whistles between his words.

"Gods save the king."

"Gods save the king," the crowd of soldiers echo.

A rumble swells in the enormous room as a hundred Convex soldiers relax and mingle with one another. I slide it into the sheathe on my belt.

"Don't forget the law, soldiers!" the Tranq calls as we all trudge eagerly to the door, the taste of a cold mead practically on the tongue. "Keep your blades sheathed unless you want to meet the monsters' teeth!"

Aston slings his arm over my shoulder, and we traipse out of the repurposed king's army training warehouse nestled in the northern district of the Convex Sector near the river. Many other soldiers spill out around us. All enroute to the pub, but not before grabbing our hand-sized bag of grain, our monthly payment for choosing to enlist. A spattering of squat, thatched straw and wooden homes tumble into the cobblestone streets, brick-and-mortar buildings, and gritty air.

"Will you join me on a trip across the river this evening, Elle?" he asks, nodding a pretend top hat at a girl waving at him. "I have a plethora of goods to deliver to the finest people in our kingdom."

"Not the palace," I groan, rolling my eyes. "Can't we just grab a pint and wallow instead?"

"Oh, come on! It's the most fascinating experience, watching the Concave noblemen and ladies turn their nose up at me like I'm the piece of rag that cleaned their chamber pot," he says with a chuckle as we navigate our way east, towards the sun dying over the farms.

"And they wouldn't be wrong, Aston." I pinch my nose, waving my hand. "You stink of a disgusting mixture of boy and man."

He sniffs his underarms and puts his hand over his heart, mocking shock. "And I thought we were friends."

We laugh and crack dry, crude jokes to one another, passing the musical instrument factories, the pluck of strings trailing after us as we hit the yellow path, along the paddocks and fields, and eventually, arrive on a road of small homes, which is laid with hard-packed hay and dirt. The farmers' village. A string of farmers plod along the road, dragging along the undertow of soil, mulch, and manure as they split off into their russet brick and straw cottages that cough smoke into the sky. We follow a quick path to the front step of a cottage.

An old lady opens the door. She has sheet white hair pulled into a bun with dark, leathery skin from a lifetime of working in the sun.

"Ah, my Elle!" she says, throwing her bony arms into the air. "Come in, come in."

Her gnarled fingers wrap around my wrist, and her jagged nails dig into my flesh as she yanks me inside.

"Sit down, sit down." She pulls a rickety chair out from under a round table. An herbal allure hangs in the air like low, swollen fruit on a tree. Madam Sallow beams a gummy smile. "What brings you to my patch? Is it to tell me you two are finally getting married?"

"Grandmama!" Aston pinches his nose, hanging his head before marching down the short hallway. "For the last time, you can't just say that to people! Besides, we aren't even twenty."

I will the heat out of my cheeks and smile at the withered woman. "I am helping Aston deliver over the river, Madam Sallow." The chair creaks beneath me as she ignites the flame under the kettle. "Plus, I wanted to ask if you have any old produce in the orchard that you can give away." After the encounter in the forest, I want to avoid the place.

Madam Sallow purses her lips, her eyes sagging with sadness. "Not this time, Elle. The Tranqs are crawling in the fields." She draws her thumb across her neck. "Stealing food is a dead man's game."

She places a mug of steaming tea before me, and my frigid, calloused fingers desperately stretch around the mug. I take a sip and wince at the heat slicing my tongue like the side of a ribbon.

"I'm worried for my sister," I admit as Madam Sallow tosses the tea down her throat. "She's fading fast. This grain will not last, and my resources are… becoming more difficult—"

"You mean your spot in the forest?"

28

I forge an impassive expression, drumming the side of the mug.

"I can't go to the forest for a while. I think the Tranqs are out there, too," I say. Not entirely a lie. I'm not sure what or *who* I saw in the forest shadows.

I finish my tea, and Aston returns to the kitchen. "Ready, Elle?"

We thank Madam Sallow for the tea, bid her goodbye, and slip back onto the road. A chestnut horse whinnies and blows out her cheeks as we approach, stamping her feet. Aston fastens a wooden cart to the horse's saddle, loaded with crates of fresh goods. He helps me into the seat at the front of the cart and lifts the reins. The horse falls into step, and we head north. As we move further from the farms and closer to the river, Aston reaches behind him, snatching a dark grey cap from his trunk. He tosses me another hat.

He smirks at me, cocking his hat. "Don't you think this hat makes me look handsome? Like a prince?"

"More like a fool."

The horse leads us to the bridge and the river. The half-mile-wide river splits the kingdom in half, gliding between luxury and famine like a snake. We fall quiet for a beat as the horse pulls the cart up the slight incline, and I watch the water sink further away, the moss clinging to the landscaped wall, dancing into the depths of the murkiness.

Aston leans over to me. "Do you think we could blend seamlessly into Concave society, Miss Elizabeth?" he says, assuming a hoity, tight accent that the most esteemed members of the royal court tend to have.

I simply swat him, sticking out my tongue.

As we dismount the bridge, I lose myself in the disarray of senses. We pass through a road teeming with people, drinking sparkling wine from fine goblets, picking at plates of bite-sized delicacies, and smoking bronze-clad pipes. The sweet and savoury aroma of unknown dishes almost sends me toppling out of the cart. Many of the women are garbed in gowns and corsets in an array of pigments. The brighter and bustier the corset, the better. Men dress in colourful suits, too. Pale blue, orange, and red. Their slicked-back hair, clean-shaved faces, or groomed moustaches. I glance between Aston and me, dressed in threadbare tunics and trousers stained with dirt and sweat. My hair is tangled, and strands of straw spatter his head, matching the hair.

As we cross into the cobbled streets of the Concave Sector, the cart's wheels bumping up and down like a nervous knee, I notice the… lack of surveillance. I know the Tranq training building is in this half of the kingdom, but I hardly spot any of them roaming these polished streets. The only Tranq I see is hunched over a whisky at a bar, cackling with a horde of other men. His staunch gaze slides over to Aston and me.

We pass boutique shops for bridal gowns and other fancy garments. A group of young girls spills from the bridal shop, giggling like the peculiar birds in the forest that my father always adored. Seems easy for them to pretend our kingdom isn't on a sprawl of bones. We pass theatres and comedy clubs, boutique stores, and the yawning, pillared entrance of the Academy, where Concave youth go to study languages, sciences, arts, and literature. The horse leads us through a residential area of apartment buildings, with arches and mosaics of pastel hues decorating the walls. Finely carved fountains depicting figures of the God of Tranquillity and the God of Souls in neighbourhood squares spill clean, clear waters into pools. Finally, the bright palettes transcend into eggshell-white turrets of marble, practically scraping the clouds, stealing their flecks of gold from the stars. Freshly trimmed lawns reach towards us, threatening to gobble us up in their dewy and soft essence as we wobble up the wide marble path to the palace gates. The guarding Tranqs only nod at us as the gates shudder, easing open.

We ride past the grand outdoor stairs, stopping at a side entrance to the palace. A slim Convex servant, distinguishable by their dull, grey frock and white apron, scurries out and helps us unload the crates of fresh produce into the palace kitchen. By the time we are done, the pantry and fridge swell at the seams. As the sun races to drag the moon into the sky, we hasten the horse out of the palace grounds, past the manipulated hedges and violet flowers spewing their sickly scent into my face. Just before we cross the threshold of the gates, I turn around to stare at the enormous structure one last time. The chrome glimmers in the abating sunset. My heart catches in my ribs. There is a figure standing in the window frame several stories high. Shrouded in a silhouette. I cannot pick up any features. But the moving sun betrays him. The green in his eyes stiffens the air around me.

I swear his gaze locks with my own like a key finally finding its home. I flinch and whip around, staring at the horse's ears.

"Let's hurry home before Lyra worries," I say, withholding the tremble.

I open the kitchen pantry early the next morning, and a cloud of dust attacks my face. I scrunch my nose and wave my hand. My stomach growls on cue. The green eyes in the forest creep across my vision, and my palms sweat. I need to figure out something.

Lyra steps into the kitchen, winding her thick red locks into a braid. "Will you go into the forest today?"

"No," I say. "Too many Tranqs in the farms. They will see me heading into the trees."

She clutches her empty stomach. "We need food, Elle."

Of course. Not so concerned about me now when starvation has her in its vices.

"I know." I purse my lips, running a hand through my curls and frowning when I hit a knot. A bubble of irritation gnaws at my gut. "You know, it would be easier if you could work more. Earn money, so I don't have to risk my head for us almost every day."

Her jaw tightens. "I can't, Elle. You know my hands are useless since the accident."

I blow out an unkind laugh, frustration chewing at my gut. "If you hadn't fallen from the bloody ladder like an idiot, we might actually have a shot at surviving. But it's okay, as long as Elle puts her life on the line."

"I'm trying," she snaps, her cheeks going pink—just like our mother once did when she got cross with us. "I am *trying* to help."

"Hardly!" I bark, slipping the knives into my belt to prove my point. "You work in the laundromat only *once* a week. Meanwhile, I break the law every day to keep your sorry arse from starving to death."

Tears plunder down her cheeks, and the sight fuels the fury coursing through my veins.

"All you do is sit around and cry over Mother and Father's death," I say through gritted teeth, flinging the words at her like blades. I, at once, wish I could take them back.

Lyra huffs, and her bony fingers curl into fists. "Insolent bitch." Her eyes drain of all warmth, and the icy glower cleaves into my ribs.

I scrunch my hands, fire smouldering in my chest, and a hundred poison-dipped insults rise on my tongue. But I swallow them back, for now, knowing my words are forged with the flame that my father passed to me. "Fine. I'm going to the forest then. You are right about one thing. We *do* need food. The grain will not last. And at this stage, it's the only way to get it."

A curse flies from my mouth as I sling my rucksack over my shoulders and march out of the apartment, stalking through the Convex Sector, past the farms. In the rush of farmers arriving at work for the morning, none of the Tranqs spot me slipping into the shadows of the forest. Or at least, I hope.

My hands shake with the fire scorching through me. I tighten my jaw. But the fire is just a mask for the frightened girl hiding beneath. It looks like my death will happen no matter what I do. I either perish in the famine, or the king throws me beyond the walls, leaving me to whatever monster or mad man awaits.

Just as I leap over the stream and duck beneath a low-hanging branch, emerging in the clearing, my heart jumps to my throat. My skin crawls, and the breath whooshes from my lungs.

Two Tranquillity prowl through the trees like beasts hunting for souls to destroy. The clank of their armour rattles around in my skull, and an array of knives strapped to their belts glint in the blades of sunlight slashing through the canopy. They both wear helmets. But one of them wears a helmet with enormous horns that curl forward. I drop to the ground, concealing myself within the bushes and cursing my telltale red hair. The Tranqs brandish their staffs, and I gulp at the spearheads gilded in that mocking glare.

My heart careens from beat to beat so loud it may as well bounce off the trees. The breeze ruffles my hair, and I send a silent curse to the Goddess of Wind for her poor timing. My hands quiver as I reach for my knife, my father's knife with the family emblem carved into the wooden hilt. They slither into my clearing and spot the potato spouts.

"Looks like someone has a creative way of committing their crimes," one of them says, voice rough as the bark around them.

The other chuckles, the sound so entwined with the shadows that I wonder if the man was borne from them. Trust them to find amusement in our starving misery. I spin the hilt of my blade. My legs burn from the uncomfortable squat. The first Tranq shakes his head before digging his heel into the soil. He yanks the potatoes from the dirt and stomps on them until they are crumbs. My stomach lurches into my throat as the Tranq grabs a small bottle of plant poison from his belt and pours it over the soil. They chuckle as the earth hisses and crackles in lament.

Red burns across my vision, and my muscles tremble with fresh, burning waves. I lose my balance and flop over, rustling the surrounding bushes. The Tranqs snap their heads up. They hide behind their ebony-coated brass amour like lions in the grass, waiting only to strike when their prey isn't prepared to jump away.

"You!" one of them bellows, pointing at me.

My guts twist into a knot, and I scramble to my feet. But not quick enough. The Tranqs launch themselves at me, gripping my arms. They wrestle me to the ground as I wriggle and scream a string of curses.

"The king is going to have a field day with you," the first Tranq says, pinning me to the ground.

"Go to hell," I spit, refusing to yield even a sliver of fear on my face. And yet, my heart clatters into my ribs like it wants to break free and flee into the safety of shadows. "Destroying a starving person's garden. Filthy cowards. The both of you."

I shoot a glare at the other Tranq, who backs away, standing idly. The Tranq pinning me snatches the dagger from my hand and grazes it against my throat. Through the helmet, I can see the feral blaze in his eyes.

"*Your* garden, aye?" He presses the tip of the blade into my skin, and I cry out. "This land belongs to the *king*. So, your pathetic garden belongs to him. *You* belong to him."

"Then so do you. You are nothing but a pawn in his little game."

I kick out, and he flails, loosening his grip on the dagger. He barks as I shove him off me, rolling out from under him. We grapple and wrestle with one another, the blade waving around until I push him, and he gasps. The Tranq pulls his helmet off on instinct, lips quivering as he stares wide-eyed at the knife in his chest. Blood oozes from his ribs, dripping onto the forest floor. He collapses to the side. His mouth opens and closes, gurgling and dribbling bloody saliva until his eyes see no more.

The other Tranq stumbles backwards, panting and cursing. Panic claws through my ribs like a monster, and I fight the scream stinging the back of my throat.

"Stay right there," the Tranq stammers. He spins around and crests the small mound, heading back into the town.

No.

With bile churning my insides, I grab my other knife from my belt and hurl it. The blade spins as it soars through the air, and the Tranq lets out a strangled cry as it hits him. Tears blur my vision as his knees buckle.

Chapter 4

I bend over, vomiting stomach acid next to the Tranq's face. The forest spins and clouds in a haze as I stumble forward, slurring curse words. I grab my father's knife and bolt. Running and running. Hot, blinding tears dribble down my burning cheeks as I desperately try to drink in the air. I run until the forest gives way to the outskirts of the town, and I gather my wits, slowing my pace to a brisk walk. When I arrive at Aston's cottage near the farms, he isn't home. He is working, of course.

"Will you tell Aston to meet me at my place after work?" I ask Madam Sallow, trying to steady my voice.

She narrows her wrinkled eyes and purses her thin lips. "Are you okay, Elle?"

"Right as rain." Tears burn my eyes anyway. But luckily, she doesn't press the matter.

I stumble into my apartment, collapsing onto the floor. Panic, at last, finds its home in me. It stretches its claws around my throat, digging deep into my flesh. I cannot breathe. I cannot move. My body tremors and splutters. My skin burns, and I cry out at the blood staining my arms. The Tranq's blood.

The coppery scent of blood swirls around me as I stagger to the wooden tub and tip buckets of water into it. Muttering prayers to the Gods, I peel my tunic and trousers off and lower myself into the tub. I grab my sponge and a bar of soap. The Tranq's unseeing, soulless eyes leer at me as I scrub the drying blood from my skin and from under my nails. Thank the Gods, Lyra isn't home to see this.

Once I scrub myself raw, my knees inch towards my chest. I blow out my cheeks, remembering the trick my father taught us when we felt our minds slipping from reality.

"My name is Elle Fallon," I mumble, staring at my toes. "I'm eighteen, and the water is cold. I can see the apartment building across the road through the window. I can smell the mildew on the walls. I can hear footsteps in the stairwell. My sister is Lyra..."

I repeat this three times until tendrils of sanity creep back into my limbs. With a whimper, I rise out of the tub and dress, anticipating Aston's arrival.

He arrives as the sun yawns above the buildings, glaring into the apartment, reminding me it's almost time to head to training. Aston flops onto the couch with a loose smile. But it drops as I tell him about what happened in the forest.

"You killed a *Tranq*!" Aston throws his arms into the air, the colour draining from his cheeks and his eyes glinting like the rabbits' in the forest who freeze at the sight of me before diving into their burrows. "Actually, *two* of them. You killed two Tranqs, Elle? *Two*?"

"First of all, it was an accident, really, and I had no other choice," I snap, sawing a knife through a loaf of stale bread I purchased at the market yesterday, cutting around the mouldy bits.

"We always have choices, Elle." He paces back and forth in my apartment, pausing at the window and gripping the ledge. His glare reflecting in the glass boils my blood, and I resist the urge to toss the loaf at the back of his head. "Look, I am all for the crash and burn of the Tranqs as much as the next idiot, but you know what that means… for you. For Lyra."

"The choice was them or *me*." My voice is rising in anger, and I saw the knife faster. "We both know they would have thrown me out of the city gates the first chance they got. As one of them said, the king would have a field day with me. Nothing like a starving lawbreaker to seize the town in fear again!"

"Shit," I hiss when the jagged blade of the bread knife slices into my finger. The sting plunges through my hand as I stagger backwards, clutching my bleeding hand. He whirls around, rolling his eyes.

"Serves you right," he mumbles, snatching a cloth from a wooden rail in the kitchenette. He wraps it around my finger as I fight the blurry, nettling tears.

"Will you help me bury the bodies?" My voice cracks as he squeezes. Blood infiltrates the cloth like maggots to a corpse.

Aston widens his eyes so much I fear they will roll right out of his head. "You're an even bigger idiot than I thought."

I grind my teeth, yanking my bleeding hand away. "Care to say something other than an insult?"

He shakes his head, reaching for the bucket of water Lyra fetched from the village fountain this morning. The water splashes as he pours some into a mug. "We need to bury those bodies right away if you have so much as a chance of getting away with this," he says, softening his harsh demeanour. I stick my bleeding finger over the sink, and he pours the mug of water over my wound. "It sounds like the Tranqs might have started patrol in the forest. If so, they will find the bodies in no time. Perhaps they have already found them."

"We bury them and never speak of it again," I say, staring at the red-tinted water swirling into the rusty drain.

"Fine."

Aston wraps my wound in another clean cloth. "Meet me after midnight tonight at the forest's edge. We can bury the bodies then."

We eat the slices of bread. It's dry, but I force it down, knowing my body needs every crumb.

I shoulder past Lyra, who returns to the apartment, staggering, oh-so-slowly, up the creaking stairs. Her polar eyes slide over me, burning like rum on a fire. But I don't so much as utter a greeting to her and exit the building, making my way to training for the day. But my stomach churns, struggling to digest the bread. I feel like a puppet as I move through the drills of training, glancing over my shoulder at the supervising Tranqs as if they might announce my crime to the entire fleet at any moment.

When we finally leave for the day, I wave to Aston as he heads towards his farms, and I begin the short trek back home. The smell of mould on the floorboards strikes me as I enter our tiny apartment.

Lyra sits on the tattered couch, buried in the words of her book. She glances up. Her cheeks are puffy and stained. Pride ripples through me, desperate to tug me back into its net. But I shove it aside with a release of my jaw. I gather my thoughts and force myself to act accordingly.

"I'm sorry for being horrible, Lyra," I say, trudging towards her, the floor protesting underfoot.

She places the book beside her and presses her lips together, the pink in her face deepening. "You are right, Elle. You're the one who risks your neck every day to keep us alive. I'm going to see if I can pick up more shifts to help." A deep breath. "Mama and Papa died a... long time ago. It is time I let go and... be a big sister."

A sick feeling plunges into my gut, and I chew the inside of my mouth. "But you said it yourself; your hands are too injured."

"There are other tasks I can do to help." She stands, padding into the kitchen and pouring tea from the pot. "I just made the brew. You could do with its healing properties."

I almost snort at her words as she hands me the steaming mug. But I keep my snarky thoughts entombed and slump onto the couch.

"Did you bring anything back from the forest?" she asks, pulling the window shutters tight. That stubborn icy draft sings in, anyway.

"No. I'm sorry. The Tranqs were teeming by the forest entrance," I lie, cringing.

As I lift the cup to my lips, a rumble ricochets up the steps, slashing into the apartment like claws, the low, deep, thundering cacophony plundering my insides. The hammering noise increases in proximity, impending doom leering and looming, and I am on my feet, yanking the sword from the kitchen bench, pulling it out of its scabbard and planting myself in front of my sister in the same breath. The candle lights dance and twirl in the blade's reflection. A flurry of Tranqs crashes into the apartment, and Lyra screams, sending my other hand flying to the dagger in my belt.

"Which one of you is Elle Fallon?" one Tranq bellows, his armour clanging through the apartment, ringing in my ears.

"What do you want?" I say through gritted teeth, spinning the hilt of my sword.

He pulls his helmet off and snarls. An older man with bronze, wilted skin, and greying hair. "Pulling a blade on a Tranq—*you* must be Elle Fallon."

"Yes. I'm Elle," I say, pushing the tip of the sword closer to his throat, revelling in the way the muscles in his neck flinch at the cold, sharp touch. I can feel Lyra's horrified eyes on me, silently begging me to stop committing yet another treason. But I focus on steeling myself and sending a glare contrived from the darkest shadows to this ancient, miserable man. "What are you doing in our home?"

"His Majesty, King Talin, has ordered your arrest," the Tranq says, tapping the butt of his staff onto the floorboards, and Lyra flinches behind me.

"Under what charges?"

"You have reportedly committed a heinous crime. A crime punishable by exile into the madness. We have reports of a girl who has a deadly skill with knives," he says, his words dripping poison.

"Rot in hell." I take a step forward, letting the droplet of blood weep down the Tranq's neck as the shiver nettles mine. *They found the bodies.*

The Tranq sneers and the others chuckle. Before I can react, a sharp pain ruptures up my leg. Phantom stones thump into my mind, and my muscles droop towards the floorboards like the dying limbs of a tree. The room swings, and my head lolls to the side as I collapse to the ground, oblivion luring me with bitter whisperings. All the while, my sister's scream melds with the cold, distant voice that belongs to my father, rising unwelcome into my ears. "You did not keep your promise, Elle."

Chapter 5

My temple throbs, and a groan falls from my lips. I roll my head to the side, and a bright glow permeates my eyelids. A thousand needles pierce my eyeballs as I ease them open. I hiss, my hand flying to my face. As I gradually adjust to the blinding light, a nasty gash stings across my forehead and dried blood sticks to my cheeks like tacky syrup.

Grimacing at the blood, I glance at my surroundings. I'm slumped against the wall of a cramped cell. The walls are built of cold stone that bites into my bare skin, and the door has barricaded bars. There is no bench or seat, only a wooden pail in the corner. The cell reeks of vomit from the stomach contents splashed in the other corner, and I wonder if it is my own. My stomach churns as I crawl to the door. A bundle of orange and red blur across the hall, and a figure sprawls the floor, brows knitted together even in sleep.

"Lyra!" I hiss, hitting the bars with my palms.

She wakes like she's been jabbed, and her eyes dart around wildly before settling on me. "Where are we?" Her lip quivers as she shuffles to the door of her cell and grips the bars. She snaps her head from side to side, trying to peer down the hallway. Dozens of candles mount the walls along the passageway, spattering the stone in fiery luminescence.

I swallow, unsure how to respond.

"We must be in the palace dungeons," she says, running her hand down the stone wall. "I recognise them from a drawing in one of our mother's books."

"We need to find a way out," I say, as if it isn't obvious.

"Why are we here at all?" she asks, pinning her tear-filled eyes on me.

I look away, regarding the barricaded brass door at the end of the hallway.

"Did you do something, Elle?" she presses, shifting her weight and sitting cross-legged.

"I did what I had to do to keep us safe, but it looks like my luck finally ran out."

I haul myself to my feet, ignoring the ache of my muscles and the sharp throbbing in my skull. Lyra's gaze remains on me as I prowl around the cramped cell, searching for a sign of escape. A weak patch of wall or floor. Or a scrap of metal I could use to pick the lock. But, of course, there is nothing. I trudge back and forth, ignoring Lyra's protests.

"Forget it, Elle," she says. "There is nothing we can do."

Sweat coats my forehead and my palms as my heart slams into my ribs. The flickering lights dance and twirl, mocking me. I do not even realise I am weeping until the salty tears dribble into my mouth. My stomach clenches, and I lean against the wall, sliding to the floor. I blink, and the candles snuff out, wisps of smoke tainting the darkness like the first clouds of a summer storm. Velvety blackness gobbles the dungeons, and the air leaves my lungs.

I bite my tongue, waiting for Lyra's soft snoring before I let the sobs spill from my chest.

When I finally fall into a restless sleep, I dream of my father. A memory from when we were small children.

"Papa!" I shriek, running through the door, crashing into my father's looming yet warm figure. "Lyra grazed her knee!"

Lyra hobbles in after me, blood dripping from her knee. My father's eyes are soft as the evening sunlight playing with his reddish hair. He cleans her leg and wraps a clean cloth around her.

"Someone shoved her, and I punched him back," I brag, clasping my hands behind my back. "I will always look after my big sister."

He chuckles, the sound ebbing and flowing with the melody of the stars. "You will always look after one another. Never leave the other behind, even when your mother and I are no longer here."

A deep, quaking shudder jolts me awake. I sit up, taking in the flickering candlelight. Lyra's chapped lips quiver in fear.

Heavy-soled boots reverberate off the iron walls as they stalk through the corridor of prison cells. Black pants, black tunic, and black-stained bronze helmet. Carved with designs of exquisite swirls, leaving only slits for the eyes. The curved, sharp horns glint in the orange light. His breastplate and body armour clang together with each step, plucking at my nerves like a string instrument. I grimace as he approaches, instinctively reaching for my knives but realising they have stripped me bare of my weapons.

My heart lurches into my stomach and renders me silent, still.

The Tranq stops in between our cells, glancing at us each in turn. But his head lingers on me. His breaths, short and sharp, echo through the helmet. Even though I cannot see his face, his gaze burns into me. He spins the staff in his hands, slamming the butt into the floor, and I startle.

"It's *you*," he says through the mask of the helmet, voice low and smooth and somehow ethereal. The Tranq leans the staff against the wall and takes a step closer so the upturned ridge of his helmet is only inches from the barricaded cell door.

He grabs his helmet and pulls it from his head. I hold my breath, gripping the cell bars, refusing to back away. Although I can't help but stare. His eyes are green. Brilliant and demanding. Pools of jade, emerald, and pockets of amber in the centre. The forest itself. Flecked in the golden candlelight and leaking with tendrils of darkness, like ink in water.

"What do you want with me?" I splutter, wanting nothing more than to sprint away from this terrifying man.

"Is your name Elle Fallon?" he asks, ignoring my question.

My body trembles, and my mouth dries out as I fight the fingers of fear tightening around my throat. "Yes. My name is Elle."

"Elle," he says, dragging out the name, sounding out the single syllable. Something about his voice and the way he says my name caresses my bones and stirs my insides.

"So?"

"So, Elle." He runs a hand through his dark brown hair as his lip winds into a sneer. "It is nice to put a name to the face of the girl in the woods."

Chapter 6

I stare at him, afraid to blink. A shiver rakes my spine as a frigid draft oozes into the prison from the open door at the end of the hall.

"You must also be the girl who grows the illegal crops in the southern forest," he says, as his green eyes glint like a hunter sizing up his snared prey.

"What is it to you?" I stammer, gripping the cell bars. My eyes flicker to Lyra, who presses herself flat against the furthest wall of her cell, her cheeks white as bone, eyes wide.

"It is treason to grow your own crops. A crime that the king will not take lightly. The Convex have their farms." He shifts his weight, angling his head. "Don't they?"

My bared teeth do little to hide the tremble in my hands. "Don't act stupid. You know about the blight," I seethe, and he raises his thick brows lazily as if we were merely discussing the weather. "Our crops are nothing but rotten mush. The Convex Sector is starving. A forced, man-made starvation, might I add."

"Oh? That would explain why all you Convex people are falling like flies." His voice is hewn from stone, but a muscle ripples in his jaw, and his eyes flash with a hint of... guilt. Knowing.

"Pig," I snap, slamming my hand into the bar, flinching as the crash rings in my ears and Lyra squeaks.

He blows air through his nose and his mouth twitches. As he prowls back and forth with feline smoothness, my displeased leer traces his movements. His pale skin glints in the candlelight, and a dark essence oozes from his clinking armour. Shrouded in shadows and eyes flecked with light, he is dripping with the night itself. As if he carries the darkness, the moon, and the stars.

"Are you actually going to uphold this innocent façade?" he growls, examining the dainty point of his spear with his gloved finger.

"Word spreads fast, does it?" I say, swallowing my rising panic.

Where have I seen this man before?

He lets out a low laugh that slithers down my spine. "I didn't have to hear about what you did through mere gossip. I was *there*, Elle."

"What do you mean?" The words fall from my mouth too quickly. I swear he can hear my hammering heart by the unkind smirk on his face.

He clicks his tongue, taking his time to respond. "You killed my friend in the forest."

50

Lyra gasps, and tears dribble down her cheeks. She backs into the stone wall, her watery gaze meeting mine, and the guilt threatens to yank me into its storm. How could I do this to her? I *promised* to protect her. The Tranq throws her a nasty glare.

"You killed my friend, and then you tried to kill me." He pulls down the shoulder of his linen tunic, revealing a deep, red gash.

My head rings as weakness seeps into my muscles, and I want to melt into the cracks of the stones like tar. "You were there," I say, trembling like an idiot.

"Sure was," he says, pulling the fabric back over the wound with a cat-like scowl. "I must say, it took me by surprise. A girl from the Convex Sector, hurling a knife at the king's Tranq. It is certainly not something you see every day. You have a skill... and apparently enormous, stupid balls. But that skill needs to be honed since you failed to hit my heart."

I chew my lip, any counter-response dying on my tongue. He lived. The second Tranq lived. The air vanishes from the dungeon, and my hand flies to my throat.

"Such a cold, hateful creature." He flings the insult like food scraps.

"I didn't do it on purpose," I finally snap, coals smouldering within me. His eyes meet mine, dancing in the darkness, and it makes me want to scream. "You both attacked *me*. The first Tranq's death was an accident."

"He is still *dead.*" His voice rains with creeping fury, but his chiselled face remains carved from granite. "Besides, I think we both know the second attempt on me wasn't by *mistake.*"

Heat bursts into my cheeks, and I spin around, stalking across the prison cell, desperate for fresh air. But I swallow back the terror festering in the back of my throat and find my voice deep within the parts of me that belong to my father. "I'm not sure what delusional, well-fed world you live in. But sometimes, Convex must be selfish. And I made a promise. I will not let my sister starve to death."

He scowls, shaking his head. "Your actions might not have been pre-calculated. But it was a cold move. You threw the knife at my *heart*."

"Oh, get over yourself." I lean against the wall, wishing I could slap the smug look off his face.

"Careful, darling," he says, grabbing his staff and spinning it in his hand. "That is no way to speak to your prince."

"The prince?" I bite the inside of my cheek, fighting a bubble of laughter.

He raises his thick brows, leaning his staff against the wall. "The king is my father." A flicker of feral amusement nettles his eyes. "That makes me the prince, does it not?"

The prince. We always knew the king had a son. But his identity had been a secret for as long as I could remember. The king would display the odd picture of him growing up, and I am told he attends ceremonies and parties in the palace. But his name is a secret. Other than his title, Prince Talin.

"What is your name?" I dare ask.

He smiles. It's a surprisingly lovely smile that dollops warmth into my chest. "You know we would both get in trouble if I uttered my name. I must wait until my wedding day to reveal it." His pout makes

52

me want to reach out and tear his mouth off. "Although, I suppose you won't be there."

I roll my eyes. "So, why are you *actually* here, Your Royal Highness? You've told me I killed the Tranq and that I almost killed you. I couldn't escape your brooding, hateful glare if I tried. What else could you possibly want?" My words ring into the stone around us, and I almost smirk at the bemused look on his face. "If it is to make me feel guilty, don't bother. Because I am not sorry for looking out for my own, Crown Prince."

He sneers at the drawl I hold on to his title. "You have made a grave mistake, Elle. Monsters and madness await you upon your exile."

"I didn't realise you cared."

He sighs, the weight of my words settling into the green of his eyes. "I am not heartless. You better hope the monster's teeth are sharp and that your death is quick."

I snort and let out a giggle. "Have you ever tried just downing a pint and discovering the wonders of *relaxation*? You have *got* to try to have some fun and loosen up a little."

The prince flashes me a sarcastic smile. "Let me introduce you to dignity. I hear you two haven't met yet."

"And you haven't met laughter, clearly." I gesture vaguely to his face and then make an exaggerated frown and pout. "It might help with that wounded, bland personality of yours that makes me think the monsters beyond the walls would be more pleasant than your presence."

A cold breeze whispers along my skin, and I wait, amused, as he opens his mouth to retort. That's when a howl tears from his throat.

He staggers back, clutching his other shoulder. Blood runs from a fresh laceration, and Lyra's eyes almost pitch out of her skull. She startles, dropping the spear, the clang making my teeth chatter. The spearhead is coated in fresh crimson blood.

"You need to leave us alone," she musters our mother's cool, steady voice despite the quiver in her lips.

His lip curls into a snarl. "Creatures," he spits.

He reaches into the cell as Lyra jumps away in fear, snatching the staff and marching out of the dungeons. The slamming door rings in my eardrums long after he stalks away.

I have little indication of the time or if it is day or night beyond the prison. The only thing that gives some hint is the two meals and jugs of water the Tranqs bring us. But the prince doesn't show up again for a while. I suppose a prince has better things to do than tend to the prisoners in his dungeon.

When he, at last, bothers to return to the gallows, he stumbles down the corridor, muttering something indecipherable. The hungry, feral glint in his gaze sends a needle scraping down my spine. Night darkness billows from him as he stalks down the hallway, his boots snapping and echoing. I scramble to my feet, giving him my fiercest glare.

He prowls up to my cell, and his cheeks are blotched with pink as if he has been crying.

"Did it feel good?" he barks, slamming his fist against the barricades. "Huh?"

Lyra startles from her stupor and cries out. "Elle!"

"Did what feel good?" I ask, ignoring the roar of blood past my ears.

"Killing him," he slurs, his breath reeking of liquor. "Did you enjoy killing him? Are you so full of hate? Like he meant nothing."

I scrunch my nose, wanting to slap that tight frown from his face. "You *are* joking. You know I was defending myself. And you know that the famine is making us desperate. The famine fed by *your* father."

"He's gone," the prince's voice cracks as tears swell in his eyes. "*You* took him away."

"If you weren't out in the forest stalking prey, perhaps he would still be alive." I tighten my grip around the cell bars, refusing to back down.

"You were the one breaking the law."

"Laws *your* king created. Laws enforced by *you*."

The prince flinches, his teeth clacking. "He's your king, too."

I scoff and let out a dry laugh. "No. He isn't." My face burns, and my father's words rise around me. *No king of mine.*

The prince clenches his jaw, and I notice he is not brandishing his staff. "It was his funeral today." A low breath falls from his mouth as he snickers. "He had a daughter. A little girl. His wife loved him. To me, he was—"

He cuts himself off, hanging his head before shooting me a dark-cast gaze.

"What do you want me to do?" I bark, tightening my grip on the cell bars. "Do you want me to kneel and beg for your forgiveness? Your father killed my parents."

His eyes flash, and he grinds his teeth, loosening his shoulders. "Whatever heartless monster you picture us as, Concave or Tranq, we are still human."

"And so are we." The words are smouldering coals. I heave a sigh. "I am sorry for the loss." I fight the bile rising in my throat as the image of the dead, blood-soaked Tranq chars my mind. His eyes unseeing, his arms limp, sprawled around him. The same arms that once hugged his daughter and his wife. *The same arms that destroyed a starving girl's garden.*

He waves his hand in dismissal. "Don't lie to me. Now, please stop talking, for once, while I get on with my job."

The prince gestures for me to approach him with his finger. He angles his head, pouting. My blood boils at the mere sight. His change in demeanour unsettles me. I clench my fists.

"Go to hell, Prince."

He sloppily places a hand over his heart, mocking offence. "I've got something interesting to tell you. I suppose you may know since the monsters await you, and if truth be told, I am tired of keeping it a secret."

"Just say it."

He shoves his hands in his pockets and sways, stumbling on his feet like a fool. "I must whisper. Voices have a way of travelling far in this palace."

I grind my teeth and march up to the cell door, bracing myself. He leans his head close to the iron bars and smirks.

"My name is Ruben. Ruben Talin," he says with a hush that shoots a bolt down my veins.

Without another word, the prince steps back, withdraws a key from his pocket, and sticks it into the lock of Lyra's cell.

Chapter 7

My stomach lurches into my throat as my sister cowers in the corner of her cell, her entire body shaking. And yet, my own is frozen. My voice catches in my mouth, terror ripping it away.

"Get out," the prince snarls at Lyra.

"Why? Where are you going to take me?" she asks, her squeaky.

"Just get out before I have to force you." His shoulders tense, and his fists clench.

"She wants to know where you are taking her," I bark.

The prince, Ruben, ignores me as I roil the cell bars, prattling a slew of insults. He slips into Lyra's cell, who cries out, putting her hands over her face and scrunching her eyes shut as if she might wake up from this nightmare. She struggles against his strength as he pulls out a pair of metal handcuffs and shoves her wrists behind her back.

"What are you doing with her?" My voice cracks as panic claws and thrashes in my guts, and bile stings my tongue with its bitter vengeance. "Hey!"

He chews his lip and snaps his head at me. "The king has ordered her exile," he grumbles, refusing to look me in the eye. "He hasn't quite decided what to do with you yet."

Suddenly, I am eight years old again, tumbling out of the tree my sister told me was too fragile for my weight. "Please don't," I croak, not even ashamed of how pitiful I sound. "She is all I have left."

Something wild and human from the snares of torment flashes across his face. His chest heaves. "I don't have a choice."

"Yes, you do." My voice takes on an unhinged, pitchy tone. Darkness threatens to cave into my ribs. "You have a choice to not hurt others. Please don't hurt my sister. Don't exile her."

I am begging, literally on my knees and weeping. But I do not care.

"Why must you punish her? I am the one who broke the law. Kill *me*. Not her."

"She is being exiled *as* your punishment. It's what the king wants. I can't do anything about it," he murmurs as if he doesn't quite believe his own words.

"Bullshit. Are you not the *crown prince*? Can you not make your own choices? Such as the choice to barter with the king?" The world spins and screams around me as my pulse roars and my father's dying wish rises from the depths to greet me like an old, unearthed phantom. "Take *me*. Make me the king's slave. Let me become a Tranq." The words tumble from my mouth before my mind has the chance to catch them. "One of his slaves. I'll do anything."

"Elle!" Lyra snaps. Splotches of red form on her cheeks and neck as she wrestles under the prince's death grip. She yanks herself free.

Ruben's face is stone, other than the war waging in his eyes. "You would become the king's slave to save your sister's life?"

"Yes," I snarl, dragging myself to my feet, though I'm not even sure how Tranqs become Tranqs. All I know is that it's an elite career that Concave youth can apply for—those who wish for the nobility of serving the crown and enforcing its laws. "Wouldn't you for someone you love?"

He tilts his head, examining me. I can almost see the cogs turning in his head as he contemplates my offer. "I cannot promise it would work. Convex aren't even meant to be Tranqs. The king does not take lightly to those who dare barter with him. Even me." A ragged breath. "He will punish me, too."

"Please."

Gods, this locked cell is driving me insane.

Ruben chews his lips, staring at Lyra and at me. Heat creeps into his face, and after an eternity, his shoulders slump forward. "Fine. I will try." He unlocks the handcuffs. "I… hate seeing people exiled, you know."

Lyra staggers towards me, weeping. I reach out and grab her thin shoulders, pulling her into a hug. "What have you done, Elle?" she mutters, and my knees knock together. But she shoots the prince a glare formed from the storms of grief.

"I will take you back across the river. But I will still have to establish punishment for you since you bore witness to your sister's treason and didn't report her." He swallows back the grimace. "But we will discuss it on the way."

His armour clangs together as he stalks to the end of the corridor, leading her out of the dungeon. When Lyra doesn't follow, he glances over his shoulder and rolls his eyes. "Do you want to go home or not?"

"I will not leave my little sister," Lyra says through gritted teeth.

Ruben purses his lips. "I think your little sister is the resourceful one out of the two of you. I am sure she can handle herself."

"Pig!" I say, and he merely blinks at me lazily.

"Are we going, or would you rather I lock you back in the cell to rot?" He pretends to check a watch as if we are just minor inconveniences to his day.

"Just go, Lyra," I say, fighting the pressure building in my chest. Not yet. "I will be alright. The prince is right. I can handle myself."

"What if he hurts you?" Her pale blue eyes crinkle on the sides, and I notice the lines between her brows, a permanent reminder of how she never recovered from our parents' deaths.

I glower at Ruben before schooling a smile on my face. For her. "Find Aston. He will help you. Maybe he can get you some food from the farms. Ask for more hours at the laundromat. But whatever you do, don't go into the forest."

"This isn't right." Tears dribble over her lips, and her voice trembles, tearing my heart anew. "I'm the eldest sister. I should have been looking after you. Not the other way around."

"Never mind that." I squeeze her hand. "We did what we had to survive."

She sucks in a harsh breath and reaches out, tucking a loose red curl behind my ear before catching the tear racing down her cheek. "I don't want to say goodbye."

"This isn't goodbye. We will see each other again." Although, with the terror chewing through my gut, I'm not sure if I believe my own words.

We hold each other's hands, and I memorise those lines on her face. Her blue, hooded eyes, our mother's eyes. Her pointed nose and hollow cheekbones. The splatter of freckles on pale skin.

She pulls away and turns, scurrying after Ruben and out of the dungeons. Only then do I allow my chest to heave for the sobs to consume me.

Loneliness is a silent, invisible monster. It creeps up on you slowly, then all at once, like a festering wound. I huddle in the cell's corner. My eyes sting from tears, and there's an ache in my stomach from the wracking sobs. Dirt crusts my nails, and my hair both tumbles around my shoulders and sticks out around my head in frayed knots.

Ruben hasn't returned to the prison in what must be two days. Other Tranqs still deliver meals of stale bread and cheese. They ignore my questions about the prince or my sister.

In between meals, my mind sweeps into delirium. Flashing memories of my childhood, laughing with Aston as a ten-year-old, running through along the farms. My father, a tall, burly man with red hair, and a reddish-brown beard, hunched over a pint of ale, shrouded in the shadows and quivering orange light of the pub. Huddled with his other men. Whispers of *"Death to the Tranqs"* rattled between my ears as I scribbled drawings with a stick of charcoal next to my sister on the neighbouring table. We drew carrots. Or bread. Or fruit. As if the pictures would come alive and rescue our growling stomachs.

As I am about to drop into another stupor, the scraping of metal startles me. I push myself to my feet, gripping the cell bars, too weak to trust my legs to hold me upright. Ruben prowls towards me. Shadows practically swirl around him.

"You look like you have seen better days," he says, a flicker of amusement on his face.

"Glad to know my suffering is a joke to you." I don't bother to hide the disdain from my tone.

He angles his head. "Luckily, I will let you out now." His keys jangle together before he shoves one into the lock with a satisfying click. I freeze for several beats, heart racing, debating how much I can trust him.

"Where are we going?"

"To the servants' quarters." He sticks his thumb over his shoulder. "We will feed you and clean you up. You look horrid."

"Could you not have done so sooner? I almost perished in here," I say, stepping out of the cell but keeping a wary eye on him.

He shifts his weight, and I flinch back. "I would not have allowed that to happen. I was... caught up and couldn't help you sooner."

I decide it's unlikely he will provide information if I try to probe. "I am hungry."

The corner of his lip tugs into a half-smile that makes my stomach flip. He inclines his head, and I fall into step after him. Our footsteps echo through the prison, bouncing off the surrounding walls. We cross the threshold of the doorway, leaving the cells behind. Ruben leads me up a short flight of wide stone steps illuminated by candlelight. Through an arched entryway, we arrive at the lower levels of the palace. We follow a wide hallway of light brown brick walls, past a dozen closed rooms.

"This is the scullery," Ruben says, pointing at a door. He nods at another. "And this is the laundry."

We turn into a room, and my jaw drops. An enormous kitchen. Brown brick scatters the walls like a cobblestone street, intermingling with the panel of black gas ovens and stoves. Oil-fuelled lamps droop from the ceiling on long wires. A wide, rectangular wooden table gobbles up the centre of the room, and darker brown bench tops cling to the walls like wings of a beast, filled with cabinets and polished brass knobs that glimmer chrome in the spattering of orange-yellow light.

"Where is everyone?" I glance around.

"It was just lunchtime. They get an hour break, and the ladies tend to enjoy the sunshine in the courtyard."

Indeed, velvety sunlight streams in through the large, arched, crisscrossed window above the sink. I traipse forward, revelling in the feeling of warmth on my skin and the brightness on my face after my days below ground. Faint, feminine laughter trickles in with the light like summer rain.

Ruben grabs a woven basket from a cabinet. Instinctively, my mouth waters and my stomach rumbles. A fresh apple and banana, cheese, fresh bread, and a bowl of some sort of creamy rice dish.

"Risotto," Ruben says. "Leftovers from lunch. Eat." He places it on the wooden table, gesturing for me to sit on a chair.

I simply stare at him. "Surely, the king would not allow this."

"No, he wouldn't. So, let's not tell him."

I hesitate, narrowing my eyes at him. "Why are you doing this? You don't even know me, and I killed your friend."

He drops his gaze, trudging around the table to stare out the window at the freshly manicured field. "I do not always agree with the king's methods. The man-made famine and the exiles—it's too much. Too much cruelty and suffering. He's an unkind, miserable man, and I don't want to be like him."

I flip over his words in my mind like stones. "Then what did you do with sister?" I dare to ask the question.

Ruben turns to me, running a hand through his dark hair. "She is back at your home. But we had to reduce her hours at the laundromat."

My heart slams into my ribs, and my stomach clenches. "Why?" Heat surges into my cheeks.

"I must give some sort of punishment, Elle. I do not make the rules, but I must follow some of them. Not unless you want her thrown into the madness outside the kingdom."

"She has no other way to feed herself," I snap, marching towards him, stopping only inches from his chest, scrunching my nose as stomach acid churns up my throat. "She will starve to *death* without my help."

"I didn't have a choice," he seethes. His jaw slams tight, eyes feral.

"Heartless monster. It must be easy for you when you have an abundance of food. Meanwhile, the Convex crops are rotting as we speak. The people are rotting themselves."

"I am not heartless," Ruben says, sucking in a breath. "I could have followed the king's orders and exiled your sister from the kingdom. But I chose to not throw her to the wolves. Be grateful."

"*Grateful?*" I stifle a dry laugh. "She will wither to dust and bones just the same if she cannot work."

His chest sinks as he blows out a deep breath through his nose. "I have taken care of her, Elle. I may have had to reduce her hours at her job, but she will not starve."

"How?"

"The less you know, the better. She will be alright. She will not starve. Trust me."

"Trust you?" I shake my head in disbelief.

"Just eat, Elle," he growls, pointing at the food on the table. "No more questions."

If I had any strength, I would protest. But I know the effort would be wasted. So, I grumble, slump into the chair and eat. Nausea crashes through me as I bring a spoonful of risotto to my lips, the aroma overwhelming. Flavours, foreign to me, dance on my tongue. Twirling and crackling. I think there are mushrooms in this dish. I stare at Ruben wide-eyed, lowering the spoon.

He raises his brows with a faint, amused smile on his face. "Mushroom and wine risotto. A personal favourite of mine. Eat up."

Without another thought, I plough through the bowl, sighing and groaning with utter relief. I chomp through the apple and banana and polish off the cheese and bread. My stomach swells and aches as if it's going to burst. But the hunger has eased at last. For now. I wipe the smeared creamy rice from my mouth.

"Thank you," I say.

"Of course." His voice is soft. He offers me a smile. His smile is so lovely I could stare at it for hours.

"What do you need from me now? What kind of payment?" I blurt out.

He smirks, taking me in for several beats as if he's never interacted with a Convex person for longer than an order. "Nothing. Other than a bath, maybe. You stink."

Chapter 8

Ruben leads me through the servants' quarters, past many more rooms—offices, bed chambers, storage closets, parlours—until he pulls up short in front of a wooden door with a polished bronze handle. His uniform clinks as he raises his fist and knocks.

"Larissa!" Ruben calls through the thick mahogany door.

"Come in, Your Highness," a meek voice calls back.

He hastens inside, and I scurry after him. I find myself in a large dressing room bathed in sunlight. The bathtub, raised on curled marble legs, sits on the left of the room, the light simmering within its iridescent marble. A vanity with a gleaming, round mirror takes up the furthest wall from the hearth. An open, walk-in wardrobe flanks the other side of the room, an array of clothing and fabrics spilling from the shelves and racks. I flinch at the girl in the mirror. Scrawny, bony, and smudged in dirt and dried blood as if she's been dragged from the gutters. My hair is a wild, flaming mess. I traipse over to the mirror. Hollow, frightened eyes. The dark circles beneath make the grey colour of my eyes look like a swirling, ominous storm.

"Thanks, Larissa. You're about to do the Gods' work," Ruben pipes up, and I forgot he was lurking behind me.

He nods at me before stalking out of the room.

Ice creeps into my gut like maggots to a corpse. Larissa, who stands by the vanity with her hands clasped, opens and closes her mouth.

"His Royal Highness, Prince Talin, said I need to help you look your best," she says finally, offering a sheepish smile as she smooths the corset that holds her slim, tall frame.

I grimace, stifling a laugh. "It might take more effort than you think. For that, I am sorry."

She waves her hand, the lines creasing between her brows, and I wonder if she's ever known how to relax them. "None of this is your fault."

Larissa's brown eyes hold mine before she crosses the room, fidgeting with the wispy strands of hair that have escaped her otherwise tight chestnut bun. Water gushes into the tub as she sprinkles in some powdery crystals, and a floral scent disperses into the air. She grins at me with yellowed teeth before clapping her hands together. The door crashes open, followed by a flurry of five other women dressed in the same white corset, grey frock and creamy apron pinned to their waists. They are all Convex. They descend on me like vultures, stripping the ragged, dirty clothes from my body and ushering me into the tub.

I hiss as the water scorches my cold toes but sigh as it seeps into the pores of my skin and loosens my taut muscles. Soap bubbles grow around me into tiny mountains, and the floral scent cuts through the lingering smell of grime. The women scrub me down with sudsy sponges and wash my tangled, oily hair. I resist the urge to tell them I can do this all by myself.

I sit there, letting them dunk my head under the water and rinse me with fresh water. All the while, they chirp at one another like gossiping birds.

"Did you see His Royal Highness in the hallway?" one of them says, voice trilling like string music, glancing around as she absentmindedly runs a razor blade over my bare legs.

The girls respond with giggles and gushes.

"He smiled at me when he passed. He's so handsome," the same girl says.

"I think we have a bond," another says, blushing. "He always greets me by name. Maybe one day he will tell me about *his* name on our wedding night."

"I wonder what it is," another girl chimes in, grinning.

"I'll tell you as soon as I know."

They cackle, and the sound makes the corner of my lip twitch up. Heat prickles my insides. He told me. *Ruben.* A secret. My secret. He must have just told me because he thought they were going to kill me. It must be hard to keep your identity from everyone, and a to-be-dead-girl offers safe ears. Yet here I am.

The girls hoist me from the tub, wrapping soft towels around me and rubbing my skin. They lather my limbs with rose-scented lotion before plucking and waxing more hair from my body in crevasses that make me shriek and curse. I am a chicken ready for the spit.

Someone slides a white robe over my shoulders, and the girls scurry out of the dressing room just as quickly as they came. Larissa materialises from the flurry. She rifles through the gowns in the wardrobe.

I blow out my cheeks, slumping into the seat by the vanity.

Larissa laughs, glancing at me with a sparkle in her eyes. "They are a lot of energy."

I smile, feeling warm for the first time in a while. "I think they're wonderful."

She purses her lips, stepping up behind me. I almost flinch when she reaches for my damp curls and grabs a paddle brush. "They tend to bicker like angry old ladies. The prince apparently put them in a good mood." Her honey-sweet scent puffs past me as she gently rakes the brush through my hair, pulling out the tangles.

"The prince is that powerful, huh?"

She swats at me. "Let's not fuel his already full-to-the-brim ego."

I laugh, watching the flush of my cheeks in the mirror. Larissa towel dries my hair and massages a thick cream into the ringlets, her nimble fingers rubbing my scalp, and I almost start purring. She arranges the curls around my head and drapes them down my shoulders.

"I am surprised you aren't going to give me one of the hairstyles that all the young Concave ladies wear," I say, catching her eye in the reflection.

"The braid updo?" Larissa snorts and shakes her head. "Not for the king. He should fear you just as you are."

"The king?"

"Yes. Didn't Prince Talin tell you? You're to meet His Majesty, the king." The words spill out, almost catching in her throat, as if she realised that I wasn't meant to know.

"What for?" I cringe at myself. As if the king wouldn't want to clap eyes on the girl who defied him.

"Well, he knows what you did. A few of the servants know, too. From when the crown prince stumbled into the palace after you… hit him with the knife." A nervous pause. She chews her lip. "We know about the girl who dared to kill a Tranquillity. But we have been sworn to keep it secret from others."

"Almost the prince, too," I remind her, waggling my finger.

"It is a dangerous game you are playing," she says, again in a way that tells me her conscious and subconscious are at war. Drawers of the vanity grate together as she pulls them open and digs for a palette of colours. Pinks and browns. She dusts powder onto my cheeks and swipes my lashes with black and my eyebrows with brown pigment made from dyes and oils.

"I didn't ask to starve," I say, a lump forming in the back of my throat as my father's voice, masking my own, rings in my head. *What have you done, Elle?* I push the panic back. "The Tranqs attacked me first. It was self-defence."

"King Talin won't care." Her eyes, like molten earth, burn into me with a ferocity that turns my limbs to stone, and my heart clubs, instinctively rallied by her rebellious spirit. "You have made a grave mistake, Elle. The people you love will suffer for it.'"

"I know," I say, guilt chipping away at my mood, piece by piece.

"He is afraid of people like you—people who defy him. Growing your own food is an act of defiance because it means he doesn't entirely control you. Killing his Tranquillity is another. Both are crimes no one has ever dared to commit."

"How do you know this?"

She tightens her jaw, and a wave of grief crashes through her face. "My brother committed a crime in the king's eyes. He tried to find a cure for the blight. Eventually, he found a treatment that would prevent the blight from growing in the first place. But someone in the village tattled on him before he could announce his findings to the Convex mayor. The king swiftly destroyed his fungicide treatment. Then they destroyed him."

My spine tightens, and I am reminded of Aston's mother, the woman whose similar crime and exile led me to meet her son.

"They banished him, didn't they?"

"The king simply ordered the execution of my parents in the gallows and banished him. But, of course, exile is far worse than a quick execution."

My stomach churns, and bile stings in my throat as my palms moisten with sweat. Larissa sweeps into the wardrobe and plucks a red dress from the rack. Dark and vibrant as blood. As she helps me into the fabrics, she says, "I feel sick with anger at the way they destroyed him." Her nose wrinkles and her eyes redden. "I think the monsters got him."

73

"You believe in the monsters, too?"

"Don't we all? Creatures of the night with sharp teeth and no soul." She fusses over the placement of the material, pinching and pulling. Her eyes flick me up and down until she sighs, stepping back.

"You're still alive, though. How did they let that happen?" I ask, clearing my throat when she gives me a strange look. "I mean, how are you here?"

"I was only a young child when my brother committed his crimes. So, they sent me to the palace to learn to become a king's servant."

I bite the inside of my cheek, my mouth filling with saliva. "Do you still live in the Convex Sector as a servant?"

"Yes. But I also have a room in the servants' quarters. We rotate in and out every few days."

Larissa smiles, tilting her head to the full-length mirror beside the vanity. I turn and gape at myself. The dress, bold and demanding, makes me look like I strutted straight out of the depths of hell. Tethered to the flames and raging heat. My orange-red curls tumble around my face and down my shoulders. The paleness of my skin is a stark contrast to the red adorning my hips, and the collar cuts low across my breasts. I cringe at my bony collarbones. But my eyes, though grey, are, for once, bright, as though the storm waging within me has been forged from the essence of the Goddess of War and Hope.

"Too few are brave enough to do anything to protect the ones they love," Larissa says, her voice a hush no louder than the wind brushing the windows outside. "Even at the risk of their neck. You would have gotten along well with my brother. I have a feeling about you, Elle, like we might have been looking for you all this time."

Heat seeps into my cheeks, and a knot tugs at my gut. "You have done the work of the Gods, Larissa."

She grins, and something wild glints in her eyes. "Let the king tremble at the mere sight of you."

That's when Ruben returns, leaning against the doorframe, an expression hewn from the darkest reaches of the forest etched on his face. I clear my throat, shooting him a glare. He rolls his shoulders back, and he swallows as he takes in my appearance. My skin bursts aflame.

"You look... like a human and not a dirty creature dragged from the gutters."

"Pig." I roll my eyes, stalking forward.

"You can just say she looks beautiful, Your Highness," Larissa says, clasping her hands together and glancing at her feet like she's afraid of her own voice.

He scrunches his nose and swallows bodily.

"Don't bother," I snap. "Gods forbid the crown prince from uttering something nice. A complete fool." However, a strange feeling stirs in my chest as I stare at him, the man seemingly handcrafted by the Goddess of Night.

His gaze meets mine, and he scoffs, running a hand through his dark brown hair as he paces towards the window. "Do I finally hear an insult other than *pig*? I will take it."

"You have the wit of a butter knife."

Larissa giggles from a few paces behind us as we slip through the corridors and mount a wide, spiralling staircase. The higher we ascend into the palace, the faster my heart hammers in my ribs and the louder the blood roars past my ears. We pass an arched window, and the sun has long since raced beneath the horizon, revealing the star-freckled night. Outside, a winter squall brews. The wind sings, battering the glass.

Ruben, leading the way, turns around. He heaves, blowing out his cheeks. "Are you ready to meet the king?"

Chapter 9

A deep shudder reverberates through my skull as the enormous doors grate open on their hinges. The door shines with its freshly polished marble kissed with gold. My thumping heart practically echoes off the walls of the expansive hall. The floor is blue and white marble, with pillars rising to the roof. Monstrous arched windows border either side of the hall, and candles surround the room, washing the room in flickering yellow light.

I draw in a ragged breath, schooling my face into neutrality. Ruben steps across the threshold into the courtroom, his strides smooth and seamless. Yet, he fumbles with his fingers, and I can hear his jittery breathing. His hand quivers. Fear. His anguish sends my heart slamming into my ribs. My instincts scream at me to turn and run from the wolf waiting to devour me at the end of the room. But I force myself to keep up the pace.

Candlelight tumbles through the room, drenched in the aroma of sharp perfume and burning wax. The faint pluck of string instruments tangles with the heavy tapestries hewn to the century's old marble walls, dancing between the carvings of erupting volcanoes, trumpeting elephants, and curling waves. The king himself rises from the bone-white throne, his cape draping as if the night sky spills around his shoulders. He slithers forward, practically scrunching his toes over the ledge upon which his throne sits.

His eyes never leave mine, like a viper silently stalking its prey. A poisonous essence cascades from the man's black suit, which is flecked with silver stitching. The golden crown sits so comfortably on his head that I wonder if he sleeps with it pinned to his scalp. A shudder slides its fingers down my spine. My skin crawls, and I squirm. We approach the bottom of the stairs, pausing a few feet before them. Ruben bows low, and I stick my foot behind the other, curtseying. Every instinct urges me to run, run, run. But Ruben's face remains as stoic and solid as stone. And I can't bring myself to commit another crime. Not when Lyra's life hangs on by a very thin thread.

"Are you mute, girl?" the king barks, and I flinch. His deep, braying voice bounces off the surrounding walls and slices into my bone marrow. His hair is dark, greying, and thin. He has groomed facial hair and a tan, leathered face from too many years trapped in the snares of utter misery. "I *said*, what is your name?"

Ruben nudges me in the rib and clears his throat. If we weren't standing before the king, I would toss him an ugly gesture.

Instead, I pluck up my courage and muster my voice. "No, Your Majesty. My name is Elle Fallon."

"Elle," he says, dragging out the name as if it tastes like a bitter memory from his childhood. "Is that a nickname?"

"Yes, Your Majesty. My full name is Elizabeth Fallon. But everyone calls me Elle."

"Elle," he says again, lowering his brow and looking at me through his lashes. "Do you know why you are here?"

"Yes, Your Majesty."

His eyes rove me, and he bares his teeth. The king clicks his gloved fingers, and a man scuttles across the podium. He grips the hilt of a knife. The blade gleams in the twirling candlelight as if it might spring to life and slice someone's throat. My mouth dries as the herald presents the knife to the king before bowing and ducking away just as gracefully as he came.

"Does this knife look familiar to you, Elle?" The king's voice rattles around in my skull, dripping with authority. He twirls the knife, examining the sharp blade, before flicking his venomous gaze back to me.

"Yes. That is my knife." I choke out the words, and my face burns.

"The knife you used to murder my Tranquillity." He throws the words at me, laced with poison. "Then you almost murdered the prince, too."

I shift my weight, grimacing at the thought of the nasty wound on Ruben's shoulder.

He blows out his nose, and his lips curl, showing off his pointed, yellowed canines. "Our kingdom relies on the function of a delicate balance. If you break the balance, we will lose everything we know. Everyone has a place and rules to follow. In your actions, you have defied me. With the growing tensions across the river, I must make an example of your crimes."

He rises and stalks down the stairs, my impassive expression fighting for its life against the obnoxious clack, clack, clack of his boots. The king sticks his chin into the air, but his gaze on me doesn't waver. A phantom blade runs, icy, down my back.

"If a scrawny girl from the village can dare to kill a Tranquillity, who is to say others will not follow? Who is to say others will not try to kill more of my Tranquillity?" His brows form an arch, and he clasps his hands in front of him like he's trying to withhold some feral, gnashing beast.

"It was an accident, Your Majesty," I blurt out. I wish I could catch the words and stuff them back in my mouth.

He breathes a laugh, and his lip twists into a snarl. "Don't lie to me," he says, voice a low hiss. "Was it an accident when you threw the knife at my *son*? It was almost cold-blooded *murder*."

Ruben stiffens.

"As opposed to the rotting potatoes in the Convex fields. That isn't murder?" My nails dig into my palms, and I mirror the king's bull-like stance.

Something utterly wild and... grief-stricken flashes across the king's eyes.

"Elle, shut up," Ruben mutters.

His mouth stretches up, and his throat bobs as he swallows bodily. "Do you know what lies beyond those mighty walls, Elle?" The way he spits my name makes me want to gag, or curse, or hurl my fist at his smug face.

"I have another idea," Ruben says, clearing his throat.

The king smiles, but his eyes glint with creeping malice. "What could be more fitting than what I described?"

Ruben fidgets with his finger behind his back. "We make her become a Tranquillity."

The king blinks at Ruben before tossing his head back, laughing with such force I flinch. "A Tranquillity?" he bellows, wiping a tear.

"Think about it." Ruben straightens his back and takes on a steady, demanding tone only a prince could have mastered. "We show the Convex she is one of us now. Show them her loyalty and that *their* loyalty should be with you. Think of her as a symbolic bridge, connecting the Convex people with us, not pitting them against us."

He narrows his eyes, prowling around us like a starving snake. "There is something else, isn't there, son?"

"Yes," Ruben says, glancing at me.

I tilt my head, pursing my lips together. Did I miss something?

"Elle will marry me," Ruben says.

The room spins, and my stomach drops, just like it did when I was ten, just after my parents died, and I tried to steal a bread roll from the pocket of a little boy. He whirled around without warning and put his rusty knife against my throat. My knees wobble, and my chest swells with panic that dribbles out into the hall in the strangest form. Giggles.

Both men glare at me as I stuff the chuckles back into my mouth and shove a nonchalant expression onto my face. I wonder if they can hear my untamed heart. My teeth scrape together, and frustrated tears nettle my eyes. But I blink them away and push past the scream scalding my tongue.

"Marry you?" I splutter, stumbling backwards.

"I agree. This is utterly ridiculous." The king shakes his head, grinding his jaw. He stops and surveys the prince. "We will publicly exile her to show the people across the river what happens if they try to stand against us. Simple as that. The easiest way to *move on*."

"Think about it, Father," Ruben says, voice strained. "Give the people a distraction. You said it yourself, the Convex are festering in their misery. Distract them and the Concaves from the actual problems with the wedding of the prince. A public exile could backfire and just fuel their tensions. Many of the Convex have nothing to lose because they have already lost enough. So, they would be more likely to retaliate."

King Talin rubs his beard and paces back and forth. "But the ensuing terror would quickly snuff out any future idiotic plans in the villages."

"I need a bride, Father!" Ruben snaps, a muscle rippling in his neck. "You need a succession. Let's punish Elle by getting her to enforce your laws while distracting the kingdom with wedding parties, balls, and trying on gowns."

A vein pops out in the king's neck, and he snarls in such a way I almost wonder if a set of venomous fangs will sink from his gums and flash in the light of the chandelier. "Fine. Elle can train to become a Tranquillity, and she can become your betrothed. We will announce the forthcoming union to the kingdom tomorrow night."

"Thank you, Father," Ruben says, bowing his head.

I murmur my thanks and mimic him.

"But I have one more thing to add, Elle," he says, drumming his fingers together.

I snap my head up and clench my jaw.

He massages his chin as he stops pacing and glares at me. "I don't trust you," he says. "So, I need you to prove your loyalty to me. And to prove it to the Convex and Concaves. You will need to pass a series of tests to prove your loyalty. It is more than wearing pretty dresses and sleeping in my palace. Understand?"

"What tests?" Ruben asks, shifting his weight.

"You will see, my son." He smirks but doesn't so much as glance at Ruben.

I squirm in place but roll my shoulders back. "I will convince them."

"And me," he says in a low growl. "Convince *me* of your loyalty. As my son said, you will be the bridge. *Show* me this is true."

I gulp, and Ruben stiffens.

He claps his hands, and the herald materialises again.

"Frederick, will you show Elle to the empty bed chamber in the east wing? Instruct Miss Larissa and the maids to make up the room."

The herald slithers towards me, locking his bug-like eyes on me and inclining his head. With one last glare at Ruben, who refuses to look me in the eye, I follow the herald. He leads me back out of the hall and into the corridor, where he leads me through the maze of the palace. We pass through a hallway of tall walls with large oil paintings. Each painting depicts the lineage of kings throughout the history of the kingdom. The kings have always had something in common. Brown hair and green or blue eyes. They have prided themselves in their features for generations. King Talin's grinning portrait is no different.

The herald stops. I pull up short, almost knocking into his shoulder. He rotates his torso and stares at me with his enormous eyes. He pushes a door open and ushers me inside. It's a large bed chamber, with a four-poster framed bed in the centre of the room, stripped bare of sheets. There's a bathroom off one corner of the room and a dresser and vanity pushed against another wall with a full-length mirror. A couch and bookshelf swallow the last wall. Rows and rows of titles burst from the shelves.

As the herald slips out, Larissa barges in, followed by her flurry of gossiping women. They carry bundles of fresh sheets, blankets, and clothing. Larissa frowns at me as she approaches.

"I am surprised you are still here," she says.

I sigh, shrugging. "The king has other plans for me worse than death."

"That sounds about right."

"So, I'll be sticking around to annoy you for a little while yet."

She rolls her eyes and claps. The girls disperse. White sheets billow like clouds as they toss them onto the bed, tugging them into the corners, and their chatter trills in the air.

"Let me help," I say, reaching for a blanket.

Larissa gives me a good-natured shove to the velvet couch next to a bookshelf. "It is our job to help you. It is the least we can do after today." She roams around the room, lighting the candles with a match. One candle must be scented because the room fills with the smell of vanilla.

I watch the girls prepare the room as pressure builds in my chest. They laugh and giggle with one another. Meanwhile, the primal urge to curl into a ball and weep grows heavier, demanding more and more of my attention, like the illness people get from the unsanitary water in the Convex Sector. But I chew on my cheek, fighting the feeling as the tang of blood crawls across my tongue. The sensation tethers me to reality. I breathe a sigh of relief as they scurry away but keep the urge at bay while Larissa lingers back.

Larissa studies me, her breath fanning my face. She puts her finger under my chin, forcing me to look at her. Her lower lip sticks out. "What have they sentenced you to, Elle?"

The pressure bubbles up, and hot tears blind my face as I cup my mouth, muffling the sobs. What have I done?

Larissa kneels before me and gently squeezes my shoulder. "Whatever it is, you will always have an ally in me."

I try to smile, but the tears spill down my cheeks as I splutter. "I must prove my loyalty to the king, no matter the cost."

Chapter 10

I toss my hands into the air, storming across my bed chamber. "Marry you?"

Ruben barrels into the room without even knocking, muttering a flurry of curses as if I should somehow be falling over my feet with excitement to marry him—*marry* him. I square my shoulders and sink into a brooding cloud, ready to refuse before he even tries to drag me out to my first morning duties.

His scent swirls past me, fuelling the rage brewing in my hands, face, and chest. "Good morning to you, too," he says, clicking his tongue.

I roll my eyes, pacing to the window and leaning against it. My back to him. It's a dreary day. Grey clouds billow in from the east, coating the sky with the foreboding of more snow. Yet, lazy fingers of sunlight reach over the kingdom. Frost spreads across the window frames like cobwebs.

"The wedding won't be for several months," he says, blowing out his cheeks in such a way that I have a feeling he tossed and turned all night, too. Good.

"You never mentioned this part of the deal." I whirl around, glaring.

He shifts his weight, stuffing his hands into his pockets. Today, he doesn't wear his armour. Only the black pants and long-sleeved tunic. "The idea came to me after we spoke. I wanted to tell you earlier."

"Lies," I spit, stalking forward until I am only inches from him. "I don't want to marry you, Ruben."

"Oh, gee. Thanks." He crosses his arms over his chest, and a vein in his neck pulses. "Did you think I wanted this?"

I simply shake my head. "I cannot believe I agree with the king. It would have been easier to exile me and get on with it."

His eyes narrow. "Why are you acting so ungrateful when I saved your life?"

"Because this is a trap!" I find myself leaning forward as the heat surges throughout my body.

"A trap?" The morning light gilds his face, and his forest eyes glimmer like pools of jade.

"I don't want to pretend to be happy for the rest of my life, stuffing my belly, wearing fancy stones and gowns, while my people across the river starve to death each winter! It just isn't fair." My voice trails off, and a single tear slips down my cheek. "Nothing about the Sectors has ever been fair."

He flinches at my words, scrunching his nose. Ruben steps back and traces the edge of the vanity with his fingertip. "I couldn't banish you, Elle. I couldn't be responsible for that."

"Why?"

"Because my father loves watching people go. Because it is the quickest way for him to regain his control, to remain relevant without having to see the consequences of his cruelty. Except for each night that those city gates open and close on a person, he turns to the drink to console himself. To dampen the impending, instinctive guilt of the blood on his hands. It is one of the reasons you'll never catch the king in the Convex Sector. He can't handle seeing the bones of the people *he* starves."

The whistling wind fades into the background as I swallow his words. A cruel yet *remorseful* king. Too cowardly to change. "So, you don't want to end up drunken and miserable either."

His eyes flash as if he's remembering something horrific. The darkness roils around him as he presses his lips together. "Not if I can help it. I am not like him."

"A delicate balance," I echo the king's words from last night. "That's why you've suggested the wedding. To keep the balance."

He sighs, and his shoulders slump. "It was still a dangerous move. If we tried anything more dangerous... my father would just send more Tranqs into the Convex Sector to keep everyone doing what he wants them to do. No one would dare lift a finger, not even in their own home, or... or in the forest."

I chew my lip, my stomach churning at the possibility of the Tranqs realising that Aston, indeed, sells illegal produce. "I don't even know you," I say, smacking my lips at the bitter taste in my mouth. "Let alone like you."

He snorts unkindly, rolling his eyes. "No one cares what you want at this stage. This is bigger than you, and you're damn lucky to even still be alive. This might prevent more Convex exile if you can prove to the king that you are *loyal*."

"The Convex… my people are masters at dancing with the God of Souls. Besides, my death would have at least promised my sister staying alive and being able to work. Now, with me in the palace, she is just a target. He could and will use her against me."

"You killed my friend," he snarls. His voice is the shadows themselves, low and dark and inviting. "I am doing you a favour."

Unpleasant pig. I swallow nausea as the wide-eyed Tranq flashes across my mind. My knife embedded in his chest, cocooned in his blood.

"Your king would have killed my sister and me by starvation if I didn't bend the rules and grow the potatoes."

"And look where it got you." He gestures to the room. "Under the king's scrutinising cruel eye. Don't be so naïve to think he won't find his own selfish way to punish you further. It's coming, Elle. Being betrothed to me might shield you from some of that blood and loss."

"As if I didn't know that, *Ruben*." I fling his name at his face and grind my teeth. "Did you come in here to argue and gloat about your heroic moves? If so, please leave."

"Gods, you're odious." He yanks the door open and strides into the hallway, tossing a stony face over his shoulder. "Come on."

"I suppose you will not tell me where we are going?"

He flicks his hand up and down my body like it's obvious. "You're a Tranq now. Curvy, red dresses will not cut it, darling."

I tug at my linen dressing gown, feeling exposed. "Pig," I say.

"Nice one," he drawls, stalking away before his voice echoes back into my chamber. "Come *on*, Elle."

He leads me through the maze of the palace, winding through corridors, passing servants scurrying about their morning tasks. We descend a set of stairs and arrive outside, my footsteps crunching, the frost clinging to the manicured grass. The sweet scent of grass tints the air as we cross the wide field, the blades tipped in white frost, crunching beneath my feet. Another building flanks the other side. Short and squat compared to the palace, its dark stone and wood.

I revel in the warm sun on my skin until we slip into the building. Candlelight shimmies back and forth along the obsidian walls of the narrow hallway.

We arrive in a room that appears to be an enormous wardrobe. Racks and shelves border the walls, bursting with Tranquillity uniforms and helmets. Ruben shoots me a smirk. As if that were a cue, Larissa scurries into the room, switching her small briefcase into her right hand and then back again, her eyes flicking between Ruben and me as if she's trying to assess the level of tension that she must wade through.

"What are you doing here?" I ask, looking over her shoulder as if the rest of the girls are about to follow her in like ducklings.

"I am here to help you look like a Tranq," she says, shrugging. "Tranqs are also typically Concaves. They look put together."

"Do you need my help, Larissa?" Ruben asks, his mouth flopping upwards. "Shall we fix Elle with more knives so she can kill us?"

"Get out, Your Highness!" She swats him with her briefcase.

Ruben chuckles, tossing his hands up into the air as he hastens away.

Larissa rifles through the rows of pants and tunics, plucking out the pieces. She helps me into the clothing, and fits me a new pair of black leather boots. I can already feel the material biting into my skin, forming blisters, as I pace back and forth, making sure they fit.

Larissa opens another closet, revealing an array of shelves brimming with fresh, gleaming Tranq helmets, the shade of dead coals. She glances at me, narrows her eyes, and plucks a smaller headpiece from the bottom shelf. Her lower lip sticks out as she holds it above my head. I nod and suck in a breath. Larissa slides the helmet over my head, and the heavy, warm metal jabs into my skull.

She fixes my clothing with a chest plate and armour for my shoulders and arms. My thin frame looks like it may collapse under the armour, but it's all lightweight and moves easily as I swish my arms around. Larissa fastens a belt around my waist and disappears to a shadowed part of the room. She returns with two knives. My mouth falls open.

"Why do I have these?"

She slides the blades into sheathes, pinning them to the belt. "Every Tranq has a special weapon. Yours are the knives. Perhaps we can fix you with a sword, too." Larissa quirks her lip before grabbing a spearhead staff from another shelf. She fastens the long body onto the straps on my back.

"She has a sword," Ruben says, and my gaze snaps up. He leans against the doorframe, crossing his arms against his chest. His smirk drops. "We found her sword in her apartment during the arrest."

My cheeks burn. He nods to the wall of lockers on the opposite wall. There is already a locker with my name. *E. Fallon.* "Go on," he says.

I toss him a glare, pry the door open and loosen a gasp. My father's sword, with the Fallon family emblem, rests on a hook. The light above our heads gilds the... freshly polished blade.

Ruben clears his throat. "I had the palace blacksmith give it a polish and sharpen."

My heart creeps into my throat, and I reach in. A chill plunges into my gut. My dagger... the one I used to kill the Tranq, rests on the small shelf in the locker, engulfed in the dim of the brass walls. A tremble rips through my hand as I grasp its hilt, running my thumb over the grooves of the twin snake emblem. My stomach convulses. For a moment, wisps of the coppery scent of blood drip from the shining blade into the air. "Are you... sure, Your Highness?" I swallow bodily.

"Larissa said it herself," he says, closing the space between us. "Your weapon is the blades."

I open my mouth to respond, but his scent... citrus and the forest, renders me silent. Still. My breath echoes around my head in the helmet.

Ruben reaches over me and opens the locker next to him. He pulls out a sleek bow and a quiver teeming with arrows clad in iron-carved points. "Mine is the bow."

Larissa ushers me into a brown leather couch in the room's corner. She pulls the helmet off and winds my hair into two braids along the sides of my head and down my back. Then, she adds a dusting of makeup to my face. Concealing the bags under my eyes. Swiping black onto my lashes.

"Won't my face remain in the helmet?" I ask, suddenly wishing for it to hide any sliver of expression from the prince and his odious lingering glances.

"We are just going for a tour of the Concave Sector," Ruben says, fixing the bow and quiver to his back. "You don't need the helmet."

He takes the sword from the locker and places it across my back, the strap of the scabbard crossing my chest. Everything in me wants to set fire.

"Careful," he says, waggling his finger, catching my gaze. "Your eyes are going to fall right out of your head."

Larissa giggles, and I shoot her a glare. I thank her for helping before slipping out of the building after Ruben. "Would you like to see my town?" Ruben asks as soon as the sunlight drenches us. He gestures to an approaching horse pulling a large mahogany carriage.

The horse snorts and stamps his feet. A manicured, polished beast. Aston's voice pipes up in the back of my head, reminding me of how stupid I am. But I brush him away and climb into the carriage despite myself. My body sinks into the plush cushioned seats, my hand trailing the velvet. Ruben slumps across from me. He jolts back as the horse trots into step. I try not to pick at my nails as he stares at me, considering, while the carriage circles the expansive palace grounds until the smooth paths become stone-paved roads. We have entered the Concave streets. I fight the urge to press my hands against the window and stare. These people always leave me amazed and angry at the same time. Their bright-coloured clothing, full bellies and jewels bury needles of envy deep into my gut.

"Where are we going?" I finally ask, leaning back in the seat.

"My favourite bar," he says, and his lips quirk up. "It's the one place I can feel... a little less like a prince."

"Let me guess. You're going to get me drunk and humiliate me?"

He laughs. A deep belly laugh that warms my blood. "Have you ever interacted with a regular Concave?"

"Only once or twice. My friend Aston is a farmer, and sometimes, he brings me with him on his delivery runs. A Concave once chased us out of his restaurant with a meat cleaver because he said we smelled of dirty horses. As if we hadn't delivered his produce with the help of a horse."

"He wanted to kill you?" He rests his head against the window, his eyes drooping. I realise, fleetingly, how exhausting being the prince must be. The son of a miserable man. Having to put on a mask every day, going against your morals.

"I am sure he would have killed us if he could. But his restaurant was full, and it would have been a grim look for business."

"He could not afford such a dirty look on his restaurant." Ruben's face brightens with amusement. I notice he has a couple of freckles on his nose and cheeks. Only visible in the light streaming in through the carriage, warming his skin.

I jerk forward as the horse pulls to a halt. We dismount from the carriage, thanking the horseman, whose scruffy hair, dark grey pants, and brown tunic show he's from across the river. I am thankful when

94

Ruben places a handsome pile of silver coins into the man's gnarled palm.

We step away from the carriage, and I glance at my surroundings. Pastel hues of blue, yellow, rose pink, and dusty orange stain the buildings looming over the smoothed stone road. Carefree laughter flecks the wind, and arched pathways stretch overhead. Two gleaming Concave men, with their slicked-back hair, clean-shaven faces, and blue and violet suits, perch on their balcony like birds fawning over a nest, sipping bubbling wine the shade of a waxing sun, their curious eyes tracing my movements.

"Redhead with Prince Talin," one of them mutters to the other, loud enough to warrant a wave from me as I plaster a smile on my face. They eagerly return it.

"The Concave people adore the Tranquillity," Ruben whispers as he nods at them. "But they love their prince."

"Do you ever listen to yourself speak?" I ask, shaking my head as we turn the corner. A soft, high-pitched melody fills my ears, and we move through a pocket of Concaves hovering around someone playing the violin. His dark-toned hands dance back and forth across the beaten-up instrument like it's a race, like his life depends on the music. Because it does. Fury ripples through me. Yet another Convex person used for the whims of the privileged. The Convex man peaks his eyes open in between the notes. His weathered gaze locks with mine. Lingering. As if he just knows I'm not from here, too. I elbow Ruben in the ribs, who tosses another handful of coins into the splayed violin case.

Ruben slips past the Concave throng and into an alleyway. But not before the Concaves pepper him with cheerful yet obsessive greetings, grappling out their limbs in a desperate bid to feel a hair of royal flesh.

A warm glow permeates the bar as we cross the threshold of the arched doorway. Ruben cringes as we leave the crowd, shaking his arms as if to rid himself of their unwanted touch.

Only a few other Concave people scatter the round wooden tables of the diner. A low rumble of chatter thrums, and heat billows from the crackling flame in the hearth to the left. I shiver. Hundreds of bottles filled with various kinds of liquor line the shelves behind the bar. The barman's eyes pin onto the prince, widening. Fine glass tumblers clink together as he grabs a bottle of unopened whisky from the shelf.

"Only the stars themselves for His Royal Highness," the bartender says, bowing his head before carefully pouring the liquor into the glasses. I catch the year 2152 engraved into the bottle. Almost 50 years ago. Likely the most expensive bottle of liquor in the entire kingdom. He hands the glasses over, and my jaw falls open. Tiny flakes of *gold* float in the liquor—bobbing up and down like a couple on the ballroom floor.

Ruben raises the glass to his lips and tilts his head, eyes roaming my face and glimmering with amusement. Yet, darkness settles over him. He is swathed in the night as if he knows the language of the moon. I wonder if he's ever known the light. "To the stars, Elle," he says.

"To the stars, Your Highness."

We tap the glass rims together, and I take a sip. Indeed, the stars themselves murmur over my tongue. I stare at him, and he chuckles. The liquor warms the back of my throat. I take another sip.

"Do you know what's being done about the supply shortage, Your Royal Highness?" the barman pipes up. His thick brows furrow, and he flicks his prying eyes between us.

Ruben shifts on the barstool, shaking his head. "It is the same as the past few winters. Things will pick up again in the hotter months."

"Useless Convex," he grumbles, knocking back the last dregs of his bourbon. "Taking too long to grow decent crops. I am sure the Tranqs will whip them into a sense of urgency, right?"

Ruben kicks me as my chest burns. I drink deeply while a figure slumps into the seat next to Ruben's and glances at him sideways. Her eyes are hollow, her cheeks puffy and stained with old tears, her stomach swollen.

"Only a lemonade, please," she says to the bartender.

As he slides the bubbling glass before her, she grinds her teeth. Her face reddens. "Your Highness." A half-assed bow. "When will you have news about the person who murdered my husband?"

Chapter 11

I welcome the rest of the liquor burning down my throat. Ruben tenses, but his composure remains granite. He presses his lips together. "We have them imprisoned. The king will determine their execution date shortly. We will notify you."

My grip tightens around the glass at his lie, and I am grateful for the bartender when he tops me up. The pregnant woman weeps, fresh tears dribbling down her brown cheeks. "How can someone be so hateful?" she says, pulling a cloth from her pocket and holding it to her leaking nose. "How can they rob a child of their father?"

Ruben heaves a sigh. "They were thoughtless and selfish."

I resist the urge to crash the glass on his stupid head and resort to kicking him under the bench. He ignores me, placing his hand gently over the lady's trembling one. "We will find you and your child justice, Lily."

She clutches the handkerchief and squeezes her eyes shut. Another tear escapes. The room sways, and my muscles grow heavy. A merciful relief despite the acid burning my throat and sizzling beneath my skin. Lily drains the rest of her lemonade before trudging back out of the bar, nodding goodbye to Ruben.

He scowls. "Don't even try to get angry at me."

"I'm not," I say with a slur, gripping a fresh glass of gold whisky. "She's right. I am hateful. I tore a father from their child." A chill slithers into my gut as the raw honesty and reality of my words reverberate around us.

Hateful. The thought rattles around my head with icy resonance, like the chime of temple bells. Am I hateful? *No.* I *had* to save my sister from those Tranqs. We'd both be long rotting beyond the walls now if I hadn't found the potato garden in the forest all those years ago or defended myself against the Tranqs. Sometimes, *within* the walls, we must be selfish. I did not enjoy tearing a father away from his child, of course. I know that feeling all too well. Their deaths prowl through my mind with reckless abandon, reminding me how utterly alone I am in this kingdom if it were not for my sister, who I must... I just must protect. Selfishness keeps one alive in this kingdom. It is how we survive.

"It is quite suffocating in here," Ruben says, downing the last of his drink. "Shall we continue our walk through the streets?"

I nod, thanking the bartender. We stumble out of the bar, dodging the crowds still filling the alleyway and the street. Ruben leads me past the fairy-tale hue buildings, balconies, and underneath stone arches. Horse hooves clatter in the distance. But carriage wheels do not screech or shake against the smooth pavement. Savoury and sweet aromas splash past my nose, competing with one another, and my stomach rumbles in protest. We continue through the streets until the buildings thin out, and we arrive at a park in the north of the Concave Sector. Across yet another arched bridge, over a gurgling, bubbling stream, and onto the freshly mowed grass. Evergreen hedges and plants border the sprawling grassy field, and bronze park benches dot the landscape. Thickets of bright violet flowers shift in the icy breeze. Concave people mingle about. Walking, hands entwined with one another. Children shriek with laughter as they kick a ball between them.

My eyes linger on the water fountain in the centre of the park. A round marble pool, elevated from the grass, with porcelain sculptures of two female figures. Naked and sitting with their backs against each other. One of them wears a necklace with a crescent moon and cries tears of stars. While the other wears a floral headpiece.

"The Goddesses of the Night and the Day," Ruben says, his gaze roving my face, not theirs.

"I know," I say. "Tutella and Ruaris. Two sisters separated by Curos, God of the Earth, who cast a spell on the planet, making it so the sisters could only perform their duties without each other."

"So, they *do* teach you of the legends in Convex schools."

"Pig. You know our school system is basically non-existent," I say, rolling my eyes. "If it weren't for my mother, I wouldn't have even learned to read."

We leave the sculptures behind, stepping onto a narrow path that stretches to the furthest end of the park. Sparse trees welcome us. Their limbs, bony and cold, stripped bare of their leaves for the winter. Sodden brown leaves glue to the forest floor, crunching under our boots. A sickly sweet smell clings to the air, and the frost speckles the trees. We lose the path in our wake, moving deeper.

My instincts crackle to life in the depths of my gut as the landscape shifts, greens, browns, and whites blending with one another, like the work of a drunken painter, his brush stumbling over the canvas. Where is he taking me?

"My father is trying to drink himself to death," Ruben says suddenly.

We step over another narrow stream, crunching fallen twigs beneath our boots. I raise an eyebrow.

"He is afraid." His voice sounds like a molten night sky. "My father is afraid of being alone."

I swallow the lump in my throat. "How?"

"The Convex people are festering in their suffering. Any spark of hope, any brave act of defiance, such as yours, is an opportunity for them to muster their courage collectively."

"He has agreed to cover up my… crime, though, hasn't he?" I draw in a gulp of air as we reach an open alcove of trees. The Goddess of the Day spills her canary sunlight into the clearing, glinting off the patches of old snow like the chandelier in the king's throne room.

"Yes. But a scared, hateful king has never fared well in the history books. With the growing tensions outside the kingdom, he will want the Tranqs to tighten things in the Convex villages."

I shake my head. "What are the growing tensions?"

His shoulders tense, and he tightens his jaw. "We believe the outsiders want our resources, Elle." He pauses, running his finger along his shirt collar. "When our ancestors began building the city walls, they chose a piece of earth with the healthiest soils. The ridiculous levels of carbon dioxide deposits poisoned most of the planet's soil. Not to mention, much of it has also been ravished by the blight. The outsiders are starving and angry. We have been hoarding the good soil within the walls for the last 150 years."

My gut plummets to my feet. Aston has been, of course, right all along. This… war with the people beyond the walls has always been a battle between human desperation and greed.

"So, they're threatening to invade us, right?"

Ruben leans against a bare tree trunk. "He's haunted by the threats of outside the kingdom and within."

"Who are the outsiders, Ruben?" I pace back and forth in the clearing. My chest swells with anxiety, scorching and demanding my attention. "Are they the monsters?"

He flinches at my use of his name but grinds his teeth.

"Can you not tell me?" I press.

"No, Elle," he snaps, stuffing his hands into his pockets. "I am not even sure who they are. I have only heard the few things my father has told me."

I cross my arms. "Fine. Then can you tell me what you mean by tightening up the Convex Sector?"

He hangs his head, refusing to meet my eye. "We will have to increase surveillance again. There will be more exiles. More demand from the farmers to provide for the Concaves, or further punishments and torture."

Panic slithers around my throat like a snake, sinking its poison-dripping fangs into my flesh. Before he can react, I yank a knife from my belt, lurch forward, and press the blade against his throat. A string of startled curses falls from his lips. His nose flares. But as the blood slips from his face and utter terror sinks into his eyes, heat pulses through my veins with the ferocity of the wildfires my father used to battle in his youth during the summer.

"You're a coward," I say through gritted teeth.

"What the hell?" he seethes, shadows billowing around him. The night itself.

I snort, shaking my head. The sharp tip of the blade presses into his delicate skin. His Adam's apple trembles. "You're full of shit. Acting as if you care about me, about the Convex. But it's nothing but an act to protect your ego, to help you sleep better at night. Show me you *actually* care, Prince. What happened to the Convex have nothing to lose? Won't all this oppression simply tip them over the edge? Make them hungrier for rebellion?"

He grunts. "You're drunk." The breeze blows the loose strings of my hair into his face.

"And you're a fool."

He lets out a low laugh that makes my skin tingle. "I don't make the rules around here, darling."

"Yet you blindly follow them." A droplet of crimson oozes from his flesh, and my blade glints like the bared fangs of a venomous creature drenched in moonlight. "Nothing but a pawn in his little game."

His lip stretches into a sneer, a feral glint in his reddening face. "Then you should have had better aim when you tried to kill me. Hateful little creature."

"Coward." I spit the word at him, hoping it hits him in the gut. But my voice cracks, betraying me. My arm weakens, and I lower the knife, stumbling backwards.

He gasps, holding his throat. "I am not your enemy, Elle."

"An enemy wouldn't force me into marriage or put me in a position to kill to survive," I say, scrunching my fists, feeling the embarrassment as my words pepper our ears. He did save my sister… I think. "Nor would an enemy claim to help the suffering… when all they do is enable greater suffering."

He scoffs and clicks his tongue, shadows gathering into the jade of his eyes and the grooves of his face. "*Ungrateful*, hateful creature," he growls, stalking back out of the clearing the way we came. "I *saved* your life."

Okay. Fine. He's right. But somehow, it just isn't enough. Not with the population of skeletons across the river. "You are going to let hundreds of men, women, and children… *people* starve to death, Ruben. This is a famine made by man. You said it yourself; we have access to healthy soil. Yet, the Convex Sector is denied its harvests." If the prince can't demand justice, how can any of us have any real hope of seeing change in our lifetime? "A famine fuelled by cowardice and greed."

"King Talin just doesn't believe that our… wedding will unify the Sectors. Doesn't believe it will be enough of a distraction and only knows to grip onto power for dear life."

"I wish the lives across the river mattered more than his seat on the throne." My voice is low, drenched in disdain. "Never mind the fact that people are eating animal feed and drinking diseased water out of pure desperation!"

He flares his nostrils, his face darkening. But he doesn't speak.

I roll my eyes. "Are you going to tell me why you brought me out here?"

He pauses, throwing a smirk over his shoulder. My blood boils. "There is a stream up ahead." He inclines his head past me. "In the warmer months, when I need somewhere to escape, to think without the king breathing down my neck, I come here. I thought you might want to know of the place in case you need to do the same in the years to come."

Years.

Ruben brushes past me, and I fall into step behind him. Sure enough, a bubbling stream materialises from behind a tumbling façade of bushes and gangly naked trees. A school of tiny grey fish dart upstream. Snow coats the rocks and surrounding plants, turning the water licking the banks of the stream into strips of cloudy ice. It cracks like shards of glass underfoot.

"My mother used to bring me down here as a child. She taught me to swim and read me stories." He smiles fondly, sitting on the edge of a frosty boulder. "Sometimes, I think her spirit still lingers here."

My eyes suddenly spring with tears, and I blink them away. I sit next to him. "What happened to her?"

He heaves a sigh, running a hand through his hair. "She died of pneumonia."

A cool heaviness settles into my chest, and I blow out my cheeks. "I'm sorry."

His eyes flick towards the treeline, and I know there is more to the story. But I don't push it.

"I know my father let her die. Her way of thinking, her radical mind, it was too much for him."

I fumble for the right words to say but find silence sinking into my chest, permeating the forest around us with its airy chill. Somehow, the only sliver of comfort I can accept. A vague memory of the announcement of the queen's death floats into the recesses of my foggy childhood memory. My heart twists, and a lump swells in the back of my throat.

"She asked me to say her eulogy at her funeral. To tell a memory. Or simply to utter the words *I love you, Mother*. Anything. She just wanted her child to honour her. As anyone would, knowing that the king would try to erase your memory before your spirit even arrived at Netaris, the God of Souls." He sucks in a breath, hanging and clicking his tongue as if the words sting his mouth. "I didn't show up. Too afraid to face the reality of her death. Instead, I came here to cry until my father sent the Tranqs searching for me later that night. I was barely ten."

I can almost hear his heart thumping against his ribs. The surrounding trees sigh, and a little black bird swoops across the stream, slicing the space between us. The brush of air beneath its beating wings grazes my face. My vision glazes over as I lazily watch the bird perch on a low-hanging branch, cocking its head.

"Are you going to tell me something about yourself?" Ruben says, almost a growl. Demanding, but laced with the embarrassment of the realisation he might have spoken too much.

"What do you want to know?" The little black bird bursts into song, locking its eyes with mine, before darting into the shadows with such purposeful, knowing energy, as if it knows the language of the darkness between the stars.

"Anything. As you said, I know nothing about you other than the fact you are terrible at throwing knives." His low-humming laugh settles into the fiery leaves on the floor.

The sound stirs something warm in my chest, and I want to bottle up the feeling forever. I stifle a scoff. "Well, my father is the reason I believe in love. That people can be good, expecting nothing in return." I suddenly pick at my nails, my body burning.

Ruben leans back, placing his hands flat on the rock. "I doubt he would have liked me much," he says wryly.

I roll my eyes, revelling in the feeling of the fresh breeze tangling with my hair, flecked with the sweet scent of moss and the muskiness of the earth. A smile creeps across my face as I pluck a lonely dying flower from the foliage, twirling the stem between my fingertips. "He went to secret meetings every night. Told me he was trying to find a solution to the... way things were. Every night, he would come home with a bundle of flowers from the forest for my mother. He used to make Lyra and I giggle till we forgot about our empty bellies."

Ruben shakes his head, drawing an indecipherable pattern into the frost, his fingers turning pink. "Trust a commoner to have more class and compassion than a king."

"Strange what having nothing can do to a person." A bite of panic dips into my blood, along with the urge to flee. I want to scold myself for the ember growing and burning in my chest.

"What happened to them?" he asks, clearing his throat. "Your parents." A genuine question, coming from a place of concern, not judgement, and yet, I still cannot bring myself to release the blade of resentment embedded in my gut. The ember within me catches alight into an untamed blaze, and sweat springs to my forehead. I taste nothing but bitterness, and any merry feelings vanish into the wind.

"Your father killed them." I stand and march away, back towards the park.

Chapter 12

I startle myself awake, trapped in the snare of a nightmare. The clanging of the cell bars and my rapid, panicked breathing echo off the cast iron walls. Darkness and hunger. No sign of day or night.

Sweat drips from my nose, dribbling into my mouth as I gasp. The world around me shifts and stretches as I throw the heavy blankets from my body and stumble into the bathroom, cranking cold water from the faucet. A sliver of moonlight slices into the room and quells my racing heart. My fingers flinch as the water bites into my skin. But it tethers me to reality as I sink into the tub, sitting there until shivers scuttle through my body. When I step out and slip pants and tunic on, I realise the clock only reads 4 a.m. But I cannot sleep any longer. Not when the claws and fangs of nightmares loom over me, taunting and teasing. My stomach aches with hunger, too.

I traipse to the door, expecting it to be locked. But it opens with a click. Raising my brows, I step out of the bedroom and pad, barefooted, down the marble hallway. I navigate my way through the east wing of the palace. Silence saturates the corridor, light skittering off the polished marble walls like moonlight on a rippling sea. I pray to the Gods no one will see or hear me. But my stomach rumbles, and it may as well screech.

I hasten down a set of stairs into the servant's wing. The kitchen door thumps shut behind me, and I reach for the matches, circling the room like a bird of prey, the feverish flame brushing the wicks of the candles around the kitchen. A shriek spills from my mouth when the light splashes onto a figure. Clothed in a white linen shirt and yet cloaked in darkness, Ruben hunches over the table in the middle of the kitchen, munching a slice of bread.

"Elle!" He chokes, coughing and whacking his chest until his eyes water.

"What the hell are you doing?" I ask, crossing my arms and tapping my foot.

He inclines his head to the bread. "I'm eating. What does it look like?"

I quirk a brow. "At four in the morning?"

He bristles, those green eyes darting to the window, where the moon kisses the clouds in the distant sky. "Yes. My meal schedule is a little... inconsistent."

"What does that mean?"

"None of your business." He takes another bite, chews, and swallows. "What about you?"

I gnaw the inside of my cheek. "I had a nightmare. Then I woke up and realised my reality was worse."

He smirks and his eyes are bright, almost feline, sharp, and calculating. "As if seeing me in the middle of the night is a nightmare. And anyway, it appears someone has a message for you. He asked me to pass it on to you this morning. But your presence is... *perfectly* timed, Elle. He literally just stepped out the door."

I angle my head. "I'm not sure what you're talking about."

He brushes the breadcrumbs from his lap. "Come on, Elle. Who delivers fresh produce to the palace at an ungodly hour?"

"Elle," a voice hisses.

I turn my head on instinct, my heart racing at the all-too-familiar voice. I widen my eyes at Ruben in disbelief. "Are you playing a cruel joke? Can I see him?"

"Of course, Elle. He said you two are best friends." He leans back in his chair and winks. "As I said once, I'm not a monster."

The owner of the voice remains hidden behind the side kitchen door—the one that leads to the courtyards and garden. With a giggle bubbling in my throat, I slip out into the night. Aston clings to the shadows like a vampire hiding from the sun. Brows pulled together; jaw tightened. He doesn't say a word, motioning for me to follow. I throw Ruben a look over my shoulder, running my fingers over my throat. He nods in understanding, pretending to zip his mouth shut and throw away the key. I bite my lip and follow Aston. His sandy blond hair catches a chord in my heart, and a smile slides across my face. We skulk into the shadowed corner of a small garden surrounded by hedges. Their leaves glimmer dark green in the ghostly light like fish scales. A low breeze raises the hair on my skin and rustles the leaves like chattering hyenas.

"What are you doing here?" I whisper.

Instead, he yanks me into a hug. Tears unexpectedly pool in my eyes as his arms tighten around me. Safe and sound. Warm and earthy. He smells of the forest and the farms. "Is he unkind to you?"

"The king? He would rather see me in the jaws of the Shadowtooth outside the walls before anything else."

His eyes flash, and his teeth clack. "What about the prince?"

I blow out my cheeks. Lyra must have filled him in on the prince's Tranq duties. "He is a jerk. But I don't think he wishes me dead. I'm a pawn in his own game, too."

"Don't let your guard down, Elle. Do not trust him for a minute." He glances out of the nook as if expecting Ruben to pop out and drag us into the prisons.

"I won't."

He nods, leaning against the wall and folding his arms across his chest, thin but strong despite the famine. His face becomes stone, other than the flicker of terror crossing his eyes. I feel it crackling under my skin and resist the urge to fidget. "What is it, Aston? Is Lyra hurt?"

His Adam's apple bobs in his throat as he swallows. "No. She's okay," he says. "Look, Elle. Things aren't going so great across the river."

"What is it?"

"You aren't going to like it—"

"Spit it out," I snap, panic stirring my pulse.

112

He heaves a sigh. "The Convex people are standing up to the Tranqs, Elle."

His words knock the wind from my lungs, and I place my hand on the marble behind me. "How?"

"Some of them are getting brave. Famine and starvation drive them to stupid desperation. One man knocked out a Tranq who arrested a young boy for sneaking into the Concave farms for food. Another group looted a Tranq headquarters of their uniform and weapons."

I close my eyes, grimacing. My stomach aches.

"I am sure you can guess how they paid for their crimes."

Sharp teeth and no soul. Insanity.

My entire body goes numb, and a scream burns in my throat. No. A *thousand* screams. The cries of all the dead beyond the walls. "Why are they doing this? They know they're risking their heads!" A crack cleaves into my words.

He chews his lip and heaves a sigh. "They do not know you killed the Tranq. But I think some farmers know you've been hiding something from the Tranqs. What with them seeing you wander past the fields almost every day."

Gossip is a powerful weapon.

"Are you saying I inspired them?" I ask, a coppery tang spreading across my tongue. *What have I done? What have I done?*

He shrugs. "Well, if you could get away with defying the Tranqs, who is to stop them from doing the same?"

"I don't want to inspire them to get themselves killed," I say through gritted teeth.

"You cannot control what other people do, Elle. Besides, it's just my theory. The famine is enough of a drive. But they will have many reasons. Many of them have nothing else to lose besides their heads, anyway."

"I don't want anyone to get hurt," I say meekly, dropping my head.

He places his fingers under my chin, forcing my face up. "Starvation will hurt them. Tranqs will hurt him. Monsters outside the kingdom will kill them."

I nod, feeling foolish. "You are right."

"Our people are finally doing something. Finally, they are showing courage. It's only the beginning. We were born in his world. We will die in our own, Elle. Mark my words."

I catch his promise in my chest, soaking in the warmth. Letting the flicker of hope wash over me.

"How is Lyra?"

"She's... struggling. I'm taking care of her the best I can. I also understand the prince did, too."

A sigh. "He's trying to help in his own insufferable way."

Aston shakes his head but pulls me into another crushing hug, and my tears stain his shirt. Gods, why am I crying so much?

"I'll find you again, Elle," he says, nodding as if trying to convince himself.

"I want to go home," I blurt out, voice cracking. "I fear them changing me here."

Aston shifts his weight and brushes a piece of straw from his threadbare pants. His eyes soften, and he reaches out, tucking a loose curl behind my ears, and I want to sob. "Eat the food, Elle. Gather your strength. We will find a way out of this soon. All of us."

Aston disappears into the shadows and the wind as if the very elements flow through his bones. When he's gone, hollowness caves into my chest. Aching. Alone. I'm so alone. My knees shake, and I fight the urge to collapse into the garden and weep.

"Is he your lover?" a voice pipes up from around the corner. Heat cascades up my neck and into my face.

"Piss off, Ruben." I stalk past his smirking face, slamming into his shoulder.

"Cannot be too good a lover if he didn't rescue you," he says with a drawl, following me back into the palace kitchen. He lets out a dry chuckle.

I grimace. "I am going to bed. Good night, Your Highness."

"I heard he told you about the uprisings," he says, rendering me still.

"Insufferable bastard," I snap, whirling around. His green eyes glint in the moonlight, so beautiful it makes me dizzy. But the frown on his face, pretending he could care about the Convex people, makes me want to slap him. "Listening to us, were you? Were you ever going to tell me about the Convex leading themselves to their deaths?"

He clenches his jaw, pursing his lips. He inclines his head deeper into the garden, pressing his finger to his lips. I glare but lumber after him. A slight wisp of wind curls around my limbs, drawing the hairs

115

up. We slip into a narrow path, hidden by walls flanked by hewn hedges dotted with white flowers. The leaves chatter together, sharing stories of the night. Finally, Ruben stops. His chest heaves and leans against the hedge gently, propping a heel up.

"How did you know?" I hiss, resisting the urge to squirm. Ruben's tall, broad figure swallows the path, towering above my short, scrawny figure. His furrowed brows and demanding eyes are close... too close.

"At dinner with my father last night. He was discussing it with the other high-ranking Tranqs."

"What is going to happen to them?" I brace myself for the answer as the guilt unleashes its temper within my gut.

He holds my stare for several long, reverberating beats. There is a war behind those eyes. "It's about to get violent for your people, Elle."

My stomach aches with such intensity that bile oozes up my throat. "What can I do?"

A muscle twitches in his nose. "You can get to sleep for the last few hours until dawn." A blend of despair and hope laces his voice, like fire burning through snow. "Let Larissa make you all pretty, and let the king announce our marriage to the kingdom."

I ball my fists, fear gnawing at my gut. A lifetime of the kingdom snaring me within its trap. Of sitting idly by while the Convex people starve year after year. Of sharing a bed with the prince. A shudder ripples through me.

"Be prepared. You're a Tranq now. So, your duties may include things that will go against your morals."

"What does that mean?" My voice croaks, and my hand flies to my chest—the thump, thump, thump against my palm.

He turns and stalks back through the hidden path, into a clearing, into the garden, past the sculptures, and into the kitchen. I blaze after him.

"Cool. Ignore me," I snap.

He whirls around. "I can't give you details because I have none. It's up to the king. He will tell us. Goodnight, Elle."

Ruben flees the kitchen, blundering into the hallway. "Bastard," I say, marching after him.

"I heard that, Elle!" he calls, letting out a low laugh that warms my blood despite myself.

I groan, storming out of the kitchen and to bed. Sleep is merciful and quick, but not long enough. A flurry of babbling women barging into the room wakes me with a start. They literally drag me out of bed and strip me of my nightgown. Larissa trails in, an amused smirk on her face as she watches, as if they are completely beyond her command. I wince and groan as the girls drag me into the bath chamber.

"Gosh, Elle. You look like you've been run over by a wagon," Larissa says with a giggle.

"Gee, thanks. I did only just wake up." I roll my eyes as the ladies hustle me into the steaming tub. They scrub me raw until my skin and hair smell floral.

Someone hands me a freshly baked pastry as they towel me dry and sling a robe over my exposed body. Before I know it, the ladies help me into another glorious red gown and style my hair, tying half of the curls up. They polish my face with powder and rake an inky pigment onto my lashes. Someone grooms my brows with a light brown hue.

Larissa pushes me in front of the mirror, grinning. A gasp falls from my lips. There is a stranger in the mirror. She is fierce and demands attention. Nothing to reflect the frightened girl beneath the glamour.

"Whatever King Talin wants with you today, make him afraid," Larissa says, her voice forged from the essence and spirit of a lion learning her roar.

I turn to the ladies, now flocked together like swans. Smiles and fearful hearts. "Thank you," I say.

"He's waiting," Larissa says, angling her head to the door.

"The king?"

"No, silly. Prince Talin."

I grimace, rolling my eyes. Ruben prowls into the room without knocking or waiting for permission. He draws to an abrupt halt when his gaze falls on me. My cheeks burst into flames as he takes in my appearance, piece by piece, biting his lip. He nods. I scold my body for being far too reactive to his mere presence. As if any man deserves such power.

"I am sure the king and his men will approve," he says, clearing his throat.

"Do *you* approve, Your Royal Highness?" Larissa chirps, and I want to swat her.

He runs a hand over his chin, licking his lips as they pull into a half-smile. "You look…"

"Like the very flames themselves," Larissa finishes for him.

The girls behind me are practically in a frenzy of raging hormones, all giggles and whispers. I glare at him. "Incessant bastard."

The night sky and the stars ripple from him. He fidgets with the silver cufflinks pinned to his black suit, and a silver necklace drapes down his chest, disappearing behind the fabric. His forest eyes catch alight in the streaming sunlight. Ruben is so beautiful he makes me weak in the knees. Too bad I hate him. He smirks, holding out his hand. He is smug, having revelled in me staring a moment too long.

I click my tongue and groan, accepting his hand. He pulls me to his side, sauntering out of the bedroom and into the corridor. My heart careens from beat to beat as my blood heats. His body is warm against mine. He smells of the forest, too, and the citrus scent of lemon.

"Larissa is right, Elle," he murmurs.

My insides stir, and I mutter a curse beneath my breath. "Why don't you wear something more colourful, like the Concave men in town?" I ask as we round a corner. "I think you're not as dark and ominous as you want people to believe."

He breathes a laugh. "Do you think I'm dark?"

"You pretend you don't care. Like you're afraid of feeling things too deeply."

His shoulders tense, and his jaw clacks. "I care. But I cannot save everyone. I can't feel the weight of the entire kingdom… how could anyone? Not unless I want to lose myself completely to the darkness of it all."

"But then nothing changes," I say, swallowing the bubble of frustration. "Compliance fosters oppression and cruelty."

His grip on my arm tightens. He opens his mouth to say something but stops for the rumble of an ever-stretching crowd beyond the palace walls. My heart thunders, and my mouth dries up. Ruben huffs.

"Time to introduce the Concaves to the flames," he says.

Chapter 13

The thrum outside the palace booms and pulses into the hallway, the bass plucking at my ribs. Ruben drops my clammy arm and studies my face.

"You are afraid."

I scoff, taking a step back. "You're not? Stage fright is a thing, you know."

He presses his lips together, a thousand thoughts no doubt bouncing through that head. "They are about to either hate you, fear you, or envy you, Elle."

"Because you are such a snatch, right?" I roll my eyes.

He reaches out and tucks a loosened strand of hair behind my ear. My lungs deflate. His lips tug into a smile, and heat scorches through me.

A herald opens the door, and the rumble grows in decibels tenfold, scattering into the walls around us, roaring in my ears. I fall into step after Ruben, schooling my face into a pleasant smile. Erasing all signs of the girl who killed the Tranq, of the girl who tried to kill the prince.

A gale lashes with icy vengeance, swirling the skirt of my gown around me as we skulk into the centre of the marble stage. An enormous courtyard spills into the field behind the palace, packed with what appears to be every Concave in the kingdom. Thousands of eyes pinned on me. They shift and sway like a forest enraged by a storm.

King Talin slumps on another of his thrones. A coat the shade of a lonely sea drapes down his broad shoulders, flecked with the licks of gold. His sinister grin raises the hair on my arms. His snake-like eyes rake over my body, sizing me up like a meal, and I can almost feel them like claws running down my spine. I shiver. But I shove a bigger smile onto my face, desperately hiding the terror quaking within me.

For once, I am grateful for Ruben's presence. However, with each step closer to the throne, his arms quiver and his fingers tremble, that jaw clenching so tightly I fear he'll shatter his own teeth. Like a child about to receive discipline from their schoolteacher for poor behaviour. His eyes grow distant as if he's picturing himself as a small boy, shaking at the sight of his mighty father. I wonder if the king loves his son.

We stop in the centre of the stage. King Talin rises like a cobra, assessing its prey before the strike. The crowd drops silently all at once. So silent, I can hear Ruben's ragged breathing and the distant sighing of trees in the morning breeze. Talin slithers forward. We bow before him. He nods smugly, holding my gaze.

"Kingdom of the Floodgates, welcome," King Talin bellows to the crowd. His voice bounces off the castle walls and carries over the throngs in the wind. "May the Gods bless us. Ruaris, Goddess of the Day, certainly has with the abundance of sunshine recently. Perfect for the farmlands."

The shadows of the northern forest stretch and contort over the furthest reaches of the crowd, and I wish I could disappear into either.

"Today, I have an announcement for our kingdom." He points a meaty hand to us. "His Royal Highness, your prince, my son, has declared his engagement to Lady Elle Fallon of the Convex Sector. The historic marriage will take place in the summer. A pairing which will unify both sides of the river!"

They meet his words with a crackling cacophony. The Concave people fire hateful, mocking glares my way, their whispers and bickering peppering the arid air.

"She's a Convex!"

"This isn't fair! His Royal Highness should wed a lady of the Concave Sector."

"Not worthy of my prince."

"Silence!" the king growls. The rumble drops at once other than the odd squeak of fright, and my breath catches in my throat. "I am your king. My decisions are final, and how dare you question them?" His bellow billows through the crowd, and I can practically hear the thousands of rapid heartbeats.

I bite my tongue, swallowing the scoff at the front row of Concaves dressed in bright-coloured tunics and corsets, nodding furiously.

"This is a joyous time," the king continues, clasping his hands behind his back as he prowls across the stage, casting dark, penetrating stares at his subjects. There is not a sliver of joy on his face. "It will be full of festivities and balls. We will be happy for my son, your prince. As per the tradition for the heir in this kingdom, his name will be announced to the public on the day of the wedding."

The Concaves erupt into a round of applause and forced cheering. A sound more ominous than hateful words. My skin crawls. King Talin turns to us, a feral glint in his eyes deceiving the otherwise pleasant smile.

"May Isra, Goddess of Love, grant you eternal happiness together."

We murmur a thank you.

"Dismissed!"

I march into my bedroom, squinting at the harsh blades of sunlight cutting into the room. My stomach knots, and tears spill down my cheeks. Ruben skulks in behind me, reaching for my wrist. I hiss, yanking it away.

"You need to leave me alone, Ruben."

Hurt flashes across his face before he sneers. "What's your problem?"

"You." I toss my hands into the air. "Get out. I—I just need some time to process this. It just seems so… hopeless. How can I even live with myself… enjoying a full belly while my people perish? And now, with the uprisings… the deaths on my hands. None of this would have happened if you weren't—"

"Weren't *what*? None of this is my fault."

"No? Why were you out in the forest that day, huh? Scouring for your next victim to toss out of the kingdom!"

"We expanded our patrol, that's all!" he growls.

"If you had just left me alone! None of this would be happening. How could you… how could you punish someone for trying not to starve to death?"

His mouth clamps shut.

"You have never gone hungry a day in your miserable, comfortable life, *Ruben*." I spit his name out like it tastes bitter on my tongue, as if it comes from the darkest of curses. "You know nothing of the realities of the famine. What all of us must do to survive."

He bares his teeth and scoffs, pacing the floor. "You know nothing about me."

"Yet, I am betrothed to you!"

Ruben straightens his shoulders and runs a hand through his hair. "Perhaps we should start learning more about each other. But starting with the basics rather than getting all deep and personal right away."

"Such as?"

He folds his arms over his chest and leans against the window frame, examining me. "I had my first kiss at only seven years old."

I laugh, and my cheeks flush. "That isn't deep and personal?"

Ruben shrugs nonchalantly. "It was rather sad. Someone dared a girl at school to kiss me. So, it wasn't authentic. A heartless, childish dare stole my first kiss from me."

My expression has never been flatter. "How tragic. Now, shoo." I wave my hand at him as if he's a fly.

"Aren't you going to share something, too?"

"Maybe tomorrow, Ruben. I want to be alone."

He rolls his eyes. "Fine, we begin Tranquillity training at sunrise. Lucky for you, I will be your trainer. Enjoy your precious night of peace because I'll be back by morning!"

With a smug grin, he waltzes out of the room. Despite requesting his exit, the weight of the loneliness presses onto my chest with such force I cannot breathe. I peel the gown off, kicking it into the corner, weeping as I sink into the bathtub, praying to any God listening that they will give me the strength to face my mundane future within these marble walls, and yet, a lick of fire scorches through my chest—the familiar yet terrifying burn for rebellion. And I know my soul cannot rest here.

***

Indeed, what feels like moments later, Ruben's obnoxious voice rings into my ears. My eyes sting, begging to remain closed against the ghostly glare of dawn permeating my vision. I groan, shoving my head under the pillow. He knocks.

"I'm still sleeping," I mumble into the bedding.

"Would you rather the king train you? Or perhaps another grumpy Tranq?" he says, his voice muffled.

I fling a string of ugly curses through the door.

"Me, it is!"

I skulk into the training field with a scowl on my face. The field behind the Tranquillity building is surrounded by brick walls, keeping the field concealed from nosy Concaves. Ruben plasters a grin on his face as I approach him. He wears his complete Tranq uniform, including the armour. While I wear the same, my movements are clunky and mechanical as I allow my body to get used to the armour. Meanwhile, Ruben's movements are smooth and seamless, almost feline.

"Today, we will practice knife throwing," he says, gesturing to the human-shaped hay dummy several yards away.

I snort. "You are joking."

Ruben pulls a knife from his belt and spins around, throwing it. The blade slices through the air, thudding into the dummy's head. I cringe. "No, Elle. I am not joking. Besides, we both know you could do with the training."

"I am certainly more practised with the sword. Too bad I haven't spent more time on the knives. I might have saved myself all this headache."

"And made a great meal for the monsters." He licks his lips and smirks. "Baby steps. But we do want you to hit the head consistently. Accuracy and consistency are vital as a Tranq, especially when you need to react suddenly and quickly."

"Don't Tranqs use the spears?" I say as he stalks up to the dummy, yanking it from the packed hay.

"That is tomorrow's lesson." He furrows his brows and twists the knife. "We use the spears when banishing people. Pushing them out with the spearhead poking their backs."

"I know," I say, gulping. "I've seen it many times." My gut twists with the sense of foreboding, and I push it away. But a sour expression remains on my face.

Ruben inclines his head to the knives in my belt. "Go on. Let's see you throw, hateful creature."

"I am not full of hate," I snap.

"Then tell me, who do you love?" He scuffs his boot in the manicured, green grass.

I roll my eyes. "My sister. My best friend, Aston." A sigh. "Feel free to laugh heartily at how pitiful that number is."

He shakes his head. "I thought I told you I am not the kind."

"What kind are you?" I march up to the white line painted on the grass. Positioning my feet at a pivot angle, I glue my eyes on the target, rear back, and throw. The blade spins through the air, sailing right past the dummy's shoulder.

Ruben laughs, throwing his head back and clutching his stomach. He wipes a tear from his eye. I stick my tongue out like a child.

"No wonder you didn't kill me. You threw it too aggressively," he says, prowling over to me, and I flinch as he stands behind me. He gestures to my hand. "May I?"

I nod, cheeks burning.

Ruben gently grabs my wrist, my hand already holding the second knife. He rolls my hand over my shoulder and then gently points my hand and the blade towards the target.

"It's a two-part move," he says, voice low and tickling my hair. "Roll it back, then snap forward."

A shiver spider-walks down my spine at the feeling of his body against mine. My skin bursts into flames. My soul quivers, but I refuse to allow him the satisfaction of knowing the effect he has on me. So, I step out of his chest, shaking him off. I bite the inside of my cheek, shoving those feelings far away into the recesses of my mind, scolding myself for them. I will not let the prince so close to me again.

"I think I got it," I say.

He stands several feet away and crosses his arms, arching a brow. "Fine. Prove it."

I position my feet, adjust my grip on the knife, and eye the target. As I roll the knife over my shoulder, I block him from my peripherals. The knife spins, propelling through the air, landing with a sharp thud into the dummy's head.

Chapter 14

A rapid knock on my bedroom door drags me from my stupor. Before I can even summon him in, Ruben barges through the entrance. His face drained of colour; his lower lip pulled in between his teeth. A curse falls from his mouth as he stalks towards me, his white linen shirt rippling like a disturbed glass lake beneath the moon.

"What are you doing?" I hiss, slipping out of the bed but hugging the blanket to my body. "I barely have any clothes on."

He waves his hand, scrunching his nose. "Oh, don't flatter yourself. We have other matters."

My fingers furl tighter around the blanket. "What then?"

He paces the room, hands clasped behind his back. Frost creeps across the windowpane, and grey clouds skid across the sky, drenching the kingdom in an icy essence that I feel in my bones. His piercing green gaze lingers on the frigid river in the distance. Its quicksilver surface wrapping through the narrow gaps in the maze of Concave buildings like a forest snake coming for breath above the leaves.

He holds his fist against his mouth and closes his eyes as if he's about to vomit. "I am sure you have heard of the crimes some Convex are committing."

"What have they done?" My stomach clenches.

He swallows bodily. "One of them snatched a sword from a Tranq's back and pointed it at his throat."

He might as well have punched me in the gut, for the wind leaves my lungs. "They are out of control. Unhinged."

"Elle, there is something else you need to know," he says, struggling to meet my eye.

As he opens his mouth to respond, the king himself bellows from outside the bedroom. "Son, bring the girl outside at once. We must prepare for her first task as a Tranq."

"But—"

"Out now," he growls with such ferocity we both startle.

Ruben hangs his head and slumps out of the room. I throw my clothes on, splash fresh water on my face, and hasten into the hall. The king slides his predator eyes to me. Today, he wears black speckled with gold. His golden and silver crown rests on his thinning head of hair.

"Collect your armour and weapons, Elle. I have a task, especially for you."

I clear my throat and muster my feeble voice. "Yes, Your Majesty." When I return to the hallway, clad in armour with my sword and spear sheathed to my spine, Ruben is gone. That pair of beady eyes await me. I swallow, and a shudder rakes its fingers along my nerves.

"You look great, Elle," he purrs as we slip through the hallway.

I pluck up an ounce of courage. "What is the task for me today, Your Majesty?"

He chuckles, shaking his head. "It is time you earn your place as a Tranquillity. And your position as a woman worthy of my son."

Vague, incessant bastard. I keep my eyes pinned on the hall before us. We wind another corner, past scurrying servants who avoid eye contact, and sculptures of long-dead kings and fountains carved into the shape of the gods and goddesses, including the God of Souls, whose hands reach out, past the stream of arching water, as if he is offering his guidance into the afterlife.

"If you can complete the task today, you will be a step closer to my blessing," he says, nodding at a couple of prominent members of the Concave Sector ogling at us. "If you fail, blood will be on your hands."

My heart lurches to my throat. "Who's blood?"

He breathes a laugh. "The Convex's. Your sister's. The blond boy who works on the farms. What is his name again?" Malice creeps across that hardened face, and his lip tugs into a grin. "Oh, yes. Aston Sallow. Do you think the boy will fare against the Shadowtooth? Perhaps the God of Tranquillity and Peace will offer a swift, merciful end."

Horror crackles on my tongue like the first flames of a forest fire, but I cannot form a response. He lets out a low laugh. We arrive in the foyer, and I squint at the buttery light pouring in through the windows, a wispy shift in the clouds above. The snow-tipped grass outside glimmers like a thousand scattered stars.

A carriage awaits us in the cobbled curve before the palace steps. I glance around, half-hoping to find Ruben. The king leads me into the carriage, where the four polished black horses snort and stamp their hooves. I lean into the leather of the seat, facing backwards. The king's eyes remain pinned on me as the horses jerk forward, and we move through the kingdom. I stare out of the window. My stomach gurgles, and my pulse roars past my eats. The whoosh of water and the slight incline of the carriage crossing the arched bridge sends bile singing up my throat.

King Talin scrunches his nose as we clatter through the dusty Convex streets. Thin, skeletal people stinking of famine stare at the carriage, a hollow, knowing look glazing through them. Wide, yellowed eyes, pointy cheeks, and prominent ribs. I almost reach across and slap the disgust from the king's face.

I squeeze my eyes shut for the rest of the trip. My stomach churns, and tears sting, dribbling pitifully down my cheeks. We turn down a street, and a rumble of a crowd batters against the kingdom walls, icy blood plunging into my gut and yanking my eyes open. I stare out of the window, and panic soars through my veins. We are heading down the long, chalky road towards the kingdom's gates.

The stone gates, built by our ancestors, hold the secrets of the world behind them. They blend into the rest of the circular stone walls like storm clouds into the night sky, wrapping up the kingdom in a neat little package. No one can see past them other than the sun, the moon, and the Gods.

I climb out of the carriage with the king's breath on my neck as he follows—but not before waiting for a servant to place his wooden step stool down. A hush drapes over the throngs teeming around the sides of the street. Thousands of timid, scared, and anguished eyes trace King Talin's movements. And mine. My skin crawls, and I resist the urge to hurl up my breakfast.

The king stalks towards the gates. His chin pokes up, chest puffed out. A shadowy scowl etched into his face. Those green eyes are as vibrant as the venomous skin of a forest frog. Heads bow as he passes. Women curtsey. Children hide behind their parents, mouths curled back in dread. Mothers wrap shawls around their children before themselves for the frozen air bites at the skin. My nose stings, and my hands are stiff as if riddled with rigour Mortis.

Terror. So tangible I can feel the weight of it on my chest, the fingernails grating along my bones.

At the end of the road, the crowds grow thicker and tighter together. I wish the ground would split, and I could fall into the molten earth below. A row of Tranqs stands at the edge of the crowd closest to the gates. I recognise Ruben's distinctive helmet. Poised, dainty horns curl over his head. Face hidden behind the black-stained, bronze face shield.

I glare at him, my fingernails digging into my sweaty palms. King Talin draws to a halt, and his eyes rove over a couple of scrawny men tethered to a wooden stake with chains. I hold my breath, realising the forecast for the next few minutes. The prisoners' tan tunics flap in the singing wind like beating wings. Their faces blanched like sun-baked stones, all too aware of their impending doom. One older, thinning man meets my eyes and smirks. My very soul unsettles, like seeing the moon during the day.

King Talin wastes no time. "These criminals are meeting their demise beyond the walls today," he grinds out, pointing at them. He paces back and forth across the face of the gates. My heart thunders in my chest. "Only the Gods know what awaits them. Starvation, monsters, or insanity. They will soon find out."

He prowls towards the prisoners, sneering. "Do either of you have any final words to say before you meet with the Shadowtooth?" He flings the monster's name at them, spit flying.

One of them snarls, and his lip whorls into a feral grin. "You're no king of mine. We were born in your world, but you will die in ours."

King Talin chuckles, unflinching. "Arrogant fool. You will never see such a day."

He snaps his attention to me, and a malicious grin spreads across his face. "Elle Fallon. Step forward."

Thousands of eyes burn into my soul as I draw forward. As I do, a spot of red hair bobs up in the crowd. Lyra. Our gaze locks. Reddened eyes, tears spilling down her jittery lips. I want to scream. I want to run into her arms and sob in our apartment, hidden away from the terror of it all. The only place I truly feel safe. She nods as if she understands my thoughts.

King Talin angles his head to the prisoners, his lips crimped up in amusement. A cat playing with its food. "Push them out, Elle," he says, voice low enough to reverberate through my ribs.

No.

I shake my head, panic searing through my blood like caustic poison. "I can't. I won't."

"You will exile the criminals who dared defy my Tranquillity, my peace, or you will have the blood of *all* the Convex people on your hands," he bellows, and I flinch as the sound slams into the gates and whistles into the village.

"You're cruel. Evil," I spit as my knees knock together. Blood roars past my ears. I can barely breathe. As if a stone is fastened to my feet, dragging me to the bottom of a dark lake, to a watery grave.

He reaches behind me and draws my spear from the sheath. Its dainty spearhead glints in the fingers of sunlight reaching down from the clouds roving the sky. The point, sharp and narrow, taunts me.

"Push them out, Elle Fallon," he says through gritted teeth, words dripping with bane. He gestures to the prisoners, who stumble forward as a couple of Tranqs unclasp them from the wooden stake.

King Talin shoves the spear handle into my hands and nods. A deep shudder reverberates through the kingdom, splitting my eardrums. The stone gates groan and creak as they ease open outwards on their hinges, grating against the earth. King Talin plants his feet at the opening and draws in a deep breath, closing his eyes with a smirk.

"The scent of the monsters leads me to believe they are lurking. Death's beckoning arms await." He twists his head to me. "Push them out, Elle."

A Tranq shoves the first man towards me, who almost falls to his knees. He reeks of body odour and old ale. His jaw tightens, but I catch the telltale glint of fear in his eyes despite the defiant mask he pulls on as he shoves back his shoulders and stands.

"Do it," he says, nodding as if to tell me it's okay. "Do it. But don't let my death be in vain. You know who our enemy is. Destroy them."

My lips quiver, and sobs clench my heart and lungs. I cannot breathe. "I'm sorry," I splutter.

"Do not be sorry," he says, eyes glossy and red with tears. "Fight for us, Elle."

The way he says my name and the way the sound licks the wind makes my mind want to separate from my body. A cry falls from my mouth, more animal than human. "I will."

My feet are stiff as stone as I step behind him and aim the spearhead at his spine. My stomach surges, and tears blind my vision.

"Make haste. Show us you are worthy of the Tranquillity. Or my son's hand!" the king growls, and I cry out.

Flinging curse words at the king, I prod the prisoner in the back, and he yelps, falling into step. He strides a beat quicker, avoiding the spearhead as if he's leading himself to the end. A scream scratches my throat, like a monster's claws, red and raw and demanding to be heard. I bite the inside of my cheek, tasting blood. Weeps escape my mouth, cracking and drawing pathetic tears down my face.

As the prisoner crosses the gate threshold, he stops and turns around. He throws a vulgar gesture at the king. "Let my death be the catalyst for change." His gaze finds me, and he nods. "I forgive you, Elle."

My knees scarcely keep me upright. The prisoner wipes the tear running his colour-drained face before turning and striding into the shadows and lights of the wilderness beyond the walls. His figure shrinks as he moves towards the lake. A distant, monstrous shriek slices into my ears. As if the monster is welcoming the prisoner into its arms.

A shuddering numbness sweeps over me. Mind a thousand miles away. As if I'm a supernatural creature who can shut off their emotions at will. The second prisoner doesn't say a word as I push him out. His hungry, feral gleam finds a home in my nightmares. His face is stone, not a whisper of fear.

His figure disappears into the glare of the wilderness. The gates groan like a hundred dying beasts as they ease across the ground on their hinges, shuddering as they seal shut, but not before the prisoner's strangled scream pierces the walls. Blood splatters through the narrow gap, cascading over my face and hair. The gates close, and I vomit on the ground.

Chapter 15

Sweat soaks into the sheet. It coats my forehead, and a metallic tang clings to my tongue. A raw wound aches on the inside of my cheek, and my throat stings from the screaming. I slept in fits. Monsters swathed my nightmares with teeth dripping blood. Unseeing eyes of their victims burnt through my skull all night, their final screams rattling back and forth within my bones. Would the men fight? Or would they let the monsters kill them, knowing they didn't stand a chance?

The pillows caught my sobs all night. The bed chamber walls protected me from the prying ears of anyone in the hallway.

All I want is to fall into my sister's arms. But I am trapped in the snare of my most bone-chilling nightmare.

My numb fingers sting as I grind the faucet in the opposite direction. Blood. It cakes my soul. I sink into the steaming water and snatch the sponge from the shelf, scrubbing my hands, under my nails, my chest, and arms, even though I already did this exact same routine last night. Red seeps across the recesses of my vision, and I whimper, panting and shaking. Yesterday's blood-splattered clothes are still crumpled in the corner. Go away. Go away. I want to scream. When I rise from the tub and wrap a towel around my body, the room spins and sways. The sun peaks over the horizon, sending chops of yellow light across the kingdom and across my face. I hiss and close my eyes against the glare, but all I see is the blood. The terror. *Fight for us, Elle.* The prisoner's garbled voice rings in my head.

I pad barefooted to the bed, wearing nothing but a linen dressing robe. As I peel the sweaty sheets from the mattress, a knock sounds through the room. My hands fumble for the steadiness of the mattress as my stomach lurches and bubbles, sending surges of saliva up my throat.

"Elle?" Ruben calls from the hallway, his voice infuriatingly gentle.

"I do not want to talk to you, Ruben," I snap, tossing a bundle of sheets into a basket. Silence follows, and I nod, assuming he left. With a huff, I dress into my tunic and pants and grab the basket handles. As I open the door, Ruben's eyes send me reeling back. I curse. "Did you not hear me?"

He shifts his weight, studying me before heaving a sigh. "I thought you might want to talk about what happened yesterday."

A wildfire billows through my chest. "You are the last person I want to talk to. The last person I want to look at," I say through gritted teeth.

He opens his mouth to respond, but I roll my eyes and shoulder past him, anyway, stomping down the marble hallway. Tears blur my vision, and I blink them away, biting my lip to keep from screaming at him.

"Elle!"

I shake my head, navigating my way to the servants' quarters. His incessant footsteps follow. A vulture circling its prey. I march into the laundry room, and a couple of servants ogle at us. Instead of handing my basket to them, I tip my sheets into the large sink and turn the faucet on. I pour some fabric soap into the sink and grab the cleaning stick.

"You are upset with me," Ruben says. From the peripherals of my vision, I see him chewing his lips, and I resist the urge to slap him.

"Oh?" I say as lavender aromas fill my nose. Water splashes up my front as I stir the sheets in the sink.

"Do you think I am responsible for what happened yesterday?"

My hands tremble, and I whack the stick against the fabric. "You just stood there," I say, my voice cracking but low enough to avoid drawing the servant's attention. "You stood there like an idle fool while I *exiled* two men. You stood there while his blood splattered my face and hair."

His face transcends various hues of pink, and a storm rages behind those eyes. "I didn't have a choice, Elle."

"You had the power to save me, Your Highness," I spit his title like poison, stirring the water and beating the sheets. "But you couldn't save *them*. Furthermore, you just stood there while I shoved them out! What kind of prince are you?"

"This is all a delicate balance. You don't realise how little control I have," he says lowly. "The king needs to be convinced of your loyalty."

"So, it's okay then?" I say, throwing my hands up, my voice dripping in disgust.

"No. Obviously, it is not okay."

I scoff, pulling my lips back in a sneer. "You promised me, Prince, that you weren't my enemy. That you cared for the Convex. How on earth can we do that to people?"

"Ask the king, Elle," he says, tossing his hands to the ceiling. "He is the cruel one. He is the one responsible for all of this."

I shake my head, grinding my teeth. "But what of the Tranquillity? They are responsible for following the king and for enforcing such cruel laws, for being so full of hate and the complete inability to think for themselves." My tone takes on an intensity that scares the recesses of my consciousness. "I do not believe you are much better than him."

He stumbles back, and his eyes grow icy and distant. As if reeling from a slap in the face. He blows air through his nose and angles his head, studying me. "I am not my father, Elle," he says, voice strained yet calm. I know I've hit him in the spot that hurts the most.

"Aren't you?" I counter, shaking my head.

He grinds his teeth, his eyes glistening. "We have a royal tour of the Concave Sector today. Can we just act civil until it's over?"

"I'll bat my eyes and swoon like the rest of the ladies seem to do around you," I say.

"Gods, you're odious."

My lip quirks. "Only the bane of your existence."

I wring my sheets out and hang them on the racks before marching out of the room, shaking my head as he follows me.

"Can you meet me in the foyer in an hour?" he says,

"Only if you leave me alone."

He clicks his tongue as he slips away. "Don't be late."

When I arrive back in my room, Larissa is already there. She paces the room, brows pinched, the two lines deepening in her porcelain skin. "Gods, Elle. I heard what King Talin made you do." Her voice quivers, and my heart cracks. "I can only pray to the Gods that they will bring you peace."

Words die on my tongue. She nods in understanding as she ushers me into her chair and helps prepare me for the royal tour of the Concave Sector.

My burgundy corset dress pushes my chest up and straightens my back. Larissa arranges my curls in a half-up, half-down situation. I hitch up the skirt as I stride through the hallways alone, trying to remember my way to the foyer.

He stands by the enormous arched main entrance. Sunlight streams in through the open doors, kissing his green eyes in a golden hue. His lip tugs into a smile, eyes softening as I approach and loop my arm around his. I draw in his scent. My heart would flutter if it weren't for the anger still yanking at my heart. The blood of the exiled men still lingers on my soul like ghosts, now cold and tacky.

"You look…," he starts to say, leading me down the stairs to the outside courtyard. "Like fire."

"You don't look too bad yourself."

It's true, unfortunately. His black linen collar cuts down his chest, revealing the muscle beneath. The sleeves tumble midway down his forearms, and a couple of gold rings adorn his fingers.

Grand pillars and blaring trumpets surround us, making my heart thump. The horses snort and swing their heads, and the sun glares into my eyes. But the air is still bitter and frigid. I shiver as the wind plays with my hair. We climb into the carriage as the trumpets end their song with a flourish.

As soon as we enter the Concave streets, fear leaps into my mouth. Hundreds of thousands of Concaves crowd the sides of the streets. Waving and cheering and calling our names. Ruben winds down the windows with the levers on the door and sticks his hand out, waving right back.

"Come on, Elle," he says. "They'll love it."

I school my face into a pleasant smile and wave. Bright and pastel colours merge and mingle with one another as people shout my name and chase our carriage along the cobbled street. The carriage, without warning, jerks to a halt.

"Why have we stopped?" Ruben leans forward, pinching his brows.

The horses erupt into panicked whinnying, rearing back on their hind legs and jolting the carriage. Screams and shots fling around us.

"It's the Convex!" someone yells, and my blood pools.

I throw myself out of the carriage on instinct but curse myself when I realise my knives are not on my body. They are stowed uselessly in the palace.

"Elle!" Ruben barks, scrambling out after me.

Utter chaos envelopes our carriage as the crowd of Concave flees in all directions. Many grab their children, tossing them on their shoulders as they run for their lives. But bodies already sprawl on the ground. Concave bodies.

That's when I spot them. Three Convex men, identifiable by their scruffy beards, dressed in stolen Concave garb, gnarled hands clenched around crimson-dripping daggers.

"There he is!" one man bellows.

He throws his knife at us. I yelp, jerking aside as the knife slices through the air, cutting between me and Ruben's head and slamming into the carriage door.

Chapter 16

I huddle in my room that night, tears streaming down my face as the gates in the far distance ease open on the hinges. The groans of a dying God of War permeate the kingdom. My breaths fall short and sharp as I hug my knees and pick at my fingernails, the only thing I know how to do tonight.

Every single one of the Convex who stormed the parade today is being exiled.

I have already vomited up all my fancy palace dinner. Yet, my stomach still churns and winds into knots. The crescent moon climbs toward its apex amongst the stars, reminding me of all the souls that will return to the cosmos soon. They will return home. I am unsure how long my journey is to the stars, but I'm certain that when I get there, I will not fear oblivion. But can I be forgiven for all I've done?

I don't think so.

I want to be.

Someone knocks on the door, and I cringe, burying my face into the pillow. "Please go away."

"It's me," Ruben says.

"Even more of a reason to leave," I bark, shivering as the bitter draft blows in through the open window and tickles my skin.

"I have two people here who want to see you."

"Elle?" a voice says that makes my heart leap.

"Aston?"

I peel myself from the bed and fling the door open. Aston and Lyra stand behind Ruben, and he ushers them into the room, glancing over his shoulder.

"Ruben…" I say, voice dripping with a warning. "You haven't put them in danger, have you?"

"It will fall on me. I promise," he says, tightening his jaw and not quite meeting my gaze. "We don't have long, so please be quick."

And suddenly, I am staring at my sister's face. "Are you…?" she starts to say. She's here. It's *her*.

A cry spills rampant from my chest, and I pull Lyra into a hug, tears prickling my eyes at the feeling of her too-thin, frail body. Her bones practically prod into me.

"Oh, Elle," she says, pushing me back with surprising force, regarding me with watery eyes. "You look so strong. So full of life."

Her red hair is dull and frizzy, even in the braid draping down her back. There's a tremble in her hands as she tugs at her threadbare frock, and my heart aches. "I'm still stuck here." My voice quivers, and I clench my fists. "I'd rather be home with you, listening to you read one of Mama's books."

Her smile is an effort, and I see the little girl who once tripped over her feet to make our parents proud, the little girl who wanted to finish school and dreamed of working her way into the Concave Sector so we could enjoy life. "Hopefully, when all this is over, you can do that. Maybe after your wedding."

Aston and I both grimace at the word. Ruben recoils into the wall. "She will be my wife. Once my father dies, I will be the king. So, she will have free rein to do whatever she likes."

Aston elbows me, wagging his brows playfully. "Do you want to see if your knife-tossing skills have improved? Perhaps we can hasten along His Majesty's death."

I swat him, shushing him. "*Aston.*"

"You aren't alone, Elle," Aston says, voice low and hushed, hardly louder than my breath.

"What do you mean?" I furrow my brow, feeling embers of fear crackle in my throat.

"There's more of us. The rebels. There's more to come."

An icy sting grazes my spine like the claws of an awakened beast. "They can't. Did they not see what happened to the rebels tonight?"

He swallows, and his Adam's apple bobs. "They all know the risks."

I shake my head, my stomach churning like a storm. "They are idiots. Nothing will come out of it other than their deaths. I can't have more blood on my hands." My fists clench and unclench as if my spirit is too restless for my rigid body.

"You do not bear responsibility for their actions, Elle," Aston says, pacing the room and examining the fine furniture like a baby bird exploring a forest for the first time. He stops at the window, hands clasped behind his back. "You gave the Convex a spark of hope. Many of them do not have anything to lose. It's either fight and die trying or starve a slow, painful death. They have told me they owe it to their ancestors who were too afraid to fight, and their descendants who deserve a better world."

The wind blows his bronze hair, and I shudder. "When did you become such a soldier?" The little boy I once knew is gone. Small, scrawny, timid. The young man before me is strong. Weathered, yes, but ablaze with the reckless spirit of rebellion.

He chuckles, pulling me into a side hug. "You and I were born soldiers, were we not?"

Lyra settles on the corner of the bed, and Ruben lingers awkwardly in the background. I soak in Aston's embrace. The rough canvas of his clothes scratches my cheeks, and Madam Sallow's herbal tea that has long since stained the fabric stretches around me. "I cannot lose you, Aston." My voice is a mere squeak. "Other than Lyra, you are all I have."

He shifts and smiles, planting a kiss on my head. "I think a certain dark and brooding prince may also care for you. But remember what I said about trusting him."

We both glance over our shoulder at Ruben, who flushes pink, and our laughter melts together—the only sound that has ever made sense since my parents' death.

"While the Convex people are perfectly capable of the uprisings themselves," he says. "They need a leader. I think you'd be the lady for the job, Elle."

The wind whistles outside, and the curtains flap. "I can't." I tighten my fists, shaking my head. "I am too weak to handle any more death on my account. Nor do I have any of the skills to lead them into battle against the king. I don't even have a reliable knife shot."

We cast another smirk at Ruben. "Clearly not," Aston says with a light laugh, earning a scowl.

"And the world still has its dark and brooding prince," I say, smirking.

"He has ears!" Ruben says, crossing his arms over his chest.

"Gosh, you're odious!" Lyra speaks up, earning a laugh from all of us.

All too soon, Ruben reminds us that our time is up. I pull Aston into a hug, burying my face into his shoulder and his tunic catching my tears.

"Now, don't get soppy on me," he says, chuckling, but his voice wavers despite himself.

"I'm so afraid. I don't want you to leave me." My voice cracks, and I sound pathetic. But I don't care.

"You are a storm of fire, Elle. The king should be afraid of you." He places his sturdy hands on my shoulders. I study the shape of his face, those warm, hazel eyes, and breathe in his earthy scent, soaking up every inch of him, wishing I could bottle him up and keep him in my pocket.

"I think he is a little." My voice is hardly louder than my breath.

He presses another kiss to my forehead. "Good. Even if you do not agree to lead the Convex rebellion, I need you to understand they will take action anyway. These people have nothing else to lose. They believe they owe it to future generations to fight. Many of them have voiced that they hope you will fight *with* them at the very least."

My stomach clenches, and I wonder if my supper will return to the land of the living. The memory of the prisoner I banished rises to greet me, his final words scalding my skull. *Fight for us, Elle.* "I understand. For now, my role remains in keeping my loyalty to the king. But don't worry, we will figure out how to end him without the deaths of thousands of Convex and Concaves, too." I can't risk it. I just can't.

"Hopeful. Optimistic. Please don't be too naïve, Elle." He hugs me again, and it takes every ounce of strength to not fall apart. "I love you, Elle."

"I love you, too. I will see you again." My lip quivers, and I bite down on my cheek to stop the rising panic.

"I better receive an invite to the royal wedding," he says, throwing a wink to Ruben before stepping aside.

Lyra steps forward, reaching for my curls and tucking a strand behind my ears. "You will invite me, too, right?" Her eyes water and my knees almost buckle. It is like regarding a small, helpless child. A sliver of resentment burns in my gut, followed by a roar of guilt. Her limbs are so slim and brittle that I am surprised she is still standing upright. The way her cheekbones poke out, the sagging of her cheeks, and the yellow of her skin make me want to peel my own flesh off. It is almost a relief my father isn't here to see her like this.

"Yes. But I fear you will not make it, Lyra," I say, my voice sharp as blades. Shame grips me like a hand tightening around the throat. I can almost hear my father's voice. *"You promised me, my Elle. What happened to sticking together?"*

She bristles, sticking her chin into the air. "No need to fret over me. You spent your entire life doing enough of that." That ember of resentment glows again. And suddenly, I realise that Lyra has simply drowned in grief. All that has remained since our parents' exile is a sallow, faded ghost. I lost her that day, too.

"So, are you eating? Are you working?" The words tumble from my lips like the kingdom's waterfall. My nose burns.

Her gaze hardens, and she brushes her red braid behind her shoulder. "Yes. But Mr Pollins refuses to give me any more hours, and the food is still scarce. Even with Ruben's help."

The way she speaks, her eyes not quite meeting mine, tells me she isn't being truthful.

"Are you eating?" I say again, my nails digging into my palms.

She purses her cracked lips. "Yes. But also, there's a pregnant woman on the street with her two children. I've been giving them some of my food."

I want to scream at her, throttle her. But my heart aches at her compassion and selflessness, knowing I would do the same thing. "Please just eat," I squeak.

She reaches out and takes my hands. Hers chill mine to the marrow. "Elle." Something deep and primal within me captures the way she says my name and tucks it into my heart. My throat bobs, and I cannot utter a word without melting into a pool of sobs.

"Tales of a girl with the spirit of a snake have spread throughout the kingdom. I hear your name on the wind like it's a war cry, Elle. They say this girl will spark forever change." Lyra's cheeks go pink, and her voice trembles. "That rebellious spirit of yours comes from father. Let it guide you. Let it make you brave."

I open my mouth to respond, but she grabs my temples and plants a whisper of a kiss between my brows. My sister scurries away, her hands clasped in front of her, as she disappears around the corner into the white blade of moonlight.

Aston holds my gaze for a moment more before nodding sharply at Ruben, who leads them both away, leaving me to the torrent of my thoughts and the groaning kingdom gates in the distance. For a moment, I swear I can hear the monsters screeching, their howls calling my name as if I am one of them.

Chapter 17

The hallways are still laced with the essence of a silent night as I slip through them. Only the odd handmaiden and servant scurry past. Lyra's words keep me company, whirling around me like a phantom trying to complete business they did not finish in life.

Rain patters and drips down the arched windows, yielding beams of grey light as I stride past them, and a chill creeps over my arms. I enter the kitchen downstairs, earning a squeak from the servant reaching for a sack of flour. She flips around, leaning against the stove with a hand over her heart, eyes bulging. For a moment, I wonder if she's afraid of me.

"Oh, Miss Elle," she says, voice pitchy as she steels herself, pulling at the apron pinned to her frock. "What are you doing here at this hour? I'm not sure you may be here without His Royal Highness or an escort."

My cheeks burst into flames. "I am… hungry." The rumble echoes from my stomach on queue, the feeling grazing the deeply rooted instincts. I know the feeling all too well. The weakness. The desperation. "I suppose I'm still learning the rules. Hopefully, he doesn't scold me. He has quite the temper."

She smiles, reaching back for the wooden spoon in her large brass pot. Steam dances from the bubbling liquid. "He has a temper. But something about him… is lovely."

I scrunch my nose. "He's the most obnoxious person I have ever had the misfortune to meet. He is the bane of my existence."

The girl arches her brows, spilling a giggle. "Careful, Miss Elle. It sounds like you might actually like him."

"Never," I say, letting out a braying laugh as I march into the scullery, grabbing a loaf of bread and olive oil.

I cut the bread on the bench next to her as she sprinkles a pinch of salt into the hissing pot. "Miss Elle. I envy you."

My serrated bread knife slams into the wooden chopping board as I glance at her. "How so?"

"You are marrying the crown prince," she says, pursing her lips like it is the most obvious answer in the world. "You are never going to have to worry about anything again. *And* he is gorgeous. I wish he looked at me the way he looks at you."

The lump in my throat is a struggle to push past. I shake my head, releasing a laugh. "He doesn't look at me in any way."

"He looks at you like he's never known warmth, and you're a dancing flame," she says. "Not to mention, you are going to change our world. We have been waiting for you."

I stuff the bread dipped in olive oil into my mouth. "I am just a girl. And I almost killed the prince. Might I remind you?"

"Well, how many people get away with such crimes?" she muses, pressing her lips together. "If you can get away with it, the rest of us can do it. You have given us hope we can fight."

"You better keep your voice down," I say, tightening my jaw.

"There's no need to worry about me, Miss Elle. I have nothing left to lose. I can only hope you will fight with us."

The hairs on my arms spring up, and a shudder ripples down my spine. Those words. Like she's echoing the man I exiled. Parroting Aston's warning, too.

I finish the bread and bid her goodbye, wondering, for an agonising beat of my heart, if anyone was lingering in the corridors or the shadows, listening to her treasonous words. The hallways are still swathed in the blanched shadows of dawn as I make my way back to my room. But as I reach my door, I wonder if I should ask a servant for directions to Ruben's room. Something about my interaction with the servant makes me want to see him.

Curse words fling back and forth in my skull.

What am I becoming?

He is just a prince with pretty eyes. Nothing more. I can't fuel his enormous head by ever uttering... by ever daring to admit that he might make my soul want to come undone.

Someone clamps a hand over my mouth, and I cry out, the sound muffled. The rough hands shove me into a broom closet in the hallway, their putrid coffee and liquor breath fanning my face as they huff like enraged animals. I thrash and writhe against them, but they're simply too strong for me. Dull pain explodes in the back of my skull as they slam me against the wall. They grab a broom and shove the stick against my throat, cutting off my windpipe, and I gasp, struggling for air.

"*You* killed our friend," the Tranq says, his voice cracking with the wrath of a grieving soul.
His face and identity remain hidden beneath his helmet. The only telltale feature is those light brown eyes, watery and red.

Another Tranq lingers behind him, his blade pointed at me, glinting in the streak of sunlight reaching into the room through the single window, catching the dust particles alight.

"What do you want from me?" I splutter, trying to push the broomstick from my neck, but the man holds firm.

"We can't let you live," he growls, voice echoing through the helmet. "You've caused a lot of trouble, Elle Fallon. You killed our friend and almost killed the prince. Now, there are uprisings in the Convex Sector. King Talin may place a feeble bet on your little wedding uniting the Sectors. But we know better. The Convex will only get greedy. And we don't have enough food to share. Our kids will go hungry."

Flames burst into my cheeks. "They're not greedy. They're starving, you big idiots."

"They will destroy our way of life, our livelihoods if given half the chance. Feral, hateful creatures."

"Look at you both." I release a harsh bark of laughter, which they cut off, pressing the broomstick tighter into my throat. "You are afraid of a bunch of people taking back what was robbed from them for generations. Freedom. Security. The Concaves and the Tranqs have had it for years, and meanwhile, the Convex starve to death, slaves to the ghost war beyond the walls. We are destroyed for even thinking of rebellion."

"You killed our friend," he says, voice wavering.

I snarl, curling my lips. "I am sorry. But it had to be done. They were going to kill me."

"Would that have been worse than where you are now?" he says with a sneer.

His words bore into me like spores of a fungus, deeper and deeper until they became a part of me. I stop fighting against the broomstick. My glare falls.

He hisses, shaking his head. "That's what I thought. You should have died when you were meant to, Elle. Now, look at the blood on your hands. Your sister and the Convex rebels."

"My sister is still alive." The words fall from my mouth before I can stop them.

"I cannot imagine King Talin will let her live for long. Or she will die from the famine, which I hear is worsening with the winter."

I notice his grip has loosened just enough on the broomstick as he gloats. My heart pounds as I reach for his belt, grab the knife, duck, and roll out from the broomstick. I stand and jab the knife at them.

"Don't move," I say, my tone forged from the darkest parts of the kingdom. "Unless you want to be another dead Tranq on my list."

They turn to stone, eyes wide with fear, apart from the quiver in their lips. They truly fear me. The realisation jolts me like a burn to the flesh, and I back out of the closet, my chest building with pressure, a lump forming in the back of my throat.

I shut the door behind me and bolt down the hall, pulling up short as Ruben approaches my room at the same time I do.

He arches his brow, head tilting. But his mouth drops at the sight of the blade in my hand, and he shoves me into the room, glancing over his shoulders for any watchful eyes.

"Can you people stop manhandling me?" I snap, jerking from his grip as soon as he closes the door.

"What the hell were you doing?" he barks back, pacing across the floorboards, his face dark.

"Getting breakfast." I toss the knife on the bed and cross my arms in defiance. "Is that a crime, too?"

"You shouldn't be wandering the palace alone." He plants his hands on the window ledge, turning his back to me.

"Why? Because vengeful Tranqs might try to kill me in a broom closet?"

His head snaps to the side. "They fear you."

"How do you know? What have you seen?"

"At dinner last night with the Tranqs, some of them voiced their... opinions. They didn't exactly say they were afraid. But they said other things. She's ignited the uprisings. She should have died. Killed our friend."

"Charming." I press my lips together. "Why have you come so early, anyway?"

He twirls around, his face lighting up. "I want to take you across town. To meet my friends."

I swallow back the laugh of disbelief. "*You* have friends?"

"Now I know it's hard to believe," he says, his lips tugging up in amusement. "But we've been friends since we were young boys. Brothers not by blood but by fate."

***

I glance at my reflection in the carriage window, smoothing down my frizzy curls. The bags under my eyes are prominent from my sleepless nights since the rebel exile. I pinch my cheeks and bite my lips to draw colour to them. Ruben blows out a breath of a laugh. "Who are you trying to impress?"

I glare at him. "Do you *have* to say whatever comes to your mind?"

He shrugs, picking at a bit of thread on his loose linen white shirt. The collar cuts low down his chest, and I refuse to stare at his skin. "My friends already know what you look like, what with our pictures all over the town."

"I just don't want them to see the swamp rat I truly am."

My freckles have faded from the lack of sunlight, and I arrange my ringlet curls down both the front and back of my shoulders. I wish I had my mother's eyes, as my sister does. But those cold, calculating eyes belonged to my father.

"Swamp rat." He laughs as the horses whiney and the carriage jolts to a stop. "Quite the contrary."

I bite down on my cheek, furiously willing the blush in my cheeks to recede. His gaze lingers on me for a moment before he reaches for the door, and we tumble out. "They will love you, Elle. Ajax and Killian are the least Concave-like guys I know."

"I'm sure I'll fit right in," I say dryly.

Apartment buildings flank either side of the uneven cobbled road, some of the outdoor corridors connected by low arching stone bridges that crisscross over our heads. Market stalls spill out from the bottom of the buildings, the smell of fruits and vegetables, meats, and loaves of bread playing with the morning sun. Everything is fresh. The smell of baking bread almost brings tears to my eyes. I have never seen such abundance.

Concave people dressed in corsets and tunics dyed pastel hues of pink, blue, and greens mill through the markets, perch outside cafes, and sip coffee, their chairs scraping the stone pavement and their delicate mugs clinking. Low, airy chatter winds and tangles in the frigid breeze. Many of them trail our movements as we pass with varying expressions of anger and envy.

Ruben leads me into a building's foyer and up a set of spiral stairs that doesn't so much as creak. My body shivers and yearns as I try to soak in the sunlight rolling in from the arched window.

"Ruben," I whisper as we stop outside an apartment. "Will *I* like them?"

He flashes me a grin and opens the door without knocking. I'm surprised it's even unlocked. The sweet, earthy scent of herbs and spices swathes the apartment as I scuttle in after him. Something bubbles in a pot on the stove, the steam oozing through a hole in the lid.

A boy pokes his head out from the hallway, a grin growing on his face. "What a sorry sight you are, Ruben."

161

The use of his name startles me, and I glance at Ruben. But he just lumbers up to the boy and pulls him into a big bear hug, slapping him on the back. "You are quite unsightly yourself, Ajax."

The boy grins, his teeth white as snow. His appearance takes me by surprise for a moment. His hair, dyed green, stands out like a beggar in the palace. A ring sticks out from his left brow and the middle of his lip. "You must be Elizabeth," he says, voice kind and warm like tea on a winter's night.

"Call me Elle."

Curiosity brims in his glacier-blue eyes, but he bites back the question. "I'm Ajax. Ruben has told me lots about you. You are as pretty as the wind, just like Ruben said."

Heat bursts into my cheeks and neck, and I want to scream and run away.

"Thanks a lot, Ajax," Ruben says, shaking his head to mask the embarrassment.

"Are you named after the Greek hero?" I ask, diverting the subject.

"You know your history," he says, ushering us further into the apartment with a soft, welcoming gesture. "Your rather ancient history at that! My father thought the name was strong. Masculine. He thought it would help me stand out amongst the noblemen in the Concave Court."

We are enveloped by the buttery allure of a scented candle, flickering and dancing in the kitchen. Ajax himself practically twirls into the living room, casting a mischievous grin at me over his shoulder. "My father would be appalled to know I continue to rebel against his whims and wishes. Gods rest his soul."

My hand trails up my chest, pinching the fabric. "And here you are, speaking to the girl who supposedly ignited uprisings in the Convex Sector."

He scrunches his nose, and his eyes are what I imagine the ocean looks like, both harrowed by storm and thrilled by the wind. "I never did fit in with my people."

"I sense a rebellious spirit."

Ajax scoffs, the light of a party billowing through him before darkness clouds his features, and he jabs his finger at me. "We are going to help you kill the king," he whispers, as if his father's spirit is in the room, listening and brooding.

Chapter 18

*K*ill the king. As Ajax's words knock the air from my ribs, another figure lumbers around the corner from the bedrooms. A tall, lanky boy with brown skin and dark auburn hair sizes me up and down. He points his long, calloused finger at me like I'm a peculiar, caged animal.

"So, you are the girl who almost killed Ruben?" he says, arching his thick brow and tightening his jaw. The cosmos sparkles in those hooded eyes, and a curious smile slips across his face.

I open my mouth to protest, but words die on my tongue.

Killian throws his head back and howls with laughter, pretending to wipe a tear from his eye. "I am sure you humbled our beloved crown prince."

"Killian, let's not be weird today. We have an important matter to discuss," Ajax says, pinching the bridge of his nose and letting out a groan.

"What matter?" Killian tosses me a side glance, almost as if I cannot hear the pair speaking. His hair falls into his eyes, but he doesn't bother to flick it away.

"The uprisings across the river." Ajax points in the general direction of the Convex Sector before shooting me a sympathetic smile. "The rebellion against the king."

"Keep your voice down," Ruben hisses, putting a finger over his lips. "Anyone could be beyond that door."

Ajax scoffs and shakes his head. "I thought you *wanted* to save the world from your old man." He crosses his arms, elbowing Ruben in the ribs.

"Just the kingdom. I can think about the world another time. I'd just rather not have to worry about you two." Ruben paces to the window as if he's expecting to see a cavalry of Tranqs barrelling down the road, coming to arrest us all.

"So, you're the one who's sparked all the chaos, Elle?" Killian says, marching into the kitchen and grabbing a knife. I flinch, but he just carves a loaf of fresh bread.

I click my tongue, letting out a shaky laugh. "I didn't mean to."

"We are glad," Ajax says, throwing me a wink. "We have been waiting for someone like you for years. Now, the Convex are finally seizing their chance to fight."

"But you're Concave, right?" I tilt my head. "I didn't think Concaves would want to change the status quo."

"Well, we aren't all selfish idiots." Ajax shrugs and pours us each a shot of whisky. We collapse around the small round table. "There's a few Concaves who understand the absolute unfairness of our society. We have power in our voices. If you believe that giving people equalities is going to take things away from you, you have never been without."

I feel Killian's sunken eyes on me as Ajax's words ring into the space between us all, his brows furrowing. "You're a *Fallon*, aren't you?" he says as he shoves a piece of bread into his mouth.

"Yes. The Fallons have had a name for themselves for a while, thanks to my father." I sip the whisky, cringing at the sharp, bitter taste. It is what I imagine venom would taste like.

"And now you continue the legacy." Killian tips his glass towards me, something shifting in those copper eyes.

"I suppose I do."

He shoots to his feet and practically lunges into the kitchen, yanking the oven open. Steam bursts out. His curses mingle with the warm, nutty scent of the tray of cookies that he slams onto the bench. "Almost burnt them! Mama would wring my neck." He tosses his chin up at me. "She's a baker. One of the king's bakers."

"Sounds… fancy. And like you have a legacy to uphold, too."

He bats at the air, dispersing the steam. "I'm not usually this careless with my macadamia cookies. They are Mama's favourite. She… made them for my father before they got married. But she wolfed down half the batch before he'd even had a crumb." Killian scoops the cookies onto a ceramic plate and slumps back at the table.

Ajax snatches a cookie and shoves half of it in his mouth. "Your cookies make me think that maybe there is good in the kingdom. That we aren't entirely stripped of decency."

"My mother says sugar can cure the black heart of any man," Killian says, reaching for his glass of amber liquor. It glints in the candlelight as he takes a swig.

"If we ever got so lucky to get sugar as children, my mama would put it in a pot on the stove until it turned golden," I say, drinking. "My sister and I would go crazy. Literally."

Killian swirls his finger through the condensation on his glass. "My mother said that many Convex children don't ever know the taste of sugar. She never wanted my sisters and me to miss out on one of life's simplest pleasures."

I shrug, taking a gulp, trying to ignore the burn that comes with the impact of his words. It is hard to stomach the fact that Killian grew up just across the river, across the bridge, never knowing the hollow ache of hunger. How odd that fate can determine so much suffering or an abundance of luck. "I was eight when I tried sugar for the first time." I hope my voice does not yield the jealousy pricking my heart. "And yet, my grandmother worked in the sugar cane fields right up until the day she passed. Said the very smell of them made her stomach turn."

Killian clears his throat, reaching for the bottle. "Perhaps... perhaps we can create a world in which every child knows the sweetness of sugar and not the pang of starvation."

"Here, here!" Ajax says, shoving his glass into the air. His smile makes it hard to resist the one crossing my own face and part of me relaxing around him. I probably would be more relaxed if it weren't for the stony eye coming from Killian.

We drink until the night falls and the moon ascends into the sky. I awake the following morning back at the palace with a pounding head and spend the rest of the day curled up in bed, feeling sorry for myself.

***

I rub my eyes as I traipse into the kitchen, finally emerging from my gremlin-like state as the palace falls asleep again. Pockets of shadows have hidden away from a couple of flickering candles. My stomach rumbles as I dig out a roll of bread from the pantry and cheese from the cool room. They quell the ache. I sit at the table, staring out of the window at the fingers or orange light stretching lazily over the walls. An icy breeze blows drafts through the windows, not quite sealed. But I revel in the coolness against my cheeks. Drying the sweat from the nightmares that snared me.

My mind travels elsewhere, dreaming of my father brewing tea for my sister and me every winter morning as children. But their brutal exile from the city, with nothing but the clothes on their backs, flashes across my mind, and I cringe. My heart aches, and my stomach curdles, my cheeks scorching. I push the thought of my father away like I always do.

I couldn't wait until morning in that room. By myself. With only my thoughts for company. As I sit hunched on the table, a knocking sound startles me from my still-hungover, groggy state. A shadowy figure emerges from the back kitchen door.

Aston.

Joy and bewilderment ricochet through my body, and a shrill laugh falls from my mouth as I bound up to him, flinging myself into his chest. Warm, soft, and smelling of pine and the earth. He pushes me forward and holds my shoulders.

"What the hell? How did you get here?" The words rush from my mouth.

"Breaking in to find you. What does it look like?"

I blink, opening and closing my mouth like a fish in a net.

"You need to come with me," he seethes, jaw tighter than the closed kingdom gates. "Don't ask questions."

Of course, a hundred questions nettle my tongue. But I nod and follow him outside. Darkness hugs his bony horse and grocery wagon. Aston nudges me, and I hoist myself into the seat. With a gentle flick of the reigns, we lurch forward. I fight the tears brimming my eyes as I regard Aston. His head remains facing the back of the horse's ears. But I keep my mouth shut while we navigate through the Concave Sector and across the bridge. I lean back, smiling at the star-freckled sky and liquid night. Have the stars ever known the darkness surrounding them?

Fear raps against my ribs. What am I about to see?

I swallow my impatience and wait. We skirt through the outside of the Convex Sector, along the river, and towards the network of streets, drawing closer to the heart of my village. The run-down, red brick building looks no different than the day the Tranqs arrested me. Sweat springs to my forehead in beads. I am a far cry from the girl who foraged for measly potatoes in her illegal forest garden. What, with the blood soaking my hands, day by day. The thought makes my stomach lodge into my spine. We dismount the cart, leaving the horse with a pail of water and fastened to an oil lamp post as we slip into the building. Dust and grime cling to our nostrils as we climb the groaning steps and arrive at my apartment.

Aston holds his hand out before we enter, his brows knitting together, his eyes clouding over. "Elle," he says, tone gentle. "Brace yourself. I will explain the best I can once we are inside."

I nod, gnashing my teeth. We enter the apartment, and I almost kneel over. Lyra hunches on the torn couch. Her eyes travel to me, hollow and distant. Her ribs poke out from beneath her shirt, and a yellow tint stains her skin, blotchy in the crevasses of her prominent cheekbones. My mouth dries, and I snarl at Aston. "What the hell happened?"

He throws his hands up defensively. "With the Tranqs crawling in the fields and the markets, I haven't been able to steal food for her. I understand Prince Talin provided some goods, but whoever he sent has clearly tampered with the food. It was poisoned."

My heart lurches into my throat. Lyra's lip quivers as I scurry over and crouch before her.

"Elle," she rasps, her head lolling to the side as if it's too heavy on her fragile bones. "I think I'm dying."

"That is ridiculous," I snap, shaking my head.

"I'm sick, not just starving," she says, her cracked, pallid lips trembling and my toes curl. "I've been vomiting my guts out for days. Can barely keep water down, let alone food. I am... I am going to finally join Mama in the stars." The finality of her words makes my vision blur and my cheeks burn.

No.

"I'm going to be right back." I rise to my feet, making for the exit, reaching for the wall to steady myself from the grief crashing through me, the world trying to knock me to my knees. "I will talk to the prince and deliver you fresh food myself." A tiny voice rises into the back of my head. That incessant, gut-wrenching reminder. *Lyra never did recover from our mother's death.*

"Stop, Elle," she says, voice firm enough to render me still in the doorway. "Come back. Sit down."

But I am a little girl silently screaming for my sister to stay, stay, *stay with me.*

My muscles urge me to do no such thing, but I sit before her anyway, crossing my legs. I raise my brows at her expectantly. "You have to save us, Elle," she says, her voice so sure a sliver of me is rallied by her. Awoken. "With the handsome prince by your side, you can destroy this kingdom from the inside out."

I blink at her, my mouth going so dry it's an extra effort to swallow. "Why are you saying this?"

She heaves a ragged breath. "Because word on the wind is you have sparked something in us."

"What could I have possibly sparked other than uprisings that keep sending our people to the monsters beyond the walls?"

"Hope," she says, a tear slipping down her cheek, over her lips. "You have sparked hope in some of the Convex that we will not always live in *his* world."

"You are talking nonsense," I say, letting out a low laugh. I glance at Aston leaning against the window ledge, chewing his lips, his face a blend of white and green.

"I am not, Elle," Lyra says, drawing in another gasp of air. "You must take accountability for what you have done. Stop denying what you have sparked. It does no one any good to wallow in self-pity." She pauses, reaching for the wooden pail at the end of the couch and retching into it. It's only red splotched bile. She groans in pain and curses. "My throat feels like it's been shredded by a bunch of tiny blades."

I hold the pail, biting the inside of my cheek and gagging at the stench hitting my nose.

"The kingdom knows of the girl who killed the Tranq." She smears the vomit dribbling down her chin with a handkerchief. "No one else has dared such a crime. The fire is spreading. Be ready for it. You must be getting to know the prince quite well now. If he has a shred of decency, he will help you. Perhaps the king's maliciousness will end with his bones on a pyre."

Weeps bubble up my throat, and I fling myself into her arms. Her skin is cold to the touch, and for a moment, I fear I'm too heavy for her. She struggles to push me out with her brittle hands, resting her trembling, icy fingers on my shoulders. Her eyes blaze.

"Father would be proud of you. He wanted this, too. You are his legacy."

***

Silvery dawn light stumbles across the sky when Aston ushers me back into the palace kitchen. I throw myself into his arms, drawing in his scent and trying to swallow the panic surging up my throat. Trapped. I am so trapped. I turn and scurry into the hallway, navigating my way through the palace to my room. I light the candle by the door to chase away the shadows and almost yelp. Ruben lounges on my bed. His arms over his head, snoring lightly. He wears nothing but black pants and an unbuttoned white tunic as if he threw it on hastily before racing to my room.

"What the hell?" I growl, marching over and poking his shoulder.

He sits up so fast I stumble back in fright, and he snorts. "The same question I have for you." He shakes his head. "Where the hell have you been?"

I cross my arms. "Didn't realise it was your business, Ruben," I retort.

"Unbelievable." He clicks his tongue, throwing his hands into the air as he stands from the bed. "You fled across the river, didn't you?"

I open my mouth to respond.

"And don't lie to me."

"What does it matter?" Heat creeps into my cheeks. "I returned."

His braying laughter boils my blood. "Naïve, hot-headed fool. You better hope the king does not find out."

"My sister is dying," I bark, balling my fists. "Someone is poisoning her food, and Aston has nothing to give her because of the rotten crops! He's scarcely more than a skeleton himself. If I lose the only two people I love—"

"Then you need to stay on this side of the river, Elle," he says, grinding his teeth. "It is the only way I can promise they will stay safe."

"Your promises mean nothing, Your Highness. She is dying anyway!"

He flinches, but the harsh glint in his eyes softens. He heaves a sigh. "I will investigate what is wrong with the food I'm sending her. It... shouldn't be poisoned."

"But it is, probably thanks to a Tranq," I say with a sneer. *Or the king.* More likely, it's King Talin.

He winces, pacing to the window. "We need to show up for lunch today. The king will give us his blessing. I came here this morning to wake you for an early training session, only to find you missing."

I blow out my cheeks and shift my weight. "Then let's get breakfast and get on with it."

We traipse back through the palace into the kitchen, and my jaw drops. The doorway and kitchen floor are covered in a layer of squashed tomatoes. Larissa mutters curses under her breath as she mops the creaking floorboards, shooting her frown to *Aston*. His cheeks match the tomatoes, and he plunges another mop into a wooden pail. His wide eyes flick between me and Ruben.

"What the hell, Aston?" Ruben asks. Meanwhile, Larissa tuts under her breath.

Aston swallows, chewing on his lip as if he's withholding a laugh. I stifle an uncomfortable breath, giggles welling in my chest. "I dropped a crate of tomatoes," he says, voice snapping with breathy chuckles.

Ruben blinks at him and then turns to me and throws his head back, howling with laughter. "What an entrance, Aston," he says, shaking his head. He turns back to me with a warning glint in his eyes. "And I thought your friend was cunning and careful."

I nod, opening my mouth to speak.

"I apologise for the wasted food, Your Highness," Aston says, squeezing the excess water from the mop and swiping it along the floorboards.

Ruben waves his hand. "I'm not worried about the food. I'm worried about your little journey across the river with Elle overnight."

The shadows falling over Aston's face shackle in my stomach. "Her sister is sick. She's on death's door."

"I understand, and I'm so sorry. But if the king finds out... we were lucky he agreed to the wedding, Elle." He shoots me a pointed look.

"Lyra wouldn't be in this situation if Elle was home. If you hadn't been in the forest that day," Aston snarls, stalking forward until his chest is inches from Ruben's. "Do not try to fool me. You are not a good person either, Prince Talin. You are using Elle to distract the Concaves from the real problem."

"Might I remind you, Elle killed a man, Aston," Ruben says through gritted teeth, any humour from moments before vanishing into the floorboards. "A treason punishable by exile. I *saved* Elle. I convinced my father that her exile would just fuel a rebellion."

"And what the hell are you doing about the bodies piling up in the Convex Sector? About the man-made famine?"

"Bodies?" I say, my stomach churning, trembling from the rage.

Aston doesn't even look at me. "In the square. The cemetery men are working overtime to load the bodies into their wagons. The blight has just gotten... so fucked up. People are about to turn feral from the insanity of starvation." A pause and a flicker of the lips. "I am sure the prince knows nothing of hunger."

Ruben and Aston stare at each other, eyes blazing, jaws tight. The prince swallows bodily, his Adam's apple bobbing in his throat. "You know nothing about me."

Aston scoffs and stalks to the exit.

"Wait," Ruben says. He trudges into the dim-lit scullery and emerges with a woven sack filled with fresh, healthy potatoes and spinach. "Take this."

"I won't take scraps from you," Aston snaps.

Ruben's eyes flash. "I am not your enemy, Aston. Take the food. Give it to Lyra and take some for yourself."

Aston snorts, shaking his head as he prowls to the exit. "If you are not my enemy, let me take my best friend home so she is safe with me."

"Just take the food, Aston," I say, and my voice cracks. How have I not crumbled from the pain?

He glares at me and presses his lips together. "Fine." Aston snatches the food from Ruben's outstretched hand and disappears into the yawning shadows of sunrise.

Chapter 19

The storm clouds roll in like a beast creeping across a desert plain, coating the sky in fiery hues as the sun cascades into the depths of the horizon. Snow will likely fall tonight. I drum my grown-out nails on the window ledge, grimacing at the shiver running down my spine. My stomach twists and clenches. I need to figure out how to get Lyra more food. Perhaps I can sneak her some of my own meals. I know the route home. Could I sneak out?

If I don't... Lyra's too-thin body, so akin to a skeleton, could send her soul back to the stars. The very thought of it makes my eyes prickle with tears, and a shudder ripple through me.

A knock yanks me from my thoughts.

Ruben peeks his head into the room. "Ready for dinner?"

Biles burns the back of my throat, but I bury the surge of emotions. "Yes." I have never sounded so disinterested—so unready.

My dress, a pale pink number with a beige corset, flows around my ankles. Ruben wears dark pants with his classic white linen shirt and suspenders over his shoulders. A loose strand of brown hair falls into his face. There is a moment, a pause, when all I can see is the little boy behind those eyes. Swimming. Drowning in his terror, in his father's cruelty. Before I can stop myself, my hand flies out. His lips part. And I brush the strand of hair off his face. "Elle," he says, breathless. And I am weightless. I don't move—can't move. For that moment, there is only him. And I. In this room with the candle-flecked walls and the utter breath between us. He says my name again, and his voice ignites a spark that licks the side of my neck, plummeting into the base of my spine.

"You are afraid." The words tumble out of my mouth before I can catch them, and they make their impact like icy rain, running its claws down his chest.

He stiffens. A slight scowl flicks onto his face, like a cat's mere breaths before it scratches. A warning. "I cannot show him a lick of fear."

"I think we both know that the king is smart enough to see you."

"Apparently, you see me, too."

"How could I not? You are right there, so blazingly obvious. It's like I am looking into a mirror."

"I thought you said we were nothing alike," he says with a scoff, somehow looming closer.

I let out a bitter laugh. "I think we both know that isn't true."

There is a freckle on his lower lip and a tiny scar on his chin. Details.

Ruben releases the tension in his jaw and blows out his cheeks. "Let's just get this over with. I can think of a hundred other people I'd rather share a dinner with other than my father and you."

"You say that as if I arranged this meal," I bite back, pulling myself away from the trance that is him, and turn to the full-length mirror, trying to untangle the knots in my hair. I whirl back around. "Now, do I at least look presentable for a royal dinner with His Majesty?"

Ruben's throat bobs as his gaze slowly, agonisingly slowly, traces the shape of my body, eventually arriving back at my face. "Yes," he says, practically shoving out the word.

"Great. Let's go. I'm starving."

***

The dining hall is an enormous room adorned with sparkling chandeliers draping from the coffered marble ceiling, splashing between the greasy aromas of glazed ham. I gulp. Different shades of marble splatter the floor, deep purple, blood orange, blue, and white, like a mosaic for a giant.

A long table gobbles up the room, stretching towards the arched, stained-glass window like a sword to the throat. King Talin perches on the grand, hand-carved chair at the head of the table. He grips his goblet, and those venom-green eyes trail my movements as we approach and sit. The servants scurry forward and push our chairs in before pouring fizzing wine into the goblets.

Ruben and I clink the goblets, the sound ricocheting across the room and back as the king takes me in, bite by bite.

"Elle," he booms from the head of the table. His voice scrapes down my back, and I shiver, gritting my teeth. "So kind of you to join us for supper. I'd like to get to know one another this evening."

I lower the goblet and wait as the servant scoops steaming mashed, herby potatoes onto my plate. My stomach rumbles, still unused to all the food. I wonder if I can sneak bread into my serviette and take it across to Lyra.

"I'd like nothing more," I say, forcing a pleasant smile. But it's made of glass.

"Perfect. I'll start." He leans forward, clasping his hands together in front of his dinner plate. "Did you know that when my son was small, we used to paint together? I taught him how to hold a brush and how to move it across the page with just the right looseness and precision. I taught him how to mix colours and let his creativity run wild."

I resist the urge to grab my goblet and drink the entire thing. "It sounds like a lovely father-son bonding."

The king turns to Ruben. "You were quite talented. Loved to paint pictures of the garden and of the sunsets and night sky.

Ruben clutches his goblet so tightly that I fear it will break. Red blooms into his cheeks like a fresh wound seeping into a linen shirt. "I don't paint anymore."

The king grabs his fork and stabs his asparagus. Our cue to eat, too. "You should pick up the brush again."

"You didn't exactly like my last picture," Ruben says, bringing his goblet to his lips.

"Well, it only seemed that... portraits of people were not your skill." King Talin turns back to me. "I also taught Ruben to read. His mother was busy, you see. I didn't want the nannies to help with reading as I believed a young boy should learn from his father."

Ruben rubs his lips, pulling down the smile forming on his face. "You only let me read books from the Old World," he says, shaking his head, eyes sparkling with amusement.

"That's because all the New World literature is codswallop!" The king throws his head back in braying laughter, and I almost catch myself smiling. "You loved some of those books, too, my boy."

My boy.

A jolt snaps my spine straight. I can see the word strikes a strange chord in Ruben's heart, too, by the flinch in his eyes. But he somehow still smiles.

"My mother used to read with me, too," I say, sawing through my lamb with the steak knife. "She let me read anything. Books from the New World and Old. Poetry. Children's' nursery rhymes. Novels. Whatever I could."

"And your father?" The king raises a brow, the glimmer in his eyes draining like water down a plughole.

"He... taught me to not fear my own strength and abilities."

King Talin pulls his lips into an odd combination of a grin and a sneer. "I just wanted to say how you have taken me by surprise the past few days."

There is an edge to his tone that at once sends my heart slamming into my ribs. But I school my face into neutrality. "How so, Your Majesty?"

"I am warming up to you. A girl plucked from the streets of the Convex village to marry my son. I think it is a great way to unify the Sectors. A perfect little distraction, you are. Perhaps my son's ideas hold some value after all."

His words are dainty, poised knives held to my quivering throat. A cat playing with a frightened mouse.

My stomach drops. My mouth dries, and I choke down my sparkling wine as the blade slices through me. Cold as a winter storm. And those royal eyes flash with satisfaction as he sees that I realise what he knows.

He knows I left the Concave Sector.

Chapter 20

Dirt stains the snow. It splashes its murky sludge up the sides of the cart as we bumble along the rickety cobbles, past the piles of it shoved to the side of the Convex roads. The horse's hooves clatter, and clouds of steam burst through her nose with each breath as she draws me through the streets toward the gates. Biles burns my throat, and my stomach churns with the impending test. Another exile. My fingers tremble as I place them against the window of the carriage, staring out despite the exhausted sting in my eyes.

I catch the eye of several Convex people. A bony elderly woman whose cheeks sag into the earth and grey whiskers that stick towards the sun as if they're searching for hope. Her ribs poke out from beneath her tattered oat-coloured tunic. A dead rat hangs from her belt. I offer a smile, but her cracked lips quirk into a sneer. Jealous of the food in my belly and the colour in my face.

Startled, I lean back into the cushioned carriage seat and close my eyes. Only as the carriage jerks to a halt do I force them open. My stomach lurches into my throat. Hundreds of Convex people line the street leading up to the gates. Just as they did the other day. Hundreds of heads turn to me, faces filled with terror as if I am an inferno ploughing through a village.

I force my concrete feet forward. One in front of the other. Keeping my face impassive, I acknowledge each group as I pass. A small band of musicians slams enormous canvas drums before them, the deep, rhythmic thud booming in my ribs, drowning out the scream in the back of my throat.

When I draw closer to the gates, a wisp of fiery red hair catches my eye. Fastened to the stake behind her, Lyra hangs her head in exhaustion. The sun burns her scalp. Her weak body can barely remain upright, and a yellow tint stains her skin. My knees tremble and buckle. I collapse to the ground as pitched wail streams from my mouth, transforming into a scream.

She is the prisoner today. She's about to be exiled.

Hot tears blur my vision as my face twists, the agony paralysing my muscles. A blond scruffy head materialises, and warm arms wrap around me. Aston's pine needle scent coaxes a sliver of sanity into the recesses of my mind. I swallow. As I wipe my tears and let Aston help me back to my feet, he presses a kiss to my forehead. "I'm sorry, Elle," he whispers.

I shake my head. "No, it's not your fault." With another squeeze of my hand, he nods in the gate's direction. I throw up my breakfast.

My teary, hate-filled gaze lands on King Talin. A faint, amused smirk twitches onto his face, and I see nothing but red. I yank a knife from my belt and toss it. The blade spins, slicing through the air as it sails past the king's ears, landing on the dirt behind him. An animalistic scream tears up my throat as I pull out my sword and lunge for the king. Finally, I understand. Every ounce of hatred I once felt for the Tranqs redirected to one miserable man in only a moment. His Adam's apple bobs in his throat as my blade brushes his jugular vein, and I sneer.

"Let her go," I growl. My muscles waver, and my voice cracks, but the fusion of ice and fire burns so furiously it startles even the king.

The brief flash of fear disappears. Schooled into the practised look of indifference. "I see your shot still hasn't improved."

He turns to the crowds and puffs out his chest. "Clear the gates!" he bellows so loud it prompts squeaks and squeals from the Convex throngs. "Curfew for the Convex Sector begins in half an hour. We will arrow anyone on sight caught out in the streets!"

With that, the crowds disperse at once. Mothers grip the hands of their children, yanking them away. Younger people gather their friends and loved ones, helping carry the elderly and disabled out of the streets. The rumble of hundreds of feet and terrorised voices dissipate, and my glare remains on the king. But I slide my sword back into the scabbard across my spine.

When not another soul remains other than Lyra, the king lets out a low laugh and I gnash my teeth. "Time for your next test, Elle," he says with a hiss.

"Are you going to make me exile my sister?" I ask, stepping forward, reaching for the blade—my father's blade—resting against my hips.

The king smirks, prowling forward like a snake slithering toward its prey. I am the rat. "You will find the monster in the lake beyond the walls."

"The Shadowtooth?" I say, the air leaving my lungs. The monster with no soul. "Why?"

"If you can return a pint of the Shadowtooth's blood, I will spare your sister." He sticks his chin into the air and puffs out his chest.

I swallow, an icy sea surging through my blood, crushing my spine. "How do I know you are not bluffing? That you will not kill her, anyway? It is not like you will stop her from dying of starvation."

He shakes his head. "Return with a pint of the Shadowtooth's blood, and she returns home, safe and sound. Albeit, the blight is out of my control."

Liar.

"What is the catch? Why do you want the Shadowtooth's blood?" A strange feeling creeps across my skin as I utter the creature's name again. Such a creature should remain buried from sight, sound, and human consciousness.

His teeth appear yellower in the light of day, as if the palace chandeliers cast a glamour of pristine health and beauty over him. "No catch other than a happy king and a step closer to earning my blessing."

The gates boom, groaning like a beast from the depths of the earth as they ease back on their metal hinges. A gust of bone-chilling wind blows through the widening gap, swirling my hair around my head and running its fingers down my spine, whispering the call of death.

My eyes snap shut. The world simply screams. I brace myself to be slashed in half by the monster. But… nothing.

The lake, a dark blue chasm of unknown monsters, glints beneath the grey clouds. The shore is a sprawling sandy marsh riddled with weeds and grass-like bushes, brushed with the scent of dying things. Ducks and their young quack and waddle across the sand, picking at morsels. A long, narrow wooden canoe moors the shore. Other than the ducks and the gentle lapping of the water against the shore, the silence of the lake is absolute, as if all life and light have been sucked into the depths of the water. Beyond the lake, far, far in the distance, another land mass rises into the horizon.

Nothing but an eternity of emptiness beyond the walls. Perhaps the legends and stories were right after all. Why am I even allowed to see this?

King Talin drags me from my spell by grabbing the knife from the ground and handing it back. "You will need this. One can never have too many blades, right, Elle Fallon?" A flicker dances in his gaze, and every instinct urges me to slap the smirk off his stupid face.

I snatch it back, slipping it into my belt. As I muster my courage, I stow my dagger in the scabbard strapped to my hip and glance back at Lyra. Tears stream down her swollen, reddened face.

"Don't do it, Elle," she says, a mere breath away from melting into a weep, as if the king isn't there, lapping it up. "Let me go. I am dying anyway."

"No," I bark, scrunching my fists, my jaw muscles pulsing with the rage scorching through my limbs. "When have I ever turned my back on you? I will always protect you."

"You'll die." Her voice is a desperate rasp, as if she has swallowed burning coals. She winces against the tight bonds slicing into her skin.

"I can do this," I seethe, and she flinches.

Shadows hug the grooves of her yellowed, sallow cheeks. But she nods. After snatching the small bottle from the king and tucking it into my belt, I prowl closer to the gates.

I sweep my gaze around the perimeter of the gates, half-expecting to find Ruben. But he is nowhere to be seen. I shoot King Talin a hateful glare once again. The crunch of the beach pebbles beneath my boots strums along my arms, helping distract me from the knots in my gut. My hands tremble as I remove the armour, tossing it aside. I freeze. Someone's skull is half-buried into the sand and stone.

The frigid water sinks its fangs into my ankles as the canoe slides over the lapping waves. The Gods cackle at me, lashing me with their opinions, tossing my hair about as I jump into the canoe and glance back at the king, who leans against the towering gate. A smirk rests on his face. I throw him my middle finger before shoving the oar into the water and pushing off.

Muttering under my breath, I row further and further from the shore until the king is a mere ant. The sweet scent of moss tinges the air, and the thump, thump, thump of the water against the hull of the boat finds rhythm with my heart. There is a figure who looks vaguely like Ruben. A spark of fury blooms, but I force it away, saving it for later. I am surrounded by the darkness and depth of a watery abyss. The wind snaps away without warning, leaving the silence and stillness rippling around me, the furrows of the lake melting into glass. I peer over the edge. The darkness stares back. Mirroring my soul. But my hair is a fiery mess. Silence roars in my ears.

Where is the Shadowtooth?

The canoe wobbles beneath me as I stand, twisting the oar and smacking it into the water. Splashing and yelling for the monster to show itself.

A screech from the depths of the water chills the marrow of my bones. It emerges from the water, one arm at a time. No, one *tentacle* at a time. Covered in scales and suctions, bathed in deep violet, and flecked with blue. Its enormous body remains submerged. A fiery orange eye fixates on me and narrows. With another shriek, the creature flings its tentacle at me. I grab my sword from the scabbard and slice through the flesh. The monster screams like an enraged goddess, the sound ringing in my skull as the tentacle bucks into the air. Its blood cascades down on me like a sick rain shower. A low laugh falls from my lips. A feeling simmers deep in my gut. The brief euphoria of power. Is this what all the great men have chased throughout time?

The Shadowtooth roars, swinging at me again. My reflexes are not fast enough; it knocks me flat. I cry out as my head smacks into the bottom of the canoe. Spitting crimson saliva, I pick myself up and grab my cast-aside sword. I need to get the blood.

The Shadowtooth throws its tentacle at me again, and I yell, swinging my knife. It cries out, smacking an arm into the top of the canoe, propelling me into the air. I tumble into the lake, dropping further and further into the inky darkness. The water sinks its icy talons into my skin, bubbles racing to the surface. But I merely suspend in time and space. Weightless.

The two men I exiled skulk across my mind. The glint of terror in their eyes as I pushed them out. Then, my sister's face, her scrawny figure. Aston. The two people I love most are going to be killed because of me.

"You know who our enemy is," the prisoner said before I shoved him across the gate's threshold. *"Fight for us, Elle."*

My lungs burn as I kick up to the surface, gasping for air when I break through. The Shadowtooth smacks its arms into the water, sending waves pummelling toward me. I spit the water from my mouth and swim towards the canoe. Just as I reach for the edge of the boat, the monster wraps its tentacle around me. Dragging me under. Surrounded by the darkness, cold slicing into my nerves, my muscles grow weak. I want to scream but keep my mouth clamped shut. I pull my other knife from my belt and shove it into the monster's flesh. It shrieks, loosening its grip, and I wrangle free.

An idea strikes me. Hysteria bubbles in my throat. I swim to the surface and scramble through the water to the boat, hauling myself bodily onboard as the monster reels itself. I wait for the enormous squid to move toward me before I spin my knife and leap from the boat. With a grunt, I propel myself through the air and land on the top of its head. I crouch and grip the scales, large enough for my hands to dig beneath. It swishes around, confused, no longer able to see me. I'm in its blind spot.

A war cry tears from my throat as I plunge the knife into the Shadowtooth's head. It roars and thrashes, but I hold firm as the blood gushes out. What a dramatic creature. The tiny knife relative to the squid's size is nowhere *near* its skull. Dark crimson blood oozes out, and I stick the lip of the bottle into the flow, filling it quickly. Just as I screw the lid on and tuck it back into my belt, a tentacle sweeps across its head, knocking me off. I fly, landing in the water once more. When I break the surface, the angry Shadowtooth's eye lands on me.

Heart hammering, I swim fast to the boat, dragging myself onboard. I grab the oar and push off. But not fast enough. Into the water once more, the canoe flipping upside down. Frustration builds into a roaring crescendo of blood coursing past my ears as I swim to the shore. I gasp as a mighty, sticky arm wraps around my torso and lifts me into the air, pinning my hands at my side, but I keep my grip on my dagger, screaming and writhing in the beast's grip. But it's useless. The monster hoists me high into the air, and water cascades from us both. Its burnt orange eye pins on me, and I wonder, for a moment, if I'm staring into the universe. It squeezes me tighter, and I brace myself for death, hoping the crushing of my bones drags me into the arms of the God of Souls quickly.

But the Shadowtooth's eye darts, only an inch, to my father's dagger at my side. Something strange passes through its gaze. A knowing expression.

The Shadowtooth lets me go. It hurtles me across the lake, and I plummet back into the inky depths of the lake. A wince rumbles through me when my blade catches through the flesh of my forearm as I fight my way to the light. As I break the surface, coughing and spluttering, a bubbling growl tears from my throat. With every morsel of strength and grit, I swim my way to the shore. My muscles give out as I feel the sandy bottom under my feet, and I collapse onto the shore. Coughs and splutters tear through me. A flash of quicksilver. My sword thuds into the sand, hurtled from the depths of the lake. The jar of Shadowtooth blood tips, and the lid falls off. Its shimmering blood splashes out onto my arm, mixing with my blood. I cry out, grab the jar, and stamp the lid back on before I roll over, hair sprawled around my head. My chest heaves as I splutter up wads of bloody water and blackout.

Chapter 21

My vision blurs as the Tranqs shove me back into my room in the palace. The king's cackles and chortles echo into my ears as he stomps away down the hall, clutching his precious jar of Shadowtooth blood. What does he even want with it, anyway?

The room spins. A strange sensation comes over me, like I've both ingested poison and swallowed an entire cup of vodka. Sweat pools on my forehead and drips down my face as I pace back and forth around the room. Strange shapes morph around me. The bed posts stretch and bend. The windows shatter, and I scream, ducking and covering my head in instinct. But when I look back, the glass is still intact.

A rage unlike anything I have ever felt explodes into my veins and billows through my body like a rolling storm, rushing and surging, and the room is on fire. I am on fire. I want to pull my skin off my bones.

A scream. Mine. It cuts through the rattling percussive sound in my ears and jerks me to my knees.

What is happening to me? I want to shout. But my mouth is sewn shut. I stumble to the bed and collapse.

Finally, the noise, the pain, and the nausea vanish. The fury is all that remains. It's deadly. Thirsts for blood and heads on spits. A feeling I've never known.

It drains every bit of my strength as I lay in bed, sweating and trembling, and I, at last, tumble into merciful sleep.

***

"Elle." A voice stumbles into the recesses of my consciousness.

A groan tumbles from someone... from me.

"Elle!"

My skull throbs as if the blade of a sword has been wedged between the bones, deep in the mushy flesh. But my eyes cannot open, will not open. There is nothing but oblivion awaiting me, and it is just calling for me.

"Elle!" Someone jolts me, and my eyes fly open. A figure swims and blurs before me. Him.

"Ruben," I mumble.

"Gods! Elle, wake up... please." A tear slips down his face, and those reddened eyes search me with a desperate frenzy. "I just spoke to Aston. It's—it's your sister."

I sit bolt upright. My heart lurches into my throat. "Is she—" I rasp.

He opens and closes his mouth like the trout the Convex fishermen haul out of the river, and I have my answer. The room spins and sways as I fling myself out of the damp bed and stagger into the bath chamber.

"What the fuck happened to you?" Ruben snaps.

I realise my clothes stick to me like tar. There's a strange violet stain on my forearm mixed with the crusty layer of blood. My hair sticks up in all directions like the mane of an enraged lion. I smooth it down. "I'm okay. Now take me to my sister."

He grasps my hand and tugs me out of the room. We run. Through the hallways and around corners, leaping down staircases until we fly out the foyer doors into the awaiting carriage. Ruben orders the horseman to make haste, and the reigns crack before the horses yank us to speed. My stomach rises and sinks as the carriage ascends the slope of the bridges, canters down, and into the rickety streets of the Convex Sector. The stench of death seeps into the closed windows of the carriage. Ruben gags and covers his mouth and nose with his sleeve. My knee bounces up and down, and a scream festers and churns deep within me.

Not my sister. Not Lyra.

I throw the carriage door open before it even comes to a halt outside my apartment building. Ruben calls after me as I launch myself into the familiar shadows of the tight-knit street and stumble into the grimy apartment building, the smell of mildew and rotten wood coiling around me.

"Lyra," I wheeze, lunging up the staircase, each step feeling slower, the stair stretching away from me like a bad dream. Suddenly, I am five years old, waddling after my big sister from the schoolyard, brown oil-slicked rain dripping down the back of my neck, her hair a flash of fire against the landscape of evening blue flecked with the ominous grey.

"Don't leave me behind, Lyra!" I said, sludgy water splashing up my legs as I wobbled down the street.

Her giggle rang in my head above the rain and the torment of my growling stomach. She grinned at me over her shoulder and stopped on the side of the road outside the apothecary. "Never," she said, sticking out her hand. "I'll never leave you, Elizabeth."

The air is tainted with the foreboding essence of death as I stagger into the apartment. Ruben has the good sense to come in quietly and move to the window, where he shoves the pane a few inches out with a creak. Lyra's final puffs of fresh breeze. Aston hunches over my sister, who sprawls in the bed, her chest rising and falling ever so slowly, her scraggly hair strewn around the sweat-soaked pillows, the red faded and dull.

Aston dabs her sweaty forehead with a rag while I choke on my sobs, taking the gut-wrenching steps to her side. I take her hand and flinch at the iciness. Those once bright eyes now look up at me with a deeply entangled exhaustion, as if she's on the verge of tumbling into a bewitched sleep.

"You made it," she says, her voice hardly louder than a breath, a ghost of a smile playing on her lips. The effort. "You made it in time."

"Please don't leave me," I beg, voice cracking as I weep. Ruben flinches by the window. Something about his presence, his scent of citrus and sandalwood, in that moment, keeps me grasped onto tendrils of sanity. But if it weren't for Aston... My best friend kneels beside me, tears streaming down his splotchy cheeks. He dips his chin but keeps his warm, calloused hand resting on my knee. *I am here.* Is he about to be the last person left here I love?

"I love you, Elle," Lyra rasps. Her rattly breath pitter-patters onto my face. "Now, Elle. When I am gone, remember I am not truly gone. You'll see me around. I promised you I wouldn't leave you behind, didn't I?" Her grip on my hand tightens as if swept by a final burst of strength. "You know who the enemy is. Bring the kingdom to its knees. Promise me you'll kill the king."

Ruben stumbles back, smacking into the wall. But I ignore him.

A growl spills from my mouth, and I furiously wipe the tears from my eyes, determined to capture one last clear image of my sister. To bottle her up forever. "I promise," I say, blinking as hot tears drip from the tip of my nose.

She smiles one last time. Lyra leans back into the pillow, and all the thoughts she's ever had, all the love she's ever given, and all the dreams she's ever pondered, are gone forever.

***

Only three people bothered to show up to Lyra's wake. Besides myself. Ruben. Aston, of course. And the elderly lady in the apartment across the hall, who has always had a soft spot for my sister.

For the past week, I have been anywhere but within my body. As I slump in the porcelain bathtub and prop my feet onto the faucet, the storm outside brews with a vengeance, flashing its angry teeth at me, illuminating the walls for a split breath. The faucet squeaks as I turn it on and off with my big toe.

My eyes sting. My throat is raw and scratched from earlier days of screaming. I have not seen Ruben since. Another Tranq has trained with me the past week. Swinging swords, launching blades at dummy heads, and firing arrows have kept me from completely drowning in myself.

I relish the burn on my skin as the heat seeps into my achy muscles, glad to feel something other than the rage of a hurricane. My stomach churns, and pain plunges through me. But I have run out of tears. I lean against the head of the tub, staring blankly out of the bath chamber window. The lightning throws itself across the sky, revealing a sliver of sunlight reaching through the tempest of clouds. A sign from Lyra, I am sure of it.

Her final words reverberate in my ear, and a chill sweeps across my arms draped over the sides of the tub. My hair stands on end. *"Promise me you'll kill the king."*

I swallow, although my mouth is bitterly dry. With a yank of the plug, I rise, shaking, and step out of the tub, hugging a towel to my naked body, muttering curses beneath my breath. Red stains my vision. Images mar my consciousness—of blood as dark as onyx spilling from the king's throat as he gurgles, face blanched.

I nod to myself. Ruben was right about the enemy all along. And the decision sinks into my gut, forged from the cold depths of shadow from which I come from. For Lyra, for the kingdom, for the starving Convex, I will kill the king.

A smile creeps across my face.

I am not a girl. I am the shadows. And the king will soon know what it means to fear the dark.

A knock on the door drags me from my trance. I smear the drool from my lip, tasting metal. Larissa scurries into the room, eyes wide, hands clasped in front of her apron. The kindness in her pink cheeks, so akin to my sister's, makes my belly cramp.

She throws her arms around me. "Oh, Elle," she says, squeezing tight. "I am so sorry."

"I couldn't save her," I splutter, knees giving way, and I slump into her. Fresh weeps rack my body. "I have blood on my hands. It's so dark."

Silence slithers between us for several beats.

"Do you think I can be forgiven for all I've done?" I ask.

She grips my shoulders and frowns. "Yes, Elle. You never turned your back on your sister. She was lucky to have you. Your soul is not tainted by the darkness. I know it. I can feel it. You can be forgiven. I believe it."

But dread engulfs me. I hang my head, certain I do not believe her.

"Now, listen," she says, placing her finger under my chin and lifting it, forcing me to look at her. "The crown prince is on his way. Please be gentle with him."

I almost ask her why when footsteps echo through the hallway, and Ruben pokes his head around the corner. The colour drains from his face, and he chews his lips. My muscles shake with pulsing fury as he prowls into the room, swathed in misery.

"You have a lot of nerve showing up here, Your Highness," I grind out, completely disregarding Larissa's warning. She clears her throat, hastening around the room, melting the shadows with each candle blooming to life. "Where were you?"

He purses his lips and stalks closer anyway. "I couldn't be with you, Elle."

"You hot-headed fool," I say, tasting the bitterness of the venom coating my tongue. "You left me to fend for myself in the days I needed you most. Right after the wake... what were you thinking leaving like that? Leaving *me*. I have sobbed myself to sleep *alone* for the past week. Did you not hear my screams?"

His vein pops from his reddening neck. "It wasn't my fault." His voice is lifeless. "The king dragged me into... other duties. I had no other choice."

Heat flushes my face, and I ball my fists, stalking back and forth. "What duties?"

He slumps his shoulders, inky darkness clouding his face. "I cannot tell you, Elle."

In the beats of heavy, tangible silence, Larissa leaves the room.

"My sister is dead, Prince," I seethe, voice drowning in hatred and quivering in grief. "She is *dead*."

The word hits me with such sudden finality I fall to my knees.

"I know, Elle."

"You *promised*, Ruben. You promised she would be safe if I stuck by you. You said I could trust you. Her death is on *you*."

He grabs his stomach, and his face twists, eyes brimming with tears. "I tried to save her."

I throw my hands into the air. "That makes two of us." The ferocity in my tone startles him.

"This is the king's fault, not mine. I sent her food for weeks, but someone poisoned it. He let her die."

The truth settles into my gut, but I stifle a cold, dry laugh, refusing to think a man could be so utterly cruel. "You would think the prince who could wager my life could save another."

He poisoned her.

The king poisoned my sister.

"The king has the final say in everything, Elle. King Talin has your sister's blood on his hands." Ruben finally stops his pacing, and his body deflates, defeated once again by the relentlessness of his father's cowardice. "It is always King Talin."

Ruben's eyes burn into my own like a storm of darkness and death. His terror and sorrow thrum through me.

As the kingdom falls asleep, draped in the liquid night sky, I slip out of bed. I dress in linen pants and a tunic and pad out of my room, but not before slipping the blade of my dagger up my sleeve. Wisps of candle wax dance past me as I cling to the shadows like a vampire afraid of the sun. Past the ballroom, the foyer, and deeper into the palace maze. Eyes of previous kings in portraits leer at me as I pass. Eventually, I stumble across a wide marble staircase, polished white and flecked in deep purple, spiralling up into oblivion. The passage to King Talin's quarters, towering above the rest of the kingdom.

My lip curls into a sneer.

Tonight, I will kill the king. After all, revenge is a brother of grief.

Chapter 22

I prowl up the stairs the way dusk creeps through a town. Silent and stealthy. Swallowed in darkness like a storm of death. Around and around, higher into the God of Souls' realm. As I arrive, at last, on the landing, a light cough pulls me up short, and I paste myself flat against the wall. Of course, the Tranquillity guard the king at all hours. I draw in a breath, slip my knife behind my back, and plaster an arrogant smirk on my face before waltzing into view.

"Elle," one says, recognising me at once. "What are you doing here?"

The pair swap frowns of differing severity, shifting their weight.

"The king asked for me especially," I say, offering a sincere smile.

The first one angles his head, and the other opens his mouth to speak. But before they have the chance, I lunge forward, swinging the butt of my knife into their temple, knocking them out cold. Their limp bodies collapse to the floor. I know I only have moments before they wake. Casting them a wary glance, I reach for the gold-plated doorknobs, pushing them open with only a creak. Darkness grins back at me. Pockets of candlelight splatter the shelves, stuffed with tattered leatherbound books that I wish I could browse as I shuffle deeper into the obsidian. Dust scatters into the air like lazy hornets, flecked in chrome and threatening to find a new home in my throat. Musk and liquor stain the otherwise stagnant air. My heart taps against my ribs so hard they bruise. I flinch as my boots crunch a patch of glass shards.

A deep laugh, dripping with malice, startles me so abruptly that I clamp a hand over my mouth to stop the squeak. A silhouette claims the shadows. He sits on a plump, red leather couch. Fiery light flickers onto his face as if he's a ghost, frozen beneath the moonlight, staring at its tombstone.

"Did you come for my head, Elle?" he says in a grating tone that turns my blood to ice.

"Would that not be fair?" I say, grinding my teeth and twirling the blade. It glints orange, and its reflection appears in the king's glass of whisky.

He chuckles again, and my skin crawls. The king sips his whisky, and I notice bubbles of a dark, inky substance bobbing around in his drink, not quite mixing, like oil and water.

"Sit." He points to the chair across from him.

The sharp authority in his voice sends me sinking into the seat like a frightened schoolchild. "You should be ashamed of yourself. A coward and a murderer," I spit, feeling the darkness creep through my body in wispy tendrils, burrowing into my marrow. Powering me.

His lips bend up, and his eyes flash. "I was sorry to hear about your sister, Elle."

"Were you?" I smack the table with my palm. "You literally bend over backwards to make sure that people... *my* people keep starving. *Want* people to remain skeletons."

His nostrils flare as he takes a slow sip of his chipped glass, keeping those jade eyes like he waits for me to lunge forward and slash his throat. "Hunger keeps the Convex from gathering the strength to overthrow me."

"Why are you like this?" I say with a shadowy scorn. "If not to simply torment us? You must have a reason for your obsession with control and power."

"An obsession?" He quirks a brow.

"Your grip on control is loosening," I bite back. With a sneer, I snatch the decanter of dark liquor and pour a healthy shot into a tumbler. The liquor burns the back of my throat and tastes of poison. But I revel in the feeling.

He lets out another laugh, shaking his head and clearing his throat. "In my younger and more naïve years, I did believe in the power of rebellion. I know it sounds... strange coming from me... I'd call it childish."

I continue sipping the whisky, narrowing my eyes at him. The candlelight performs exotic dances on his face, and a shiver plunges into my spine.

"When I was a boy, a small but promising group of rebels from the Convex Sector infiltrated the palace. They so desperately wanted power and control over their lives, as my father had taken it from them during his reign on the throne. But they wanted revenge, you see. For the men lost their wives and children to the famine that chilling winter. And those men were feral for vengeance. When they broke into the palace, their targets were any of the royals. Myself included, if they could get their hands on me. But my mother tried to fight them off, blocking me from them with her body. I watched the *leader* slice open her throat with his rusty dagger."

The king swallows bodily, eyes glimmering as if the phantom of his mother stands before him. No doubt, those memories scalding red in his skull.

"I held her hand as she bled out," he says, his voice catching. "She told me to remember who the real enemy is."

I startle, slamming into the back of the chair.

The king breathes a bitter scoff. "The real enemy, Elle, is human nature. By nature, we are cruel, power-hungry monsters. More dangerous than the Shadowtooth or any other monster beyond the walls. Once we harness power and control, it catalyses our cruel nature. We are all the same. If I am not cruel, they will be cruel to me. So, I may as well be selfish. If I do not want to be cold and alone."

My heart thumps against my ribs, and my skin crawls. I toss the remaining liquor into my mouth, forcing it down. "You are a coward. One man cannot hold so much power. It defies the laws of the earth. The laws of balance. It is time to take off that crown, Your Majesty."

I smack the tumbler onto the mahogany table and stand up. Our eyes lock for several beats, and for a terrifying moment, something rises to greet me in him—unwelcomingly familiar. Determination. Loss. I march away, crunching over the broken glass and to the exit. *I will never bow down to you.* The words crackle on my tongue, but that

204

royally icy glaze kills any sliver of confidence. I grip the blade harder. Kill him. *Do it.* But the wind sucks out of my lungs, and I am nothing but a Convex, forever at the mercy of the terror that the king inflicts, scampering away to phantom safety.

"You had better keep up the game, Elle," the king calls. His bark reverberates off the surrounding walls, and I flinch, stomach knotting. "For if you do not convince the kingdom of your love for my son and your loyalty to the throne and my Tranquillity, the blond boy will be next."

Bile and alcohol sting my throat as I whirl around. I ball my fists.

King Talin grunts as he rises to his feet, wobbling. I wonder if he can even see me straight. "Imagine, the girl who dared kill my Tranquillity loses the last person she holds dear. The loneliest hateful creature."

"At least I have someone in this god-forsaken kingdom I genuinely love. And someone who loves me back. You cannot say the same."

His lips twist into a sneer, and crimson stains his teeth. My stomach churns at the sight. He tilts his glass. "I will see you at the winter ball, Elle."

Chapter 23

A brisk wind coils between us. "I want Aston invited," I say, my voice sharp as the side of a ribbon.

Ruben rolls his eyes. "It is not the kind of ball for the common folk, Elle. The highest, most honourable members of the Concave Court will be in attendance."

I stare at him, face granite. "Then you will not see my face there either. Might I remind you; I *am* the common folk."

"Not anymore, Elle," he says, wrinkling his pink nose. The alabaster ice clings to the bare hedges in the courtyard, the path beneath our boots slick from the dew as the sun climbs into the sky. A warm glow permeates the kingdom, reminding us of the slowly approaching spring. "You will be a royal soon."

I scoff, leaning against the frost-slicked barrier, gazing into the stream below the narrow, gold-accented bridge. Orange and black fish lazily swim in the cool, obsidian water. "You cannot look me in the eye and tell me you want to be a royal. Not in this life." I gesture in the general distanced direction of the Convex Sector.

He sighs, chewing his lip. "No. But it might be the only way to ensure we can carve a new world for our children. Perhaps when the king dies…"

"Given our luck, that could be a hundred years away. And you will not take a step further unless I hear you say that Aston can attend the ball," I say, throwing my arms out and blocking the path.

He gently pushes my arm down. My skin scalds at his touch. "Fine. Aston can join us. As long as you wear a curvy red dress. I want the Concaves to understand the true fire that you are. I want them to fear you, just a little bit."

Heat pinches my cheeks. "You're a waste of breath."

He throws his head, laughing from deep within his belly. "Oh, but I know you enjoy my company, Elle. The blush in your face tells me so much."

"A moment of silence, please, for the crown prince's humility. He seems to have lost it." I whirl around and march away, Ruben's laughter tickling my ears.

The palace becomes a frenzy of bubbling excitement the moment the king announces the ball. Daughters of high court members giggle like a bunch of squawking birds any time Ruben waltzes past them. Yet, they send scorns and frowns of varying severity my way. Sometimes, I want to tell them to take Ruben. I could not care less. But then a tiny, peeping voice in my head tells me I might miss his attention. I shake the thought, wincing as the servant in the parlour tears every follicle of hair from my legs and underarms and places I would rather never experience so much air around again. At one point, I almost yelp and slap the woman.

"Gods, you're a wriggly thing," she says, ripping the final strip of wax from between my legs. I wince, gripping the side of the bench. By the time I slip back into the linen pants and tunic, my skin stings, and I feel like a plucked, raw chicken.

"I hope Prince Talin knows the worm he is about to bed," she says with a snip as I make to leave.

I only bother to glare at her before skulking away. Bed? With Ruben? I will do no such thing.

The servants race around like hungry ants. Arranging the ballroom with the décor and peppering the room with dozens of polished, round tables. Placing goblets and cutlery before each chair. They hardly cast me a glance as I hasten through the palace and back into my chamber.

Larissa perches on the chair before the vanity. She taps her foot, sweaty brow knitted together. "Took your time," she quips, slipping into the bathroom and turning the faucet. "Get in the tub."

I do as she says. Fruit and vanilla infuse the steamy room as she lathers my skin and scrubs my hair. Larissa wraps me in a towel and coats my dry skin with lotion until I'm shining. She slips a robe over my shoulders and shoves me into the chair in front of the vanity, chewing her lip and frowning at me in the mirror.

"What?"

"Have you been civil with Prince Talin since…your sister's wake?" she asks, choosing to grip the point.

I sigh as she ruffles my damp hair with a towel. "Yes. But we somehow always end up bickering."

She purses her lips, catching my eye in the mirror as she oils my locks. "I think you should forgive him." Her breath catches in her throat. "Or make it look like you do. Remember, you need to convince the Concaves in this palace that you are madly in love."

"Don't people in love bicker?"

"Well, I am not sure how much I know about love." A whimsy look crosses her face, which gives me the suspicion that she is thinking of someone. A certain pair of green eyes dance with my shadows.

"He does care about you," she says, offering a sly half-grin as she untangles the knots. "He told me himself."

"You speak to the prince?" A strange, airy feeling cinches my gut, and I gnash the extra questions I want to ask between my molars. "I didn't realise you were friends."

"Of course. We speak all the time." She finishes drying my hair and combs it out before pulling a handful of locks behind my head. Her smirk widens into a grin. "He said he told you his name."

I open my mouth like a blubbering fish.

She laughs a wonderful, tepid sound that draws a smile from me at once. "Prince Talin wouldn't disclose such a secret to anyone. I think our crown prince may have a crush."

I giggle like a schoolchild and swat at her. She leaps away, and I chase her around the room, shrieking profanities until we both collapse onto the floor, laughing so intensely my stomach hurts and tears slip down my cheeks.

"You are ridiculous!" I say, voice shrill as I flop back into the chair.

"Maybe." She shrugs. "But I tend to have a feeling about these things. Plus, Prince Talin has girls flocking to him and batting their eyes every day. I have never seen him look at them the same way he looks at you."

My heart flips into my throat, and I swallow. "Let's just get ready for the ball. Best not fuel the prince's already bursting ego."

A tread of footsteps rumbles through the door, and we snap our gazes up.

"Is Elle in here?" a voice echoes through the hallway. Aston's voice.

Warmth washes over me. As if on instinct. My heart settles as the person I feel most at home with enters, his brows knitted together as the Tranqs wait for a beat at the threshold before they march away.

"You look beautiful, Elle," he says, closing the space between us with a hug. His face brims with adoration, and tears spring into my eyes as he pulls away. I wish he'd never let me go.

He is not wrong, though. Larissa has dressed me in a dark red dress that hugs my curves and accentuates my collarbone and breasts. The skirt spills to my feet and pools around me like liquid flames. She pulled my hair into a half-up, half-down style, braiding the locks around the back of my hair. My blue-grey eyes are vivid against the earthy tones dusted onto my eyelids.

"Sit, Aston," Larissa says, snapping her fingers at the chair.

He throws his hands into the air, doing as she says. His pursed lips and raised brows coax giggles from deep within my belly. Larissa rakes a comb through his hair and wrinkles her nose.

"Did you bathe before you came here?" she asks, straightening up.

Aston clicks his tongue and lets out a small chuckle.

She rolls her eyes and points into the bathtub. "Clean yourself at once!"

Once spotless and smelling like soap, Aston sits back in the chair. Larissa combs his sandy blond hair, styling it with gel. She instructs him to change into his suit. My friend mutters bewildered curses beneath his breath before strutting into the bathroom to change once more. When he emerges, I smile. The black suit clings to his slim yet sturdy frame, reminding me with a pang that he doesn't get to eat enough food. But that easy grin fills the dull room with colour.

"Do I look fit for the royal ball?" he says, pretending to tilt a top hat.

"The fittest of them all," I say with a grin.

"What about me?" Ruben says from behind me. His voice is a low husk that stirs my insides and tickles my neck.

I whirl around, schooling my face into neutrality. But for the sight of him. The night sky incarnate. Glimmering with stars and smouldering with the dark in between. His lips quirk. "You look…"

"Dashing? Handsome? I can help with the adjectives if you are feeling lost for words," he says, shrugging and stuffing his hands into his pockets before nodding at my friend. "Aston. A pleasure to see you, as always."

"Right then." Larissa claps her hands, unleashing us from the spell of mutual irritation. "Your Highness, it is time you take your lady to the ballroom, followed by her friend."

Ruben smirks at the jolt of annoyance on my face at Larissa's use of the words *your lady*. He offers me his arm. I roll my eyes, grab his arm, and we waltz out of the bedroom, waving goodbye to Larissa. Aston brings up the rear, several paces behind.

"You may as well be dressed in flames," Ruben whispers as we round the corner, stepping into the main hallway. "Gods, you *are* the fire."

My chest tightens. "You said I should frighten the Concaves."

He stifles a chuckle. The rumble of the ballroom invades my ears. Percussive booms reverberate with the pulsing gleam of entranced chandelier light that spills into the hallway, the strum of string instruments blending with the scent of wine, fermented delicacies, and the sharp tang of coins. Chatter hums in my ears, joining the crescendo with untethered bounds, the noise growing and growing.

"And frighten them you certainly will," Ruben says.

My heart thunders in my chest to the beat of the drums as we round the corner and cross into the ballroom. The warmth of the room reaches and engulfs me whole at once. The musicians change to a violin number, the thrum of the song pirouetting in my ribs. Hundreds of eyes shift towards me, to Ruben. I tense against him. At this moment, I am grateful for his presence. Envy and hatred, and adoration. Even the servants and the musicians scarcely keep their thoughts off their faces. I spot Aston sticking out from the crowd like a swollen wound, even though he's looking handsome and clean. He nods and smiles. Yet, even his presence doesn't calm the throbbing pulse in my skull.

Ruben clears his throat and steps away from me. I want to scream and sink into the ground. But I roll my shoulders back, raise my chin, and push a somewhat confident smile onto my face. Ruben bows. "Ladies and gentlemen of the Concave Court, I present to you the brave, the cunning, the fire, Elle Fallon. My betrothed."

An awkward silence follows. For only a beat. But enough to send the blood rushing to my cheeks. Aston is the first to clap, and the partygoers fall into action with him. But Ruben's words are the only thing I can hear, rattling in my head, sharpened nerves plunging into the base of my spine. Brave. Cunning. Fire.

The violin reaches a high note, and the crowd merges back with one another. Ruben smiles at me, and my insides stir.

"Come with me," he says. "Let's wander and meet people."

I fall into step alongside him, moving with grace through the swaying throng. We flaunt through the expansive room, and I allow my senses to blur. At some stage, he hands me a goblet of sparkling wine.

"To the stars, Elle," he says, smiling and clinking his glass with mine.

"To the stars, Your Highness."

That's when I catch the glinting eyes of King Talin. He sprawls on his throne at the head of the room, limbs tossed in all directions. A sloppy grin on his freshly groomed face. The goblet of wine held loosely in his hands. He catches my gaze and shakes his head—a hewn, poised warning. My skin crawls. But I plaster on a smile and raise my glass at him.

Aston brushes up against me. "What a piece of work," he mutters, loud enough for only me to hear.

I laugh, spluttering into my goblet. "That is one way to put it."

"Dance with me, Elle," he says as the music changes tempo, offering a hand.

I drain my sparkling wine, and he rolls his eyes. "Of course, royalty changes a person. But you can never quite take the tavern spirit out of any girl who lived and breathed it." He chuckles as I hand the empty goblet to a servant and take his hand.

"I can't imagine I'll change that much," I say, waving to Ruben. He nods before slipping up the stairs to his father's throne. "I will always be your Elle." Even as I speak, I am not sure I believe those words. This palace, all the deaths... Lyra's death... it's all chipped away at me, carving me into something else. And it's all made me wonder whether I have ever truly been a good person at all. How can I call myself one when I execute prisoners who cannot help themselves? When I cower in silence while people across the river eat animal feed and drink brown water and toss their loved ones into overflowing mass graves?

"Gross," he says with a scoff, mocking a gag, and I swat him. "Truth be told, I haven't quite known who to spend my evenings with beneath the stars. No one quite understands my cynical jokes the way you do."

I push past the lump in my throat. "I cannot come back. Not yet. I must stick to the king's demands. Otherwise, he will kill you."

Amusement tugs at his lips, but the glint of fear is unmissable. "Charming."

I open my mouth to respond when a whisper from behind catches me off guard. "Nothing but Convex dirt," they say, the grate of their whispers scraping down my eardrum. "She does not deserve the crown prince."

214

"Not when I hear she's planning a rebellion!"

"How do you know?"

"What? With all the attacks on the Tranquillity in the Convex," they hiss, clicking their tongue. "The Convex just want everything handed to them. An entitled group of people."

I glare at them, and they flinch. "Careful how you speak of my people. You haven't felt the pain of hunger in your entire pathetic existence." The words spill from me like poison, and the feeling awakens a deep, ancient rage within me.

Aston tugs me away to the buffet table and hands me another goblet. "Drink up. They are not worth it."

"But did you hear them?" I murmur, sipping the wine. "They think we are starting a rebellion."

"Are we not?" he whispers.

I resist the urge to slap him. Instead, I clear my throat. Someone taps my shoulder. My soul almost leaps from my bones when I meet the king's examining eyes.

"May I?" he asks Aston, sticking his chin in the air.

Aston bows his head deeply in and steps back, throwing me a tight glance. I press my lips together, silently telling him that I'll be okay.

Shackles claw at my stomach as the king leads me onto the dance floor, reeking of liquor and shrimp appetisers.

"How is the night for you, Elle?" he says, placing his hand on my waist and holding my other hand as we twirl and move around the room.

"Pleasant," I say with ease despite the roar of blood in my ears. "There is a lot of food, though."

"I hope you have indulged." We slip through a part in the crowd as the music hums and swirls with my deep crimson skirt, the organ booming in my ears.

I release a bitter scoff. "Yes. Full bellies are important. Too bad the ones across the river are no more than shrivelled-up skeletons."

"Ah, yes." His lips crinkle, and the candlelight flickers in his green eyes, so alike and *unlike* Ruben's all at once. "The uprisings and attacks are a favourite topic of gossip among the court and common Concaves."

"Take a hint," I bite back.

He chuckles. "Oh no, Elle. *You* should. After your sister's death, I thought you would understand by now."

I press my lips together, thumbing for a decent retort but coming up short. The music increases in intensity, the beat thumping with my heart.

"The blood is dripping from your hands already, Elle," he says through gritted teeth. "Let's not add the blond boy's blood to it."

I jerk free, chest heaving. "Murderer."

A servant scurries up to us, and the king takes the goblet from her tray. He drains the liquid quickly, and I catch the thick, dark substance in it.

"What is that?" I say, and the realisation hits me. "It's the Shadowtooth blood."

He smacks his lips together, and his breath stinks of death. "An acquired taste."

My eyes narrow, and I let him spin me around to the music. "Why do you drink it?"

"It makes me strong, Elle," he says. Malice glints in his eyes, rising to greet me like ghouls in a timeworn house. "It's important in my older age. And there are ancient legends about the properties of the creature's blood. That it can turn a man into a god."

I almost laugh at the crazed king but remember the agony and mind-bending trip I experienced after the Shadowtooth blood spilt across my wound. My heart pounds, but I school my face into a pleasant smile before, finally, the dance ends. Then, I slip into the safety of the ebbing and flowing crowd. Ruben sips from his goblet, none the wiser. I march up to him and grab his hand before fleeing the ballroom.

Chapter 24

A shrill giggle falls from my lips as I lead Ruben through the palace and into the grounds. The thrill of leaving the king's ball crackles in my blood, pushing me onward into the shadows, towards the stars glimmering in the garden pond. I suppose rebellion burns in my blood. Servants and guests mill about and toss themselves to the side as we pass. Eyebrows raise. Ladies chatter and whisper.

I soak in the sweet smell of the flowers drifting past on invisible tendrils as we hide in the maze of hedges in the north of the grounds. The inky night sky looks like an ocean. As if one could jump up and swim in it. I lean against the hedge, the prickling of the branches keeping me grounded in place. Ruben heaves a sigh, his gaze landing on me. He stands only inches from me, and I can almost feel the thump of his heart, so close to my own.

I grind my teeth. "He is closing in on me. I must convince them and the king that I am one of you, that I am not with the rebels."

Ruben nods, blowing out his cheeks. "We need to show our affection for one another."

I scoff, rolling my eyes and shifting my weight as I cross my arms. "What affection?"

He raises his brows, a flicker of amusement dancing on his lips. Ruben leans forward so his mouth is against my ears. "Come on, Elle. I know you're obsessed with me."

He barks with laughter as I shove him away, scrunching my nose. "That arrogance will be the death of you. Ask the ladies in the court for their affections. I am sure you will not be limited in your choices," I say, tossing my hand at the palace. Even as I release the words, my stomach pinches with envy.

He smirks, resting his shoulder against the hedge. "Is that what you want? My attentions elsewhere?"

"Fine," I snap, balling my fists. "I will pretend to swoon over you."

"Are you sure it will be feigned?" he says, eyes glimmering. The nerve of him. I am merely a toy for him to play with. "I think we both know there is something in you that is not going to pretend."

"Stop messing around. Stay focused, Prince," I hiss, swatting him. "I also need to find my way across the river to join the rebellion, but don't think I can be both a loyalist and a rebel without winding up with blood on my hands. But I believe I need to try."

He straightens, letting out a sigh. "We need to redirect their attention to the king, not the Tranqs."

I press my lips together. "I don't think the king's demise will not work unless we dismantle his army. They are protecting him, after all. If we can turn them against him…"

Ruben turns away, pacing back and forth. He glances at me over his shoulder. "We need to turn his own Concaves and the court against him, too."

"We begin with the Convex, who will help strip the Concaves and the Tranqs of their resources."

"So, we continue to keep the king on our side while draining him dry." Ruben rubs his chin, a darkness creeping across his handsome face.

"You do not think it will work," I say, tilting my head. "It is a delicate and precarious game that we will play."

"I am afraid," he admits. "Afraid of what will happen if it doesn't work."

"Me too."

"Let's begin with the Convex, especially since many are already uprising. They will be the easiest to sway into action. The Concaves will need more convincing." He pauses, staring at the sliver of moon in the sky. "I know Ajax and Killian will help."

"Spring is coming," I say, stepping away from the hedge wall. I stand beside him, our hands so close I can feel the warmth. "Perhaps the blight will ease, and the Convex will have more strength to help. We will need to come up with plans to drain the king of his resources."

He wrenches his hand away, and my stomach clenches. "I am afraid the king is doing the same as us. Draining, I mean. Drain the Convex of whatever they have left. He will not allow the famine to ease. He knows that mass death and famine will ensure they are too weak to retaliate."

"I fear they have nothing to lose," I remind him.

He nods, glancing down at me. "You sparked hope in them, Elle. I can only pray to the Gods that your people will be brave enough to take the opportunity you have given them… ideally without killing any more of my comrades. They can direct their weapons to the king."

I stare at him, trying to swallow past the lump in my throat. "You will never forgive me for killing your friend."

Ruben sighs, and his shoulders sag. His eyes meet mine, burning jade in the sliver of moonlight. "Let's not talk about him," he says, voice sharp.

"You practically brought him up. I did what I had to do to survive, Ruben," I say, grinding my teeth. "You either let it go or at least stop hounding me about it."

He tightens his jaw. "Fine. Sorry."

I allow several beats of silence to pass. "I am not sure how to get across the river unseen by anyone who licks the king's boots."

His face brightens, brows raising. "The underground tunnels."

"What?"

He puts his finger over his lips and gestures for me to follow. He leads me out of the hedge passageway and into another corridor. My stomach curls with a distant yet familiar sense of foreboding as we wind our way through the garden, sticking to the shadows like monsters ill to the light. We slip into another clearing, and a phantom claw scrapes down my spine. This garden is different from the others. Hedges stretch into the middle of the clearing like the last desperate drop of paint on a brush, limbs scraggly and unmanicured. Leaves smother the stone path like a cloth over a mouth, gathering in rotting piles of amber. A rogue park bench springs from the ground, faded blue brass from years bathed in the sun and no one bothering to polish it. Ruben nods at the fingers of vibrant grass forming their own microcosm.

"What is it?" I ask, taking cautious steps toward him.

A small handle pops up from the ground. As I brush the grass away, I gasp. It's a trapdoor.

Ruben pulls it. Dust bursts up, and he waves it away. A sooty abyss yawns up at us, at the sky. It smells of old stone and dirt and death, like an ancient tomb, and cold, damp air blows up and over my arms. I shiver.

"This is one of the many entrances scattered across the kingdom. There is an entire network of underground tunnels criss-crossing the city. Tranqs use it to move around uninterrupted by the kingdom traffic."

"Take me now," I say, rising from the crouch to lower myself inside.

But his hand flies to my wrist. His grip is gentle, but his skin burns my own, stirring my insides, and our eyes lock.

He flinches away, clearing his throat. "We should go back inside. Lest the king wonder what you are plotting." His amused smirk sends the blood rushing to my face.

I stand up, brushing the dirt from my palms. "You understand how imminent the king's death is, right?"

Ruben blows out his cheeks, standing up. "That man haunts my—" he cuts himself off, hanging his head and letting out a sigh. "Never mind."

I open my mouth to respond, but a voice calls through the gardens.

"Prince Talin? Elle?" Larissa steps into the clearing. She angles her head as she takes us in together. "What are you doing out here?"

My cheeks heat up. "I needed some air," I say.

She stifles a giggle. "Of course. But do make haste inside. Wouldn't want the court thinking you share affection for one another."

Larissa smirks, sauntering away and laughing as I toss curse words in her wake.

Chapter 25

The quivering orange lights and thrum of voices and music twirl around us, blending with the cigar smoke and whimsy cackles as we file back into the ballroom. Jokes spit across the bar, far too loud and revolting. Concaves have a way of billowing their thoughts like an untamed storm. Hundreds of heads turn our way, one by one. A crackling energy ripples through the limbs and scorns. I gulp, grabbing a goblet of sparkling wine and draining the entire glass, and Ruben stifles a laugh, red flushing his cheeks.

"It isn't so bad in here, is it?" he asks, taking the goblet and handing it to the closest servant.

I roll my eyes. "Aren't you meant to ask me to dance?"

An amused smirk tugs at his lips, and he holds out his hand. "Will you do me the pleasure of a dance?"

"I would be delighted," I say, feigning a sweet voice and smiling.

The king leers as he sips his goblet. He lounges on his throne, watching us like we are all prey, ready for his claws to sink into.

"You are still signing your allegiance to the Tranquillity tomorrow, right?" Ruben says, voice a low husk as we step and twirl around the room. His hand on my waist burns, and my pulse thunders in my skull.

"I cannot wait," I say loud enough for those around me to hear. "To complete my initiation and officially join my comrades. Although, I understand my training will continue."

"Yes. More knife-throwing lessons with yours truly." He lets out a feigned chuckle, tossing a pleasant smile to a staring Concave man. "I know you look forward to it."

"As long as it's more time with you," I say through clenched teeth, earning a glare from a young lady next to us.

I draw closer, leaning my head on his shoulder as we spin slowly on the spot. He smells of the forest and oranges. Sweet and earthy.

Someone clears their throat, and I lift my head. King Talin smiles at me, but his eyes carry the coldness of a glacier. "Pardon me for interrupting the betrothed, but may I have a word with you, Elle?" A vein tremors in his throat, and I grimace.

"Of course, Your Majesty," I say, offering a tight-lipped smile with my curtsey.

Ruben squeezes my hand before letting me go with a bow. I toss him a reassuring nod over my shoulder as I follow the king. He leads me through the crowd, ignoring those throwing themselves at him, trying to speak to him. We step out of the ballroom, and he leads me into a hallway.

"What do you have to say that cannot be discussed inside?" My voice is taut like a bow, the arrow nocked towards his throat.

We pause in a hallway adorned with an enormous portrait of the king's father. Those cold, hateful eyes scratch into me like a prisoner trapped in a burning dungeon, desperately trying to escape. The king towers over me, puffing his chest and angling his head, but not enough for his crown to fall. "I hope you and my son are getting to know one another better. After all, the wedding is in the spring."

I swallow, letting out a short breath. "He enjoys getting under my skin."

He presses his lips together. "I am sure you are looking forward to your signing tomorrow."

I open my mouth to respond when a gloved leather hand clamps over my mouth. A pungent, floral scent bursts into my nose, and the powder in the person's palm coats my lips. Clouds seep in hungry wisps through my head, filling my muscles with lead. Oblivion beckons me with warm arms, whispering my name, coaxing me into it. I cannot fight it. It grasps my conscious, dragging me into the darkness.

I wonder if I *am* the darkness.

***

A rotten smell warps and jabs my nostrils. I pry my stinging eyes open, coughing at the dryness in my throat. My head aches as I sit up and glance around. Stone walls and cast iron stretch upwards and sideways, as if I'm buried in nothing but obsidian and silence. Phantom hands tighten around my throat, and I splutter, the air leaving my body as I realise that I am trapped. Yet, as I glance around, rising to my feet, this appears to be a different set of dungeons from the ones I was in when they first arrested me.

"Ruben?" I say, flinching as my voice slams into the walls around me.

He does not respond, for he is not here. I whimper, stumbling back and bumping into the wall, sliding to the floor. Cold water gobbles up my fingers, and I flinch, a whimper hurtling from my mouth. The water coats the floor in a thin layer, spreading throughout the cell. I cannot see a pipe in the wall nor any indication of the water source nearby. My fingers trace its path, but the water trail disappears into the shadows further into the dungeon hallway. My heart thumps against my chest, and my stomach twists. As if my body knows something my mind doesn't yet. The water grows like it's a monster of its own, coming to life before me. It reaches the opposite wall of my cell, stretching along the sealed concrete before trickling out of the door and into the hall, into the next cell.

I stand, the water skidding past my shoes, soaking my red skirt.

"Ruben!"

"*Elle*," something hisses low, and it grates along my bones. "Elle." The noise reverberates against the walls and my skull, and it doesn't sound human.

"Hey, can you let me out?" I march up to the door, gripping the handle.

Footsteps. Squelching towards me, splashing the water like Convex children in the river on a summer's day. They say my name again. Another animalistic hiss comes from the shadows, raking down my spine and raising the hair on my arms.

"Hello?" I say again.

It emerges into the dim candlelight. My guts sink into the stone floor. It is a human-sized lizard. With black scales and no eyes. It snorts, tossing its enormous head as it prowls towards my cell with its webbed feet. I reach for my sword but grip only the air at my waist.

"Elle! Elle!" it hisses, a serpent of a tongue flickering out as if it might try to lock around my neck.

The front claws reach for the cell door, the metal groaning as the beast tears it from its hinges. It lurches for me, but I dive under the creature's arms, ducking out of the cell. It screeches, the sound scraping my eardrums and spurring me onward. Adrenaline pumps through my veins as the beast sniffs me out and launches itself into the hallway.

The lizard beast chases me through the dungeons until we reach the furthest door. It's oddly unlocked, and I fling it open, throwing it shut behind me. But the lizard crashes through, and a shrill shout spills from my throat. I barrel down the next corridor of dungeons, the water coating the floor and splashing up my back and legs. The lizard thrashes after me, grappling for me, claws snatching at my flesh, and I cry out, driving my legs harder, faster.

I skid to a stop at the end of the hallway, which droops into a sweeping underground chasm, and a waist-deep pool of murky, grey water rises from the charcoal blend of stone. The monster roars in my ear as I leap out, wading through the water to the far end of the pool. As I reach the middle of the pool, I duck beneath the surface, holding my breath. My heart echoes in the water as I count to ten, waiting to disorient the blind monster. It snorts and hisses my name over and over until it's the only sound pounding around me. But my lungs burn. I poke my head out, drawing in a breath. The monster whips its head

228

around, trying to sense me. The dirty water won't mask my scent for long. As I glance around, the slashes on my legs ooze crimson into the water, and panic surges through my veins. The sharp, iron rods of a spare prison cell door materialise from the dust and grime, discarded on the other side of the pool, on the ledge.

"Oi!" I shout, jumping and splashing, letting my blood drip into the water.

Its head snaps to me, and its mouth widens as it screeches, showing off its stained fangs. It leaps into the water, slashing towards me, and I haul myself onto the platform at the end of the pool. I groan as I lift the door, struggling against the weight. Waiting for it to get closer, closer. It's slit nostrils flaring. Hissing my name like a parroting bird.

I scream, tossing the jagged ends of the door towards the monster. It flails, and the metal only punctures the fatty layer of its flesh. But it's enough for the creature to howl, almost splitting my eardrums, as it stumbles and crashes into the water.

"Hey!" a voice snaps my attention. A human voice from the ceiling.

I crane my neck to see a Tranq hovering over the opening of a trapdoor all that way up. A rusted ladder runs up the wall to the opening. Without a thought, I launch myself at it. It whines against my weight as I shove my foot onto the first rung. But I pick my way up the ladder, a trilling curse tumbling from my mouth when my foot slips and my chin almost slams into the rung, a breath away from plunging back into the water below. The beast, having jerked the old cell door from its flesh, its dark blood pouring into the water, averts its nose in my direction. It sniffs and hisses my name.

The beast hurdles itself, gripping the ladder below me, and the entire structure groans, jolting downward and sending dust and granules of rust erupting from the wall. I yelp, hurrying to the trapdoor, and the now two Tranq helmets hovering over the trapdoor. The monster slashes at my legs, running its claws down my calves once again, and I scream.

The Tranqs, wide-eyed and red-faced, reach into the opening. I grip their hands, and with a cry, they haul me through the trapdoor, and I slump onto the floor, coughing and wincing. Searing waves of agony blow through me. I clutch my legs, warmth flowing through my fingers and dripping onto the floor.

But I gather my strength and peer at my saviours. The two Tranqs pull their helmets off, brows creased with concern and panting. A man and a woman. The lady has sagged jowls and a birthmark on her neck, while the man has dark skin and a scar across his cheek.

"Thank you," I start to say.

"What the hell is this?" bellows the king so furiously the three of us flinch. He stomps out of the ballroom with dark, beady eyes flaring at me and sweat dripping down his temples.

I snap my gaze at him and tighten my jaw. "You drugged me and trapped me down there." I fling the words at him like knives.

The king lets out a breath and bares his teeth. He opens his mouth to respond. But the floor tremors. His face drops as a screech tears up from the trapdoor in the hallway. The lizard creature launches itself from the opening in the floor, knocking the king to his feet with a shriek. Spit flies and fangs gnash as the lizard pins the king to the floor, snarling and roaring. The king screams and curses. People from the ballroom spill into the hallway, and their shouts infuse the cacophony. But no one does anything.

The monster unhinges its jaw and forces itself towards the king's neck, all too ready to tear it open.

"Help!" the king yells, voice cracking with desperation as he pushes against the sheer force of the lizard's head.

For a moment, I don't move either. The king's imminent death dancing and singing within me. I wait and welcome it.

But Ruben's green eyes catch in the orange candlelight. Wide and glinting with the utter instinctive terror that comes with losing his father. It snaps me from my trance, spurring me into action.

I glance at the two Tranqs who saved me and snatch a knife from their belt. I rear back, mark my target, and throw. The knife spins, slicing through the air, and the beast shrieks and gurgles when the blade thuds wet into its brain. Silence tumbles over the hallway as the creature flops, dying on top of the king, spilling its blood onto the crown discarded on the floor.

I lock eyes with the king and curtsey.

Chapter 26

The liquor burns the back of my throat, and the rubbing alcohol stings my wounds. I hiss, flinching when Ruben dabs my scratches with the cloth. He lets out a sigh. As he moves around the infirmary to the sink, the scattered candle flames reach towards him as he brushes past. The light bounces across the walls and his face. The sharp smell of wax and smoke tames the panic surging within me like an angry tide.

He tips the wooden bowl of red water into the sink and refills it with the pump faucet. My pulse consumes the silence. Ruben grabs another cloth and washes the blood from my calves. The scratchy fabric grazes my skin and tugs at the wound.

"The Veckling has venomous glands on its claws," he says, voice low.

"The Veckling?"

Ruben blows out a laugh. "That's what you got from what I said? What if I told you there is no antidote?"

I blink at him as he tilts his head, a flicker on his lips. "That smile tells me there is one."

He squeezes the reddened cloth into the bowl. "I warn you. It doesn't taste like sugar and lemons."

Ruben grabs a small tumbler from the bench, plucks a bottle from the cabinet, and pours the thick liquid in. He hands it to me. I scrunch my nose at the bubbling, bright yellow liquid. The stench of rotten fruit singeing my eyes. With a deep breath, I knock it back, groaning the moment it touches my tongue. I may as well be swallowing a cup of ground-up slugs. Ruben clamps a hand over his mouth to stop the laughter as I choke down the liquid.

"I can't believe I trusted you," I say, scowling. But I can't help but release a bubble of laughter.

"Me too. I could have just walloped you with poison." He waggles his finger as he takes the goblet.

"But who will you marry? I cannot imagine any of the ladies in the court would get under your skin the way I do." The words tumble out before I can catch them.

He pauses, gaze burning into my own. He plucks the roll of gauze and wraps my calf. I bite back the wince at the pressure of the cloth against the sliced flesh, watching the deep wounds disappear beneath the fabric. Ruben lets out a breath.

"Everyone knows that you make me mad," he says, flicking his eyes up. His face darkens. "The things you… do to me."

My cheeks burst aflame. "I don't understand."

"Oh, don't feed me lies, Elle," he growls. His eyes burn jade, flecked in the chrome glow of the flaring candle. "I have never wished for the kingdom walls to fall. But I do now. Only so I can get as far away from you as possible. Perhaps the madness beyond the walls would at least make sense. Be more pleasant."

I open my mouth but do not speak. Silence flares between us. My heart… he must be able to hear it.

"But what you do to me… how can any man stay sane? I am going to be forced to surrender."

His neck muscles tense, and a vein throbs in his temple. Moisture vanishes from my mouth. I stare at him as words continue to betray me.

"I'll meet you outside your room for the Tranq allegiance tomorrow," he says, breaking the uncomfortable trance.

I clear my throat as he pins the second gauze wrapping in place on my left leg. "Thank you for cleaning up my wounds, Ruben."

He stiffens at the use of his name as if it belongs to some ancient legend finally unearthed from a dusty, abandoned library. I imagine it feels like a curse to hear out loud.

"Can you walk?" Ruben stands up, offering his hand.

I take it, rising to my feet. As I pace the room, my calves protest. But it's not enough to stop me. "Let's go."

My stomach twists as we walk in silence. There is nothing to say. Tomorrow, I am about to sign my freedoms away, all for the sake of keeping the king off my back and the blood off my hands.

***

234

Glaring morning sunshine burns my retinas as we exit the main back double doors of the palace. I nod at the two Tranqs guarding the doors as we pass and head down the stairs. With such harsh sunlight, I keep my gaze pinned on the dewy grass at my feet as we cross the field to the Tranq building.

A sharp, startled curse word falls from Ruben's mouth, and he grabs my wrist. I glance up. Two bodies dangle from the side of the Tranq building. Their now dry, brown blood cascades down the wall of the building, dripping from their bare toes like the thick syrup some of the merchants sell in the Convex markets. Their heads slumped, upheld only by the thick rope noose around their necks.

A scream tears from my throat, raw and ragged. They're the Tranqs who helped me out of the dungeons.

My knees buckle, and the stone path grazes my skin. "What have I done, Ruben?"

Tears blur my vision, and vomit surges into my mouth. He grabs my ringlets as I hurl my stomach contents onto the grass beside me, coughing and spluttering. Quivering, I scrape myself from the ground, praying to the Gods no one witnessed that hallowed unfolding.

"I did this to them," I splutter, face hot.

Ruben clamps a hand over his mouth but bends over and vomits as well. "You didn't do this." He clutches his stomach and spits, closing his eyes as more waves of nausea plough through him. "I wouldn't be surprised if the king set this all up."

"He couldn't have, Ruben." I can't take my eyes off their pallid, swollen faces. "Why would he allow me to expose his vulnerability to the entire court?"

Ruben's lips stretch up, and a darkness settles into those eyes. "You're right. Now, the most powerful members of the kingdom have seen that a girl from the Convex can take down the king by turning his monsters against him."

My insides curdle like cheese, and my chest aches. But I draw in a breath, muster my wits, and march into the building. He leads me through the hallways and to the large training room. He clears his throat. We both pull our helmets on. His, the regal black bronze, with carved swirls down the temples and cheeks. The horns, terrifying and commanding attention, curl up and over his head. Mine mirrors his, only without the horns, which signify not only his rank in the Tranquillity but also his royal status. I often forget he is Prince Talin. To me, he's only Ruben. The boy with the startling green eyes who brashly proclaims to be lost in my madness.

I let out a small gasp. Hundreds of Tranqs, fully clad in their uniform, swarm either side of the room. The king towers above the audience at the head of the room. His shoulders rolled back and taut, hands clasped before him. A sinister, smug glower etched into his features. His whiskers freshly manicured.

"Nice decoration, Your Majesty," I say through gritted teeth as I prowl across the room, head high. "It shows the entire court and Tranquillity the true nature of your character."

His chest rumbles, and he shoots a soft, close-lipped smile. "I only have you to thank for saving me from the brutes. Those Tranqs, however, put me in danger, going against all Tranquillity code."

"I am... glad I had the quick reflexes and improved aim to have helped you, Your Majesty," I say, drawing to a stop only several feet before him and sinking into my deepest curtsey, the armour clanking.

"Are you ready to sign your allegiance to us?" He gestures to the marble bowl behind him.

There are smooth, charcoal stones piled in the bowl. Dancing flames shoot up through the tight-knit gaps between.

"What is this for?"

Ruben stiffens beside me, and the king sneers. He plucks a dainty silver knife from the side of the bowl. "We only need a few drops of your blood on the stones for Tellcolite, the God of Tranquillity himself."

Ruben's armour clinks as he balls his fists. The king passes me the knife by the hilt, those eyes gilded in the flickering light of the flames. Silence drapes over the room like a smothering storm, other than the resounding boom of my heart in my ears. I grind my teeth, trying to let the throngs of Tranqs melt into a background din.

I wince as I prick the delicate skin of my forefinger. Heavy droplets ooze out. The blood hisses and crackles as it splats the searing hot stones.

The room erupts into the rumble of applause, blended with the percussive crack of the Tranqs slamming their staffs into the floor in unison. They chant my name over and over like it's a prayer to the God of Tranquillity himself.

"Congratulations, Elle Fallon," the king says, waving his hands and drowning out the Tranqs. "It's time for you to prove to the kingdom your loyalty to the God of Tranquillity and your king."

"I will not let you or Tellcolite down, Your Majesty," I say, curtseying.

***

"Elle!" Larissa's trilling voice carries into the room.

I groan, rolling over, burying my face into the blankets and pillows.

"I'm coming in." Without waiting for a response, the door clacks against the wall and she scurries in on feet as light as a cat's.

"You need to bathe and dress, Elle," she snaps, yanking the curtains open. Chromatic sunlight spills in, hitting me in the face. "You need to report to the head Tranq for your first official duty."

After another groan, I shove the blanket off and pad into the bath chamber. Larissa's already filled the marble tub, and after helping me scrub clean, she towels me dry and braids my curls down my back. She helps me dress in the Tranq issue pants and draws the corset strings tight, straightening my spine. Her humming sprinkles the room as she arranges the Tranq armour over my body. The chest plate, the boots. She fixes the blades to my waist and spine before ushering me out the door.

Armed to the teeth with blades, including my father's dagger, with the Fallon crest, I should feel confident. And yet, as the head Tranq prowls around, his hands clasped behind his back as he surveys me, top to bottom, my stomach has never felt so unsettled. I resist the urge to gulp, to fidget.

"You are rather small," he says, rubbing his chin. The Tranq, with his brown skin and hooded, almond eyes, may as well have told me I look like skin and bones for the way his gaze carries that hardened, disapproving grimace. "But I am not here to question His Majesty's decisions."

I don't utter a word, afraid to say anything.

"You will join the squadron in the Convex Sector today, particularly the trading market in the southern village." He pushes his shoulders back, reaches into my locker, and binds the spear to the leather straps and buckles on my back. His tongue clicks as he presses the helmet against my chest.

I catch my reflection in the quicksilver wall across from me, and reality lurches into my throat. I am one of the people I have feared my entire life and tried to protect my sister from.

I join the bottleneck of Tranqs heading for the queue of carriages outside the building. A bunch of us herd into the carriage heading for the markets, and I swallow the bile burning my throat as the vehicle lurches forward and the horses trot at a steady pace out of the enormous palace grounds, through the gates, and into the Concave Sector. I keep my back pressed against the seat, obscuring my view of the window, much to the judgement of the Tranq sitting across from me. She arches her thick brows and clips the last of her tight black coil hair to the top of her head, out of her face.

The sounds outside the carriage change as we disembark the bridge and arrive on Convex soil. Screams of starving, sickly children in the outskirt villages. The wail of a man. The crackle of the various brass barrel fires scattered throughout the streets. My nose wrinkles, and my stomach curdles at the stench of decay that seeps in, even through the closed windows. I chance a glance out the window, and my mouth goes dry. A scrawny elderly man crouches beneath the awning of the building's front door, braiding the hair of his dead wife, whose body slumps sideways against the porch.

"The coroner should have collected the body by now," the Tranq across from me says, her eyes narrowing at the man.

My chest splinters. "The coroners are run off their feet with the dead." I wish I could stuff the words back in my mouth.

Her nostrils twitch, and she tilts her head. "So, you are the new Tranq, employed from the *Convex* Sector." She utters the last few syllables like they taste of a bitter, mouldy fruit. "And you are the girl betrothed to the crown prince."

I gulp. "A new... opportunity for me. I am grateful for His Majesty's trust in me."

Her chest puffs out as she sticks out her chin. "Next time, keep your comments to yourself."

Poison flares in my chest, licking up my throat and sizzling on my tongue. I open my mouth to retort when the other Tranq sitting next to her groans and throws his hand between us. "Can you at least pretend to get along?" he says, rolling his eyes. "We must focus."

I snap my mouth shut, my teeth clicking together as I shoot the Tranq a spiteful glare.

The carriage jerks to a halt, and the door flies open. I side-eye the Tranq as she ducks out of the door, tossing me a sneer before shoving her helmet on. "Better not be soft out there, Elle Fallon."

I stiffen, startled by her use of my name. Does everyone know who I am?

With frantic energy, I yank the helmet on and clamber out, staggering across the cobbled stones. The scent of baking bread snarls around me at once. Other horses clatter past, dragging rusty carts of hay into the markets, while a few of them carry bodies. No one has even bothered to cover their heads. The horsemen bear withered, pale faces with droopy under eyes.

It takes an extra effort to push away the lump in the back of my throat as I fall into step, marching with the Tranqs. Shadows engulf us as we enter my beloved markets, which are tucked between a string of tall buildings shielding the sunlight. We pass the lady from the apothecary, offering her bloodletting service. Her face turns the shade of parchment as she traces our movement. Farmers flinch, turning to stone behind their stalls. My insides simmer, and I almost miss the instruction from the squad leader to stand in my position, nestled between a stall selling chopped wood and the lady who sells homemade stew. I stand as taut as possible, with my shoulders pinned back, my hands at my side, and my knees slightly bent so I can leap into action at any time. I am glad to be far away enough from Aston's stall. I don't think I could bear to see him, especially when he couldn't recognise me. Or would he? Would he recognise my grey-blue eyes behind the narrow slits in my helmet? Would his nose scrunch in utter disgust?

Or would he pity me? Try to help me escape?

For most of the morning, I remain rigid, unmoving, watching children giggling and weaving through legs and stalls or elderly couples, clinging onto one another as they shuffle through the slow-moving throngs, picking up bits and pieces from the stalls. Everyone is bone thin. Those sunken cheeks, protruding ribs, narrow legs, and yellow eyes. I don't spot a single smile from any adult. It is simply too much effort.

One young man, who looks to be about my age, lumbers past, his shoulders rolled forward, his arms dangling limply towards the cobbles. His mouth hangs open. Frost forms on his eyelashes. Those grey eyes slide to me. They do not widen. Nor do they glint.

His knees buckle, and he collapses into the dust, smacking into someone on his way down. There is a dull thud as his head hits the stone, and blood spreads onto the cobblestones.

Before anyone can react, a wail cuts into the alleyway, wrenching my attention. A little boy, perhaps no older than eight, stumbles through the mob, tears streaming down his face. He crouches beside the body, his lip quivering. He doesn't even have shoes, and his toes are purple from frostbite. A gust of wind whips through the alleyway, followed by more screaming elements. Rain runs its icy fingers down my spine, and I take a step toward the boy, a deeply entangled primal urge surging through my veins. But the Tranq across from me holds their hands up, silently commanding me to stop. The Tranqs do not interfere with the dying or the dead.

As soon as the Tranq lowers his hand, his head turns, and he and a couple of others lunge forward, arresting another young man for carrying a parcel of stolen Concave produce through the marketplace.

***

That night, sleep evades me. The moon's glow leaks into the room as it crests the sky, and the blood dripping from the hanging Tranqs' toes mars my mind like festering wounds. The wind blows over my face, and the window creaks. I close my eyes, and I see their bulging, cloudy eyes. My guts churn.

An unannounced scratching noise comes from outside the window. I sit bolt upright. It sounds like someone chipping a stone against the marble wall. I launch out of bed and yelp at the face staring back at me. The breeze blows through his green hair.

"Ajax!" I hiss, glaring at him. "What the hell are you doing?"

"Hold up!" He picks his way up the jutting-out bricks, using them as a ladder until he hauls himself through the window. "Shoot."

I cover my chest, aware of the threadbare nightgown providing little shielding from the detail beneath. "Can I help you?"

He chuckles, standing up, giving his green head a small shake, and flashing me a grin. "Are you coming?"

I flick my wrist, raising my brows. "Where?"

"To the underground, Elle. Ruben's waiting." He waggles his brows, and his bubbling energy is contagious. He's a child at the Spring Bloom festival tasting his first cinnamon apple. "We are crossing into your town."

"Tonight?"

"No time to lose. Hasten and put your clothes on, Elle. I promise I won't look." He spins around, and I laugh.

As Ajax browses the books on the shelves, tapping his foot and humming, I pull my pants and tunic on. I slip my knives into my belt and my sword into the scabbard. But I don't bother with the armour or the helmet. Too loud and obnoxious.

I catch a glimpse of myself in the mirror. Hair wild as flames in the moonlight. "Let's go, Ajax," I say.

He climbs back out of the window, glancing over his shoulder. With a nod, he scuttles his way to the ground. As I stare after him, the sheer height sends my head reeling and the world swaying. I inhale and exhale. Ignoring the voice in my head, I swing my legs over the ledge and follow Ajax, ignoring the gnawing of my insides.

Cicadas chirp, and an owl hoots deep in the northern forest. Darkness conceals us from prying eyes, but the kingdom has gone to bed. We slip through the gardens, arriving in the overgrown, half-abandoned courtyard. Ajax yanks the trapdoor open. "Ruben," he whispers.

"I'm down here!" Ruben calls from the darkness below.

Ajax lets out a braying laugh as he swings off, dropping into the tunnel. My breath catches in my throat, and I gather my wits before jumping in. I curse as the concrete slams into my boots a moment too soon. The bones in my feet may as well have shattered as I double over, groaning.

"Thanks for warning me of how shallow the underground is, Ajax."

"Whoops." He cringes.

Sprouts of orange oil light hang from lamps fastened to the walls. The hallway is so narrow I have to hunch my shoulders. Ruben's hair brushes the ceiling. It's an extra effort to breathe.

"Do you know the way?" I rasp.

He grins, and the light dances on his face. "I am the prince. Of course, I know the way."

"Apologies, Your Highness. I should have known." I curtsey for him, earning a chuckle from Ajax.

"Might be a good time to tell you I don't want you to curtsey for me. You will soon be my equal." Ruben spins around and falls into step.

Ajax quirks a brow, clamping his mouth shut when I shoot him a warning glare. But his laugh rings out. Ruben leads the way, and Ajax brings up the rear. We twist through the maze of tunnels. Water drips from various points in the ceiling, and the stench of mildew lingers in the stagnant air. Our breaths echo, so we don't dare indulge in conversation. After what feels like an hour, a deep rumbling sends tremors through the earth, shaking my ribs. My hairs rise, and I instinctively pull out my knife.

"Relax, Elle," Ruben says, voice drowned by the roar above our heads. "We are beneath the river."

I let out a tight breath. "Feels like the world might cave in."

After another hour, we finally draw to a stop. A small flight of stone steps rise to the ceiling, and Ruben shoves the trapdoor. I blink as the wisps of moonlight reach down, curling around my hair. We climb out, and the hoot of another owl greets us, paired with an icy breeze playing childish games with the amber leaves.

"The southern forest," I say, glancing around, drawing in the musky scent of mushrooms and the sweetness of flowers.

"You came," a voice pipes up. Aston's voice.

He emerges from the shadows, fingers of moonlight gilding his eyes. Pools of honey and molten earth. I frown at Ruben and Ajax.

"I got in touch with Aston during his delivery this morning," Ruben says with an innocent shrug.

"I've rounded up some rebels, Elle," Aston says, nodding. "They have scrounged up some resources."

I arch my brow. But I swallow my questions and traipse after them, letting Aston lead us through the forest to the outskirts of the Convex village. Ruben's eyes drink everything in. The red brick-and-mortar houses bordering the miles of farmland in the east. Greenery, orchards, and ploughed fields. The bitter, musty scent of mouldy potatoes festering in our fields. We pass by the sheep farmer's barn, who hauls armfuls of hay into the pens and pours water into the troughs. The bleat of sheep melts with the farmer's low hum.

We move into the town, trudging along one of the cobble-stoned streets. There are only a few people out at this hour. Drunken men with their arms around one another, swaying from side to side as they sing an old hymn. Mothers usher their children down an alleyway and into their apartment buildings. Scraggly, leathery old men hunch over a table outside a tobacco store, playing chess. Their grey, almost folded-over eyes trace us as we pass. I thank the Gods that none of them recognise the prince.

"It's so different from the Concave Sector," Ajax says, also taking in every detail. He gestures between Aston and me. "Whereabouts did you meet?"

"By the river," we say in unison and glance at one another, letting out a laugh.

"After the king exiled our parents, I found Elle sitting by the river," Aston says, sticking his thumb over his shoulder. "I thought she was a burning bush at first. It was a stormy day, and the wind blew so strong I feared those flames would catch. But I realised it was a little girl, same age as me."

"He came up to me to see if I was alright, and we bonded over our exiled parents," I say, feeling Ruben stiffen beside me.

"What a charming way to meet someone," Ajax says, releasing a bated breath.

Finally, we arrive at the old pub. Squirrelled away in a dark corner of an apartment block, the Stoned Dog is a popular spot for locals to meet for drinks and cigars. Aston leads the way, pushing through the double doors. The smell of sweat and tobacco infuses the sooty haze shrouding the room. Men and women lean against the bar while others sit at round wooden tables, drinking pints of ale and tumblers of whisky. The bartender polishes pint glasses with a rag. Behind him, dark bottles line the shelves, separated by the odd flickering candle.

An inferno blazes in the hearth, and orange light bounces and flickers across the room, performing a jig with the shadows. Partners sworn to one another by nature itself. Light and darkness. I stare at Ruben. The man who I once believed was the night, but now, he is… something else. I draw in a breath, and his presence settles the pitter-patter of my pulse. Dozens of hardened gazes avert their way on drunken paths, landing on me, and I can practically sense their scepticism, as if they are afraid to believe in hope. But some of the rebels smile and nod at me.

"Elle Fallon," someone says. A man no older than twenty-five spins his rusty butcher's knife, sitting at one of the tables alone. "I'm Baron. Are you here to help us overthrow the king?" Baron wears reddish pants and a brown shirt. His black hair is pulled back in a knot, and the ring around his deep olive finger tears my heart. Something tells me he has nothing left to lose anymore.

Fear pinches in my throat, and I shove it away. "I am. I will help. What can I do?"

"We want to leech the Concave Sector dry. Starting with the bridge—the thing that ensures the Concaves go to bed with full bellies," Baron says, his words stretched and contorted with a thick accent. Those muddy brown eyes, which come from one of the poorest Convex villages, practically burrow into my soul as if he can somehow read the terror-laced thoughts dripping from my mind into my blood. "Are you ready?"

"Baron is the bomb maker. He has a stock of gunpowder he stole from the Concave Sector," Aston says, touching my shoulder. "He's a blacksmith for the Tranqs. Helps them with all kinds of weapons."

Ruben grunts, nodding at Baron. He crosses his arms over his chest and shifts his weight. "Yes. I recognise you."

Baron stiffens, pressing his lips together. He bows. "Thank you for choosing to help us, Prince Talin."

Ruben nods again once. "I know who the enemy is."

"I am sorry it has to be your father," Baron says, swishing back the rest of his bourbon, smacking his mouth.

He shrugs. "This is no longer his world. He just doesn't know it yet."

***

I hurry up the slope of the bridge, ducking behind the enormous side rail and clinging to the shadows. My backpack slaps against my spine. I keep my tread light, running on the balls of my feet across the river until I reach the middle point of the bridge. I cast only a glance over my shoulder at Baron and my friends, who hide in the outer streets of the Convex Sector. Gathering my wits, I haul myself up and over the rail, swinging my legs onto the other side, lowering myself onto the sliver of brick jutting out. There is enough space for me to kneel and lean over, ignoring the waves of nausea at the black sheet of water far below.

There are thick, enormous planks of stone and wood stretched across the underbelly of the bridge, keeping it arched and hovering above the river. Heart clubbing in my chest, I ease myself onto the plank. I grab a large iron bolt, knuckles white as I balance myself on all fours. Letting out a shaky breath, blurring out the darkness beneath, I crawl along the plank. When I reach the middle, I slip the pack off my shoulders and pry it open. A dozen handmade bombs glint back at me. I pull them out, one by one, and fasten them to the bolts of the planks with the thick rope, making my way back to where I started. My nose wrinkles as the foul-smelling sulphur in the bombs stains my fingers. The bombs are simply old wine bottles filled with gunpowder and sulphur.

Just as I finish rigging the last bomb, a voice cuts into the air. "Oi!" they shout from the Concave side of the river. "What the hell are you doing?"

I whip my head over my shoulder, and their Tranq helmet gleams in the moonlight. They haven't seen my face, but my teel-tale red hair is seconds from giving me away.

Muttering a string of curses, I shift around so I sit on the edge of the plank. My legs dangle down. I grab the matchbox from the bag and strike the match. The small flame blooms to life, and I brush it against the threads of the rope, watching it catch. Flames hungrily consume the rope, snaking down the line towards the bombs.

My stomach launches into my throat. There's a ringing of silence. I push myself off the plank, letting out a yelp as I plummet to the river below, and the bombs explode.

Chapter 27

A monstrous groan tears across the kingdom, as if some enraged god has split the earth. The water around me absorbs the sound, turning it into a dull reverberation that churns my blood. I spin myself around and watch with a moment of peace as bombs explode, triggering one another and billowing clouds of infernos into the sky, a surging squall of bright orange and yellow. The bridge collapses. Enormous chunks of debris crack from the structure, bleating as they plunge into the river. I swim to the surface, gasping and spluttering. Ruben waves from the side of the river, shouting my name.

Panic burns through me as more debris rains over my head. I scream when a large chunk of the bridge launches me out of the water and yanks me back into the depths. I swim across the river, coughing and whimpering and stumbling up the riverbank, flinging myself into Ruben's arms.

"Come on," he hisses, grabbing my face and pushing my sopping hair out of my eyes, checking for any scrapes and bruises. "We need to return to the palace right now."

I rush a goodbye to Aston and Baron before following Ruben and Ajax through the Convex Sector and into the underground tunnels. Shivers rake down my spine, and my teeth chatter.

"We need to get you warmed up," Ruben says.

When we finally slip into a back garden entrance of the palace, the Goddess of Wind blows the water from my skin, but my hair, still damp, leeches the last dregs of heat from my body. Ruben follows me into my room and grabs a blanket and wraps it around me. I tremble as he rubs my shoulders.

"I can't believe we did that," Ruben says. "We destroyed the only connection between the Sectors. The king will retaliate." He does a poor job of hiding the quiver in his tone—evidence of the little boy who both instinctively seeks his father's approval but also fears what is to come.

My heart clubs. "This is a rebellion against the throne. Of course he will." I stare up at him, watching the sliver of moonlight brush the grooves of his cheekbones.

He sighs, pinching his brow. "Will you be okay until dawn?"

"I'm going to warm up and try to sleep." I offer a tight smile.

His gaze lingers, and it feels familiar, like I have known those eyes in another time, in another life, as if we are from the same star. "I was afraid I might lose you tonight," he whispers, tucking my red curl behind my ears. "I can't lose you, Elle. You make me… unsteady. The reason I can't sleep at night, and it's running me over."

The breath deflates from my lungs.

His lips, only inches from mine—my soul blazes like it has never known air. But he tears himself away and wishes me goodnight.

My hands shake as I crawl into bed, still reeling from our proximity. I am warm and cold all at once. Like teetering on the edge of madness. When I close my eyes, I see him. Layer by layer, I am unfolding to him like the waning moon. And I realise I want to burn with him.

The next morning, Tranqs barge into my room, startling me awake. They are dressed in complete uniform and armour and drag me out of bed, tossing my own tunics at me.

"Dress," one of them barks, her tone carved from a lashing wind.

"What's going on?" I say, not bothering to hide as I pull on the pants and slip into the tunic and corset.

Another Tranq hands me my boots, and I step into them. "He knows what you did. How could you do something so stupid, so catastrophic, Elle?" she says. "You're going to destroy us all."

Those last words rattle around in my skull as the Tranqs lead me through the palace, down the foyer steps, and into the awaiting carriage.

"Where's Prince Talin?" I ask, leaning against the window as the carriage jolts forward. The horses hasten along the path, out of the gates, and into the Concave Sector.

"He's completing his royal duties this morning," says the Tranq opposite me.

I blow out my cheeks, trying to ignore the knots in my stomach. The carriage pulls to a stop by the river. The rumble of the crowd scrapes along my spine, and I taste vomit as the king smirks from the riverside. I mutter a curse while the Tranqs direct me out of the carriage and toward the king. Hundreds of too-eager Concaves gather along the boardwalk. In the sunny haze, patches of Convex merge into distant sight on the other side. Skeleton limbs of the former bridge stick into the air. Chunks of metal and wood float in the murky water, gathered in clumps against the brick wall that descend into the watery gloom. Dozens of Convex folk haul them out with ropes. Knots tug at my insides.

"Hello, Elle," King Talin bellows, loud enough for even some of the Concaves to flinch.

"Your Majesty." I curtsey.

He turns to the horde of Concave people. "Last night, a small, cowardly band of rebels collapsed the bridge. The connection between the two Sectors of our kingdom. They wanted to cut off our access to one another and bleed the Concave Sector of their food and resources."

The king meets my eye and sneers, looking more snake-like than ever. "None of these rebel schemes will ever cut through the thick skin that is our kingdom." He waves his gnarled hand around his head, spit flying as he speaks. "The demise of the kingdom will not be ignited by some scrawny girl from the poorest Convex village."

He nods at a shaky Convex man wearing brown slacks. The man slips into the small wooden booth a stone's throw from the carcass of the bridge. The ground tremors. A deep, belly groan reverberates through the kingdom, and the water ripples as an enormous hunk of metal and wood erupts from the water. The second half of the structure rises from the other side of the river, water gushing off the material. I let out a scream. A body lifts from the water, dangling from a noose around its neck, fastened to the rising wood and metal arms. With a teeth-splitting crack, the pieces connect, sending water cascading off the sides and splashing back into the river. It is slick with moss. But it is another bridge.

I lose my balance and stumble back, leaning against the carriage. The horse snorts behind me. I swallow and step to the edge of the river, peering at the swaying body. My hand flies to my mouth. It's Baron, the bomb maker. His face is swollen, fingers water-logged.

"What have you done?" I snap my head to King Talin and fling myself at him. But the Tranqs grab me, digging their sharp nails into my flesh as I writhe and thrash.

The king chuckles as he strides up to me.

"Like I said, Elle. Thick skin." He snarls, crow's feet crinkling. Red seeps across my vision as he leans forward, his breath fanning my ears, and he lowers his voice. "You reek of gunpowder."

The Tranqs shove me back into the carriage, and the horseman leads us back through the Concave Sector and back to the palace.

They deposit me in my room and march out. But one of them pauses, gripping the door over his body, scowling at me. "You have a day off from your Tranq duties, Elle. Use it to think about what you've done and the consequences of your little uprisings. And don't expect Prince Talin to seek you. He is busy. Might be a good day to reflect or train or do something that'll actually benefit the city."

The prattle of the door chimes through the room as I ball my fists. My heart just wishes Larissa was here. Her cherry smile would be medicine. The hanging bombmaker flashes across my mind, and curses tumble into the lonely room as I traipse into the bathroom and crank the faucet, waiting for the tub to fill. I don't bother closing the

254

curtains as I peel off my clothes. No one can see me from this high up into the palace anyway. The hot water eases my tense muscles and washes the dirt caked into my skin from last night. A rattling sigh loosens from my chest as I scrub and scrub, covering myself in the sudsy soap, waves of nausea knocking through me as the sickly lavender scent imbues the steamy bath chamber. Perhaps if I keep going, I'll be able to tear the blood of the bombmaker off my skin.

Salty tears slip into my wavering lips, and a sob echoes around me. "I killed him," I mutter, my voice twisted and strangled. "I killed him."

My body shakes despite the hot water, and it takes every ounce of strength to not let the shadows—which creep around the borders of my consciousness—completely take me over.

I welcome the rough fabric of the towel grazing my skin and dress in a fresh set of the Tranq uniform, pulling on the armour and slipping my knives and sword into their respective scabbards around my belt and back. As I pull the helmet over my head, I bury the memory of Baron.

I ask one of the servants to arrange a small horse and wagon. The horseman raises his brows at the red locks poking out from below my helmet but says nothing as I climb aboard. He guides the horse through the kingdom across the newly risen bridge. Convex workers scrub and scrape the moss from the surfaces. Their curious, scornful eyes scorch into me as the sweet, earthy scent of the green sludge blows around the wagon. My telltale red hair tells them exactly who I am.

There are few with red hair in the kingdom. My family always had the brightest red, and my father's hair and beard faded into a dark auburn by the time the Tranqs arrested him, banishing him from the walls.

The horseman stops outside Aston's village, and I thank him by pressing a coin into his palm. Dust puffs up my ankles as I trudge through the northernmost Convex village, running alongside the river towards the beginning of the farmland. Plumes of sooty smoke topple out of chimneys, sinking over the children kicking a tin together in the sunshine. A slim woman milks her goat chained to her front step. I know Aston will be at work, ploughing the farms, selling in the markets, or training with the other soldiers.

A smile flicks on my face as I make my way up the freshly laid straw path, pulling my helmet off and knocking on the door of Aston's home. Madam Sallow's gummy grin greets me, and I resist the urge to weep.

"Goodness, what are you doing here, girl?" she says, ushering me inside, the whiskers in her brows bouncing up and down as she frowns and tuts at me. "I thought they'd have converted you to gowns and jewels by now."

She swipes a match against the wooden slab next to her stove and ignites the flame. The cramped kitchen soon smells of herbal tea as she spoons some of it into the teapot, waiting for the water to boil.

"I will never completely convert to royalty," I say, sitting in the rickety chair at the table. "Not really."

Madam Sallow raises those thin, grey-white brows. "I am not so sure about that. Isn't the prince handsome?"

Blush creeps into my cheeks. "He is. But he's also an arse. He's not *as* bad as his father, though."

The pot bubbles, and she grabs it with her stained mitts, pouring the steaming water into the teapot. "You must be careful of him. He is the king's son, after all. How much can he truly empathise with you?"

The question stumps me, and I allow several beats to pass as she places a mug before me. I take a sip, wincing at the burn. "I believe he has suffered more than we realise. Prince Talin has a kind heart beneath the brooding exterior."

"Taunted souls are dangerous, Miss Elle," she says, waggling her finger. "Which begs the question, will you really marry this royal boy?"

I open my mouth to respond when Aston throws the door open and traipses in. "Ah, my two favourite ladies!" he says, swatting the grass and twigs from his hair.

"Excuse me, boy!" Madam Sallow barks. "Not in my house!"

He snorts, pressing an adoring kiss to her leathery, sun-spotted cheek. "It's my turn to sweep anyway. So, I'll clean it up."

As soon as Aston changes into fresh clothes, he slumps against the wall, wiggling his brows at me. "Time to get a drink."

"Just don't come back like a couple of drunken idiots and interrupt my sleep!" Madam Sallow says, jabbing her wrinkled finger at us.

We cross through the farmlands and meadows, stepping over the threshold into the tight-knit streets. Soil swirls around my boots as I trudge over the cobbles. "You don't have a quiet bone in your body when you're drunk," I say, shaking my head and clicking my tongue.

Aston throws me a grin. "Remember when we came home from our first day in the king's army absolutely off our face, and Lyra had to nurse us back to health?"

257

I cringe, sucking in a harsh breath. "She didn't speak to me for a week after that because she missed a shift at the laundromat that morning."

"She did laugh at us, though." He waggles his finger.

"I think it was because she was trying not to lose it at us."

We laugh heartily, and I pull my hair out of the braids, letting it run wild as we slip into the back alleyway pub.

A fire blazes in the hearth to the left. Drunkards mill about, bellowing with laughter, clanking their pitchers of ale together, and smoking cigars. Candles bounce dull, yellow light around the room. But I prefer the shadows. We order ale and slump into a booth. The icy drink soothes my raw throat and settles my stomach.

"Elle," someone says.

I turn around to see an older man, tall and slim, sporting a short moustache. Moles and freckles splatter his balding head.

"You rigged the bridge with the bombmaker's bombs." Saliva splatters from his tongue, and I spot three metal teeth in his otherwise gummy mouth.

I wish the floorboards would open so I could flee. "Yes."

"And you know where the bombmaker has been today, right?" His gravelly voice scrapes like chair legs.

The world plunges around me. "I do."

"We must honour his sacrifice by not giving up." He rubs his chin. "You know the Convex have your back. It's the folks across the river you need to win over. Show them who their king truly is."

258

As he slides into the seat, a howl tears through the bar, and an arrow lodges into the man's ribs. Before I can even scream, he grunts and gurgles, ripping it from his flesh and bleeding out. His head rolls forward. I turn into stone for several vital moments. Cries erupt throughout the tavern. More arrows slice through the room, hitting their targets with shrieks and groans of agony. Five Tranqs march into the bar, flanking the exit, armed with quivers. Bodies collapse to the floor, and patrons desperately try to stumble behind the bar or duck for cover beneath the tables, but there are only so many places to hide. Terror wraps around my throat as blood splatters across my cheeks from another nearby arrow sliding through someone's throat. The warm liquid dribbles into my mouth, and I gag at the metallic taste of death.

"Aston, hide!" I shout, the world screaming around me.

I leap across the room as arrows tear past my head, diving behind the bar and grabbing a towel. The woman behind the bar whimpers as I press the towel against the bleeding wound in her stomach. Sweat trickles her forward, and her face contorts with excruciating pain. "Stop them, Elle. You are one of us," she says with a rasp, her face drooping as the life slips from her.

I glance around the room. The fire whirls in the hearth, and the arrows crisscross like dragonflies darting over a pond. Screams and screeches of death bore into my bones, igniting fury within me and a hunger for vengeance.

"Who are you fighting for, Tranqs?" I bellow, rising from behind the bar. "The king and his comforts? Or the men and women who are the backbone of this kingdom? You can kill us, feed us with poison, starve us, and exile us to the monsters beyond, but you *need* us. We are the reason you have the luxuries you enjoy and the basics to survive."

"Stand down, rebel," a Tranq barks, nocking an arrow towards me.

"You think the king cares for you? That he wouldn't kill you if you were one of us? You are nothing but a pawn in his little game. A pawn in a lonely man's desperate bid to conquer."

"The king warned you," the Tranq says, nostrils flaring. "Warned you about the price of rebellion. Now look at the blood on your hands."

As the arrows continue to sing through the room, I snap a wooden chair into shards of the material. I hold the ends of the wooden sticks into the flames until they ignite, and I toss them haphazardly around the bar. Fire catches, roars, and crackles. A searing heat fills the room.

The Tranqs scatter, ordering one another back into the street. Aston and I help usher the remaining villagers outside and into the alleyway. Smoke clings to the back of my throat, and my face burns. Vomit convulses in my stomach.

My heart tears as I see how few I saved. The woman with the stab wound. A young man coughing and spluttering, leaning against the wall of the next building. Three middle-aged men covered in soot and dirt from the farms and the flames.

"Elle, you need to go back to the palace," Aston says, his expression carved from the wind. He nods at the Tranqs standing stiff in the courtyard, far away from the burning pub.

They grip their staffs and stare at me rigidly.

Terror snakes through my limbs, burrowing into my gut as I shoulder past them, making my way back to the palace.

Chapter 28

I have nightmares of the hanging man that night. The darkness is kindling to the images morphing and stretching across my subconscious. The creak of the wind battering his body. A scream tears through the night. Mine. But the bombmaker swings back and forth as the oysters and algae grow and infect his melting flesh. Someone shouts my name as I throw the blanket off my scorching body.

"Elle!" He stumbles inside. His lip hangs open, and his brows crease. "Are you okay?"

In between gasps for air, I shove my tangled curls from my face and pull the blanket back up to my chin as the frigid night breeze scrapes my skin. Moonlight stretches into the room, gilding his shirtless, chiselled body. I suck in a slow breath, grappling for my hold on this earth.

"Ruben."

He sits on the edge of the bed and tilts his head. His dark hair is ruffled from sleep.

"I keep having nightmares," I say, voice cracking. "I keep seeing the arrows flying. Hearing the screams and smelling the coppery blood of the dying. It's my fault they're all dead. My fault the bombmaker swings from the…"

I flinch as Ruben reaches out and tucks a strand of hair behind my ear. *Breathless.* "This is the king's fault. Not yours."

"I need to go back," I say, wriggling from the bed. "I must help them bury their dead."

Tears blur my vision as I trudge across the room and grab my boots and coat. His warm hand brushes my bare shoulder. "I don't think that will do any good, Elle," he says. "Let's not dare the king to hurt anyone else."

My shoulders slump. "I can't sleep again." My voice is hardly louder than my breath. "Please stay."

His sigh is gentle and kind. "I will sit on the chair in the corner. You should try to sleep. We have a big day tomorrow."

But as I blink, the flying arrows, blood, and dying screams slice across my consciousness. "You don't have to sit on the chair."

He blinks as I crawl back into the bed, tugging the blankets to my chin. I pat the spot next to me. "Come here."

He hesitates but pads toward the bed, climbing on. Ruben leans against the wall, leaving a gap big enough for a book between us. I roll my eyes and scoot over, nuzzling into the blanket and resting my head on his chest. My heart settles as his gentle smell steeps into my nose. He stiffens, breathing unsteady.

"Elle," he whispers. "I—"

"What?"

He runs a hand through his hair. "I... I am so sorry I got you into this whole mess."

We both pause, taking a moment to let the gravity of the previous day settle between us. I try to ignore the fire grazing my skin as he rubs a spot on my arm. His heart thunders beneath my ear.

But the magnitude of it all quickly swallows me whole, and I fall asleep.

***

"So, can you dance?" Ruben says as we enter the ballroom. My stomach tightens, and my shoulders tense. A perfumed scent tinges the air in the room, and blistering sunlight spills across the floor from the arched floor-to-ceiling windows above the king's steps and throne.

I squint, letting out a laugh. "My father taught Lyra and me a few jigs when we were children."

His amused grin sends a spark down my spine. "I'd love to see those."

We traipse across the echoing room to the tall, slender man in the centre. He wears tight pants and a singlet, scratching his moustache.

"Your Royal Highness and Elle Fallon," he gushes, swinging around us like a circling bird. "I am thrilled to be your dance teacher today."

"We appreciate you taking the time to help us find our rhythm. No doubt we will need it," Ruben says, shaking the man's hand.

"Of course! What with the wedding coming up?" He clasps his hands together, and I cringe at his too-upbeat tone. "You are going to be dancing the night away. The most beautiful couple."

The dance teacher turns to the assembly of musicians huddled in the corner of the ballroom and nods. I let out a sharp breath as the slow, deep bass of the cello thrums through my body. High notes pluck at the golden light imbued in Ruben's hair and perform a gentle waltz with the delicate aroma of incense speckling the outskirts of the room.

"The most important thing to master is the *near touch*," the teacher says, wiping the bead of sweat dribbling down his temple. "It is how we develop tension and desire with our partners. Now, stand with your feet close to one another and hold out your open hands. Move them towards each other."

We mirror one another, holding out our hands and inching them closer until I can almost feel his fingers brushing against mine. Almost.

"Now stop!" the teacher barks, pursing his lips as his eager gaze flicks to me. "Keep your hands about an inch apart. Look into each other's eyes. Now circle one another."

Giggles bubble in my chest as we step around one another like lions. His breath fans my face, and his lips sit slightly apart as his eyes roam my face. A smirk tugs across his cheeks as the teacher drones on about our wedding. I furrow my brow.

"What?" I whisper.

"Sorry, this is just really different from our constant arguing."

I arch a brow. "Would you prefer to practice dancing with someone else? Perhaps you'll be more comfortable, your *Royal Highness*."

He shakes his head, and the sun shines on the freckles across his nose. "I'm happy dancing with you, Elle."

"I think you'd prefer my father's jigs over this stiff, choreographed dance."

The teacher's arm slices between us like a wood chopper, breaking us apart. His beady eyes slide between us. "Are you ready to practice the dance in which you *do* touch?" The man salivates with anticipation and smears a dribble of drool from his chin. He puts his hands on his hips. "Or are we saving the touching for your wedding night?"

Ruben coughs, and my face burns. "No!" I blurt out. "I mean, let's just dance."

Ruben rubs his temples. "I agree."

"Right." The teacher smacks his hands together. He presses me closer to the prince. "Put your hand on her waist. And hold her hand."

My skin smoulders at his touch, and my stomach bursts into a forest fire as we spin and twirl around the room. The music grows into a colourful beast roaring in my ears.

"I realised I know little about your family," Ruben says, catching me off guard. "Besides, well…"

I school my face into neutrality. "Well, there's not much to say."

We twirl on the spot, and he leans me backwards. "What happened to them?"

Bile fills my throat. "The king exiled them." I mouth the words.

"Why? What did they do?"

My jaw tightens at the peppering of questions. "It was my fault." The memories pummel my mind in agonising flashes, mixed in with the raw ones from last night. Arrows. Blood. The hanging man. "We were starving and desperate. I stole some fruit from a Tranq. My parents took the blame to protect me. End of story."

"I'm so sorry."

"My sister never knew." I stare out the window at the spattering of clouds, silently apologising to her.

He grinds his teeth as we spin, and he flicks a hateful glare over my shoulder to the doors as if the king stands on the other side. "He has a habit of exiling people who challenge him. Including my mother."

I almost stop dancing and swallow the gasp. "Oh, my Gods. I thought she died of pneumonia."

Ruben blinks, shoving back the tears. "That is the story I tell myself... and others. The easier, more palatable story. The truth is, she... tried to help the Convex people. She wanted to heal the blight and resolve the famine." He runs a finger over his lip. "But such a peaceful world would mean the king loses his power. And loneliness would enfold him. Can't have that. I was only eight. And up until then, my father had always shown my mother love. Kissed her behind closed doors. Giggled with her at the dinner table and late at night. He did love her. Protected her from the cruelty of her father. But in the end, he loved power more."

I shake my head, fumbling over my tongue. "He murdered your mother."

He loosens a taut, raggedy breath. "Had you not wondered why there is no memorial for her anywhere?"

I cannot pull my gaze from his. And my heart tears anew, crumbling at the thought of Ruben as a child without a mother. A lost, lonely little boy with only a hateful, miserable drunk of a father whose interests were elsewhere.

That's when I realise he and I aren't all that different.

The dance teacher cleaves his arm between us again, splitting us apart. "Let's pick this up next lesson. Your miserable energy is depressing me." He pinches the bridge of his nose and gestures for the door.

We slink out of the ballroom, twisting into a deserted hallway. "Elle," he says, touching my wrist.

I whirl around. "What is it?"

"I want to know what is going on?" he says, voice low and husky. "Something is going on."

"What is it?" I say again.

Suddenly, I realise it's only the wall behind me, and he is inches from me. His face is right there. Lips *right there*. A heat sears through me as every instinct tells me to *do it*. But fear jumps down my throat.

"Um, I have to knife train," I say and side-step him.

His gaze burns into me as I hasten away and around another corner. I keep walking past my bed chamber, turning into various hallways, losing myself and all sense of direction in the maze of the palace, my quickened pace matching my walloping heartbeat.

"They're dying like flies," a voice in the room I just passed catches my attention, cold and sharp, like a knife aloft at my neck.

I draw to a halt. My pulse booms, and I clench my fists as if they might hear me, like a predator sensing its prey before it sees it.

"There are too many bodies filling the mass graves, Your Majesty," another voice says, haughty and obnoxious, and my skin crawls. "I fear the population will start to decline if we keep this up."

"I fear so much, too," King Talin says, and my gut sinks. "But I have an idea. They have begun to act like there is nothing left to lose. An oversight on our part, letting the famine get... this bad. Utter desperation makes animals out of people. They will continue like this, and, well, gentlemen, I would be lying to you if I didn't say that the throne could crack. After all, there are more Convex than there are us. But it doesn't matter. Insects are no match for the tread of a lion. They'll only get squashed."

But who eats the lion when it's dead, Your Majesty? I want to scream the question at him.

King Talin's hiss digs into my nerves. "We need to give the Convex hope."

A pause. Someone shifts their chair. "Hope?"

"Yes. Just a sprinkle of hope to hinder their rebellious energy." There is another pause and the clink of glasses. I pin myself tighter against the wall as if they can see around the corner. Part of me wouldn't be surprised if King Talin could somehow detect the pitter-patter of my heart. "We give them an incentive. Those who report any suspected rebel activity to the Tranquillity will receive a week's worth of fresh food from the Concave supply chain."

"And turn them against each other?"

The king lets out a dry chuckle. "Precisely. Pit their desperation against one another."

Chapter 29

King Talin's plan booms in my head over and over like a throbbing wound. A flock of maids turn the corner, heading towards the king's bedroom chambers. Their figures blur before me as the rage and the terror burrow into my gut, finding a home there. A scream fills the back of my throat. I think those two feelings—rage and terror—are the only two I have ever truly known in my eighteen years in this kingdom.

"Are you okay, Miss Fallon?" one of the maids asks, pausing and trailing behind her coworkers. Her kind, honey eyes lock with my own, and she reaches out as if to feel my forehead for a temperature, and an image of my mother making the same gesture flashes across my mind.

"I'm fine. Thank you." The worlds spill from me with absolutely no vigour. But I turn and flee anyway, praying to the Gods that I do not bump into Ruben.

Guilt tears out chunks of my stomach as I dart down the hallway, passing an oil painting of Ruben when he was a boy. For a moment, the guilt subsides. The small child has dark hair, pale skin, and striking green eyes, vibrant like a forest snake. Would he and I have been friends as children in another life? The spiral staircase propels the thump of my footsteps into the sky before I stop by my room to sling my sword over my back and make my way to the rear of the palace, turning various corners and scurrying down hallways until, at last, I burst outside. The wild wind whistles in my ears and bites my skin as I cross the manicured, dewy grass.

I hasten down the stone path into the northern forest, skirting past the green park. Birds chirp as the moss-green shadows wrap around me. Leaves rustle like the waves of the lake beyond the walls, and the branches creak, bending their limbs towards the earth like bony beggars in the Convex Sector trying to wave others down for a morsel. The tight-knit trees begin to thin out, and I glance around and look for Aston. He did agree to meet me here.

"Up here." His voice startles me.

I crane my neck. He's perched on the thick arm of an oak tree, smiling down at me. "Why are you so cheery?" I groan, shaking my head and tapping my foot.

He pushes himself from the branch and falls to the ground with a thud. "I don't see my best friend so often anymore," he says, dusting his hands of specks. "It's a good day."

I grin and pull out my sword. We circle each other, our practised treads quiet and dull. "Then please cheer me up. I spent the morning rehearsing my wedding dance with Prince Talin, pretending nothing happened at the bar or the bridge yesterday." The thought of discussing what I overheard in King Talin's office makes my stomach squirm.

His soft eyes grow harsh and watery, and his sword cracks against mine. "I couldn't bring myself to go to the wake for the tavern victims today. It's hardly an adequate send-off for the dead. The families have no choice but to add the bodies to the... mass graves. It's sick."

The world burns around me, and darkness creeps across my mind as we dance around, bouncing on the balls of our feet, swinging, and parrying our blades. "I don't understand how so much has happened. And I miss Lyra. I wish she were here so I could ask her what to do."

He slices his blade high, and I block it. "You have to keep playing the game."

Leaves crunch and whoosh together as I stumble back, adjusting my stance. "It's hardly a game when I am doing a terrible job at balancing dismantling the throne and swearing loyalty. How can I bear to go through this stupid wedding without her anyway?"

Aston presses his lips together and loosens his grip around the blade's hilt. "But I will be there. Will I receive an invite?"

"I am not walking down the aisle without you there, Aston." I flinch for a moment as birds caw, tearing over our heads.

He arches a brow, shifting his weight, waiting for me to swing. "Perhaps the prince isn't that bad."

I chuckle, stepping and lashing the sword at his knees. He scuttles back like a little beetle, drawing a laugh from me as he blocks the blade. "Oh, he's bad. Obnoxious. Arrogant."

Aston drops his blade lightly into the dirt and shrugs, tossing me the most ridiculous smile. "He's hot, though."

My jaw drops, and my brows arch. "I should gut you right now for such a comment." I let out a shrill cackle that carries into the singing wind.

He laughs, cheeks reddening, clicking his tongue. "Perhaps it's just as good your aim was terrible that day."

I nod at his sword, and he assumes position, lowering his knees and waiting for me to parry with him. Our blades crash, snap, and clank against one another, ringing throughout the forest. "My advice? Don't tell the prince any of those thoughts. We don't need to fuel his already overflowing ego. Have you seen the size of his head?"

He pouts, tilting his head as his blade swings towards my temple, and I stumble back, catching the blow. "So, you agree with me?"

I snort, shaking my head. "He's a prick. Besides, I don't have the privilege to focus on the prince's good looks. Not when I want to kill the king."

Aston lowers his sword, face paling. "You want to give the death blow?"

"I want the king on a pyre," I admit through gritted teeth. "If I sparked a series of uprisings, it's my responsibility to lead my people into rebellion."

I stiffen. A pair of footsteps approach us, their figures concealed within the trees. On instinct, we stand with our swords at the ready, peering into the gloomy sweep of grey and green.

"Don't worry, guys. It's just me," Ruben says, emerging from the shadows and pushing a branch out of his way.

I let out a groan. "R—I mean, Your Highness, what are you doing here?"

Aston throws me a funny look.

Ruben shifts his uneasy gaze between us. He presses his lips together, blush creeping into his cheeks as he ducks his head for a beat. "I wondered if I could train with you?"

I narrow my eyes, taking in the deep purple bruise, and split on his lip. "Who hit you?"

His eyes flash, and the gurgle of a nearby stream cuts into the painful silence. "I walked into a door."

Aston and I exchange a look. That's when two other voices bound into earshot. Ajax and Killian crash through the thickets and brambles, shoving one another and chortling.

"Can we join, too?" Ajax says, out of breath, brushing a couple of leaves from his hair. "We want to strengthen ourselves for the war."

"War," Killian says, dragging out the word. "Makes it sound so much more serious than a bunch of starved Convex following a redheaded girl into the king's palace."

"You could at least try to have some faith, Killian," Ruben snarls, clenching his fists.

Killian's hair ruffles as the wind batters the trees, and he crosses his arms. "Look. I want the king gone as much as the next person. But I'm afraid he is always going to be a step ahead of us."

"There are more Convex than Concaves and Tranqs combined," Aston says, pushing his blade back into the scabbard at his waist. "We have the numbers. We only need to drain the king of his resources and overpower him. Remember, the Convex have nothing to lose."

The guilt threatens to eat me alive. "Problem is, the king is trying to stop all acts of rebellion," I say, my voice dry, and I gulp. "We can't encourage them to charge right into the palace where the axe awaits them or the monsters beyond the walls. We must be more strategic. And I can't have you risking your life, Aston. You need to let me care of it before someone turns you in."

Ruben paces back and forth, chewing his lip. "You overheard the king, didn't you?" he says, as his back turns to us. "When you left the... dance lesson."

"Yes. It was hard not to. He didn't exactly whisper." I shove my sword back into the sheath.

"What did he say?" Aston asks.

"He wants to...get the Convex to report any signs of rebel activity," I say, my voice catching in my throat. "In exchange for Concave food."

Killian lets out a huff through his nose. "See? King Talin doesn't let girls from the Convex Sector spark rebellion. He's too... focused on kingdom security."

"Security?" I snort.

"Do you want to go kiss the man on the arse cheek while you're at it?" Ajax barks, shaking his head. "I didn't know you were his biggest fan."

"I'm not," Killian seethes through gritted teeth. "I just... don't want anyone getting hurt trying to take him down. No one else has succeeded in killing him. Why do we think *we* will be the ones to do it?"

I pull my father's dagger from my belt and tighten my brows. "I almost agree with you." I turn to Aston, my hands trembling around the dagger, panic surging up my throat. Who am I kidding, wanting to lead my people into rebellion? "We must warn the Convex. I can work on my own. I can kill the king without their help. They must just go back to their lives and let me deal with it."

"And go back to what?" he growls, scarlet flushing his cheeks. "Famine? Misery? Watching their children die from starvation and disease? Meanwhile, you and the prince enjoy a wedding that will cost hundreds of thousands."

I flinch, sucking in a harsh breath. "So, I just let them charge to their deaths?"

"No, Elle," he says, shaking his head. "They are charging towards our new world. Get ready. It's coming soon."

"As long as you promise to not do something stupid. You are all I have left."

He grunts and nods. "You won't lose me."

***

The snap of blades rings through the forest. Killian's auburn hair bounces as he skips a step and lunges forward, swinging his sword at my ankles.

"Gods, not bad for a baker's boy!" I say, blocking the attack with instinctive speed.

"I have been practising," he says, tossing me a grin that brightens the shadows around us. We pause, slouching our shoulders as we catch our breath, and I notice spots of blood around his fingernails, as if he's been picking at them. "Ruben started teaching me not long after you arrived at the palace. It is like he knew what you were, that you would revolutionise a kingdom."

I chew the inside of my cheek. "I hope you know that I won't let anything happen to your sisters. They will not go hungry. If Aston's mother could invent a way to cure the blight, we could heal the crops. We could make sure there is enough food for everyone."

Killian taps his sword into the dirt and tugs at the collar of his sandy-coloured linen shirt. "I just… I am their brother, right? I am meant to protect them. And I will do anything to keep them safe, Elle. Anything."

My stomach tightens. "I know that feeling all too well. I do."

The tension in his face eases. "Of course you do. It's why you are even here in the first place."

"I didn't want my sister to starve, either. I had my own bloody potato garden in the southern forest, committing treason to keep her alive. I killed—I *killed* a man to try to keep her safe and almost killed the heir to the throne."

He wraps his hand around his crimson-licked fingers. "I am glad we understand each other." His blade glints in the beams of sunlight stretching down through the canopy before he sends it arching towards me. We parry one another, chortling and cursing the king. I cannot help but grin as the thrill of the clash surges through me. Killian grins back, his swings becoming harder, faster, more precise.

Chapter 30

My muscles tighten as I pull back the bow, breathing in deep and blowing out the air, focusing on the target across the room. The clack and clang of dozens of other Tranqs in training fades into the background. I ignore Ruben's lingering stare. A gasp falls from my lips as the arrow stabs the dummy's head. Strangled death cries echo in the back of mine. I squeeze my eyes shut, and the bombmaker hangs from the new bridge, creaking in the wind. My knees buckle, and I drop the quiver, hissing and gripping my head.

"Are you okay, Elle?" Ruben says, stepping up behind me.

"Clearly not, Your Highness," I snap, curling my finger inward.

Dozens of heads turn our way, and I glare at them, averting them elsewhere. I swallow the lump in my throat. "I can't do this," I say under my breath.

"Yes, you can." His voice stirs my insides, and I want to unfold into him and hide from the monsters baring their teeth at me. "You killed the dummy."

"But one day, it might be a real person." My voice is flat, and I stare at my boots. "What kind of person will that make me?"

He presses his lips together. "I'm not sure—" Ruben cuts himself off. His face draws back as he lifts his chin in the air, sniffing. "Do you smell that?"

My stomach lurches into my throat at the distinct, sooty stench of smoke coiling around us. The hairs straighten on my arms, and I snatch the quiver from the floorboards. Then I hear it. That sound. Crackling and licking and roaring, as gusts blow the scorching flames through the building. Its heat grazes my face. Sweat springs from my pores. But my feet remain stone, even when Ruben grabs my wrist.

Despite the blistering heat billowing through the target practice room, a shiver brushes my spine. A hundred voices permeate the air, growing louder and louder by the moment, transcending into a chanting crescendo that turns my veins into icicles.

"You will die in *our* world! You will die in *our* world!"

"Fire!" a Tranq bellows, bolting past me.

Even as Ruben yanks me away from the crawling fiery hues eating at the walls around me, I still cannot move. A throng of Convex men, dressed in their tattered brown pants and linen shirts, hurtle from the burning building, dashing for their lives across the grass. A sharp scream tears from my throat when the first man falls face first into the dirt, his death blow, a Tranq arrow, nocked towards the sun. Convex men tear past me, diving into the safety of the trapdoors scattered around the palace. As more Tranqs flank the palace grounds, dozens of arrows crisscross the air. The brave Convex men fall like poisoned rats. Ruben yells in my ear, and I finally stumble after him, fleeing from the blazing building.

But a yell for help stops me in my tracks. I whirl around to see a Convex man trapped under the fallen debris of a doorway he tried to escape before it collapsed. Blood pools around him, and the flames thirst for it. He desperately tries to push the hunk of wood from his chest. Blisters form on his cheeks as the flame creeps up his flesh. His howl unearths a primal terror within me.

"We have to help him, Ruben!" I cry, ignoring the fact I used his name.

Ruben lunges forward, gripping the chunk of wall on the man's lower half. Together, we grunt and groan and lift it off, pushing it aside.

We help the whimpering, blubbering man to his limp feet and drag him away from the flames. He hurls himself at the grass and rolls around, snuffling out the fire. The man lies there, whimpering and trembling.

"Elle?" a voice snaps my attention.

"Aston?"

He bounds over, blood trickling down the side of his face like a winding forest path. "I didn't realise you would be here."

Aston helps us carry the man through the cacophony, dodging arrows, towards the mouth of the trapdoor and down the stairs, where a flurry of Convex awaits. We scramble back out into the glaring sunlight and throw ourselves into the thicket of the maze garden, ducking behind the towering hedges.

"You lead this, didn't you?" My eyes narrow as we crouch.

"Why were you trying to kill us?" Ruben snarls, wiping the man's blood from his face. "You need to set the palace on fire. Not the Tranq headquarters."

Aston examines the gash on his thigh, and I cringe at the bloody-looking piece of meat beneath his torn trousers. "That's the next step. But we are draining King Talin of his resources, are we not? Taking as much as we can from him. Reminding him that he is only a man. Not some immortal god."

Ruben's shadow-brooding shoulders shift, and a spark catches in those green eyes. "Good. As long as you know what my father will do. He'll kill anyone who survives today."

Aston grins, and the glint in his eyes startles me. "It doesn't matter. Those men have nothing to lose. They knew what they were getting into."

"What the hell, Aston?" My chest burns, and my voice quivers. "Don't I matter to you? How can you be so okay with leaving me alone? You promised me—"

"I didn't promise." He grunts and pulls my head into him when I stiffen, kissing me between my brows. "Things must get done, Elle. This is bigger than us." Aston rises to his full height and peers over the hedge. "I need to join the Convex preparing for the next attack."

He steps away without even saying goodbye. "Aston!" I snap, voice strained.

"Are you going to the palace?" Ruben growls at him. Aston stiffens. Tears blur across my eyes, slipping down my cheeks, and I furiously wipe them away.

"Don't walk away from me, Aston." My voice is a crackling, humiliating mess.

My friend whirls around, scowling at Ruben, hardly bothering to look at me. I clench my jaw, pressing my lips together to stop myself from slapping him. "Yes. I'm going to the palace. Can you help us?"

Ruben clenches his jaw and nods. "There's another way inside. Another tower into the king's headquarters."

"Take me." Aston pulls out his knife, spinning the hilt around, red splotching his cheeks as our eyes meet for a moment. A muscle twitches in his temple—the shame of ignoring me or being perfectly okay with leaving me with hardly a goodbye, forcing its way onto his face. "The other men can continue through the originally planned entrance."

"I'll come with you," I say, reaching for his hand. "I can help it look like we are trying to escape the fray together."

Ruben helps me to my feet, and we follow him through the hedge maze. The shouts and screams of men rage around us like the smoke of the fire, tunnelling into my ears, into my spine, and my heart pumping harder, faster, driving me forward, around the corner. We streak across the once-manicured grass that's now crisscrossed with crawling flames, stained in blood, and littered with bodies becoming one with the fires. Heat curls around us, luring us into its grasp.

"Run, Elle!" Ruben yells as if I'm not doing just that. I barrel across the fields, dodging blades and arrows slicing through the air. My boots squeal when I skid across the marble and limestone floor of the palace, blowing out a breath of relief as I cross the threshold.

"Elle?" Servants and higher members of the court, still unaware of the fire, throw me the strangest looks and glares laced with jealousy as the prince grabs my hand and yanks me faster down the hall.

Aston growls but sprints after us. We fly down the hallways, careen around corners, passing paintings, sculptures, and dozens of doors and rooms. Finally, we arrive at the foot of the tower.

Our thundering footsteps cascade up the narrow tower wall as we circle higher and higher. My erratic breathing fills the space between my footsteps. A burn tears through my leg muscles. Candlelight jumps against the stone bricks, illuminating the path to the door at the top of the twisting spiral staircase.

"He should be hiding in here," Ruben whispers as we reach the top. "Ready Aston?"

Aston pulls out his torch, which is wrapped in oily fabric, and swipes his match on the door, holding it against the end of the torch. The blaze leaps to life. "I'm ready."

My pulse roars as Ruben shoves the door open, and we barrel in. I hold my sword out in front of me as we move around the room, throwing open wardrobes and checking out the windows. But the emptiness echoes back, teasing and taunting us.

"He's not here," Ruben says flatly.

"You said he'd be here, Your Highness," Aston says, his face forged from the wrath of a storm, holding the torch out like a blade as if he wishes it was.

Ruben paces the room back and forth, his turns as sharp as knives, chewing his lip. "I know, Aston," he snarls, snapping his fiery glare at my friend. "But the bastard is an utter coward and fled. They must have tucked him away when the attack began."

My blood pools, and I grab my friend's shoulder. "Aston. You need to run. Hide. They'll be coming for you!"

Aston's eyes glint with terror for only a moment before he gulps and nods, pulling me into a hug. "I love you, Elle."

Fear keeps my tongue rooted in place, unable to command the strength to splutter the words back. So, I kiss his cheek and memorise the lines of his face, those hazel eyes, his bronze hair, refusing to honour the thought of losing him. But he doesn't leave yet. He storms across the room, placing the flaming torch into an empty flower vase. "Let him know we were here."

He flees back into the raging chasm below.

Chapter 31

Ruben lets out a dry, braying laugh. He marches to the window and leers at the kingdom. The sun drips towards the horizon, casting red and gold hues across the sky, matching the blaze in the Tranq building below. Smoke drifts past the window, tendrils spanning into the room.

"My father is such a coward," Ruben bellows, gripping the windowsill, glaring out at the view for a moment before hanging his head. "How can he live with himself?"

My heart calls out to him, wishing I could utter words of comfort. But I only hear the screams of agony as men incinerate below and feel the terror clawing its way up my throat. "Look, we should probably leave." My voice trails off, the pitiful words dying.

He stalks back toward me, his cheeks blotched pink as the flames clamour outside. I wonder, for a moment, if they might burn the palace to the ground. If only. "He has always done this," Ruben growls with such vigour in his voice I flinch. He throws his hand at the window, indicating the general, unknown whereabouts of the king. "Runs away before anyone can challenge him. He punishes them before they can make him question anything. He can't—won't—allow himself to die a lonely and abandoned man. Even if it means others suffer. The coward."

Part of me is rallied by his words, fuelled into a renewed thirst for the king's blood on my sword. The pain in his voice and glimmer in his eyes makes my heart quake. "We will catch him," I say, cringing at the tremor in my tone, at the lack of conviction, feeling like little more than a rabbit in a trap.

"How?" His voice wavers and strains. "Killian is right. He is always steps ahead. And the thing is, I'm not even sure if I will have the courage to kill him myself. But I feel it is my responsibility to do so."

"You don't have to deliver the death blow." A sob festers in my gut as he paces the room, biting his cheek and fighting that wild storm within. "I can do that. I can kill him."

He clenches his jaw, running a hand through his hair. "You'd do that?" Those forest eyes render me still. Pain. It tears at my heart.

I shrug, a draft of scalding air breathing against my back as the flames climb higher into the Tranq building and the easterly wind carries the sound and smell of the dying, melting men. "I thought it was obvious I would. But yes. I'd do it. For you. For the kingdom."

He draws in a shaky breath. "Do you even know what he did to me as a child? What he *still* does to me?"

My heart pounds, and sweat soaks my palms. "No. I don't." I brace myself.

Ruben sighs and slumps down on the corner of the couch shoved against a wall. He pats the spot next to him. I sit. The burnt orange shades of the setting sun snap into the room, splashing across his face, brightening the hues of green and flecks of gold. But the darkness behind them does not waver. He draws in a breath.

"Whenever my father decided I was misbehaving or challenging him, he locked me in the prison, the same one you were in at the beginning. He wouldn't let any of the servants or chefs bring me food. I'd be locked in there for up to a couple of days at a time. I've lost count of how many times he did this to me. *Still* does to me."

He lets his voice drift off, and the words resonate in my ribs like a church bell. I shudder, swallowing the horror bite by bite.

"So, I do know, to an extent, what it is like to starve," he says, voice flat as if all the colour in him has turned grey.

I know the constant pang and throb in the stomach. The trembling weakness. The chronic haze across my mind. I know it all too well. A muscle feathers in his jaw, his eyes watery. He blinks, sending the tears away. Ruben knows suffering, as do I. He comes from royalty, and I come from the dust. But even still, we all, in some way, stumble through darkness. Is suffering just a promised condition of being human? Or is it something we create for one another? Part of me knows, deep down, that it's the latter.

"I'm so sorry," I whisper, my voice cracking and trailing into shackles of silence.

He pursues his lips and huffs. "I think we know each other a little more than we thought."

More wails of agony and commanding bellows snap up the tower into the bedroom chamber. A shiver rakes my spine.

"We should go. Someone will be looking for us." I grab my dagger and head towards the door.

"Elle, wait."

I whirl around and find the space between us mere inches. My back rests against the door. Somehow, my knife ends up back in my belt. "Do you think I am good?" he asks his voice a low husk that glides down my neck and makes the skin behind my ears tingle.

"Good?" I blink rapidly, chewing on the question, trying to not crumble to the floor.

"I… how much of his darkness do you think runs in my veins?" He drops his head as if ashamed for daring to utter such a question.

"It doesn't matter where you come from, Ruben," I say, trying to ignore his scent. "What matters is the choices we make. The people we choose to love. That's what determines whether we are a good person."

The air dispels from the room, and my heart hammers against my ribs. He is so close, and that storm, forged by a lifetime of agony and loneliness, rages within those jade eyes. My heart calls his name.

"Then I am not *that* good a man," he says, breathless. "I do love my father. How can I not? Yet I think about killing him. *All the time.* It's an agonising way to live. And I'm scared I will become him one day."

"Why are you saying all this?"

He runs his tongue along his lips. "Because I've spent my whole life afraid. Of him. And then you sprang out of the fray and gave us all hope, gave *me* hope that I won't always have to fear him, that he won't always control me. I will forever be trying to repay you."

288

"You don't have to. I didn't mean to do anything. I only tried to save my starving sister, who still wound-up dead." My words taste as bitter as liquor.

"And I will never be able to prove how sorry I am."

The silence withers between us. His eyes. Like the forest I loved so much. I want to get lost in his darkness. Yet, something about him has felt familiar since the beginning… like home. He inches closer, and a sharp breath falls from my lips. *The near touch.*

"Careful," I say, hardly shoving out the word.

"Your fire does not scare me, Elle."

My thrumming pulse seems to reverberate in the room. He cups my face and presses his lips to mine. I flinch at first. But the pounding in my chest turns my limbs to stone as I whimper, my hands flying to his shirt, gripping the buttons. He groans as the kiss deepens, and my skin bursts into fire and wind and madness. I stumble, smacking into the door, and it rattles as our tongues meet. I feel a part of my soul in that moment, reaching for his, like meeting with an old friend. An ache scorches my chest, and I know, I know, I know, I am going to take a lifetime to recover from him.

He pulls himself away, sucking in a harsh breath. His eyes roam my face, and his gaze darkens. "Elle, I… I haven't been truthful with you. Not entirely."

My brows pinch together, but the ghost of the kiss still lingers on my lips, and my mind reels. "What is it?" I say, sitting back on the couch.

He sinks into the plush cushion next to me and runs a hand through his hair. Wails and screams rise into the tower on plumes of smoke.

289

But I focus on Ruben, letting the dissonance of agony become a mere din.

Ruben draws in a deep breath before he speaks. "Many of the Tranqs have wanted to overthrow the king for several years," he says, his voice hardly louder than my breath. "They knew they were not strong enough, nor clever enough, to orchestrate their attack on him. So, they waited. For something, or someone that would spark uprisings and rebellion in the Convex Sector."

My breath catches in my throat. Dread curls in my stomach.

"You are that spark, Elle. The burning fire that caught the attention of a starving kingdom," he continues, reaching out and tucking a loose ringlet behind my ear. "They have been waiting for someone like you since your father's death."

The past tangles and snarls at me. Memories of my father hunched around a table in the tavern, surrounded by dozens of other men as they organised an uprising.

"My father and his rebels slit the throats of all the Tranqs in the square," I say, my voice cracking. "Earlier that evening, they had a religious ceremony deep in the forest. Took an oath. Sacrificed a goat. One of the druids from the witchy part of town blessed them all. It was the same day I stole the fruit. Perhaps if I hadn't... if I hadn't gotten caught, the king and his disciples might have never known who orchestrated the murder of the Tranqs. My parents might still be here."

"Your father reminded the Tranqs how little power they truly have, how little they matter," he says, voice now so hushed I scoot closer to listen above the gurgles of the dying beyond the tower. "When you... killed my friend in the forest that day and almost killed me, I learned the same lesson. Not long after, a handful of them pulled me aside and told me they want to see change, have wanted it for years."

Tears slip down my cheeks. "I'm not some goddess of change and rebellion."

"No. But you are Elle Fallon. And that is close enough."

Chapter 32

Ajax crashes into the room. His face is as white as crow-picked bone.

"What is it, Ajax?" Ruben asks, standing instantly.

I pull my dagger out on instinct.

A cool draft curls into the room, playing with my hair as Ajax opens and closes his mouth like a bemused fish, gathering his words. The silver jewellery in his eyebrow glints in the jumping candlelight. "The king... his loyalists... they're just murdering the Convex rebels."

Knots tear through my stomach, spilling my guts down my legs as I stumble to the window. A hoard of Tranqs arranged in a triangle formation, fire arrows. Sharp cries and strangled grunts nettle the tower window. Stupid, stupid, stupid. Kissing Ruben, the *king's* son, while my people die as they fight for a better kingdom. Tears blur my vision, and I swipe them away furiously. Blood and corpses speckle the palace grounds and the gardens as the final remnants of the Tranq building collapse into a pile of dust and ash.

"Where is Aston?" I demand, my voice shaking.

"He's trying to help urge as many Convex back into the tunnels as possible after they charged through the palace doors, trying to set the entire thing on fire," Ajax says with a huff. I cringe, knowing they were not successful. He pads up to me, standing so close to my side I can feel his warmth. "They were fighting back. Your people. They are strong. Brave."

"And dead." My voice now yields nothing but hollowness.

"Not all of them. Many of them have fled for the night. But they will return."

"What are we meant to do?" My nails scrape the wooden finish of the window ledge. "How can we stop the king from punishing them all?"

"What *can* he do?" Ajax says, tilting his chin towards me, forcing me to look at him. "He can only exile or kill them. Most of these people have lost everything already."

Wisps of smoke and the coppery smell of blood rise into the window, performing a morbid dance that curdles my insides. "At the very least, we can round up the dead. Build a funeral pyre."

"Actually, Elle." Ruben clears his throat, joining us at the window. "The rebel Tranqs are meeting tonight. To discuss the next move. I will be joining them."

"I'll be there." The words tumble out. My heart wrenches in two as a young man writhes and thrashes, his wail drowning out the other groans of agony. He clutches the arrow in his stomach. One more twitch. Still.

The top corner of my lip tugs up in disgust and terror. More arrows crisscross the scarlet-splashed gardens, and I squeeze my eyes shut. "Where's the meeting?"

"In the forest," Ruben says. He glances over his shoulder, sucking in a harsh breath at the sight of his father's cold, bare room. "We will stop this madness, Elle. It won't be like this for much longer."

"How can you know? You don't even know where your father is." His kiss now feels like an unpleasant burn on my lips that I want to wash away. The wrong time.

Ruben and Ajax exchange a look, and I catch a strange glint in Ajax's eyes. "I'm going to find out where he is." Ruben swallows, and his shoulders tighten, a haunted look crossing his face.

"And I will take you to the meeting spot in the forest, Elle," Ajax says, tossing me a brave smile.

Groans and sobs of the dying tease and taunt me, and I yank the window closed, turning away, leaning against the ledge. "Fine."

"I'll meet you there after sundown," Ruben says, retreating to the door. His eyes dart to my lips for a moment before he heaves a sigh. "You should get back into your room. My father's loyalists and servants will be looking for you."

I scowl before forcing a fake, sickly-sweet smile onto my face. "Must show my devotion to His Majesty."

Ruben rolls his eyes before darting out the door, his footsteps dripping into the depths of the tower.

Ajax clicks his tongue and shakes his head. "Poor dude."

I press my lips together, cringing at the pitched screech of a dying man below. "Imagine having a monster of a father." I give my head a shake. "I couldn't bear it. My father was the kindest man who loved my sister and I."

Ajax traipses towards the exit, and I fall into step behind him. "I'm jealous. My father was a true creature."

"How so?" I focus on my footing, gripping the handrail as we wind down the tight, spiral staircase. Icy puffs ooze from the chunks of stone around us.

"It's actually how Ruben and I became friends when we were boys." He casts a curious glance over his shoulder. "Let's just say I still have nightmares about him and how he died."

"How did he die?" I dare ask, wishing I could shove the question back in my mouth at once.

Ajax pauses, tugging at his ear. "He used... little bits of poison in my food to manipulate me into being sick my entire life. A sick, Concave child entitles families to privileges. A fancy home near the most pristine apothecaries and medicinal professionals. It got him close to the palace, where he weaselled his way into the king's inner circle. I killed him with his own medicine."

Silence ripples between us as we emerge from the tower stairwell and cross into the main hub of the palace. The fiery orange hues of the setting sun blow through the arched windows to our left. Maids and servants, who are usually in a frenzy of activity at this hour, are mere half-frozen shells of people. Some of them stare out the windows at the corpses. Others cower on the floor, sobbing. A few ladies polish a sculpture of the king, trembling with terror.

My heart clubs in my chest, and we quicken our pace, weaving our way through the hallways and corridors, trying to ignore the hopelessness, desperation, and despair shadowing the palace walls as the dead stiffen below the dying sun. Tears slip down my cheeks as we arrive in my room.

When the door clacks shut, a sob tears from my lips.

"Hey," Ajax says, pulling me into a hug, shushing me gently as he brushes my hair, letting me soak his shirt with my tears.

"You killed your father." Pain, for my friend, scorches through my chest, fuelled by the utter terror of the day.

"It had to be done," he says, loosening an ancient breath as if he'd held it for years. "The man beat and destroyed my mother my entire life slowly, painfully, over many years. I found her body when she decided she could no longer take the humiliation. I spent my entire childhood too sick to participate in normal kid things. He was a monster, Elle. So, my heart aches for Ruben. We bonded over our terrible fathers. I can understand what he is going through, that feeling of responsibility crushing his shoulders."

The wind drains from my lungs, and I fight to gather it back. "I am glad Ruben has someone who sees him."

"You see him, too."

I pull open the wardrobe and rifle through the array of dull and bright fabrics before selecting brown trousers and a maroon linen long-sleeve. With a smirk, I gesture for him to turn around.

He chuckles and turns, sitting on the corner of the bed.

I change into fresh clothing, grateful to wear something that doesn't smell of smoke and blood, and thread my belt through the pants.

Ajax releases a breath of a laugh. "Since we are getting to know one another, something else you might want to know is that I'm not interested in people like *that*."

"Like what?"

Thankfully, my stash of knives and my sword have been safe in my wardrobe. I shove several into the belt and pull my sword over my back.

Ajax pauses, shifting his weight. "I don't think about kissing anyone. Not guys or girls. No one. I just don't have the urge."

"Here," I say, striding up to him and handing him a spare knife. "And thank you for telling me. For the record, I think you deserve all the love in the world. I think you are wonderful."

"Trust me, there's still plenty to tell." He turns the hilt over, examining the blade.

"I look forward to hearing all your gory stories over an ale after the king roasts on a pyre." We grin at one another. But my insides twist. Heat rises into my cheeks. "Since we are sharing things, I think I just kissed the prince during the height of a Convex rebellion."

A sparkle in those freezing cobalt eyes dulls. "Love rarely has appropriate timings." He tucks the knife into his belt and grabs my hand. "Now, let's make our way to the forest."

***

As the final breaths of sunlight streak the sky, we enter the northern forest. We sneak through the back gardens of the palace grounds and slip into the deserted park. Shadows gobble up the last puffs of warmth reaching through the gaps in the canopy. Birds peep, darting above our heads. Deep jade moss cushions our footsteps as it sprawls across the forest floor, covering thick roots and rocks. The odd red and orange leaf speckle the vibrant green landscape. Ajax leads me through the stripped bare trees, along a gurgling stream, and into a clearing, where my heart leaps into my throat.

My chest fills with the crackle of nerves as I sweep my gaze around the forest clearing, taking in the dozens of Tranquillities. Armed to the teeth with knives and sheer courage, they all watch me pace before them. I can't believe it. All these Tranqs are ready, waiting, to overthrow King Talin. Another crowd of Convex rebels gathers by the end of the clearing, some of them nursing fresh wounds from today's feat. Tears prickle my eyes, and a lump grows in my throat, stopping any words of gratitude from forming on my tongue. Memories of my father's attempts at rebellion flutter across my mind, and a phantom fingernail scrapes down my spine. But with the Tranqs standing with us, an ember of my father's bravery and selflessness blooms back to life deep within my soul. If only he were here to see this.

Aston and Killian also flank the crowd. Ruben slips out from the cluster of Tranqs, standing beside me. Once the rumbling Tranqs fall silent, Ruben clears his throat.

"It's time we put our heads together and weaken the king," he says, voices low and husky and demanding attention. He paces before the crowd. "But my father cannot know the Tranqs are against him."

I press my shoulders back and knit my brows together. "The king is hiding away in his underground bunker. There is a trapdoor just beside the river, and I think we can redirect some of the flow down into the tunnels and flush him out."

Ruben snatches a red leaf from the forest floor and twirls the stem between his thumb and forefinger. "We need him to start to feel the rebels gaining on him. It is time—" A shaky breath. "It is time my father knows what it means to feel like prey."

One Tranq in the centre of the group stands forward. "The Tranqs cannot reveal their position to the king yet. We must continue to... pledge our loyalty."

"He knows *we're* coming for him," a young Convex rebel blurts out from the front of the crowd. He hoists up his rusty axe, his dark skin catching in the sunlight, cutting through the canopy above. "His Majesty would be fucked if he didn't have the Tranqs protecting him from our blades and our vengeance."

I cannot help but join my people in the murmur of agreement.

Ruben bows his head. "I can divert some of the flow of the river down into the tunnels. I'd rather risk myself getting caught than any of you."

"Do you think this will work?" Killian says, pushing loose strands of auburn hair from his face. "What if he drowns?"

Ruben scoffs, but his jaw tightens. "Now, that would be great. But I think he and his right-hand men will escape with only bruised egos and, hopefully, a burn of terror."

Killian glances at the ground, pursing his lips as he digs his heel into the dirt. Ajax steps forward, fiddling with his lip ring. "The only problem with the plan is there are a bunch of miners working in the tunnels," he says.

I nod. "I'll go down and get them out."

Ruben glares at me. "If the king finds you down there, he will kill you."

"I can do this." I curve my fingers around the hilt of my father's knife but find scarce comfort when I look at Ruben and see the little boy who suffered the king's cruel punishments staring back at me. His eyes water. Fire catches in my chest, billowing into a storm. "The king better hope he doesn't run into me."

***

My shoulders tighten as I lower myself into the tunnel, drinking in the darkness, searching for specks of light. But there are not even candles mounted to the walls. Ruben lights a lantern and sticks it through the trapdoor. I grab it and nod at him with grim determination.

"Elle, I—" he cuts himself off, pressing his lips together.

"I'll see you on the other side."

"Just… be safe."

He closes the trapdoor, sealing me within the stone walls and shadows. My breath grazes the walls, ringing back at me. I hold the lantern out in front of me, letting the jumping yellow light of the flame guide me toward the miners in the south of the kingdom. Around corners, down stretches of lonely darkness, deeper and deeper into the kingdom. The ghost of Ruben's kiss brushes across my lips, and my insides stir. I swallow, loosening the feeling from my mind. Meanwhile, I can't help but think of Ajax. Of the child forced to eat morsels of poison so that his father could use him as a pawn in his little game.

Finally, the ground trembles beneath my feet, and the walls and ceiling shudder with a groan so intense it rattles my spine. My body sways, and I palm the wall, regaining my balance. There's a thundering whoosh that chills my blood, tingles of instinctive terror plunging into my flesh.

He's done it.

He's opened the trapdoor by the river and diverted some of the water flow. Everything around me screams, screams, screams. But I do not turn and flee. After drawing in a ragged breath, I keep moving, quickening my pace, knowing I'm close to the miners and I have time to urge them out.

Their voices, threaded with panic, bounce through the tunnels. Close. I'm so close. A strange feeling ripples along my arms, and I glance over my shoulder as phantom needles sink deeper into my gut. Water creeps over the floor, gobbling up the soles of my boots, and my pulse hammers behind my ears. A deep, grating belly laugh whips down the tunnel, followed by the distinctive raspy whisper of the Vecklings, the obsidian lizard monsters with no eyes.

Chapter 33

Tendrils of whispers and hisses scrape my eardrums. I pull out my dagger and whip the lantern back and forth, staring into the inky darkness, waiting for one of those foul monsters to crawl out from the depths of the tunnels.

I arrive at the mine, the specks of chatter and tools clanking the stone splintering the gloom. A dozen men, paired in twos in an underground cavern, hack into the stone with brass pickaxes, hauling handfuls of copper and iron from the depths into wooden pails. A musky, sooty smell clings to the idle air. Hooks scratch at my throat as I recognise Barrett, my father's old friend. They all glance up at my approach, brows deepening.

"You need to get out of here," I say, pointing to the exit. "There's flooding in the north, and you'll drown if you stay."

Sensing the urgency and fear in my tone, the miners do not question me. They dump their tools and usher one another to the tunnel that leads to the exit. Barrett, a tall, scrawny figure with sluggish movements and pallid, sagging skin, staggers up to me, smudging dirt across his brow. "Are you 'ere to kill the king, young Elle?"

I square my shoulders. "I'm here to help you."

He flashes me a gummy grin as he claps me on the shoulder. "Your father wanted this. He would be proud. I am ready for the future."

Barrett stumbles away down the onyx corridor.

The miners' voices dissipate, but a cragged, distinct sound snaps into the mine. I stiffen. That voice. I'd know it anywhere. My knees buckle as a scream slices through the darkness. Barrett's scream. Followed by a dull, wet thump. A shadowed figure emerges from around the corner. The king's low laugh crackles through the cool, stagnant air as the glacial water slides around my shoes, biting my toes.

"Oh, Elle," the king says. Water splashes around him as he staggers through the tunnel, his bloodied short sword glinting in the light of his lamp. Panic bubbles up my throat, and it takes every morsel of strength to not yield. "Whatever are you doing down here?"

I scrunch my nose and march forward, shouldering past him. "What have you done?" My face and heart burn, and I fight every urge to throw myself down the hallway to find Barrett.

King Talin shrugs. "Well, I had to put the old bastard down. He had one too many things to say about the crown. But the others were let go without so much as a hair off their heads."

I stare at the water as it rises and swallows my shoes, pushing the scream back into my gut, gathering my wits. "Why should I believe you? And why would you do that for them? I can't imagine it came from the goodness of your heart."

He shrugs and prowls the other way. "I am not a heartless man. I don't see the point in killing those who mine the coal that powers many parts of the kingdom. They left with their lives upon swearing their undying loyalty to me—to the crown." His mocking pout flickers in the lantern light. "Are you coming, Elle? If you don't follow me, I fear you may drown, and what a pity that would be."

I spin the hilt of the dagger in my hand, propping it over my shoulder, readying to throw it. "Not unless I knock you out and we both drown together."

He masks a bout of fear by tugging the hem of his collar and baring his teeth. "I thought you had terrible aim."

My bitter laugh dances with the chatter of the hidden lizards. "I did. But your son has taught me better accuracy. Your head looks like the perfect target. I wonder what it would look like on a spike." The thumping footsteps of approaching lizards reverberate and infuse the murkiness as I hurl the blade, and it nicks the king's ear.

He howls like the wind and stumbles backwards, grabbing his bleeding ear as his face turns white as fangs. "You bitch."

"I wonder if the lizard remembers the smell of His Majesty's blood," I snarl, shouldering past him and heading back towards the north.

The clatter of teeth and the raspy whispers swell in intensity, different sounds and pitches overlapping one another like musicians. Water splashes up my legs as I run, dangling the lantern ahead of me.

The king barrels after me, gasping and panting with terror. I cannot see the lizards. But I can feel them. Their billowing presence and the heat of their increased proximity. I drive my legs into the stone, propelling myself forward, skirting around corners, and stumbling down long stretches of darkness.

"Elle!" the king barks. "Wait up! Do not leave your king behind!"

But I do no such thing.

His mighty roar of fury drives me onward. I cry out, pumping my arms, pushing myself faster and harder, kicking up streams of frigid water in my wake. A shriek skids off the water and stone, and I glance over my shoulder. Finally, almost melting into the darkness around it, the first lizard hurls itself around the corner behind us, lunging into the tunnel. I curse, taking in the sight of the obsidian, scaly creature with no eyes, briefly recalling the way it almost ripped the king's face off.

The king's face now twists, turning violet with sheer horror. "Elle, don't leave me!" his voice snaps, and I can't help but grin.

"Run faster, Your Majesty," I growl before breaking into a sprint.

I run until my entire body burns and screams. The three lizards stampede after us, howling and hissing and huffing. Their breath, like rotting corpses, slides down my neck.

Finally, I reach the steps below the palace and launch up the flights until I burst into the chilled, stale dungeon. The king crashes in after me, slamming the door shut just before the monsters fling themselves at it. I double over, panting, taking sweet pleasure in the king's beet-red face.

"I didn't know you could sweat," I say with a grin as it runs down his temples.

The lizards batter the door for several more beats as we catch our breath, the ancient hinges groaning, puffing dust.

The king draws in a ragged gasp as he straightens, rage seeping into his face. "You snake."

I twirl another dagger, arching a brow. "At least I'm not a lonely, miserable murderer. At least I have friends, people who actually love me. Not subjects forced to exist and serve me out of fear. You wouldn't be so lucky to know about true companionship."

The king grabs a sword from a knight sculpture and roars as he swings it towards my throat. I jump back and duck, slicing my own blade across his shins. His scream curdles my brain tissue. Blood streams down his calves, staining his pants.

I sneer as he winces and finds his balance. "Too bad the king didn't have the mind to dress in Tranquillity armour when he ran away to the tunnels like a big, pathetic coward."

The colour runs from his face as the pain weakens his muscles. But he growls and veers his sword. I bounce on the balls of my feet, smirking as we parry one another. His movements are heavy and fuelled with hatred, whereas mine are sharp, trained, and calculated. But his lumbered slices work for him when his blade catches on my own, twisting my wrist backwards against the ligaments and tendons, searing pain shooting up my forearm. I yell and hurl the sword. It clatters against the dungeon walls like teeth on an icy day.

Perfectly on cue, a flurry of Tranquillity barrel into the dungeon and swoop down on me. They snap my arms behind my back and pin me to the ground. I fling curses at them like blades, but the half-dozen of them overpower me like a pack of hyenas bringing down a bull. One of them clamps their hand over my mouth, coated in a strange, icy blue powder. I cough and gag, but the herb has already entered my bloodstream.

Dazzling sunlight stabs my vision when I pry my eyes open. Blinding white clouds blanket the sky above, swimming as the world stumbles around me, stepping on the bruises riddling my joints and limbs.

"Elle!" Ruben's voice wafts into the haze.

I sit up and glance at him. My heart jumps into my throat. "Ruben." He's bound to a wooden post like little more than a sacrificial animal to the Gods. Shirtless. Blood and dirt smear his chest and stain his face and hair. His full, cracked lips hang open.

"I'm sorry, Elle." His voice is strained, like he just dragged it out of a fiery pit.

That's when I notice them. The Tranqs. The secret rebels and the sworn loyalty Tranqs alike, clad in their full armour and helmets, arranged in rows, facing me. We are in one of the large palace courtyards, located in the gardens facing the ashes and crumbling skeleton of the Tranquillity headquarters.

The king, with bandaged shins, a split lip, and a bruised ego, hobbles out of the double doors of the palace's ground floor. A deep-set scowl lands on me, and my teeth grind together as he scrapes a sword along the ground, dragging it behind him. A visceral, instinctive shudder scrapes down my spine as I notice the whip he pulls behind him in his other hand.

I scramble to my feet, only to find two especially loyal Tranqs grabbing my arms. They yank me to another wooden post and tie me around it, my cheek pressed to the chipped, fraying hunk of timber. The teeth graze my skin, and I drop to my knees, tossing the Tranqs a curse for good measure.

Ruben mutters my name again as the king circles my post, ignoring him and snarling at me like a feral, rabid wolf. Finally, he stops and turns to the Tranqs in formation. The sword clatters in my head as it hits the ground.

"I hope you all take a lesson from today," King Talin says with an abrasive voice as he adjusts his grip on the whip. "You cannot burn me to the ground. Nor can you calculate a plan that I will not sniff out myself. I am always a step ahead. But most of you know this. You have sworn your loyalty to me, and for that, I am grateful. But there are always the odd few who try to defy me and take me down."

"This wasn't her fault!" Ruben growls from the post.

His jaw tightens, and something akin to pain flashes across his face for a mere breath, gone within a beat. "I will deal with you later." His callous, cold eyes slither to me. "Three lashings for the crime of trying to kill the king."

"Stop!" Ruben cries, struggling and thrashing against his bond. "Punish *me*. I did this. Not her."

"Were *you* the one I found in the underground, son?"

Without another word, he reels his arm back and snaps the whip onto my back. I gasp as fire cracks up my spine and sears across my flesh, splitting my skin open like a quake, forging a chasm in the earth. Before I even have the chance to catch my breath, the next one slams down. I bite back the scream with every ounce of strength I can muster. I focus on my strength. I must be stronger than the pain. Never will I yield a shred of weakness to the king. Hot blood trickles down my hips and drips down to my knees as the third and final strike licks my back, tearing open the flesh.

I shudder, wincing and fighting back the tears that blur my vision. Through the smog, Ruben's face contorts, and he damns his father to an eternity of misery and loneliness and no love.

The world around me spins as the agony ricochets through me. Thick, inky blood splatters on the stone. Copper fills my mouth. I slump forward, letting oblivion relieve me of the scorching waves.

***

My vision shifts in and out of focus as Larissa flits around me like a bird. I sit, shoulders slumped, on the marble vanity of my bath chamber, watching the lukewarm water glug out of the faucet into the tub and wondering how I'm still alive.

"He could have killed me," I say, my voice hoarse. "Should have killed me. Or exiled me. Why didn't he?"

Larissa's molten earth eyes flick up to me, washed in the moonlight, trickling in through the single window. "Probably to make an example of you. A different kind of example, I guess."

I hiss, biting my lip as I sink into the warm tub, and the water plunges into my wounds like tusks, drawing out coils of blood. "Where is the prince?"

She takes a fresh cloth and pats my lacerations, pausing as I cry out. "He will be here soon." Her nimble, bony fingers reach across my shoulder, grabbing the jar of salt. "Are you ready? It's going to hurt."

I shrug, tears muddying my vision. "Do it."

She presses her lips together, and the salt cascades into the tub. A flurry of curse words flies from my tongue as the salt penetrates my wounds, scalding and sharp.

"Elle?" His low voice comes from the bedroom.

"Wait there, Your Highness," Larissa commands. "Your lady is indecent."

I can't help but chuckle. After several moments of soaking in the salt water, Larissa helps me out, dabs me dry with a towel, and slips a robe around me.

"Come in, Ruben," I say. My hand flies to my mouth, realising I've uttered his name.

Larissa's brows arch so high they almost disappear into her nut-brown hair. "That's his name?" she whispers, her smile so bright and amused that I can't help but mirror her. "Ruben."

"Shh!" I laugh, grabbing her hands.

Ruben pokes his head into the doorway. "Great. My father's big secret revealed."

Her cheeks flush pink, and she mutters his name again slowly, spelling out the syllables, tasting the roll of the R. "I swear I won't tell anyone, *Ruben*." She sticks her finger at me. "Now, I'll return soon to put ointment on the wounds. Just... don't tell the king."

I gag and scoff. "As long as you promise to never utter the word *ointment* again."

She swats me and marches out of the room.

"Gods, Elle," he whispers, an ache jolting through his voice. "What has he done to you?"

"It's nothing," I say, ducking my chin away.

He circles me, and heat flares on my skin as he stops, touching my shoulders. Ruben slowly, slowly pulls the robe down an inch and releases a curse as he takes in the angry welts and severed flesh. "It's not nothing, Elle." His growl bounces around the chamber. "I… am going to kill him. Must kill him."

I grab his collar and kiss him. His groan ignites a fire in my heart, and I push him against the wall as our tongues brush. His hands find my waist, slipping into the robe, grazing my skin. I push his collar aside, feeling his hammering heart against my palm, his chest hot. He guides me towards the bed, his tongue gliding along my neck.

Too soon, he pulls away. "It's getting late. I should go."

"Why?" I say, panting as I lean in to kiss him again.

His moan makes me wild. "I can't have the Gods telling on me tonight. This kingdom, and my father's line of cruelty, is hanging on by a very thin thread."

"The night does not belong to the Gods," I say, uttering the phrase I have heard many of the non-worshippers bellow into storms from deep within the Convex villages when the famine's been at its worst. It is a phrase of longing for freedom.

He stares at me for several beats, studying the lines on my face. "No," he says at last, releasing a sigh of defeat. His fingers graze up my ribs, and I shiver. "The night is ours. And the stars can only dim back in envy."

He kisses me again, and I feel like tumbling into his light.

Chapter 34

On the first morning of spring, frost coats the field towards the charred skeleton of the Tranq building. The cold is bone-deep.

"A slow start to the season," Larissa says, bursting into my room without knocking. Her cheeks are rosy and splotchy, and her lips are tinted a deeper shade of pink.

I gasp, yanking the duvet up over my naked chest. "Yes. Please come in," I say, huffing into the blanket. "Thanks for asking."

She rolls her eyes and giggles, pushing the curtains further aside and cracking open the window. Frigid wind lashes the curtains like claws. "The festival will still go ahead," she says, voice tight.

I grimace, snatching the robe from the end of my bed and slipping it over my shoulders as I climb from the blankets. "I don't think the Convex have much to give for their taxes." The icy draft oozes past my neck, the hairs standing on end.

Larissa presses her lips together. "They must provide something. Everyone must pay their taxes in some form or face exile."

"I know the procedure," I say, my voice like a carved hollow.

She falls silent, padding into the bathroom and cranking the tub faucet. "Let's make sure you look your best. That way, when you stand with Ruben... I mean, Prince Talin, they might find hope and strength from you."

I scrunch my nose at her and slide into the tub, wincing at the scolding water. "I don't want anyone to look up to me. Any connection or loyalty to me is a death sentence. They know I must maintain my oath to King Talin."

She scrubs my arms with suds and a sponge. "Everyone knows who you really stand for, Elle."

I gulp and let Larissa cleanse my skin and hair. Their admiration of me could get them killed.

"I've hardly seen the prince for the past few weeks," I say glumly, watching the orange-red sun swell and stretch into the morning sky. "He's buried himself deep in administration for the wedding. Making deals with noblemen and strengthening the Tranqs."

"And how have your posts in the Convex Sector been this week?" She arches a brow, dunking my head into the water and working a lotion into the locks. "You were stationed in the Trades, weren't you?"

"It's terrible. The helmet helps hide my identity. But I'm sure they sense me there. I've got my father's eyes, and he had quite the reputation amongst my people." I blow out my cheeks, letting Larissa lift my head and rinse my hair beneath the faucet. "An elderly man collapsed right in front of me. I could... do nothing as he choked on

313

his own blood. Some sort of disease… probably from the brown water, fuelled by malnutrition. His ribs were swollen." I let out a hiss, trying to shove the images from my mind. But they burrowed deep, pasting themselves permanently to my memory.

"I can hardly bear to visit the Convex Sector. Too horrendous, with the rebels and wagons and bodies," she says and leans back, wringing out my locks and wrapping a towel around them, the smile tugging at her lips. "Can I tell you a secret?"

"What?" My brows shoot up, and I can feel the laugh bubble on my tongue before she even speaks.

"I've been… staying with a noble Concave man the last few weeks." Her words are hardly louder than a hush, but her giggle trills around us. "But you mustn't tell a soul."

I clamp a hand over my mouth, my jaw falling open. "Larissa, you sneaky thing! How? Who?"

"His name's Eros." Her cheeks flush, and her smile widens. "He's promised we will be married once the king dies, once we win the rebellion."

My eyes water, and I fling my dripping arms around her neck. "Oh, Larissa. You have made my entire year. I can't believe it."

Her laughter is enchanting magic that makes me want to sing and dance. "Can I tell you another secret?"

"There's more?" I let her help me out of the tub and into the soft fuzziness of a towel.

"Yes!" She rubs me down, squeezing the excess moisture from my hair. I slip into a robe. She taps her belly.

"No way. Now you are playing with me!"

"I'm not! It's true."

I fumble over my tongue, searching for the right words, but all I can do is pull her into another giggling cuddle.

A strange blend of fear and hope spiral around in my gut. *We were born in your world, but you will die in ours.* I taste the salt of my tears as I realise, with utter joy and breathlessness, that maybe, just maybe, this child will be born in our world. Not one where they will belong to a crown.

Someone knocks on the door an hour later as Larissa tugs and pulls at the hem of my dress. She plucks a stray eyebrow and fusses over the placement of my curls. "You must look like yourself," she says. "I'm only here to enhance your features, not alter them."

The red dress accentuates my breasts, hugs my hips and splays around my legs like flower petals from the depths of the earth. Rebellion glints in her eyes as she finishes fastening the knife to my thigh, draping the dress back over it.

"Come in, Your Highness," she chirps, smiling at me.

Pink creeps into my cheeks as Ruben steps into the room. He wears a dark navy coat with a white linen undershirt. His eyes drink in my body, and he smiles. "Elle." He licks his lips as humour threads his next words. "You're not blushing, are you? Getting sloppy in your royalty."

I shoot Larissa a glare when she waggles her brows at me. We bid her goodbye, and my stomach knots as I loop my arm with Ruben's, letting him lead me out of the room and down the hall.

"Don't we look like a couple fit for a wedding?" Ruben jokes, voice low and husky and light with amusement.

"Wipe that smirk from your face," I say, wishing I could swat him. "We can't have people thinking we are friends."

"Friends?" He chokes on the word.

"Oh, please." I roll my eyes as we round a corner. "I still can't stand you."

"Such mighty walls," he says with a purr. "What on Gods' Earth are you hiding behind them?"

Our first and second kiss flashes across my mind and grazes my lips. I shiver.

We arrive in the largest room adjacent to the foyer. The gates beyond the palace hang open, and a trail of Convex people stretches from the room, down the steps, out the gates and winding around the perimeter. A low rumble hums from the line. Fingers of sunshine spill in through the enormous, arched windows, staining the room in butter. King Talin sprawls on his throne, examining a cloth full of grain the elderly lady clutches before him. Two Tranqs, dressed head to toe in their armour, flank either side of him.

He grunts and flicks his nose, sending her scuttling away. The next person trembles as they hobble up, holding a plant. I recognise her from the apothecary.

Heads turn our way as we skirt the border of the room and find our place to the right of the king. I school my face into nothingness, knowing I cannot afford to show a lick of indifference to the king. So, I focus on my breathing. One after the other, the Convex people present an item of worth to King Talin. Grains, herbs, materials, animals. Someone even tries to hand over their child, which makes my breakfast almost return.

As the line slowly, painfully inches forward, I spot a familiar face. Madam Sallow. Even more haggard than the last time I saw her. She grumbles under her breath as she steps up to the king.

"Your hands are empty," King Talin says, not so much as batting an eye.

An apparition of a blade stabs my heart and a scream tears at my throat.

"Correct," she says, voice hoarse as if she's barely recovered from a cough. "I have come to say that you are a coward. Know this, a storm is coming for you. To sweep you up and turn these wretched walls into a place for us all. You may not live to see it, though. Not with Elle in your palace."

Ruben stiffens. The king lets out a dry laugh. He waves his hand dismissively. Two of the Tranqs swoop down, their armour clanking as they grab Madam Sallow.

"No!" The word flies from my mouth before I can catch it. Ruben grasps my wrist, silencing me. Tears dribble down my cheeks as they drag Madam Sallow out of the room. She doesn't protest. She certainly doesn't squirm. But she lets them take her to her fate.

King Talin makes a show of turning around and shooting me a sneer. He returns to the next Convex, presenting a bleating goat.

I focus on the warmth of Ruben's hand on my skin. He grounds me in place while the king grows drawn with boredom, lazily flicking the Convex through.

Finally, the herald beckons us and ushers us to the courtroom, which has been set up for a festival. Monstrous double doors open to the courtyard. Splotches of pastel hues swish with the jangle of gold and silver jewellery, the noblemen and ladies scattered through the sheen of sunlight tumbling through the indoor and outdoor courtyard. Fully armed Tranqs station the perimeter. Concave ladies lounge around tables, sipping wine and gorging on delicacies. Musicians clamber in one corner, the pluck of their instruments melting unpleasantly with the guffawing of men. Servants scurry around. Some tend to the tables. Others make drinks behind the bars. Some arrange and adjust the flowers and greenery planted in pots the size of tables. Towering marble pillars accentuate the space, sending curious beams of shadow reaching across the throngs.

Ruben grabs two goblets of sparkling wine from a passing servant and hands one to me. I thank the Gods silently and gulp it down, hoping it loosens my tight muscles fast and helps me forget about Madam Sallow. What am I going to tell Aston?

The question haunts me as I move through the festival. Concave citizens flaunt around us, peppering us with questions.

"Aren't you excited for the wedding?"

"What a beautiful couple!"

"Elle, what do you think of the Convex trying to crumble our kingdom?"

Thankfully, the champagne forms a light blanket across my mind, shielding my spirit from their insults. The next few hours blur by, and I practically float through the festival.

As the music changes tempo, waxing into a percussive number, a scream erupts from the end of the courtyard, piercing the sunlight and music like a blade. I whirl around, my hand instinctively reaching for my dagger. But I pin my back straight, remembering where I am.

"King Talin," a voice hisses so low it slides along my skin like the wind.

The musicians stop playing. People stand, craning their necks over one another.

There's another scream. A Veckling whispers the king's name again as it pounces, launching at a table. Chairs scrape and scatter, along with the people, except for one. The monster's front talons sink into the man's chest. His scream burrows a grave in my darkness.

The creature flings the man's corpse as it leaps towards the king. Tranqs lunge into defence, throwing their spears at the creature, piercing its thick, leathery skin. It howls and stumbles to the side, but not all the way to the floor, for the spears keep it propped up.

A thundering roar shakes the ground. Goblets rattle and clink together. Concaves shriek and retreat into the palace. Even the king doesn't move. And for a moment, neither do we.

Shivers scrape down my arms as they emerge from the haze. Rolling over the lip of the hill and barrelling through the palace gates like stampeding animals. Hundreds of Convex. Their shouts and warrior cries reverberate in my chest like a new-forged god of wrath wreaking havoc over the earth. Swords and blades waver above their heads. The Tranqs dive into the fray. Swords and spears clash. Shouts and dying yowls engulf my senses as Ruben drags me towards one of the side doors. Blood splatters the tables and walls. Some of it flecks my face as a hand clamps over my mouth and sharp nails dig into my wrist. I bark out a muffled curse and cough as I inhale the powder in the Tranqs palm.

The herb takes over at once. My muscles go limp. Clouds sweep across my vision, and the room sways and spins. In between the cacophony of the battle around me, he calls my name.

Chapter 35

I wake up to dry air grazing my arms and cheeks. Shadows, coldness, and stone surround me like a tempest from the depths of the God of Souls realm. My limbs and ribs are riddled with bruises and sores from laying on the stone floor for Gods know how long. I groan and curse as I sit up and peer into the gloom. Something or someone scratches and shuffles against the stone, coughing and spluttering. The stench of vomit, urine, and blood drench the otherwise stagnant air. My stomach churns as bile surges up my throat, and I clamp a hand over my mouth, swallowing it back down. A single candle shoots bravely towards the ceiling from its mount on the wall opposite my cell. Fragments of fiery light glint and gleam against the achromatic puddles and stone.

There's someone's skeleton propped up against the wall of the cell across from mine. A knife buried in his dried ribs. His mandible nothing more than crushed chips, pebbles, and dust beside his decay-stained pelvis.

That's when a scorching flame stretches across my abdomen and into my chest, down my arms. I hiss, reeling back. Whimpers dribble from my quivering lips as I take in the old and new blood staining my tunic. Wincing, I peel it up, and my heart sinks. There is a deep seeping wound carved into my stomach like I'm little more than game waiting to be skinned, the inky blood trailing towards the waistband of my pants. I shudder, and my teeth chatter as the fiery needles cascade in all directions of my stomach.

Where did this come from?

Why am I here?

"Ruben?" I mumble, pressure swelling in my chest.

Is he in the dungeon, too? Has King Talin tossed him down here to starve, to serve punishment for helping the girl who ignited a rebellion against his crown?

I bite my lip and tear the sleeve from my shirt. My torso shudders and trembles, my stomach muscles bouncing up and down as I gently, slowly place the grimy fabric over the wound. Fangs plunge into me, drawing sharp winces and groans from my cracked, dehydrated lips. My hands shake like a lonely leaf clinging to a tree branch, holding on for dear life before it falls to the snow. I wrap the fabric around my waist with feeble, pitiful energy. The tears dribbling over my lips taste of salt and copper.

Finally, I knot the fabric next to my hip. I reach out for the iron bars of the cell door, grateful for the frigid splinters pressing into my palms, distracting me from the pain. I pull myself closer, inch by inch.

My breath falls ragged. Blood rises into my cheeks. Sweat promenades with my tears.

"Is there anyone there?" I call out, cringing at the croak in my voice.

"Elle?" Aston's voice, so small and distant, chiming from the depths.

"Where are you?" I tug at the collar of my tunic. Air. I need air. My throat dries, and my breath catches a fissure in my throat.

"They locked us all up," he calls, his voice both distant and near, ricocheting against the cobweb-covered walls and my aching ribs. "Are you hurt?"

My whimper is his answer. But, of course, there is nothing he can do. There isn't much a prisoner can do. I shift myself back, muttering curses and yielding grunts as I lean against the wall, biting back the primal urge to scream. "It's only a... scratch."

There is a pause, and for a gut-wrenching moment, I wonder if he has passed out. "Are you dying?"

I startle at the bluntness of his question. "I'm fine."

"Let's agree to not lie to each other. We've been through too much for half-truths," he grumbles, and I wonder if he, too, is tattered with bruises and a wound leaking the life out of him.

I suck in the air, licking my lips as I swallow a wad of spit, desperate for it to coat my throat. "I'm... bleeding. Someone stabbed me. My stomach." My eyes scrunch shut as a tingly feeling creeps throughout my body, snuffling out the pain.

Aston rattles his door. The clank of metal against stone makes me flinch, and my hands fly to my ears. "Hey!" His shout reverberates into the ceiling. "We need a medic!" Aston yells and screams until his voice becomes hoarse.

The fire rolls through me like waves of nausea, snatching my breath away and weakening my muscles. Eventually, my body can no longer handle it, and I slip into a restless sleep, dreaming about Ruben and Lyra and a world without the king. I move in and out of sleep, shuddering, my teeth clattering like a dying animal in a snow desert. A bluish, purplish tint forms beneath my fingertips. Each time I open my eyes, the world bucks, and wisps of fuzz creep across my sight.

At some point, the fire across my stomach grows and throbs, demanding my attention like a rabid animal, dragging me from my stupor. A claw scrapes and knocks against my skull. Tears would flow if I had more water. A strangled groan tears from my throat as I peel off the crusty, bloody scrap of fabric, and bile burns my tongue. Puss oozes from the wound. I lean my head back against the wall and whimper, my chest rising and falling like I've sprinted across the bridge.

"Aston!" I call, forcing my voice to work. But it still crackles, drier than the skeleton across from me. "Aston!"

But he doesn't respond. Only the silence greets me. I wonder if the Tranqs let him out. But what if he's dead? Rotting in a shallow grave right now. Or loaded on the back of a wagon, ready to join the mass of corpses in the Convex Sector? Another hunk of flesh with no significance. A number.

My heart wants to shrivel up. I don't think it was designed to handle this much pain.

But he is the boy who delivers produce to the palace. How could his life not matter?

Thick tears stab my eyes and trickle into my mouth. Where is Ruben? Why isn't he helping me out of here?

The infection draws the last drops of moisture from my forehead, and they streak slowly down my temples. I slip in and out of delirium, coughing and spluttering and aching. Now and then, a Tranq stalks past like a wolf guarding pups in a den. But I don't even have the strength to tell them where to go.

The clack of the mouldy wooden door startles me from the jagged haze of my delirium. My forehead scorches, and sweat drips down my cheeks and runs cold down my back. A fever. Perfect. Footsteps scuttle along the dungeon hallway.

"Ruben?" I mumble, forcing myself to sit up against the wall. But I wince at the ache in my muscles. It is burrowing into me like a disease, and I fear…

A scruffy auburn mop of hair materialises before me, his light brown face morphing with the iron bars as the world spins. "Killian?"

"Oh, thank goodness," he says, blowing out his cheeks. "We've found you."

"Water," I mumble, releasing a dry cough. "I need water."

"How are you feeling, Elle?" he asks, arching a brow. The mole beneath his eye twitches.

"I'm… dying." I lift the cakey material from my abdomen. "See?"

Killian gulps, holding back a gag. The angry wound leaks translucent and yellowish pus. He smacks his lips and reaches through the bars, taking my cold, calloused hand. "You'll be okay, Elle. I'm going to find Ajax. We need to figure out how to get you out."

"Where's Ruben?" I ask, heaving a raspy breath. Gods, I sound pathetic.

Killian squeezes my thumb. "He's with Ajax, trying to get you out."

"Please don't leave me." My voice cracks, and all I want is to curl up into my mother's arms and let her carry me into the cosmos, where I belong. Numbness ripples through my libs. My eyelids fall as if tiny hands are trying their best to yank them closed like blinds.

"We'll be back," he says, withdrawing his hand and standing. I don't even have the strength to reach out and grab his ankle. "I need to tell Ruben and Ajax where you are. I don't have a key, Elle. I'm sorry."

I force myself to swallow the dusty pocket of air in my throat. "Come back for me. I just wanted to save my sister. I didn't mean for this all to happen."

Killian stiffens, matching the stone around him. "I know, Elle. I'll be back." His echoing footsteps beat at my eardrums like the blade of an axe.

Those little hands yank my eyes shut, and I welcome the darkness. Was I wrong about Ruben all this time? In thinking he was the night incarnate. It seems the darkness burrowed into my battered, wrecked bones long ago.

But he.

He is the light between the darkness.

His is a feeling that sunk beneath my chest at some moment in time between the moon and the shadow. Insistent. Unwelcome.

Silence creeps around me for the first time since I arrived in the dungeon. It curls and twists around my guts and rings in my ears.

"I guess my luck finally caught up with me. The Gods got tired of all my silly whims and wins," I say, letting out a braying giggle.

Am I talking to myself?

"Yes."

Look at you. Finally locked up to rot, where you belong.

"But I didn't do anything. I only tried to save my sister. To keep my promise to my parents."

And look where that got you? She is decaying in a mass grave as we speak.

"Mama," I mumble, my breath hitching in my throat. "Papa. I'm sorry to have failed you."

My words carry on wispy tendrils into the cold and stone, leaving nothing but the gaping hollow of loneliness in their wake.

At some point, a figure traipses past, wearing a helmet with curved horns. He crouches in front of my cell. Green eyes gleaming like jewels.

"Ruben," I mumble, reaching for the door. But his figure blurs into a phantom of my delirium.

Night and day stop existing. They no longer matter. Images of my sister and my parents morph into one another. Childhood memories; the good and the terror and the hunger.

A groaning creak jolts me from my trance, and I peel my eyes open. Gods know how many days I've been here, surviving off a jug of water and a hunk of bread every so often.

"Gods, you look terrible." A voice swims into my head.

I blink, rolling my head to the side. A shadowy figure stands in front of the cell, his pale fingers folded around the bars. I almost close my eyes again, convinced for a moment it's another hallucination. But the jumping flame in the lantern on the floor flecks against the person's face, gilding the jade eyes and throwing light over the ridged scar across his left cheek.

He crouches down and pulls the hood of his cloak off his head.

"Oh, Elle," he says, voice low and hushed as he brushes his white-blond hair from his face. "I have something that can heal that nasty infection and wound." He reaches into his cloak's pocket, pulling out a small, corked bottle filled with dark crimson liquid. It shimmers in the candlelight like it has captured the cosmos, stars, and the darkness between its glass walls.

Who are you? I want to ask. But my voice cuts before the words make it, too hoarse and haggard from days of dehydration, infection, and not speaking.

"Sorry for the confusion," he says, his lip twitching as if he's a monster hiding behind a mask of normalcy, his true nature thrashing against the bonds. "But this kingdom does seem confusing. I'm from beyond the walls, so it's not familiar here. But I'm wondering if I was, in fact, better off growing up outside."

My mind reels, and I open my mouth. "What the hell?" I say, voice raspy and words barely audible.

"I think you may know my brother." He pops the cork out of the bottle and reaches through the bar, tilting his head. "Would you like to feel better, Elle?"

I narrow my eyes, pressing my lips together.

He heaves a sigh and takes a swig, grimacing. "See? It doesn't taste great. But I promise, it's safe. It looks like you need it." He gestures to the grotty, festering wound on my stomach and to my sweaty, pallid face.

Against my better judgement and every instinct, I take the bottle and bring it to my lips.

Chapter 36

When I wake up, the strange man is no longer there. But the eclipse over my vision and mind has waxed away. Footsteps lumber down the hallway, and someone shoves a key into the lock of my cell. I grind my teeth as the door creaks open. The Tranq leers down at me through the slits in his helmet like a vulture eyeing a carcass. I swallow the dryness in my mouth.

"The king has requested your release," the Tranq says, voice gruff. He grips the cell door, his indifferent gaze sliding over me.

I raise my brows, pretending to nurse a bruise on my rib. "That must be a sick joke. Why now? I was about to rot away, and I wouldn't have been a problem for him anymore."

I decide to feign weakness and delirium, knowing they are not aware of the stranger who came into the dungeons. His armour clanks as he steps down the corridor. "You are welcome to stay here if you'd prefer."

Grumbling, I steel my dignity before prying myself to my feet. Despite the exhaustion still plaguing my muscles and eyelids, the injuries I sustained in the cell have shrivelled away. I am only left with poking-out bones and blood stains. My footsteps are heavy and unrhythmic as I follow the Tranq down the empty, echoing dungeon hallway and up the staircase at the end.

"Why has he requested my release?" I blurt out, curiosity driving the words into the hallway.

He glances over his shoulder. "Don't you have a wedding coming up in a week?"

I blink and try to gulp, but thirst still has me in its vice. "A week?"

As we emerge into the palace, sunlight gobbles me up. I hiss, throwing my hands up. My heart thumps, and a shiver spider-walks down my spine as light sprawls over my body. Warmth. The general shuffle of servants going about their day grows around me as I open my eyes, adjusting to the blazing light. My lips part. I take a tentative step closer to the windows, and my fingers quiver. Frost no longer coats the gardens beyond the windows, and a couple of butterflies flitter between the trees below. Time did not exist in the dungeon.

"It's spring," I say.

"Yes."

I allow myself to pause, indulging in the tepid light on my grimy, pallid skin. For only a couple of beats. I quickly fall back into step and keep moving. We round a corner, climb more flights of stairs, and arrive at my bed chamber. Larissa scurries from the wardrobe, her cheeks drawn. She doesn't even acknowledge the Tranq. "Oh, Elle," she says, voice cracking. "You look awful!"

She grasps my wrist and tugs me deeper into the room, slamming the door in the Tranq's face. Tears prickle my eyes as she draws me a bath and opens the window.

"You must be in desperate need of sunlight and air," she says, helping peel the tacky, torn rags from my skin. "Let's get you cleaned, and you can sit in the sun for a while."

She helps me into the steaming tub, and I almost purr as the hot water seeps into my aching flesh. After scrubbing every speck of dirt, blood, and pus from my skin, she hauls me out of the tub and into a robe, sitting me on a chair in front of the window. Sunlight pours into my hair, transforming it into flames. I shiver, letting it draw colour to my skin for the first time in weeks.

"Do you want to talk about the prison?" Larissa says in a timid voice, pulling up another chair.

I heave a sigh, thinking about it. "It can be summarised as a nice royal concoction of trauma and hallucinations." A hum trickles into the room. Dozens of Convex men mill around the skeleton of the Tranq building, sawing chunks of wood and arranging them over the charred ground, forging new foundations.

Larissa shudders and bites her lip. "Horrid."

I can hardly look her in the eye and keep my gaze pinned on the happenings outside the palace walls. "Did you hear of anyone entering the dungeons last night?"

Images of the man with white, blond hair and green eyes wade into my mind, pieces like a shattered mirror.

She purses her chapped lips. "No. Who are you talking about?"

I shake my head. "Never mind. Maybe I hallucinated something."

Her thin, dark brow arches. But she doesn't push it. "Speaking of which." She stands and grabs a platter from a table. There is a bowl of rice with crushed tomatoes, potatoes, and a bowl of pumpkin soup. I almost throw up from eating it so fast.

When I finish, Larissa snorts, pointing to the dribble of soup down my chin. I scrub my teeth and return to the chair. Larissa scurries out from the wardrobe with a dress. This time, it's black. The colour between stars.

"Have you seen much of… Ruben?" I'm afraid even uttering his name will unearth wrath in me that the Gods would envy.

"He has been lying low," she says after a beat, laying the dress on the bed and smoothing out the crinkles. "I've seen him training in the northern forest. With your friend."

"Aston?"

"Yes. The cute blond one."

I shoot her a sly grin. Silently, I hope Ruben and the others have been training to help me kill the king.

Larissa helps me dress into the gown. She brushes out my matted hair, swipes an inky substance over my lashes, kohl onto my brows, and pats crushed rose stain onto my lips. Lastly, she affixes my two blades beneath my skirt.

"I'm nervous to see the prince…" The words fly from my mouth like birds fleeing a cat. "Ruben, I mean." He *must* have a reason for not trying to save me. Must have. Could he have been locked up, too?

Amusement tugs at her mouth, and the sunlight dances in her eyes. "He has made it clear he missed you." She arranges my curls and then peers into my eyes. "Do you have feelings for him?"

I pause, and my lips part. "Um."

"I know this marriage is arranged, but... the way he looks at you, it even makes *me* blush."

My cheeks burn like the crackling hearth. "I haven't been able to think of him like that recently. I've been focused on survival." A lie, of course.

"I know. Hopefully, you can talk to him." She steps back, tilting her head. That's when there's a knock on the door. Larissa throws me a wink. "And there he is. Come in, Your Highness."

I roll my eyes, but my heart hammers.

"Elle," he whispers my name like it pushes a dagger into his heart. As he steps up to me, a muscle feathers in his jaw as he drinks in my appearance. His trembling fingers brush my cheeks. "What has he done to you?"

Rage explodes through my body, and I reach for my father's blade, shoving Ruben against the wall and pinning the tip of the blade against his throat so quickly he can hardly utter a curse. "More like where in the *kingdom* have you been?"

Larissa squeaks, but I am blinded to anything but the fury tearing through me.

A muscle ripples in his jaw, and his teeth bear. "As if I *chose to* stay away from the likes of you. He kept me away."

I gulp, feeling like I might burst into flames, scream, or run away. I step back, trying not to scoff as his hand instinctively flies to his throat, nursing the nick on his skin. "How am I meant to face him?" My voice cracks, and I want to crumble. "How am I meant to feign my loyalty now?"

He reaches out, slowly, carefully, like I might strike again, and tucks a curl behind my ear. "You will just have to fake it until you get the pleasure of slitting his throat."

Needles shoot through my chest, and I stiffen. "He's still your father."

"It... doesn't matter." Those forest eyes water. "There will be a relief of letting you put him on a pyre. I'm... tired of him."

A dry scoff falls from my lips. "We are the same, you and I."

"The same, but different." His mouth twitches upward. "And yet... you have lit a flame within my darkness."

Larissa clears her throat, and I pull away. My cheeks burn. Ruben leans back against the window ledge as I wrap her in a hug and thank her.

Her lip quivers as she smiles. "I'm ready for this to end." She touches her belly. "My child deserves a new world."

Ruben and I sweep out of the room and down the hall, arm in arm, even though that rage still scalds my insides. His warmth and scent dance through my veins, and my limbs pluck to life like a plant in the sunshine.

"You never came to find me." The words spill untethered, and a tear slips out of my eye before I can stop it.

He tenses his shoulders. "I couldn't, Elle. My father threw me in the prison near his quarters for the first few days. Then he said he'd kill you if he caught me seeing you."

My stomach drops, and I taste the salt of another tear. "I needed you." The pitiful crack in my voice makes me want to curse at the sinking sun outside the arched windows. "You… needed me, too."

His Adam's apple bobs, and he sucks in a harsh breath. "More than anything. I wanted to crawl home to you in the early hours. But I was afraid. Torn. I didn't know what was worse, letting you suffer or giving you a death sentence."

A shiver ripples down my spine, and I fight the tears prickling my eyes. "Do we have to go to this stupid ball?" His heat, his scent, makes my vision blur and my skin crackle with fire. "Can't we hide somewhere?"

"We could hide in the dungeons?"

I smack his arm. "Too soon." But the laughter spills from me before I can catch it. "Does he still want us married?"

"He does." His voice is low and husky. "We must keep playing the game. He still thinks our marriage would unite the Sectors and quell the rebellion."

"We need to convince the Concaves to… turn against him."

The rumble of the crowd in the ballroom filters down the hallway in great sweeps. Sweat pools in my palms as I realise I'm about to see the king again. Golden evening light pours into the arched windows of the corridor, igniting Ruben's eyes and setting my hair alight. I grip his arm tighter as we step around the corner and cross the threshold into the hum of the ballroom. Someone hands me a goblet of wine, and I'm grateful for the heat in the back of my throat.

King Talin lounges on a throne set up at the rear of the room, surrounded by Tranqs and heralds fanning his face and tripping over themselves to feed him and water him with wine. His snake-like gaze lands on me at once. He sneers. I force my face to remain impassive as we move deeper into the room.

"We must greet my father," Ruben whispers. "It is customary at the ball before the wedding."

I grumble beneath my breath as we cross the ballroom. Concave folk step out of our way, their envious gazes stabbing my back.

The king adjusts his violet cape as he watches us trail up to him. He sips from his goblet and arches a manicured brow. "Elle. You look... healthy."

"Good evening, Father," Ruben says, bowing.

I curtsey and shove a polite smile onto my face. "A lovely ball before our royal wedding, Your Majesty. We are grateful for your... hospitality and generosity."

His lip stretches. "Oh, Elle. Nothing but the best for my only son and his bride. You are going to teach our Convex people that your loyalty is with *us*."

Venom crackles on my tongue. "My devotion to your son should do the trick."

We curtsey and bow again before slipping away, and I blow out my cheeks, loosening my shoulders. "Thank the Gods," I mutter beneath my breath.

I sip the rest of my wine, waiting for it to taint my nervous system. As I scan the room, looking for Ajax or Killian, the king's harsh, raspy voice floats into the distance. "If this wedding doesn't quell the uprisings, I will kill her."

His words are daggers grazing my bones. But I refuse to yield a sliver of emotion on my face. Ajax sweeps up to me. "Surely, you would allow your newest, truest friend a dance?" His navy waistcoat gleams in the flickering glow of the candles flanking our right. Ruben bows and steps away, turning to greet some noblemen.

I take Ajax's hand, and he spins me around. As he brings me closer to his chest, I focus on calming my breath. "What a strange turn of events. I was… rotting in a dungeon this morning. Yet, here I am, at a royal ball, dressed in glamour."

"Have you seen Killian tonight?" Ajax asks, his voice hardly louder than a breath.

We sway from side to side, and I feign a pleasant smile, hoping to deter nosey stares. "What do you mean?"

"He's… not sure about coming to the ball. He snapped at me when I told him you'd be in attendance tonight."

I angle my head, pinching my brows as the musicians break into a string number that bores into my ears.

"Hey, have you spoken to Aston? He needs to warn you—" But his words become a din as the king's choppy tone creeps back into my consciousness.

"The true test will be the Concaves' loyalty," the king whispers, releasing a braying chuckle as he speaks to one of his right-hand men. "They are my true source of power. My most mighty tool. As long as

I have them on my side, the Convex have no hope of dragging me onto a pyre. But I daresay I'd let the Concaves starve if I didn't need them."

I almost choke on the wine. Ruben approaches, and Ajax steps aside, casting me as a strange look. But I let Ruben tug me away and plaster a grin on my face. "Shall we dance?" I say, pretending to have not heard the king.

He nods and leads me onto the dance floor. "Let's give my father something else to talk about."

As we slip through the crowd, I catch a couple of Concave men glaring at the king with such darkness and bloodthirst it startles me.

Ruben and I twirl around the dance floor as the music increases into a crescendo. The drums reverberate in my chest, and his warmth makes me want to dance on this earth forever.

"You look stunning, Elle," he says. "If it isn't obvious."

I bite my mouth, weakness slipping into my knees. His lips sit only inches above my own. As we spin, I catch the king glowering at us, scrutinising us like a viper sizing up a rat. And I want to put on a show. I grab Ruben's face and pull him in, kissing him with such fire I feel him melt into me like snow from a tree. Gasps of surprise and envy sprout around us like weeds. I smile into the kiss, pulling him closer by his shirt, slipping my fingers between the buttons, and feeling his scorching skin beneath. His thundering heart. I find myself wishing no one else was here at all.

When we part, I glance at the king and throw him a smirk. The ballroom erupts into cheers and whoops, the sound thundering through my blood. A few noblemen swarm us, nattering away about their excitement for the upcoming wedding.

Through the chaos of clinking goblets, tumbling wine, and dancing candlelight, I spot the Concave men from before slinking out of the ballroom, heads ducked. A glint of murder in their eyes.

Chapter 37

An unsettling feeling sinks into my gut. I try to shake the men from my mind as Aston swoops up to us. But those knots are bound tight.

"May I take the lady for a dance?" he says, glancing between me and Ruben. A soft look etched into his face.

The musicians change to a string-led number, the lead man plucking his cello as if his life depends on it.

"I could not say no to my friend, could I?" I kiss Ruben again and take Aston's hand.

His hand is clammy in mine as we spin around. "I am surprised you are here."

"And same to you. Where... have you been?" I dare ask, feeling my heart slow at the presence of my oldest friend.

"Preparing," he says, his voice resolute. But he studies my face, glancing at my arms, brows pinching. "How are you only covered in bruises? I thought you'd be bedridden."

"I am wondering the same. Someone… or something came into the dungeon last night—"

"Look, Elle," Aston says, breathless, his face reddening. "They are coming. Any minute now."

"Who?"

His jaw tightens. "You know who. I've been rounding them up, telling them about your plight in the dungeons. They were coming to free you, to burn this palace to the ground."

The string music melts back into a bone-picking thrum, the rhythm synchronising with my heart beating for rebellion. And the world echoes and shrinks. They are coming.

The rage, the lifetime of grief and suffering rise from the depths. Shadows the colour of the night sky, seep through my body.

"They are coming," I say.

A scream rips through the ballroom. I snap out of Aston's arms and freeze as everyone backs towards the walls, frantic energy tearing through the air like the violent gust of a storm. More screams. A blade slices through the ballroom, spinning before thudding into the herald's neck, sticking out the other side. Silence snaps around me as the herald gurgles and blubbers, eyes bulging, a single line of blood trailing from the corner of his lips. His knees buckle. The king jumps to his feet and pulls out his sword.

"Who was that?" he bellows, voice shaking the room.

His glare slices through the trembling, paling Concaves.

"It was me," I say, lying through my teeth, my father's spirit barrelling through me. I yank the knife from beneath my skirt and hurl it. Shrieks stab the room as the blade sings past the king, catching his ear. "This is our world now, Your Majesty." As I speak, the ground tremors, and my heart thumps, adrenaline scorching through my veins. A sneer carved from the very shadows forms on my face, and I withdraw another blade. My father's blade. I hold his memory close. "And you will die in it."

On cue, a roar explodes from the hallways. It billows and envelopes my senses like a raging storm of the Gods. I feel it in my chest and my gut. My pulse thrums instinctively. A battle cry. Then, a chant that chills the marrow of my bones. "Kill the king! Kill the king!"

The thunder stampedes into the ballroom, throwing the roof into the cosmos. The prisoners, the Convex, and the Tranqs charge into the crowd, knives and swords rattling before they swing, cleaving through the Tranqs still loyal to the king and through the Concaves. Metal clashes against metal and bone and flesh as the chaos rips into the king's precious reign of control, prying his grip open inch by inch. For a moment, all I can do is stand there. The death and screams and darkness swarm and surge around me. I spot Aston parrying his sword with the king's Tranq. Ice tears into my chest as the Tranq knocks the blade from Aston's grip and him to his back. I shout his name, launching into the flurry to find him.

"Elle!"

Ruben yells, grabbing my arm and slinging his bow and quiver over his shoulder. "We need to move!"

343

But I cannot. Some of the Concaves are still fighting for the king. Tranqs battle with one another, spears and swords and blood flying and colliding. The clang of blades crashing against one another builds and thrashes around me. Someone slams into me, knocking me to the floor, and pain bursts across my skull when it hits the marble. I cry out, reaching for my other knife. But a boot slams onto my wrist, pinning the limb to the floor. Whimpers and curses fly from my mouth.

Auburn hair sways across my teary vision, and my heart jumps into my throat. "Killian?" I hardly get the name out before his hand clamps around my throat, and his other brings a knife to my jugular vein.

I blink and gasp as he presses his fingers into my windpipe while the pandemonium ensues around us.

"You've ruined everything, Elle," he growls, tears streaming down his splotchy face.

"What the hell, Killian?" I splutter, wheezing in primal desperation.

"You killed my friend," he says, lip curling, nose running. "You almost killed Ruben."

My stomach clenches. "He was your friend, too."

"Of course he was." Spit flies into my face as his knife cuts into my skin. He jerks his head to the wild battle around us. "Look at the anarchy you've caused. This is all your fault. My sector is hanging on by a very thin thread."

"I thought you wanted equality?"

His tear splashes onto my face. "My mother told me about how she used to starve. How she was once one of you."

344

"One of me?" My mind stretches and whirls, and the world laments around me. "She was a Convex, wasn't she?"

A vein pulses in his temple, and his face transcends a shade of violet. "I can't have my sisters starve like the kids I see playing on the other side of the river. My mother can't know hunger again."

An utterly feral gleam settles into his eyes, and he bares his yellowed teeth. For a breath, I wait for the blow, for his knife to slice into my throat. But his dog-like yelp clatters around my ears as someone yanks him off me. He releases a twine of almost indecipherable curses, slipping across the marble. Ruben casts him a tight look of disdain. Killian crawls away, cowering against the wall. But a calm demeanour washes through him, his jaw closing, his shoulders loosening. As if the terror-laced, protective instincts have snapped away, replaced by the stoic person I thought was my friend, my ally.

"Come on, Elle," Ruben says, clenching his fists. "We have things to do that are better than this traitor."

I give a sharp nod.

"Ruben," Killian murmurs, scrambling to his feet. "You must see where I'm coming from. She killed our friend. If we share the Concave resources with the Convex, we will all suffer. There won't be enough to go around. People will... my family will go hungry. We need order. Not the likes of Elle."

"She is fire, Killian," Ruben snarls, taking a heavy step forward, that cosmic darkness churning around him. "She is hope for *all* of us. And far braver than any of us ever were. You have made a mistake."

He grabs my wrist and tugs me away into the fray of knives and blood and screams. Killian disappears into the hell of it all, and I frantically glance around for Ajax and Aston.

345

"They're okay, Elle," Ruben says, seeming to read my thoughts. "Let's go. The king's gone."

He releases my hand, and we shove our way through the ballroom battle, scarcely squeezing out with all our limbs intact and the blood within our flesh.

"Do you have a knife?" He glances at me as we jog through the walls of portraits. All the kings of our history watch us as we hasten to kill the one in reign.

"Yes."

Ruben leads me through the maze of the palace, into the northernmost wing, where a wide, spiral staircase shoots into the sky. My stomach churns, and I fight the urge to pause and throw up as everything spins around me from all the twists and turns of the never-ending staircase.

Ruben crashes into King Talin's foyer—which is enchanted by darkness. Someone whimpers on the floor. Moonlight cuts into the window, criss-crossing over their figure and the telltale crimson blood spilling from their chest.

"Elle." A weak, trembling whisper. That voice, I know all too well.

"Larissa," I gasp, crumbling to my knees beside her.

A knife is embedded in her ribs, and blood splutters out, thick and taunting. Ruben tears his shirt off and crouches down, pressing it into her wound.

"What happened? Who did this?" His words crack, and his lip wavers. "Was it my father?"

She nods, weak. Tears slip down her face, falling into her ears. "I caught the king trying to escape." Her voice is raspy and staggered like she's downed shots of vodka. "Tried to stall him. But he stabbed me."

"Why on earth would you do that?" Fury ploughs through me as my body tries to shield my spirit from the impending reality before me.

Her cracked lip tugs into a smile. "I wanted to be brave like you, Elle."

The silence after lays my soul bare. "I'm going to get you help." I hardly shove the words out as I scramble to my feet, but she reaches out, grasping my hand.

"No, Elle," she says, her brown, doe eyes glimmering with tears but draining of light. "Stay."

I shake my head furiously. "I am not going to let you die."

"Just..." She trembles, sucking in quick, rattling breaths. "Find my love. Tell him I am sorry. My child and I will be waiting for him in the stars."

"No." My eyes burn, and my vision muddies. "You will live."

Her hand tightens around mine. "We will be safe now."

"You have to fight." I cry out. "You have to fight, for your baby, for you!"

Her teeth clack. "You have been the truest friend, my dear Elle. My hero. Thank you." More tears dribble down her paling cheeks. "You have changed our world. The fire has found a home in you, and I am grateful."

Ruben takes Larissa's other hand, his eyes blurred.

She smiles. "Ruben. Ruben." She says the name slowly, tasting the sound and the syllables. Her eyes flit closed. "I am glad I got to hear your lovely name. Thank you for being my friend."

Her lips part, and her hands loosen as she heaves a final breath. One final tear trails and drips into the pool of her blood.

"Larissa," I say, grabbing her shoulder and giving her a shake. "Larissa!"

He touches my shoulder. "She's gone, Elle."

"No!" My voice rocks as I pull her into my arms. "Larissa." Sobs clatter through my chest.

But I startle at the footsteps bounding up the stairs and down the hall. The door crashes open, and Killian bursts into the room, red-faced, nose and mouth contorted in anger. His sword drips with fresh blood, and he swings at us.

I leap up in an instant, pulling out my dagger and blocking his attack. He growls, and we push one another.

"Killian!" Ruben bellows. "Back down."

We parry one another, and he screams and hisses, slashing at me with such thirst for blood that the terror builds and crackles in my throat and chest. My heart pounds, and I can't even cast Ruben a glance as our blades clash with one another with the desperate speed of a hummingbird's beating wings.

"Stop, Killian!" I cry, voice breaking. Tears stream down my face, and I swipe them away with my spare hand.

"You've ruined everything, Elle!" he shouts, smacking the blade at my face and catching my cheek with the sliver of the tip. "You took everything from us. Killed my friend. You burrowed your way into Ruben's heart. And now I must protect my sisters and my mother from the consequences of what you are doing to this kingdom."

"There will be enough food to go around! We will figure it out." Ruben's words split as the anguish demands attention, and he pulls out his bow, nocking an arrow, pointing it at us. But he can't fire. Not while we flounder back and forth too quickly for him to aim at Killian with precision.

A sob flies from Killian's mouth, and he spits bloody saliva. "My mother has been through enough. Not again. She can't go back."

Our blades reverberate as they slap one another. Adrenaline and darkness surge through my bloodstream. Killian has never starved a day in his life. Never seen his loved ones fade into mere shells and skeletons of themselves. Never watched them be shoved from the gates like lambs forced into a slaughterhouse. Nor had to fight for his rights. And yet, I hear his words loud and clear. He knows that his loved one's suffering is a constant looming threat within these royal walls and is consumed by the need to protect them. I know that feeling all too well, and I know the pain of failing. I scream and shove, and he stumbles back, slamming into the wall and smacking his head. He grunts, grinding his teeth and whimpering. In one swift movement, I snatch the sword from his grasp and send it scattering across the floor. He curses and grapples for my throat, but I press the tip of my blade against his jugular, letting a droplet of blood ooze out. Killian cries out and squirms against the wall.

Finally, Ruben fires, hitting Killian in the shoulder. He howls, almost shattering the windows and my heart. Bile scorches my throat as he collapses to the floor, screaming and wailing and writhing. I back away, tremoring.

"You got this?" I say to Ruben.

His widened eyes dart to me, and he steps forward, grabbing my bloodied face and kissing me with such fierceness he must hold me steady. "I got this," he says. "Go, Elle."

I glance at Killian. Then, one last time at Larissa's body before I flee higher into the tower to find the king.

Chapter 38

My breaths echo off the narrow tower walls as I climb up the spiral staircase. Sobs fall from my lips each time Larissa's death flashes across my mind, gripping my heart in the claws of shock.

Screams and shouts snap up from below me, cold as the king's heart. I don't stop. Even though every instinct urges me to help Ruben. Wind batters and howls through the cracks in the windows as I pass, the glass rattling. I simply stumble blindly through the raging tempest of night and lament.

Finally, I arrive at the top of the spiral stairs and slam my shoulder into the wooden door, shoving it open. Thick shadows drape over the room, not a single blinking candle, as if the king has only ever known darkness—as if he's never seen the light.

The king chuckles from somewhere in the gloom, and a chill plunges into my gut. His gaunt figure looms before the arched window of the tallest tower, overlooking his kingdom, the moonlight gilding his stubble and green eyes. Fires and riots consume the Concave and Convex Sectors. Smoke plumes into the night sky, melting into the inkiness of it all, smothering the stars.

"I should have trusted my intuition," the king says, voice low, dripping with disgust and the distinct waver of fear. "Never should I have allowed you to live. Look at what you've done."

"It's finished, Talin," I say, trudging closer, spinning my knife. The pungent stench of soot drifts in with the wind. "Step down."

"Of course, *Elle*." He spits out my name, turning his chin, his body following. I startle at the severed flesh on his cheek, the blood smeared and dripping down his face, soaking into his gown. He removes his crown and holds it out. The pathetic encompassment of human greed to little end glints at me like the fangs of a beast. "I suppose you think this belongs to you. That you have the right to pry it from me with your blood-drenched hands."

I scoff, suddenly feeling an inch tall and wishing for nothing more than to flee. But I square my shoulders and take another step. "The people will decide who will lead them."

"You do not understand what you have done." He places the crown back on his head and paces the small room. "There is not enough food to go around. Not with the blight. Now, the Convex people are going to grow arrogant and take the Concave food. I predict a civil war within the kingdom, Elle."

"Don't lie to me," I snap, echoing his own words. "You don't care about that. You are afraid of losing control, of losing power. And most of all, you are afraid of being alone."

"You think you're a perceptive thing." He waggles his finger and releases a shredded cough, patting the already blood-stained cloth to his mouth.

"It doesn't matter anyway." I lunge at the king, kicking him in the gut. He staggers back, smacking into the window ledge. I grab his collar and shove the knife against his throat, gathering the primal, inhuman will to slice his neck open. I can do this. *Do* this.

He gurgles and groans, leaning back out of the window as rioters below shout his name and launch knives and spears, cursing his name to the depths of the God of Soul's realm.

An icy, hollow look, awoken by ancient instinct, slithers into those green eyes as I press the blade against his neck, letting the blood drip, drip, drip out. He whimpers and cowers. I lick my lips, revelling in the sight and feeling of the king beneath my blade... my father's blade. The serpent Fallon crest reminds me of who I came from and the man who planted the fire and the shadow within me from a young age. Would he be proud of me? Would he cheer me on?

Yes, I would, my father's voice, the one that never left my memory, echoes in my head.

"Stop," Talin hisses, trying to thrash. But I push harder. His eyes bulge, and his face turns the shade of the bodies that clog the Convex carts before mass burial—the bodies *he* created. "Elle!"

"Give me one good reason," I say, my voice a rusty knife as he recoils, leaning out of the window.

"Let me go first," he says, spluttering saliva into my face. An arrow whizzes past his temple, and he cries out, trembling beneath me.

"Pathetic," I say, clicking my tongue. "I should throw you out. Let the wolves below finish you off. You killed my entire family, Your *Majesty*. Made my people starve for decades. Made them train for a phantom war. Destroyed your son. I don't believe there is a lick of goodness in you."

His eyes flash, lips curling as a flaming spear launches past his head. "Ungrateful bitch."

The throngs of vengeful Convex and Concave rebels pile hunks of wood below. Others run deeper into the palace ground, stabbing Tranqs in the neck with kitchen knives while gripping chunks of wood and handfuls of kindling. A dozen men march forward with their torches and ignite the piles of wood.

"Burn the king to the ground! Burn the king to the ground!" the war cry ripples past my ears, and I smirk.

"It seems they all agree with me. You have taken everything from us. All because you couldn't stand to lose power. All because you were afraid of us spilling into the wasteland and finding our own community. Because you are too afraid to be alone. You know you couldn't survive without us."

He writhes and jerks, almost tossing me off, but I move the knife along his throat, cutting the skin. "I'd survive as long as the Shadowtooth remains swimming in the lake," he snarls, baring his teeth. "As long as she reproduces offspring. She has kept me going for a *long* time."

I loosen the pressure of the dagger. "What are you talking about?"

"Remove the knife, Elle. Let me step away from the window so I can explain."

354

The war hum pummels my ribs as I narrow my eyes. Tendrils of smoke twirl and leap into the window, coiling around the king's neck like a noose.

"Fine." I step back but still point the knife at him. "Prove to me you have something worth redeeming."

He clears his throat, tugging at his coat, giving his head a small shake. I tap my foot impatiently as he peers out of the window, grimacing as the rioters continue to bellow out the same chilling chant. He gestures for the seats cluttered around a small round mahogany table. A decanter of whisky and tumblers sit atop.

I spin the blade, keeping it hanging at my side as I sit and wait. The king takes his time, watching the wisps of smoke rise past the window. A muscle ripples in his cheek. He reaches for the cut on his neck, dabbing it with his fingers and grimacing at the crimson stain. For a fleeting breath, I get a glimpse of who the king really is... who he has been all along: just a man. A tear slips down his cheek as if he can sense it too, as if the fires and chants below have stripped him down, revealing the human, the threadbare soul beneath.

A lump forms in the back of my throat, and a sliver... just a sliver... of my raging urge for retribution sheds away.

"My son Ruben is not *entirely* from the kingdom," he says, his voice made of stone, pouring the whisky into the glasses. He smacks his lips together as he gulps it down, casting a wary gaze at the window. "But my other son—it is he I am afraid of. Who *anyone* should be afraid of. He is the true monster of us all."

"I beg your pardon?" I'd swig the whisky, too, if I didn't need all my senses.

He pours another drink, and his green eyes roam my face, relishing in my confusion. "I am from a kingdom far away from here. Far beyond the walls. I committed a heinous crime myself. Would you believe it? I murdered the guardsmen who… did what they wanted to my wife."

"Ruben's mother?" I raise my brows in feigned indifference, trying to hide the thundering of my heart.

"Not quite. A different wife. I presume she is long dead after my crime and exile. But my eldest son, the one I had with her, is still alive, born after I left." He rolls his shoulder, rubbing his greying beard. Another tear dribbles down his wavering lips. "I travelled for days until I arrived at this kingdom and blended into the Concave Sector. Soon after, when the time was right, I killed the king, claimed to be the son he hid from the public within the walls of his palace, and his only heir, as he had daughters. No one would try to exile me because I was the king. *Am* the king. The public still believes the previous king died from infection."

A vague memory of learning about the previous king's life and death floats across my mind. But the room spins and sways like I've swallowed five shots of whisky, like I've run across the entire kingdom in one burst. *Ruben has a brother.*

"How do you know your other son is still alive?" I manage to force the words out.

"I then married Mae, Ruben's mother," Talin says, barrelling on with his story as if I hadn't spoken. "My sons are four years apart. Ruben's twenty. My other son should be twenty-four, if I remember correctly. The war is with my eldest son, Elle. He wants the throne. Wants his revenge on me for abandoning him. His letters are written with more vengeance and blood than ink."

The chair scrapes against the floorboards as I stand and pace to the window, gripping the edge and closing my eyes as aches shackle around my ribs. "Ruben doesn't know any of this, does he?" Wind lashes at my hair, and the fires roar below us, a thousand hues of red and orange, the heat blazing skyward, scorching past my face. I know my time with the king is running out.

"When is he coming?" I say, turning my head over my shoulder.

The glass breaks as he smacks it onto the table, the alcohol already affecting the mighty yet miserable king. "He speaks in cryptic. It is hard to understand his taunts and teasing. However, I suspect he will weasel his way here no matter whether I am alive or amid the cosmos."

My hand tightens around my dagger. "You haven't told me his name. And what of the Shadowtooth? What does it do? You said it... keeps you alive."

He opens his mouth to respond when Ruben staggers into the room, face drawn and brimming with a lifetime of simmering hate. An arrow glints like angry eyes as he wields his bow, aiming it directly at the king's heart.

"My son," the king says, his voice as unsteady as his crown. "Have you come to save me from the witch?"

Fire spikes my blood, but I keep my cool, twirling the blade by my hip.

"She is the only one who ever cared for me, Father," Ruben says, his eyes watery and red. "The only one since Mother."

The king blows out a breath and pours another shot. "You are my son. I have always cared for you." His eyes water some more, and he draws in a shaky breath. "Why don't we work together to patch this kingdom back up, huh? Some father and son time. It has been a while since we did something, just the two of us. Remember when we used to read toge—"

Ruben releases a harsh bark of laughter. "Nothing but a miserable liar. You killed my *mother*. Elle's parents and sister. She is not responsible for the Tranq's death in the forest. Nor is she responsible for the riots and the rebellion. You only have yourself to blame."

The king rises like a hurricane over a small village, his eyes flashing as he curls his lips, showing his teeth. "You wouldn't kill your own father, would you?"

Ruben draws in a shaky breath. "No, Father. I am not like you." His mocking, hateful gleam fades into granite resolve.

I yelp as he shifts the arrow an inch and fires. The king screeches and howls, stumbling backwards, his face contorting in agony. Ruben lunges forward and pushes his father up against the open window, grabbing him by the collar as he cries out, head drooping out the window. The rebels chant and holler, slamming their stolen Tranq weapons against each other and the ground. Rebel Tranqs rattle their shields, and the cacophony cools my blood. By the look in the king's eyes, I can see it does the same to him.

"Ruben, I—" the king gurgles but trails off when his son wraps his other hand around his throat. He gathers every last ounce of strength and heaves a sigh that sounds like something between defeat and relief. "You always had your mother's heart."

Ruben leans forward, spilling a sob. His eyes burn as he snarls, not bothering to stop the tears that dribble down his cheeks and onto his father's face. "Long live the king."

My heart wallops into my throat as Ruben hurls the king out the window, and he plummets into the flames and blood-thirsty slew of blades below.

Chapter 39

Ruben's eyes are cold and distant as I grab his hand and yank him out of the room. We crash down the spiral staircase, bolting through the next room, past Larissa. I don't yet bother to ask about Killian, who's no longer in the room. Fires crackle and roar through the lower hallways of the palace as we burst out of the foyer, emerging into the rioters and crowds of rebels who chant and shriek, crowding a particularly bloody hunk of royal meat below the tallest tower. Ruben swallows, his eyes finally watering.

I grab his hand again and tug him through the fray, ducking my head so hopefully, no one spots me. The king's truth sizzles like poison on my tongue. But I bite it back. Now is not the time. Wounded and dead rebels litter the palace grounds, blood and severed limbs making my stomach curdle. We help haul the injured into wagons, sending them off to the infirmary. Medics pour in from the Concave Sector and pitch in. Children scream, and women wail for their lovers. I hold mine tight, not letting him go.

More Convex and Concave men run through the palace gates with pitchers of water and hoses connected to the fountains outside. Hisses and spits add to the chaos as they drown the fires. Smoke crests the stars, pushing them into the furthest reaches of the cosmos. I scurry up to a young woman as she frantically rounds up her children, blood dribbling from her eye. A medic swoops in and helps me carry her and the children to the wagons.

As they hobble away, a thousand tiny needles shoot through my bloodstream, plunging into my gut. My breaths fall sharp. The world spins and sways. Sheer panic. I move away from the carnage, blood, and death, stepping into a secluded courtyard in the garden. My breath falls short and sharp like rain pattering the ground. Tears dribble down my cheeks, and I lean against the walls of hedges as the sobs spill from my chest, like some battered beast awakening, finally safe to come out of hiding.

This is all my fault.

All my fault.

All my fault.

The bodies. The blood. Ruben killed his father because of me. They're all dead.

The pain is a knife in my chest twisting, digging. I clutch my stomach and double over as the phantom fists wrench my guts like wringing a cloth. As I hug my knees to my ribs on the ground, a bird sweeps down, landing before me, scraping its talons against the stone path. Its gleaming black feathers shimmer a hint of emerald as it waddles up to me, holding a small envelope in its little brass-coloured beak. It drops the envelope and then darts back into the night, blending into the obsidian, as if it were born from it.

Curiosity getting the better of me, I wipe my tears and pluck the letter from the ground, prying it open.

"Elle," is all it says.

I startle as a figure steps into the courtyard. His tall, slender frame faces the sculpture of the Goddess of Tranquillity and rinses his hand beneath the fountain.

"I presume you are the one who wrote me this fine letter?" I say, grateful for the smoothness in my tone.

He releases a low, deep chuckle and tugs at his coat, not unlike the king, as he twirls around. "You would be right. I suppose words failed me. Other than your name, which I have heard like a war cry for weeks. No wonder my ears are still ringing."

"I killed a Tranq trying to protect my sister from starvation." My voice is bitter. "Instead of kicking me out, the king let her starve to death. I failed in the one thing I swore to my mother I'd do. And now, bodies litter the city."

"As opposed to how they'd keep littering the wastelands if King Talin still ruled?" he says, tilting his head over his shoulder. His jawline is sharp and chiselled as if he were carved from the marble itself. "The kingdom owes you. You gave them the courage to fight for what they deserved. Freedom from the king."

"How do you know so much about me?" I ask, taking a step closer, reaching for my dagger that's still stained with the king's blood. "Are you one of his heralds?"

The harsh laughter scrapes against my ears. "Not at all, Elle." He spins around and prowls up to me with the delicate tread of a lion hunting its prey. The moonlight pushes through the murky sky and ignites his eyes. His forest eyes. I recognise his scarred cheek and white-blond hair. The memories, though foggy and tainted with the weakness and sickness from my time in the dungeon, form a moment of clarity.

"You saved me from dying of infection in prison," I say, lifting my chin and spinning the blade as I ignore the impending exhaustion shoving into my muscles.

"Yes. The king locked you up. You fired up the rebels, I remember so clearly." His eyes, those green eyes, so painfully familiar.

"Who are you?" I say, afraid to confirm what I already know.

His eyes flash, and his lips quirk into a smug grin. "You know who I am, don't you?"

"No, I don't." My jaw clenches, and I scrunch my nose. "Who *are* you?"

"My name is Edward," he says, hissing the name like a snake. "Edward Mallory. First son of the mighty King Talin and my mother, Greer Mallory."

"Edward," I say, testing the name. "He warned me about you. How long have you been here?"

"Oh, Elle. Elle. Elle. I have been watching you for a long time. Since the first moment you spotted me in the southern forest all those months ago."

A gasp tumbles from my mouth, and I stumble back, grabbing the hedge. "It was you?" Everything around me spins and sways like I've swallowed five shots of whisky as the memory of those startling green eyes from all those months ago prowls through my mind. So, it *wasn't* Ruben.

"It was you," I say again, my skin crawling at the realisation and his prideful sneer. I lunge forward, about to slice him. But his striking features render my hand still. His eyes, so like Ruben's and the king's, yet his face has a combination of Ruben and someone else. I imagine his mother had white hair, too.

"You truly propelled yourself to the spotlight when you nearly killed my brother," Edward says, circling me like a scavenger bird waiting for morsels of a corpse.

I school my face into neutrality, swallowing back the fear. "You know about Ruben?"

"Of course." He licks his lips, clasping his hands behind his back. "As I said, I have been watching. Funny, I always wanted a brother when I was little. Turns out, my father, so disgusted by his first bastard son, created his new, *perfect* child."

"So, you *don't* know Ruben at all."

His scarred cheek twitches. "Well, the night does not belong to the king anymore. Nor does it belong to the Gods. It belongs to us. Why don't you tell me about him? I'm listening."

"What do you want?" I stick my chin in the air, trying to ignore the surging sea within me.

Edward pulls to a halt before me as Ruben calls my name from somewhere in the garden. His eyes glimmer like dying coals, and his lips flicker as he bends forward. "Thank you for ridding the world of my father, Elle. I promise we will meet again."

Then he vanishes around the corner, into the shadow and wind, staining my heart with wisps of darkness.

Chapter 40

I march after him, ready to shove a blade against his throat until he spills answers and blood. "Edward!" I growl, but the rain splats my cheeks, and the petrichor smell permeates the air with such melancholy I wonder if it has brought the ghosts of the rebellion with it. A hollow carves into my chest, and I know that only the water trailing its icy fingers down my spine keeps me tethered to sanity. But that madness, that darkness, scrapes at my soul and calls my name.

I let out a grunt as I slam into someone's chest. The smell of citrus and pine needles curls around me, and my thundering heart eases.

"Who were you talking to?" Ruben asks, tilting his head and running a blood-stained hand through his dark hair.

I heave a sigh, resisting the urge to glance past him. "No one. Shall we go find the boys?"

He pulls me closer and presses a soft kiss to my lips. The palace gradually clears as we exit the courtyard. I sweep my gaze around the grounds as if half-expecting to catch Edward blending in, as he has apparently done so for months.

Every instinct tells me to send all remaining Tranqs after him. Instead, I help the rebel Tranqs load the last of the Convex and Concave rebels into wagons or escort them out of the palace gates.

"Elle!" Aston calls as he emerges from a small throng of Convex men, blood, dirt, and charcoal smeared across his cheek.

"Are you okay?" I pull him into a hug.

He nods, rubbing his face and grimacing at the blood. "We… disposed of the royal body," he says, voice low, flicking a wary gaze to Ruben, who stiffens.

"What did you do with it?" I whisper.

"There's a pyre around the other side of the palace. Should be all done by morning." Aston presses his lips together as he slaps Ruben on the shoulder. "I'm sorry, man. I know he was your father."

Ruben nods once and shrugs, doing a terrible job of masking the grief swimming in his eyes. "It had to be done."

Ajax hobbles up to us, a group of men following him. Soot stains his cheeks, hands, clothes, and hair. "We've put out all the fires… except the pyre, of course." He pulls Ruben in for a tight embrace. "If you go say goodbye, just be aware of the Tranquillity worshippers singing hymns. Creepy."

I grab Ruben's wrist, feeling his racing pulse thrum beneath my fingers. "Do you want to go?"

He opens his mouth to respond when a spot of reddish-brown hair materialises from the thinning crowds and vehicles. Killian. My jaw tightens, and I lift my chin.

"Elle," he says, in such a pathetic whimper. I almost feel sorry for him.

"Killian."

Ruben grips my hand tighter. But I do not yield. My gaze is forged from the coldest reaches of the kingdom.

Killian's reddened eyes swell with tears. "Will you forgive me, Elle?"

"For all you've done?" I shake my head, raising my brows, and he startles. "You will need to prove yourself. Do a little soul-searching and figure out why you can't handle compromising some of your privileges so others can suffer less. Your little mishap didn't just almost kill me. But if we failed tonight, the king would have taken everything from the Convex Sector, burnt their crops and spilt their blood like wine."

Killian's face pales, and he casts his brown eyes to his feet. I wonder if he truly understands the gravity of my words or if he's just ashamed that he's exposed his true character. He mutters another pitiful apology. I roll my eyes as he draws back, muttering his condolences to Ruben.

The chants of the Tranquillity worshippers curl and swirl around us as we turn the corner and approach the wall of flames. A sea of hooded cloaks surrounds the whooshing and roaring pyre, and the smell of burning flesh clouds the air. The sound of a crackling, bubbling royal body draws vomit into my mouth. I bend over and hurl it out.

"Such a mighty beast of a man," Ruben says, his voice hardly louder than a murmur, his resolve as sharp as stone. "Now, he's little more than melted mush and bone."

"Quite the sight, huh?" a voice says from behind us. Ajax presses his lips together in a sad smile.

He and Aston step up beside us. "Thought you had things to do, boys?" I say, raising my brows.

"Whatever they are, they can wait," Ajax says, clicking his tongue. He throws his arm over Ruben's shoulder. "Our friend just lost his father. We are here to support him."

Ruben pretends to tip a hat. "Thanks, man."

"We do have a lot to do," Aston says, taking on that grim tone that makes my shoulders stiffen.

"Cleaning up the city, deciding who will lead." Ajax counts on his fingers. "Preparing for this massive, impending war with the people beyond the walls."

I furrow my brow and step back as the wind changes direction and blows the heat of the flames toward us. "A leader?"

"Well, yes. We can't let the kingdom run into complete anarchy." Ajax examines me with a sense of wisdom beyond his years. But I still see the boy in him. The sparkle in his eyes for adventure. "What about you?"

"Me?"

"Yes. People followed you from the moment you killed that Tranq." He sticks his thumb over his shoulder. "You have leadership qualities, Elle."

"I'm not sure I can handle it," I say, heaving a sigh. "You saw how I reacted when people died because of me. I can't have any more blood on my hands. They're already dripping red."

"What about you?" Aston buts in, elbowing Ruben in the ribs.

"Definitely not. My royal line ends here." He nods to his father's sizzling corpse.

Ajax shrugs, pursing his lips. "Think about it, Elle. Or maybe I'll put my hand in."

I twist my torso, crossing my arms. "I couldn't think of a better person in the office."

"With my good looks, charm, and delightful personality, I might just agree with you, Elle."

"Not another arrogant man in power," Aston says with a groan and laughs.

"That's exactly why we should run an election," Ajax says. "Like our ancestors in the Old World did. They were onto something."

I snort, shaking my head. "They also collapsed from their own greed. Almost drove humanity to extinction. Might I remind you that they caused the floods, rising seas, and disease that left us in this predicament?" I gesture to the kingdom walls that have protected us for the last century.

"Your pessimism will drive you to your grave, Elle." He wags his finger at me.

Smoke billows from the pyre, and we all groan and curse, waving our hands in front of us.

"Let's get out of here," Ajax says, pinching his nose in disgust. "Have we been supportive enough, Ruben?"

A couple of eyes from the worshippers turn our way, and I laugh aloud, realising that they've heard the prince's name. Ruben realises, too, and shoots Ajax a glare. But even he cannot hide the humour for long. We all burst out laughing.

"More than enough," Ruben says.

"Let's go get a drink," Ajax says.

Finally, Ruben wishes one final goodbye to his father. The boys walk away.

I linger back for a moment, staring at the dead king. Bile swells into my mouth, and the stench *should* send me scattering away. But the knots in my gut and clubbing heart root me to the spot. I scold myself. He's dead. We killed him. I should be celebrating with the boys over a cold one. A lifetime of terror, grief, starvation, and desperation flashes across my mind. My parents' exile. Lyra's death. Larissa. Every bit of my suffering has been because of this man, and now he burns on the pile of wood, reminding me how fickle human nature is. We are only on this earth for a mere moment, and we can choose the path we take. Destruction and greed, or kindness.

The distinct rolling storm of dread settles into my chest, and I know this isn't over yet. Guilt scrapes against my skull at my inability to confess to Ruben. But I push the feeling away, swallow it down, knowing I will figure it out. I always do.

"Goodbye, King Talin," I whisper, nodding my head in respect like the worshippers.

As I catch up with the boys, Ruben grabs my hand. "Shall we hide from all this mess in the forest for a moment longer?"

"Only a moment or two," I say.

The shadows of the northern forest welcome us. As the drizzling rain eases, a cool breeze runs past our arms and tangles in my hair, making the trees dance with one another. Birds skim the branches, and insects chirp. Dew drips from the leaves.

"Summer might be on the way." I grab a flower and smell its petals.

Ruben grabs my waist and presses me against the trunk of a tree, kissing me with such ferocity I melt against him. We kiss, and I wonder if I still taste of war as warmth stirs in my chest, fire licking along my skin. I feel him deep in my soul, beneath my battered bones. It's running me over and over. *It seems that the darkness in me finally found the flame.*

He pulls away just as suddenly as he moved in. "I cannot let it happen," he says, panting.

"Let what happen?"

"I cannot become him. My father."

I angle my head, tightening my brows as his eyes dart around my face. "You won't," I say. "He is gone. You can now forge your own path."

"Do you think I can be forgiven for all I've done?" His voice strains, and his eyes water.

The wind blows, and I nod as the trees chatter. "Yes. I believe so. It is our choices that carve our path to the stars, not where we've come from."

"I want to be forgiven."

"Me too."

For a moment, I swear I can feel someone watching us from the depths of the darkness. As if I've finally understood the silent language of wind and shadow. But I shake my head. Let them watch me. We will meet again, he and I. A bird soars over our heads. Obsidian feathers with a shimmer of green. Like Ruben's eyes. Like Talin's eyes. Like his eyes. Green. Green. Green.

I may drown in the colour still.

Acknowledgements

When I was 6 years old, and in primary school, I wrote a story about a strawberry who got his piano stolen by an apple. The story got published in the school newspaper. I'd like to thank Sarah Burnett (who I knew as Miss Hall) for telling me, so early in life, that my writing was worth reading. The fire inside me lit that day.

In the years that followed, I wrote stories about my stuffed animals. I printed them out, folded them into a book, and read them to my parents. I'd like to thank Mum and Dad for always listening patiently and enthusiastically, even though those stories probably made zero sense.

I'd also love to thank the world of fanfiction, for teaching me how to write in worlds, and how to build my own. I, of course, would not be here, with this story in print, if it weren't for the unwavering support of my Wattpad readers. Each read, each vote, and each comment, gave me the confidence in my writing, and in Elle's story, and without you all, I truly don't think it would have evolved into this final version, let alone, made it here, into your hands. Thank you, Wattpad readers, for keeping me humble and for always being so kind and supportive.

I also could not leave these acknowledgements without thanking the most important group of girls in my life. To Ariana, Breanna, Christabel, Gabby, Georgia, Hannah, Holly, Kaela, Mi Rae, Paige, and Siobhan, thank you for everything you do for me, for cheering me on, for listening to me vent, and for simply sticking by my side like gum on a shoe.

And to Darcy, thank you for listening to me talk about my world and my characters as if they were real, for being my sounding board, and for being my best friend.

Lastly, to Elle Fallon: What a hell of a ride it's been. Thank you for growing with me.

Emma

About the Author

Emma Jackson is a lover of cats, an array of music genres, poetry, coffee, fantasy and dystopian literature, and brunch. She is a content writer by day in Auckland, New Zealand. But much prefers to snuggle up on a rainy Saturday afternoon watching The Vampire Diaries. If she is not doing that, she is likely travelling the world (or dreaming about it), on a mission to discover as much as possible in this lifetime.

Instagram: emma.jacksonwrites

Tik Tok: emmajackson33